The Young Knight and His Metal Steed

A.I.V. Esguerra

Ukiyoto Publishing

All global publishing rights are held by

Ukiyoto Publishing

Published in 2022

ISBN 9789356972605

This is a work of fiction. Names, characters, businesses, places, events, locales, and incidents are either the products of the author's imagination or used in a fictitious manner. Any resemblance to actual persons, living or dead, or actual events is purely coincidental.

www.ukiyoto.com

Dedication

There are too many people to acknowledge so I will start with some people.

First is my family for encouraging me into becoming an author. There was some reluctance from them but they understood why I want to be an author.

Second is someone I will simply call "Marq". He came up with the "Jolt-Vee" nickname for the JLTV vehicle. Next is someone who told me to simply use "Eagle". Eagle had helped me figure out how to work the premise of "alien ship crashing into war-torn Afghanistan in 1985" for this story.

Another individual I wish to acknowledge is a man simply calling himself "Dana". Dana assisted me with usage of Farsi in this novel. There's also "Jegor". He assisted me in the usage of Russian for this story. Not exactly a wise idea at a time like this but I did it anyway because if it was done before (the original 1984 Red Dawn and The Hunt for Red October coming out while the Cold War hadn't ended yet), why can't I do the same by putting Russian-speaking characters in this story despite what's happening now. Either way, "Jegor" has been of great help.

Lastly, there's one individual I wish to acknowledge, a professor of mine whom I will simply call "J.P.". He helped me find this path I chose to be worthwhile considering he was willing to answer any question I could think of when I was his student in the university I studied at, no matter how ridiculous it is.

Contents

Prologue: A Faltering Voyage

Iron Dutchman; Pacific Ocean. March 2, 2030; 1755 hours (Pacific Standard Time)

A lone ship traveled the Pacific Ocean with its name, *Iron Dutchman*, found on both sides of its bow. Mostly a cruise ship, its rear was built with a metallic square. This would have confused any that saw the ship. At the bow proper, Tarou Ganji and Sunan Wattana practiced *Muay Thai* against the sun that was to set in less than eighteen minutes.

Tarou, aged seventeen, simply wore green trousers held together by a brown leather belt and brown boots, showing most of his body that had a spare build and very light skin. Wattana, aged twenty-eight, wore the same trousers, belt, and boots, but wore a white-colored tank top, covering most of her dark skin and short, muscular build.

As they practiced their *Muay Thai*, both the boy and the woman also wore protective gear. It comprised of helmets, boxing gloves, and knee pads. The helmets, however, didn't cover their respective black, especially with Wattana tying her hair in a ponytail. While the boy and the woman practiced, Anita Hamilton approached.

In her late forties, Hamilton had very light skin, short blonde hair, and green eyes. She wore a white-colored button-up shirt underneath a lab coat that hid her tall and athletic build, a black skirt, and high-heeled shoes that were also colored black.

"Are you two done?" the Hamilton asked.

"Doc, it's you," Tarou said as he and his sparring partner stopped. "We were just about to finish."

"Bart finished making dinner. I suggest you get to washing up now."

"Got it, Doc," Wattana replied.

1813 hours

Tarou and Wattana arrived in the dining room of the *Iron Dutchman*. The dining room used to be a bar and lounge back when the *Iron Dutchman* used to be a cruise ship and yet it still stood, albeit as a common dining room.

Both found a table whose chairs weren't entirely filled out as one table's seats were entirely filled and one table remained void of occupants. Also on that table was a man of an average height and weight, with short black hair, light intermediate skin, and light brown eyes named Federico Diáz.

"Hey Fed," Wattana said as she and the boy sat down. "Where are Semir and Vikas?"

"Still getting washed," Diáz answered.

"It's ready!" Bartolomeu Moura, a dark-skinned man with his black hair in a shape-up and dark brown eyes, shouted as he appeared with a tray with wheels filled with bowls. Despite his fat body, Moura had muscular arms as a result of his days in the Angolan Army.

In each bowl were green bell peppers, an onion, shitake mushrooms, and two minced cloves of garlic above white rice. The dark-skinned man began distributing one bowl at a time to those occupying the tables. Those who got their bowls began to eat. Jason Luke Crawley, a man in his thirties with very light skin, an angular body, short blond hair, and light brown eyes, didn't eat despite receiving his bowl.

"Barto… this isn't bell peppers and beef if there's no beef… " Crawley said.

"It is," Moura replied.

"BUT IT ISN'T!"

"It is when we're broke," Wouter Vos, another man with very light skin, replied before he continued eating his meal. He was in his late thirties with blue eyes, a slim body with broad shoulders, and blond hair in a crew cut.

"What happened to the two million South American dollars we got from the last job?" Wattana asked.

"We've already spent most of it for fuel that's about to expire in two days, clothes, and the food we currently have, Wattana. Let it be remembered that it was supposed to be eight million until Bandjar shot himself and how much damage was wrought from Ganji's tussle with that Donian pilot. We should even be thankful that Rodrigues allowed us to leave with a submachine gun and additional 9 millimeter rounds."

"I found us a job!" a teenage girl with a short and thin build exclaimed as she appeared in the dining room with two men. She and the two men filled the seats on the empty table. The girl had light skin, dark brown eyes, and black hair arranged in a ponytail. She wore a white short-sleeved shirt, Daisy Dukes, and black slippers.

"What kind of job, Tatev?" Tarou asked as he and everyone else on the dinner table converged on the table the teenage girl placed a laptop computer on.

"Hold on," Tatev answered as she opened her laptop computer.

After opening the laptop, Tatev opened a program that made a small black square appeared on the screen and inside was a smaller rectangle that was colored cyan with the word "NUN"; the word being colored white. The words "New United Nations" were above the cyan rectangle with the words "Continue" or "Leave" below the rectangle.

"This job's from the New United Nations," Vos said. "Press Continue."

"Will do, Mr. Vos." Tatev pressed "Continue" on the black square. As a result, the cyan rectangle vanished and in its place were words and numbers. Below were the words "Accept" and "Leave".

"Says here that they're looking for protective detail," Hamilton said as she read the words in the black square. "Nine hundred thousand a month."

"Not bad," Vos remarked.

"Do we take it?" Wattana asked.

"While I didn't appreciate what Senhor Crawley said about my hard work, we could use more money for food," Moura suggested.

"We could use more clothes," Tatev added.

"Anyone here disagree?" Vos asked to the other men in the ship.

"I'm in," Crawley replied.

"Miss Wattana and I could use some rubber shoes for *Muay Thai* training," Tarou replied.

"Wait, aren't there any other jobs?" Wattana asked warily. "I mean, was that job from NUN the only one you found?"

"There was one offer from the Euro-African Alliance," Tatev answered.

"We're taking this job from NUN," Vos declared sternly. "We don't have enough fuel to cross into the Atlantic."

"Fine," Wattana replied with defeat evident in her tone.

"Then it's settled," Vos declared before turning to Tatev. "Mirzoyan, press Accept."

The Iron Dutchmen

FIS Headquarters, McLean, Commonwealth of Virginia; United States of America. March 2, 2030; 2345 hours (Eastern Standard Time)

Alberto Pérez, a man with no hair on his scalp, dark skin, and dark brown eyes arrived at his office in the headquarters of the New United Nations' Foreign Intelligence Service (FIS). Sixty-five years old with his blazer and suit hiding his body with average height and broad shoulders, Pérez was born in the Republic of Cuba early into the rule of Fidel Castro as the descendant of Africans brought to Cuba back when it was a Spanish colony for slave labor. Upon coming of age, Pérez was conscripted into the Cuban military when it was sent to aid the government created by the *Movimento Popular de Libertação de Angola* (MPLA) while it fought a civil war throughout the former Portuguese colony that was Angola. After two years as a conscript, Pérez studied at the *Instituto Técnico Militar* (ITM) José Martí and after his graduation, became an intelligence officer later throughout his prolonged career in the Cuban military.

The office Pérez occupied was once the office of the Director of the United States of America's Central Intelligence Agency (CIA). After the Third World War, the US banded together with many countries to create the New United Nations and one thing that transpired with this was that the member-states of NUN had to dissolve their respective foreign intelligence agencies, the US's CIA amongst those agencies. Yet, with the threat of other supernational unions also created from the chaos of the Third World War, NUN created the Intelligence Collective where the intelligence agencies of its member-states were to work together to determine threats to NUN but a branch of the Intelligence Collective was created to serve as NUN's sole foreign intelligence agency—the Foreign Intelligence Service. The FIS was given the old CIA headquarters in the unincorporated community of Langley, a part of McLean, as its headquarters.

Alberto Pérez, due to his record within Cuban military intelligence, joined the Intelligence Collective's FIS as his country downscaled its military when it joined NUN. He was made Director of Foreign Intelligence as of recently.

The door opened. Coming inside the room was a man with very light skin, graying brown hair, and green eyes. This man was Stanley McAllister, the Deputy Director of the Covert Action Center.

Fifty-nine years old, McAllister knew of the United States of America prior to the Third World War. Upon turning eighteen, he enlisted into the United States Army just as the war started. However, his hometown was destroyed by nuclear fire yet despite that, he carried on with his life to the point he continued his studies. He joined the Intelligence Collective's Foreign Intelligence Service and worked his way up to Deputy Director for Covert Action, where all of the FIS's clandestine activities were handled by him.

"I was told you needed to see me?" Pérez asked.

"I have an update about Maria Hoshikawa," McAllister answered.

"Do tell."

"One mercenary group finally took up the offer we posted through PriMilNet".

"Where's Caguiat?"

"She's keeping an eye on the mercenaries who've accepted the offer?"

"Who are they?"

"Iron Dutchman Services."

Pérez's face dropped. "Y… You're joking, right?" he asked.

"Sadly, no," McAllister answered. "I can understand why you reacted this way, Al. Caguiat and I were surprised too."

"Why exactly does Iron Dutchman Services have our attention again?"

"Their last contract was with the South American Union in the form of assisting in the arrest of small-time arms dealer Kirk Bandjar, who was selling the last of his weapons to one Rolf Núñez."

"*The* Rolf Núñez*?*"

"The same one. The whole thing snowballed and while Núñez was arrested, Bandjar shot himself to avoid arrest. It's for that reason, and the damage from a fight Iron Dutchman Services' Walgear pilot had against the surviving Walgear pilot under Bandjar's employ as a mercenary, that Iron Dutchman Services as a whole was only paid twenty-five percent of what the SAU promised to pay them."

"And how much were they offered at first?"

"Eight million South American dollars. All the damage from the fight between the two Walgear pilots and Bandjar's suicide reduced that reward to two million."

"And where are they now?"

"In the middle of the Pacific Ocean. Caguiat's tracking them now."

"Get her to tell those mercenaries that they need to go to Hawaii."

#

Iron Dutchman; Pacific Ocean. 2103 hours (Pacific Standard Time)

"Mr. Vos, I got a response!" Tatev Mirzoyan shouted as she barged into the *Iron Dutchman*'s bridge with her laptop.

Wouter Vos, manning the ship's helm, turned to Tatev. "What is it, Mirzoyan?"

"Someone from NUN gave us instructions."

"Jake, take the helm," Vos ordered to Jason Luke Crawley upon turning to him.

"Aye aye, boss," Crawley replied.

As Crawley took the helm, Vos walked up to Tatev. As Tatev opened her laptop, she showed the program she used earlier. Vos then found the instructions Tatev spoke of.

"Says we have to go to Pearl Harbor," Vos read from what he saw from Tatev's computer. "Someone from the FIS will see us there."

"You're kidding, the FIS?" Crawley asked while rearing his head toward Vos and Maria.

"Does it matter now?" Vos asked to Crawley. "We said yes. We're doing this."

"Aye aye, boss."

Off Naval Station Pearl Harbor, City and County of Honolulu, State of Hawaii; United States of America. March 4, 2030; 1450 hours (Hawaii-Aleutian Time)

"Attention all hands, this is your Captain speaking," Wouter Vos announced throughout the *Iron Dutchman*'s PA system. "We are nearing Pearl Harbor, so except for me, Mr. Crawley, Dr. Hamilton, and Miss Wattana, please report to the briefing room. Our client will be boarding this ship and we're to allow him or her onboard."

Throughout the *Iron Dutchman*, people began to converge the ship's briefing room, an old movie theater. This was because the *Iron Dutchman* was once a cruise ship that was destroyed during the Third World War that was refloated and turned into a mobile headquarters that Wouter Vos won in a game of chance. He named the ship *Iron Dutchman* and the mercenary outfit he established as Iron Dutchman Services as a result.

One by one, people throughout the ship reached the briefing room. Last to go inside were Tarou Ganji and Tatev Mirzoyan.

I wonder whom Mr. Vos will allow on board the ship? Tarou pondered.

#

Naval Station Pearl Harbor. 1506 hours

Three men waited by one of the ports in Pearl Harbor. All of them had very light skin and wore sunglasses. One of them, who had a slim build and broad shoulders, no hair at all in his scalp, and a scar between the scalp and his right ear, brought out a pair of binoculars, seeing the *Iron Dutchman* as a result.

Pearl Harbor was once the headquarters of the United States Navy's Pacific Fleet. After the Third World War and the creation of the New United Nations, the United States of America, one of the founding nation-states of NUN, downsized its military and because many ships were destroyed during the war, the US Navy was dissolved with the surviving ships used for NUN's own navy, the New United Nations

Maritime Force (NUNMF). The old naval base in Pearl Harbor was acquisitioned for NUNMF's Pacific Fleet.

"I see the *Iron Dutchman*," the man with the binoculars said.

"Good," another man replied.

#

Iron Dutchman. 1519 hours

The *Iron Dutchman* then made it to a port normally reserved for NUMNF vessels. As the ship stopped, it lowered its starboard anchor. A gangway was then connected to the *Iron Dutchman*. The three men that spotted the ship boarded and see Vos, Jake Crawley, Anita Hamilton, and Sunan Wattana.

"Welcome aboard the *Iron Dutchman*," Vos announced. "I'm Wouter Vos, owner of Iron Dutchman Services."

"We know," one man replied. "Call me 'Fred Smith'. We're with the Foreign Intelligence Service of the Intelligence Collective and we're here to explain to your entire mercenary group as to the full details about this job you applied for."

"Then follow me to the briefing room."

"You have a briefing room?"

"Of course we do," Crawley answered. "Follow us."

#

1538 hours

Vos, Crawley, Wattana, and Hamilton reached the *Iron Dutchman*'s briefing room with the three men who boarded the ship. Everyone already inside the briefing room except for Tatev, already in the projector room, turned to those who've entered until they made it to the stage.

"Everyone, these gentlemen, as you could guess, represent the New United Nations," Vos announced to those facing the stage. "One of them will go to the projection room and show us what we will be doing, so please pay attention. Only ask once an explanation has been finished."

One of the three men with sunglasses then walked his way toward the projector room. Tatev then stepped away from her laptop upon seeing the man. The man then connected a universal storage bank (USB) device onto the laptop and opened the files found in the USB.

The file was then projected onto the screen with everyone watching. A picture of a girl as old as Tarou and Tatev was shown on the screen. She had long blonde hair that reached past her shoulders, blue eyes, light skin, and wore a high school uniform for girls that consisted of a button-up shirt with long sleeves underneath a black blazer with the school's emblem on its left, a skirt, socks that reached as far as the knee, and leather shoes. The button-up shirt and the socks were colored white, while the blazer, skirt, and shoes were colored black. A red-colored bow tie was tied around the collar of the button-up shirt. The emblem consisted of a yellow-colored shield with a large "N" in white inside.

"This girl is Maria Hoshikawa," "Smith" explained. "Seventeen years old, she'll be the individual you are to protect. I can imagine you want to know why, so I'll cut straight to the point: certain individuals might have a particular interest in her. Either criminal groups or any other supernational union's intelligence services."

"Wait a second, is this Maria Hoshikawa the daughter of Daisuke Hoshikawa, President of the Hoshikawa Group?" Anita Hamilton asked.

"She is. However, no one but him and his wife Miku must know that we've hired mercenaries to protect their daughter. Not even Maria herself can know of this."

"And why is that?" Vos asked.

"We have yet to ascertain who she really is, much less why people are after her."

"Smith" turned away from the mercenaries to his subordinate in the projector room. "Kirk, next slide, please!"

Without saying anything, the agent named "Kirk" projected another picture toward the screen. Now on the screen was a newspaper clipping and a picture of a destroyed ship.

"As you can tell with the blonde hair, Maria Hoshikawa is not the biological daughter of Daisuke Hoshikawa. As an infant, she was discovered by Daisuke and Miku when they took a sailing vacation off Rebun Island."

"This newspaper clipping, this is that incident involving the Gatekeepers of Knowledge, isn't it?" Crawley asked.

"You're correct," "Smith" answered as he turned to Crawley. "We detected a mysterious plane above Rebun Island an hour before Maria was discovered. We had already collected information that the Gatekeepers had built their own military to defend Enlightenment Point and to test their response, we leaked our findings. Naturally, the Gatekeepers responded the way we expected them to."

"And what does this have to do with the Gatekeepers?"

"That's why we've been watching Maria. Because you took up the job offer, you're to protect Maria until we've found enough information to connect Maria to the Gatekeepers. Again, you must not reveal who you really are."

"Next slide, please!" What followed was a picture of a walled building with a clock at its center top shown on the screen.

"This is Nishi High School, located in the State of Japan's Kansai City," "Smith" continued. "Maria studies in this school and seeing that among the individuals I'm looking at is a teenager himself, I need him to infiltrate the school as a recently enrolled student to keep an eye on Maria."

"Wait, you mean-"

"Yes. Tarou Ganji."

The adolescent male stood up. "Acknowledged," Tarou replied.

"Isn't this too risky?" Hamilton argued. "Tarou may be of the same age as Miss Hoshikawa but he hasn't associated himself with people of the same age."

"I have to agree with Doc here,' Vos added. "Ganji may have learned a few things but-"

"I know of his past," "Smith" replied. "We can use it as a cover for him to be enrolled into Nishi High School. Also, we aren't asking you to go to Japan immediately because we need to conduct an 'immersion procedure'."

"Immersion procedure?" Vikas Mistry, a man in his early twenties with a body of an average weight yet a short height, black hair in a crew cut, dark skin, and light brown eyes, asked.

"Mr. Ganji will have to learn the ways of a Japanese teenager," "Smith" explained. "Kirk, next slide!"

Now on the screen was a teenage male whose face was deliberately covered in black to protect his identity. The teenager wore a uniform similar to what Maria Hoshikawa was shown to wear but as the individual now shown was a male, his uniform included trousers, as opposed to a skirt, that was also colored black. Instead of a bow tie around the button-up shirt's collar, it's a necktie.

"This is the male uniform of Nishi High School," "Smith" stated. "We've already acquired one as we've already conducted the paperwork making sure Mr. Ganji will be enrolled. Now, we need someone to act out as Mr. Ganji's guardian."

"I'll do it," Hamilton said.

"Good idea," Vos replied. "Doc may have seen action with us, but she's a doctor first and foremost."

"Now we'll offer our resources to help you do your jobs efficiently," "Smith" said. "Dr. Hamilton, what will you need?"

"A clinic to serve as a cover. I am a doctor, after all. Appropriate equipment too."

"Might I please make a suggestion?" Tarou asked.

"And what might that be?" "Smith" asked as he faced Tarou.

"Might I please have my own apartment? While Dr. Hamilton is to act as my guardian, I'd rather not give her any problems if she wishes to act out as a real doctor. In addition, I feel that having my own apartment will allow me to store equipment needed for special emergencies."

"I'll see what I can do."

"If we're to keep an eye on Maria Hoshikawa, can you arrange to have the *Iron Dutchman* docked somewhere?" Vos asked.

"We can have a dock prepared," "Smith" answered for Vos. "We even prepared a location to serve as Dr. Hamilton's clinic near the dock where the *Iron Dutchman* will be docked. However, Dr. Hamilton and Mr. Ganji will have to leave for Japan first to sort out the paperwork as part of Mr. Ganji's cover."

"If we're to go to Japan, we'll need more fuel, though," Semir Bosić, a man as old as Mistry with a body of an average height and weight, brown hair and dark brown eyes.

"We'll have more shipped. While waiting, Mr. Ganji will have to familiarize himself with Japanese society."

"I have a question myself: do we have information on Miss Hoshikawa's social life?" Tarou asked. "Who she talks to on a regular basis? Her hobbies?"

"Kirk will deliver a file on Maria soon enough," "Smith" answered. "Speaking of which, Kirk, next slide."

Projected on the screen was a map of a city. Its name was shown on the left in both *kanji* and English; both written in black. The name in English, found below the *kanji*, read as "Kansai City". Across the map of Kansai City were portions marked by red circles.

"To sum up what you need to know about Maria, you must memorize these locations to keep an eye on her," "Smith" explained before pointing at a circle found at the right side of the map. "This is where the Hoshikawa mansion is located. Now that you know these locations, you are to be positioned here almost every day to keep an eye on Maria but remember, do not let her know you're there. I suggest assigning one individual to a certain location for one day only.

"The following day, another individual must be assigned there. Also. Make a rotation chart to figure who is assigned where and when."

"Sure, sure," Wattana replied. "Now, what about alternative jobs?"

"What do you mean by 'alternative jobs'?"

"What Miss Wattana here is saying is would we be allowed to accept other jobs other than this?" Vos asked. "Nine hundred thousand UN dollars is a lot. But preferably, we like to earn more than that for certain needs."

"Such as?"

"Plate targets for shooting practice."

"Additional parts if we're allowed to keep a Walgear," Federico Díaz added.

"We've considered that. It will depend on the client as to what additional jobs we will approve of."

"Thank so much," Vos replied.

"Any more questions?" "Smith" asked.

"I have one: I assume you're giving us smartphones to use for this job?"

"We are. We feel that it's crucial you need a quick way to communicate with each other."

"Are we allowed to keep them after this job is over?" Hamilton asked.

"Of course. Though we will need to make modifications when it does end, which I assure you that we will. As to when, that's not my place to ask."

"What modifications are you talking about?" Tatev Mirzoyan asked as she appeared at the front center row of the briefing room.

"You'll know soon enough," "Smith" answered as he faced Tatev then turned to every other member of Iron Dutchman Services. "Any more questions?"

A collective "no" from every member followed. "Good," "Smith" replied. "Now then, I have questions for you. Before I ask my first one, you must know that this is simply for information collection to make sure we didn't make a mistake by recruiting you for this job."

"Smith" began looking amongst the members of Iron Dutchman Services. Some showed that they were nervous, but "Smith" didn't notice for varying reasons. Ultimately, he stopped at Tarou.

"Mr. Ganji, this is my first question: where were you born?" "Smith" asked to Tarou.

"I honestly do not know, sir," Tarou answered. "I was found as an infant amongst of a refugee community of Balochs who fled to the Islamic Republic of Iran when the alien ship *Revelator* crashed into Afghanistan in 1985. I am named 'Tarou Ganji' because someone gave a note to the people who found me by my dying mother that contained the name."

"And how long have you been with Iron Dutchman Services?"

"Two years. I was a child soldier who fought during the Eurasian Tsardom's invasion of Iran seven years ago. Since then, I've wondered across the desert until I ran into Iron Dutchman Services in Libya two years ago. Since then, I learned more than what I learned prior to fighting."

"I assume that's all you know about your past?"

"So far, yes."

"And what do you think about this mission?"

"I have nothing negative to say about this mission. I do, however, feel like as if I could learn something about my past through this mission."

"I assume Maria Hoshikawa will relate to this?"

"I don't know but… the fact that Daisuke and Miku Hoshikawa aren't her biological parents makes it feel as if there is a connection."

Wow, Crawley thought. *If Ganji were to use that while talking to a girl, he'll definitely get kicked in the groin.*

"I… see… " "Smith" coughed before facing Vos. "Mr. Vos, what about her?"

Vos saw "Smith" open his right palm and direct it toward Tatev. "Who is she?"

"Tatev Mirzoyan," Vos answered. "We met her in our contract with the African Federation where we put an end to a human trafficking ring operating in Mogadishu. We took in Mirzoyan after that and somehow, she knew her way around computers and other electronics that she gets us contracts, such as this one."

"Mind if she comes down here, please?"

"Sure."

"I'm on my way down!" Tatev shouted as she began to leave the projector room.

Everyone looked at Tatev walking toward the briefing room's stage. Their heads moved just as Tatev continued to climb to the stage, joining Vos and "Smith".

"What do you wish to ask me?" Tatev asked to "Smith".

"I'm surprised you do such work for these mercenaries," "Smith" replied. "Do you mind if I can ask you about your past?"

"My… past?"

"I see. I've heard about it from Mr. Vos. You don't have to tell me-"

"I don't mind, but… mind if I just whisper it to you. I… don't really feel comfortable talking about it openly yet… "

"Alright."

Tatev moved toward "Smith's" right ear and began whispering. Vos promptly moved away, yet he, along with his subordinates, looked on with interest at what Tatev whispered to "Smith".

Tatev then finished the whispering and moved away from "Smith". Vos moved closer again.

"Now I can understand why you took in this girl, and why she hasn't told you about her past yet," "Smith" said as he looked at the rest of the Iron Dutchman Services members. "At this point, I do not have any other questions."

"Smith" then turned to the FIS agent behind. After using body language, the latter gave to the former a piece of paper and in turn gave it to Vos.

"This is the formal contract," "Smith" explained to Vos. "You have until tomorrow to go over it and sign it. If you haven't signed it by tomorrow, consider this opportunity forfeit."

"Got it," Vos replied.

The FIS agent named "Kirk" then joined "Smith". "We'll return tomorrow for that contract. Good luck with going over it and signing it if you do wish to pursue it."

"What happens if we don't accept this contract tomorrow?" Vos asked while "Smith" and his men began to walk away from the former.

"That will be up to your imagination," "Smith" answered. "To help you with your decision, you can keep that USB with you 'till tomorrow. I'd be better that your signature on the contract be dry when I come back."

#

1650 hours

Every member of Iron Dutchman Services was in their namesake's dining room. They all surrounded Tatev Mirzoyan as she used her laptop computer. The screen of Tatev's laptop now showed a file on Maria Hoshikawa. Everything from date of birth until her personal hobbies was on the file.

Tatev then continued reading through the file. Using a red-colored circle found in the middle of the laptop's keyboard, Tatev was able to move the arrow on the screen that was used as a visual marker of going from one place to another throughout the computer. Tatev moved the red circle on the keyboard to the right end of the screen, placing the arrow toward a rectangle in the middle of a longer rectangle. Pressing a button in the lower-center row of the keyboard, Tatev then moved the red circle downward.

That lowered the file from the profile on Maria that mercenaries were reading to a document. The writing was both in Japanese and English. Anita Hamilton was the first to read this part of the file and examined it closely.

"This must be her medical certificate," Hamilton surmised. "I see nothing out of the ordinary here."

"Hold on, there should be more," Tatev warned as she pressed the same button and moved the red circle in the middle of the keyboard downward.

Now shown on the screen was something similar to the medical certificate Hamilton read. As a result, Hamilton examined the document again.

"This is strange. It says here that Miss Hoshikawa was discovered on November 3, 2013."

"The Sea of Japan must have been awfully cold at that time of year," Vos said. "She should have died before Daisuke and Miku even found her and she was just only an infant."

"Hold on, there should be more to this," Tatev added as she moved the file further down.

"This is a report about that particular incident by the Foreign Intelligence Service," Hamilton stated as she saw the document now displayed on the laptop's screen.

As Hamilton said, the document belonged to the FIS, as shown with the three letters and "Intelligence Collective" on the upper-left corner of the document. Unlike the earlier documents, this part of the file was written entirely in English.

"Figures the FIS would be really interested inwhy a baby would survive cold waters," Vos said. "Anything else on Hoshikawa?"

"Hold on," Tatev replied.

Tatev moved the file further down. Now shown were records that bore the insignia of Nishi High School.

"Incredibly good grades," Sunan Wattana remarked as she was able to see the documents now shown on Tatev's laptop screen.

"Wait… that could be it," Tarou Ganji added.

"Got something, Ganji?" Crawley asked Tarou with every other mercenary, including Tatev, looking at Tarou.

"We have an infant girl that was found in the middle of the Sea of Japan and now gets high grades in the school she studies at. Then there's how she was found an hour after a boat was destroyed in the middle of the Sea of Japan."

"What are you insinuating?" Wattana asked.

"That Maria must be either from the Eurasian Tsardom or the Russian Soviet Federative Socialist Republic based on her appearance."

"And how strange is that?" Vos asked. "Other than surviving cold ocean water but even other teenagers, people the FIS shouldn't have worried about to the point of hiring mercenaries, wouldn't be the type to attract other intelligence agencies."

"I think Ganji has a point," Wattana replied. "The girl might get good grades and is skilled enough in Judo to be the president of Nishi High School's Judo club but it doesn't change the fact that all of this happened in the Sea of Japan, which its namesake shares with Soviet Russia, the Eurasian Tsardom, and North Korea. It isn't just the FIS who should have been able to hear of this incident."

"Then there's how proof the Gatekeepers of Knowledge are involved in this," Tatev added. "The Gatekeepers have not revealed much about themselves and the fact that they're creating their own military was something that was discovered around the same time. If I were Grand Gatekeeper Sergei Akulov, I'd commission a test of a bomber to see if it's capable of being used by the Gatekeepers' military."

"But why attack a boat in the middle of the Sea of Japan?" Vos argued. "Especially if an infant was bound to have survived the attack?"

"Then the Gatekeepers might also be connected to Hoshikawa," Tarou replied. "With what they did in order to gauge their response about the alleged bomber, it was natural that they would need someone to keep an eye on Hoshikawa but now we have two questions: how connected are they to a baby that can survive cold ocean waters and achieve what we've read in this file and why?"

"That's a good point," Crawley replied. "This might veer into comic book plot, but only a mysterious organization like the Gatekeepers could pull this off."

"Even if that were the case, why would the Gatekeepers be involved in the birth of an infant?" Hamilton added. "Other than that, what would a boat be doing in the Sea of Japan that the Gatekeepers could be involved?"

"Regardless, we will discuss the ramifications of this contract later," Vos said. "Everyone, return to your respective rooms and wait until Barto finishes cooking tonight's dinner."

Everyone but Vos left the dining room. *I better review this contract until then,* Vos thought.

Movement

Iron Dutchman; Naval Station Pearl Harbor, City and County of Honolulu, State of Hawaii. March 4, 2030; 1959 hours (Hawaii-Aleutian Time)

"Attention, everyone!" Wouter Vos loudly proclaimed after he and his subordinates finished their dinner in the ship's dining room while standing up. "I've finished reviewing the contract before we started eating and before I begin signing it or not, I must ask for those in favor of this contract and those who aren't.

"We will vote on either option and we will go for the option with the most votes. I'll serve as the tiebreaker vote if it comes down to it. Now, who votes that we take this contract?"

"Might I ask something before we start voting?" Anita Hamilton asked.

"Yes, Doc?" Vos asked in response.

"Why ask for votes?"

"Because if I said we're taking this contract right now, most of you will complain if I sign without taking your feelings into account."

"That's fair," Sunan Wattana replied.

"Anything else?" Vos asked.

Every other member of Iron Dutchman Services replied no. "Good," Vos replied. "Once you raise your hand, please state if you say yes or no to this contract."

"I vote yes," Hamilton said as she raised her hand first. Everyone looked at her with surprise.

"I'm impressed you're the first to vote," Vos remarked as he watched Hamilton raise her right hand.

"We could use the payment for more clothes," Hamilton replied.

"I'm in," Wattana added, followed by raising her right hand. "Same reason, as I stated earlier."

"Same here," Jason Luke Crawley added, before he raised his hand. "Besides, I've always wanted to go to Japan."

"I vote that we accept," Tarou declared while raising his hand. "However, it's only as I stated to Mr. 'Smith' earlier: to see if this will get me closer as to who I really am."

"You *really* haven't changed since that day," Vos replied.

"I vote that we don't go," Tatev Mirzoyan announced as she raised her hand.

"And why is that?" Vos asked as he faced Tatev.

"We could end up making an enemy out of the Gatekeepers of Knowledge if we're not careful enough."

"That's a good reason. Anyone else?"

"I vote yes," Bartolomeu Moura announced as he raised his hand. "I've always wanted to try out Japanese food."

"Díaz, Mistry, Bosić, what about you three?" Vos asked as he turned to Federico Díaz, Vikas Mistry, and Semir Bosić.

"Mind if we abstain from voting?" Mistry asked. "Does it even matter to us in the maintenance section?"

"Same here," Bosić, a man as old as Mistry but with light skin and light brown hair, argued. "We're still doing the same things whether we take this contract or not."

"Five yes, one no, and three abstaining," Vos declared. "As for me, I say yes. Therefore, I'll be signing this contract."

Vos sat down again and pushed his empty plate in order to lay the contract on the table. Grabbing his pen, Vos wrote his name on the portions of the contract where his name was to be written. After writing his name into the last portion where it was needed in the contract, Vos wrote his signature above his full name in the same portion.

"And now, we wait till 'Smith' returns," Vos added.

March 5, 2030; 1007 hours

"Fred Smith" and his two guards returned to the docked *Iron Dutchman.* The gangway has already been prepared for them and once they proceeded inside the ship, they found Tarou Ganji and Sunan Wattana in their way.

"Mr. Vos has been expecting you three," Tarou said to the three FIS agents. "Please follow us."

The three FIS agents opted to listen to what the teenage mercenary had to say and followed him along with the female mercenary. Like it was in the previous day, the FIS men marveled that they were surrounded by reminders of the world before it was torn apart by the Third World War.

#

1024 hours

Tarou and Wattana, along with the FIS men, then reached the portion of the *Iron Dutchman* where the lifeboats were located at. Wouter Vos waited by himself while looking at Pearl Harbor.

"Mr. 'Smith' is here," Tarou announced to Vos.

"Good work," Vos replied before turning to see those that came to him. "Ganji, Wattana, you're dismissed."

"Yes, sir," Wattana replied before she and Tarou saluted and left.

Vos then stepped toward "Smith". He brought out a small envelope and gave it to "Smith". The FIS agent opened the envelope and found the contract he gave to Vos the day before folded in half.

Giving the envelope to the agent named "Kirk", "Smith" unfolded the contract and found that Vos had signed it. He examined the contract before folding it again and giving it to "Kirk", who placed it back in the envelope.

"You did well to make sure the ink is dry," "Smith" said to Vos.

"Thank you," Vos replied. "What happens now?"

"I'll be returning to Langley to make my report on this. After that, books and other tools will be sent here for Mr. Ganji to use in learning how to blend in. As for me, I'm to go to Japan to personally tell Mr. Hoshikawa about this."

"How much will you be bringing here?"

"Enough for Mr. Ganji to learn enough to blend in. He's only seventeen, after all."

"You're going to have to bring more than that. Ganji can learn a language in a week. It's how he learned English when we first took him in."

"Thank you for the warning," "Smith" said before turning his back on Vos and using his right index finger, which in turn made "Kirk" and the other FIS agent turn their respective backs. "I must get going now. Do take care and until I return for further instructions, you are to remain here."

"Smith" and his men then left. Vos turned back to where he was facing earlier. *This better be worth the wait,* Vos anxiously thought.

#

FIS Headquarters, McLean, Fairfax County, Commonwealth of Virginia; United States of America. March 5, 2030; 0949 hours (Eastern Standard Time)

"I'm impressed," Stanley McAllister as he looked at the contract signed by Wouter Vos given to him by "Fred Smith". "Vos agreed to take up this contract. Personally, what do you think of Iron Dutchman Services?"

"I think they can do this job," "Smith" answered. "However, I believe they'll need to be given incentives that will make them more willing to work hard."

"I'll deal with that. You're dismissed for now. I suggest you get some sleep."

"Thank you, sir."

"Smith" then left the office. McAllister again looked at the contract.

Why did it have to be Iron Dutchman Services? McAllister pondered with embarassment clear in his face. *They're bound to mess this up, but as 'Smith' suggests, all they need is enough incentive for them to do their hardest.*

1028 hours

"Did 'Smith' really suggest that?" Alberto Pérez asked after McAllister came to his office to report what "Smith" had told him.

"He did, Al," McAllister answered.

"And I assume these mercenaries are still in Pearl Harbor?"

"Yes."

"Get those Japanese language materials sent there. You're dismissed."

#

McAllister Residence. March 6, 2030; 0316 hours

McAllister had returned to his house, located in Salona Village in the unincorporated community of McLean. Many politicians lived in McLean as it was near Washington D.C., capital of the United States of America. Although he didn't serve the US government, Stanley McAllister owning a house in Salona Village was a necessity, as he was the Foreign Intelligence Service's Deputy Director of Covert Operations.

Because his house was located in Salona Village, McAllister was able to return to his house to rest there for four hours at minimum due to his position. After being received by his wife Cynthia, McAllister started to undress before taking a bath.

Unbeknownst to his wife, McAllister hid a laptop computer in their bedroom's closet and activated it. Using a certain program, he began to type using the laptop's keyboard.

#

Unknown Location; Enlightenment Point. 1359 hours (EP Time Zone)

In a darkened room, a man sat alone in a throne. He hid his face by way of a hood and his entire body with a cloak as if he were a monk from Europe after the collapse of the Western Roman Empire. This man was Sergei Akulov, the Grand Gatekeeper of Knowledge.

In 1985, an alien ship crashed into the Democratic Republic of Afghanistan, a hotbed of armed conflict since 1978 that eventually saw troops from the Union of Soviet Socialist Republics intervening a year later. The destruction caused by the ship's crash forced those who miraculously survived to abandon Afghanistan. A scientific team from the USSR studied the ship. Following their studies, they announced that the ship was alien in origin, christening the ship as *Revelator* as the crash was a "revelation" to all of mankind that sentient and intelligent life existed across space.

Yet, not much had changed as this was the "Cold War" the USSR waged with the United States of America. In 1989, nuclear weapons had been detonated in the USSR's capital of Moscow and New York City in the US. The nuclear weapon that struck Moscow was found to have used materials from the People's Republic of China while the material in the bomb that struck New York City was from the Soviet Union. This started the Third World War and after the destruction many feared that came to past in this war, it was discovered that disgruntled Afghan refugees, who hated how the international community focused on *Revelator* rather than their plight, were responsible yet they were discovered to have killed themselves, the Third World War came to an end but there was a need to rebuild.

The Gatekeepers of Knowledge, created by the scientific expedition that studied *Revelator* that hid within the ship throughout the war, offered what they were able to learn from the ship to help rebuild the world. This came with a price—the Gatekeepers demanding that they acquire custody of not only *Revelator* but all of Afghanistan. Reluctantly, the international community allowed the Gatekeepers to turn Afghanistan into their own nation-state and as such, it was renamed "Enlightenment Point" as *Revelator*'s crash "enlightened" mankind about its place across the stars. Since then, the present-day order where nation-states banded together into supernational unions to rebuild after the damage wrought by the Third World War came to be associated with the Gatekeepers. Upon founding the Gatekeepers, Sergei Akulov declared himself the "Grand Gatekeeper".

Another hooded man appeared and stood before Akulov. He clenched his right hand into a fist, placed it toward his chest, and bowed.

"Grand Gatekeeper, we've received an update from our Devotee-Infiltrator in the New United Nation's Intelligence Collective," the hooded man said to Akulov.

"What is it?" Akulov asked.

"A mercenary group has taken up the contract to protect Maria Hoshikawa covertly."

"Which mercenary group is this?"

"Iron Dutchman Services."

"The same ones involved in the arrest of Rolf Núñez?"

"Yes, Grand Gatekeeper. They're currently docked in Pearl Harbor, preparing to go to Japan in a month."

"Anything else our contact mentioned?"

"Tarou Ganji will infiltrate Nishi High School."

"Wait, did you say Tarou Ganji?"

"Yes, Grand Gatekeeper."

"No doubt he'll be spending this month learning how to blend into Japan but as this is the same Tarou Ganji who joined Iron Dutchman Services two years ago, we must also keep an eye on him. As for Miss Hoshikawa, we will need Muhadow."

"Serdar Muhadow?"

"Yes. Where is he now?"

"He's training the Turkestani Army in guerilla warfare right now."

"Get him in here. Also, inform our Devotee-Infiltrator in the OVR to inform the Tsar about this."

"T… The Eurasian Tsardom's OVR?"

"Yes. I know there's someone who wishes to know who Maria Hoshikawa really is. We'll use that to our advantage, then leave it to Muhadow to figure out how to get to Miss Hoshikawa."

"By your will, Grand Gatekeeper."

#

OVR Headquarters, Nizhegorodsky District, Imperial Capital of Nizhny Novgorod; Eurasian Tsardom. 1706 hours (Novgorod Time)

In his office at the headquarters of the *Otdeleniye Vneshney Razvedi* (OVR), the Eurasian Tsardom's external intelligence service, Vyacheslav

Leonidovich Puzanov sat as he looked at a file in front of him with his blue eyes. Sixty-seven years old, Puzanov is the Director of the OVR. Like his counterpart in the Foreign Intelligence Service of the New United Nations' Intelligence Collective, Vyacheslav Puzanov served as a soldier, as demonstrated by his graying brown hair in a crew cut.

Sixty-seven years old, Puzanov was old enough to remember the Union of Soviet Socialist Republics prior to its destruction in the Third World War. Prior to that, Puzanov served as a sergeant in the Soviet Army when it sent troops to intervene in the conflict in the Democratic Republic of Afghanistan that started in 1978. When the *Revelator* crashed into Afghanistan in 1985, many Soviet soldiers died in the disaster. Puzanov was among the few to survive as his unit was under the command of one Ivan Vladimirovich Tsulukidze. When the war ended, Tsulukidze and Puzanov's unit came out of hiding to find that the USSR had collapsed as Soviet military officers fought each other over the burnt remains. Both opted to put an end to these wars in what was now known as the "Unification War", which ended in victory for Tsulukidze and his army.

Tsulukidze opted to create a monarchical state from the ashes of the USSR. This state became the Eurasian Tsardom with Tsulukidze as its Tsar. Vyacheslav Puzanov created the OVR as its foreign intelligence agency, as he was known to have contributed to Tsulukidze's victories by launching infiltration missions in the Unification War.

A buzz was heard throughout Puzanov's office with the director knowing what that entailed. The door opened and coming inside was one Tatiana Ioannovona Tsulukidze, who wore a pantsuit that covered most of her very light skin.

Forty years old with long brown hair in a bun and gray eyes, Tatiana was the only daughter of Tsar Ivan Vladimirovich Tsulukidze. Many within the OVR thought that Tatiana only joined the OVR by using her name, yet Puzanov nor her father saw it that way.

"Gospazitza Tsulukidze, glad you made it," Puzanov said to Tatiana.

"You have something for me?" Tatiana asked.

"I do. I've recently come across new information about Maria Hoshikawa."

"Respectfully, Director, but why ask me to call all this way to tell me? Why not contact me using the usual method?"

"Because I received this information while having lunch. I don't know how, but you can imagine why."

"Then I will get this information, but I will return to Japan upon doing so."

"It's for the best."

"Spasibo."

Tatiana proceeded to Puzanov's desk and received the file. Upon doing so, Tatiana left the office and, by extension, the Tsardom.

#

FIS Headquarters, Langley, Commonwealth of Virginia; United States of America. 0915 hours (Eastern Standard Time)

"You called for me, sir?" "Fred Smith" asked as he entered Stanley McAllister's office in FIS Headquarters.

"I did," McAllister answered just as "Smith" stopped walking. "You're to schedule a flight to Japan as soon as possible."

"I'm to see Mr. Hoshikawa?"

"You two were in the same unit back in the Ground Defense Force Special Operations Brigade, right?"

"We were. Need I elaborate?"

"No need. However, I suggest you don't cause any trouble to him nor his family should you approach him."

"Understood, sir."

#

Unknown Location; Enlightenment Point. March 7, 2030; 0225 hours (EP Time Zone)

A man in his forties with a body of average height and weight, short black hair on his scalp, facial hair of the same color, dark brown eyes, and light intermediate skin arrived at the throne room of Sergei Akulov, the Grand Gatekeeper of Knowledge. The former wore a military uniform for officers that resembled the uniforms of the Spanish Army from the mid-

19th century until the early 20th century made with *rayadillo* as the tunic and trousers, both of which were white, were filled with blue-colored stripes. The tunic consisted of five gold buttons and four pockets, with two on each side of the tunic. Although hidden by the tunic, a brown leather belt held the trousers and for footwear, the man wore black-colored boots.

"Glad you made it, Serdar Muhadow," Akulov said as he saw his subordinate clench his right first toward his chest and bowed.

"I live to serve you, Grand Gatekeeper," the man named Muhadow replied.

"Before I tell you why I summoned you here, I must ask: how goes training the Turkestani Army?"

"It goes well, Grand Gatekeeper. My men have been able to teach the Turkestani Army guerilla tactics that will benefit them greatly. Of course, Eurasian equipment will give them an edge."

"Glad to hear that. Now, I've called you here because I've received news that another mercenary group by the name of Iron Dutchman Services have been hired by the New United Nations protect one Maria Hoshikawa covertly and you're to abduct her."

"Wait, did you say Maria Hoshikawa? The daughter of Daisuke Hoshikawa?"

"Yes. Anything else you want to ask?"

"Why her?"

"That is need-to-know. However, I will allow you to get your mercenary unit to assist you in this endeavor."

"Grand Gatekeeper, if I may, how will I be able to get this girl? With those mercenaries around, whatever plans we can devise will be thwarted."

"You'll be assisted by the OVR on this."

"The OVR?"

"I've already warned them about Maria Hoshikawa. They too are on need to know. All you need to do for the time being is return to your men in Turkestan and await further instructions, which will be relayed to you by Gatekeeper Turkestan."

"By your will, Grand Gatekeeper."

Muhadow repeated his salute before leaving the throne room. As soon as Muhadow was no longer in sight, a woman stepped out of the shadows and before Akulov. Hooded from head up to the ankles, the woman did the same salute.

"Keep an eye on him," Akulov ordered. "Among those within Iron Dutchman Services is an individual the both of you are familiar with."

The hooded woman had nothing else to respond with Akulov catching on. Despite that, the woman repeated her salute.

"By your will, Grand Gatekeeper," the woman replied.

#

Turkestan Tachyon Particle Receiver; Turkestani Republic. 0948 hours (Turkestan Time)

A Vertical Takeoff and Landing (VTOL) transport aircraft used by the Gatekeepers of Knowledge's private air force, the Wings of the Defenders, reached the Tachyon Particle Receiver of the Turkestani Republic.

One invention of the Gatekeepers that helped rebuild the world after the Third World War was the Tachyon Particle Generator (TPG), which can generate "Tachyon Particles". Tachyon particles, once a staple of science-fiction stories, became a reality as harnessing them was a discovery of the alien ship Revelator. When the Gatekeepers of Knowledge was established, they introduced the TPG as a way to provide communications in a world ravaged by war. To connect the world, the Gatekeepers were treated as a neutral power in exchange for them making Afghanistan their own state, which the Gatekeepers renamed to Enlightenment Point.

Stable countries have established Tachyon Particle Receivers (TPRs) in order to receive the particles generated by the only TPG built in Enlightenment Point. Many have been convinced that the Gatekeepers rule the world from the shadows because they control the only means of post-World War III communications as many have understood that if the Gatekeepers' wrath has been incurred, they can shut down a country's TPR, especially after most countries created supernational unions.

Once the VTOL transport landed at the helipad attached to the Turkestan TPR, Serdar Muhadow disembarked. Three men who belong to the

Gatekeepers stood in Mudahow's way. Like their Grand Gatekeeper, they too hide their entire bodies with cloaks and heads with hoods. Two of these men carried assault rifles.

"Welcome back, Devotee-Colonel Muhadow," the unarmed Gatekeeper said. "I can imagine you slept on your flight?"

"I have," Muhadow answered. "I wish to continue resting for two more hours."

"You may. When you've finished, call up your officers because I've just received instructions from the Grand Gatekeeper himself."

Both Muhadow and the Gatekeeper did the same salute the former did in Enlightenment Point, along with the words "By the Grand Gatekeeper's will." Muhadow then left with the two armed Gatekeepers getting out of his way.

"Smith" Residence, Fairfax, Commonwealth of Virginia; United States of America. March 8, 2030; 0510 hours (Eastern Standard Time)

"Smith" was now holding a suitcase on one hand, leaving one free for the door, yet a wheel bag stood beside him. A woman as old as "Smith" approached him. She had dark intermediate skin, long brown hair, and light brown eyes.

"I assume you're ready?" the woman asked.

"I am, dear," "Smith" answered. "I apologize for this."

"You always say that before you leave. Don't worry, I understand. Just come back alive."

"I will." "Smith" followed this with a kiss to the woman's left cheek.

"I'm going," "Smith" added before opening the door, using his right hand for the wheeled bag, and leaving his house.

#

Japan Air 747-300; Above Kansai City, Kansai Prefecture; State of Japan. 0150 hours (Japan Standard Time)

"Smith's" flight reached Kansai City in Japan. Miraculously, "Smith" sat on one of the seats with a window at the side where he could see Kansai City. He saw the flooded hole where the city of Osaka once stood.

During the Third World War, Japan was targeted because of the presence of the United States Armed Forces. Cities such as Osaka, Yokosuka, and the capital of Tokyo were hit by nuclear bombardments as a result. In the case of Osaka, most of the city became a flooded crater as a result that it became to be known as "Crater Bay".

Miraculously, the nearby city of Higashiosaka wasn't harmed. Portions of Osaka not hit and Higashiosaka were merged into the present-day Kansai City with Higashiosaka itself turned into a ward for the new city. Overall, the Osaka Prefecture, which got its name from the city of the same it was centered on, was renamed "Kansai Prefecture".

"Smith's" plane began to approach Kansai International Airport. Built on an artificial island off the city of Izumisano, Kansai International Airport had been in construction since 1987 and despite the delay from the Third World War and the Great Hanshin Earthquake of 1996, construction of the airport continued that it was finished in 1996. Now, it served airliners going to Osaka, mostly for foreign airliners.

#

Suminoe Station, Suminoe Ward, Kansai City. 0429 hours

After going through customs and immigration at Kansai International Airport, along with a forty-one-minute train ride that involved transferring from the line used for going to the airport to the Nankai Main Line, "Fred Smith" reached Kansai City itself. His train ultimately stopped at Suminoe Station.

The Nankai Main Line started in 1885 naturally became a casualty of the Third World War. As a result, when it was restarted, the Nankai Main Line was now between the Suminoe and the Wakayamako stations; the latter located in Wakayama.

Once he got off his train, "Smith" began paying for a ticket to use for any turnstyles he came across. After going through the last turnstyle to leave the station, and a brief stop at a vending machine for water, "Smith" sought out a taxi stand. Once he found the taxi stand nearest the station exit where he came from, "Smith" managed to attract the attention of the driver of the first taxi within the stand's taxi line, getting him and his luggage inside the taxi.

"Hoteru Soreiyu made onegaishimasu," "Smith" requested in Japanese.

Hotel Soleil, Higashiosaka Ward. 1607 hours

In his room in Hotel Solelil, "Smith" used his laptop computer to access the Internet. Using his search engine's "Maps" function, "Smith" typed in Kansai City on the search bar.

Once the search engine showed an interactive map of Kansai City, "Smith" typed in "Catholic church in Kansai City". After pressing his laptop's "Enter" button, red dots with lines pointed to varying locations in the interactive map. "Smith" found a church located in the Rokumanjincho neighborhood whose name was translated as "Catholic Hamada Church".

You really haven't changed, Daisuke, "Smith" thought. *Now, let's see what time do they hold Mass on Sundays...*

"Smith" went to a link pertaining to Catholic churches across the Kansai Prefecture. The website, however, was entirely in Japanese. "Smith" pressed an icon on the address bar of the Internet browser that consisted of a square with the letter T inside. Pressing the square, the website was now in English.

Says here the Hamada Church holds Mass at 9 AM, "Smith" thought. *Problem is, if this is this the church Daisuke goes to and to find out, I need to install a phone tracker. I just need to find a suitable location to plant that device.*

"Smith" continued looking at the map. He found that near the Hamada Church was near a café called "Olive House".

This will do. I just need to call up a taxi for tomorrow.

#

Hamada Church/Olive House. March 9, 2030; 1047 hours

"Koko de ii desu," "Smith" said to his taxi driver as they neared the Hamada Church.

The taxi then stopped in front of the church. "Roku hyaku roku-jyu en ni narimasu," the driver stated as to how much was the trip.

"Hai douzo," "Smith" replied as he handed the driver 660 yen before leaving the taxi.

As the taxi left after saying thanks, "Smith" walked past the church. He turned to his right, where the Onji River was on his left. He then stopped as he found what he was looking for: the Olive House café.

#

Olive House. 1051 hours

"Irasshaimase!" the female owner of Olive House said cheerfully as "Smith" entered the café.

"Smith" removed his sunglasses upon finding a table. The proprietress grabbed a menu and gave it to "Smith".

"Is this your first time here?" the woman asked.

"Hai," "Smith" replied.

"Here's your menu," the woman said while offering the menu to "Smith".

The FIS agent grabbed the menu and upon opening it, had little to no trouble reading it even if it was entirely in Japanese.

"You seem to know enough Japanese to read that menu," the woman remarked.

"Arigatou," "Smith" replied.

It didn't take long for "Smith" to finish reading the menu. He then stated his orders with the proprietress, writing everything the former stated. Once the latter finished, she grabbed the menu and left to prepare "Smith's" orders.

Unbeknownst to the proprietress, "Smith" grabbed what he came to leave at the café. It was a rectangular device with a small glass circle at its center. "Smith" then pressed the button on the top end of the device and, after doing so, flipped it before landing it on his table. He then used his left hand to grab the double-sided tape he kept in his trousers' left pocket. Placing a small piece onto the device, "Smith" moved fast yet strongly in pulling the piece out of the tape as a whole.

"Smith" succeeded, yet he tore off an amount larger than what he anticipated. Despite that, he put the tape back into his left pocket and used his left hand to remove the top end's cover. After that, he took the device under his table and stuck the device underneath the table.

It was then that the proprietress appeared with "Smith's" order. The latter helped himself yet he knew that despite the kindness the woman exhibited to him, lying to her and making her an unwitting accomplice were a part of his orders.

Meeting

Hotel Soleil, Higashiosaka Ward, Kansai City, Kansai Prefecture; State of Japan. March 10, 2030; 0532 hours (Japan Standard Time)

The smartphone that belonged to "Fred Smith" rang an alarm in his bedroom at Hotel Soleil in Kansai City. "Smith" woke up as a result and turned off the alarm. Miraculously, he managed to stay awake and began to leave his bed in order to use his laptop computer.

Upon turning on his computer, "Smith" accessed an application called "Phone Tracker". The application showed a map of Kansai City with a red circle summoning bigger circles, and it was located at Olive House. As a result, blue circles popped up across the map.

"Smith" focused on a blue circle found behind Hotel Soleil. He then moved to his bathroom as he knew what that blue circle was.

Everything from his tooth brushing to his bath was done fast. After the latter, "Smith" picked out casual clothing that he brought with him for the trip and after putting them on, yet wearing the same pair of shoes he wore since he left his house in Fairfax, "Smith" rushed out of the door.

#

Nukata Station. 0619 hours

In his casual clothing, "Smith" reached Nukata Station, also located at the Yamatecho neighborhood despite its name pertaining to the nearby Nukatacho neighborhood which he entered to enter the station. Because train services started an hour before, the station, like many of it across Japan, was welcoming its first crowd.

"Smith" was undaunted by this. After getting a bottle of coffee from the nearest vending machine, he bought his ticket. Now, he got inside the station and waited for the train like everybody else.

While waiting, "Smith" drank his coffee, as that was the only nourishment he could get on such short notice. Resisting the temptation of eating even with his stomach on the line was nothing new for "Smith". Both he and Daisuke Hoshikawa served in the Special Operations Brigade of the New United Nations Ground Defense Force, nicknamed "Green Berets" as this brigade not only inherited the nickname but also the namesake and a fair number of the old Special Forces of the United States Army. Unlike Daisuke, who left the military and continued his studies that he eventually inherited Hoshikawa Group, "Smith" remained until he was approached to join the Foreign Intelligence Service of the Intelligence Collective.

"Mamonaku, densha ga mairimasu," a female voice announced over the station's PA system with its English equivalent said afterward.

"Smith" gulped the last of his coffee and rushed to the nearest trash cans. One was for plastic and as his bottle was made of plastic, "Smith" knew where the bottle went and after throwing the bottle, he rushed back to his original position just as an announcement was made.

#

Hiraoka Station/Pandoh. 0621 hours

The train now reached Hiraoka Station. "Smith" off the train and left the station. As he turned to his right, he saw a nearby bakery.

I rushed out of the hotel to avoid a large crowd, "Smith" thought. *I should see what time that bakery opens. If I'm lucky, I might be its first customer for the day.*

"Smith" left Hiraoka Station to go to the nearby bakery. The name was written in three *katakana* with one *kanji*. In total, the name read as "Pandoh". However, "Smith" found that the bakery wasn't open yet.

Figures, "Smith" thought as he read a sign on the right side of the entrance that showed times. *This bakery doesn't open until 7:15 AM. Though I can wait because Mass doesn't start until 9 PM.*

#

0715 hours

The proprietor of Pandoh, a man, came out to turn the "Closed" sign into an "Open" sign. Just as he finished, he saw "Smith" standing beside the bakery's ice cream container and briefly gulped upon seeing the man.

"Excuse me, but… how long have you been standing there?" the proprietor asked.

"Hontou ni gomen nasai," "Smith" replied with a bow. "I didn't mean to disturb you. I hoped to get some breakfast because I have something to do elsewhere and I left early to catch the first train. I only hoped to buy from your establishment."

"I see. Please come inside."

#

Shijocho Park No. 1. 0741 hours

"Smith", with the food and coffee bottle he bought from Pandoh and nearby vending machines respectively, came across Park No. 1 of Higashiosaka's Shijocho neighborhood. However, he stopped and looked at the food he bought.

I best limit how much I eat before anyone notices, "Smith" thought.

The FIS agent then found a bench to sit on. Putting down his bag onto the ground and the coffee bottle beside him, "Smith" grabbed a loaf of bread wrapped in plastic. Opening the plastic, "Smith" began to eat it, but slowly, as he knew that leaving a single crumb on the park bench would get him into trouble. As a result, only half of his bread remained, yet he continued.

After that, "Smith" looked to find a single crumb. Miraculously, there wasn't. He then looked around him.

Looks like I can at least continue with one more piece before I drink my coffee and leave, "Smith" thought. He then continued eating what he bought at Pando and, like the first loaf, he was slow in his eating to prevent crumbs from falling off the bread. As he finished, he looked for crumbs again and, like before, there weren't any crumbs.

For "Smith", now was the time to leave. He stood up, grabbed his coffee, opened it, and put the lid inside the paper bag. Finishing the entire bottle, "Smith" put the bottle inside the bag before grabbing it and leaving the park.

Hamada Church. 0751 hours

With the remaining food he bought, "Smith" reached Hamada Church. Those who served the church supervised the Hiraoka Catholic Kindergarten beside it.

"Smith" approached the church and, upon going inside, a nun got in his way. She mostly gazed upon the paper bag with the food "Smith" brought with him.

"What might you be doing here with that bag?" the nun asked.

"Actually, I plan on hearing Mass later," "Smith" answered as a half-lie. "As for this food, I ended up buying too much. I was hoping if you could take the rest of it. I'll just help myself to one."

"Are you being honest with what you said?"

"Of course."

"Thank you." The nun took the bag while "Smith" took the empty plastic he tore open and the coffee bottle he finished earlier at Shojicho Park No. 1 and one unopened bag with bread inside without the nun noticing. After that, he began to leave.

"Where are you going?" the nun asked.

"To the nearby vending machine," "Smith" answered. "After I eat this bread and get another bottle of coffee, I wish to go inside before Mass begins."

"You plan on praying the Rosary before Mass starts?"

"Hai desu."

#

1003 hours

Mass had ended that Sunday morning. As everyone in attendance moved their respective right hands' fingers, except for the thumb, to do the Sign of the Cross, "Smith" quickly glanced at the empty coffee bottle he placed close to the right legs of the chair of one attendant, Maria Hoshikawa. Unlike every other parishioner, Maria wore her Nishi High School uniform that hid her athletic build and despite it being a Sunday, Nishi High School students had to wear the uniform out of decorum, yet most students didn't obey the policy.

After everyone said "Kami ni kansha shimasu" to end the Mass, the priest began to move in order to bow before the cross. He then began to leave the altar, yet everyone wasn't going to leave yet as it was protocol for those hearing Mass to not leave until the priest left the altar. He had dark intermediate skin, dark brown eyes, and slicked-back black hair as he came from the Philippines, who contributed many workers in the reconstruction of Japan following the Third World War and that this priest had been in Japan to tend to his flock, who mostly outnumbered native parishioners like the Hoshikawa family.

Once the priest left the altar, "Smith" was the first to leave, but not before a quick kneel with his right knee. After that, he left, but upon stepping out, he heard Maria accidentally hitting the bottle with her leg.

Despite that, "Smith" continued to exit the church. Maria then picked up the bottle.

"What's a coffee bottle doing here?" Miku Hoshikawa asked. Maria's adoptive mother, Miku, was a fifty-year-old woman with black hair in a bun and dark brown eyes. She wore a lavender-colored dress with a collar and sleeve cuffs colored purple and short-heeled shoes also colored lavender.

"I don't know," Maria replied as she opened the bottle.

Maria then found a piece of paper inside the bottle and managed to remove it. "Can we please look at that paper when we reach the limousine?" Daisuke Hoshikawa requested.

As old as his wife Miku, Daisuke also had black hair and dark brown eyes. He wore a beige trench coat over his buttoned shirt and black tie, a brown leather belt, and black-colored trousers and shoes.

"Hai, Otou-sama," Maria replied.

The Hoshikawas knelt, then left. Despite his position as president of one of the largest *keiretsu* in Japan, Daisuke Hoshikawa found time to hear Mass with his wife and daughter.

The Hoshikawas then reached their limousine, parked at the lot in front of Hiraoka Catholic Kindergarten. The driver saw the Hoshikawas and bowed. As they were no longer inside the church, Maria unfolded the paper she found inside the bottle and read the writing on the paper.

"You can resume reading," Daisuke said to Maria.

"What does it say, Maria?" Miku asked.

"It's entirely in English but written backwards. 'Find me at Hotel Soleil. Preferably for the both of us, come after work'." Maria then found an "F" written at the bottom-right of the paper.

"Someone whose name starts with an F wrote this," Maria added.

"Maria, think I could please have that paper?" Daisuke asked.

"Of course," Maria replied upon turning to Daisuke before giving him the paper.

"Daisuke, do you know anything about this?" Miku asked her husband.

"I will tell you in due time," Daisuke answered to his wife and daughter. "For now, we must leave."

#

Hoshikawa Group Headquarters, Taisho Ward. 2309 hours

At the portion of Osaka now a part of Kansai City stood the headquarters of Hoshikawa Group. To many, it came as a shock that the headquarters of one of the largest *keireitsu* in Japan isn't as grand as they would expect it to be, especially in contrast to what can be found in the current capital of Nagoya.

Hoshikawa Group played a significant role in the reconstruction of Japan after the Third World War. Yet their headquarters, which paled in comparison to other corporations across Japan, stood in the portion of Osaka not harmed by the nuclear bombing as a combination of the character of the President of Hoshikawa Group and the influence they held in post-war Japan.

After separating with a group of his high-ranking employees, Daisuke Hoshikawa reached his limousine. He and the driver bowed before the former boarded the limousine.

"Ugaki, please take me to Hotel Soleil." Daisuke ordered.

"Might I please know why?" the driver named Ugaki replied.

"It's a secret."

"Wakarimashita."

#

Sakai. 2338 hours

Ugaki now drove Daisuke's limousine into Sakai. He and Daisuke used this route to return to the Kamiishikiricho neighborhood, even if traffic was to be encountered.

This route allowed Daisuke to see Crater Bay on his way out of his company's headquarters. There was a sentimental reason for this.

Daisuke was in his early adolescence when Japan was struck during the Third World War. The Hoshikawa Group was older than him and he wasn't the presumed heir to this corporate empire. His father, Junichi Hoshikawa, was the previous President because he died during the war when Soviet nuclear weapons attacked Japan to deprive the United States Armed Forces a staging point. When a nuclear warhead neared Osaka, many panicked. Despite his social standing that came from running a *keiretsu*, Junichi knew he was human above all else and helped many flee to nuclear shelters he helped developed. Just before the warhead detonated above Osaka, Junichi, his wife Sayaka, and Daisuke were the last to reach a shelter located in the nearby city of not yet filled entirely. Sayaka and Daisuke got inside first, but Junichi found another mother and her child also rushing to the same shelter. By the time Junichi helped the mother and child, it was too late for him and knowing that, he closed the shelter door despite cries from his own wife and child.

That act defined Daisuke's future. While he and Sayaka were helped by a surviving relative, Daisuke opted to build his own future based on his father's sacrifice. He started by serving in the New United Nations Ground Force (NUNGF).

Many assumed that a scion of a *keiretsu* family would cower from what was expected of those who joined the military, but Daisuke defied all expectations. As a result, he was recommended for the NUNGF's Special Operations Brigade. There, he met the man now known as "Fred Smith". Eventually, Daisuke left the military to resume his business studies in order to take over Hoshikawa Group. During this time, he met Miku Sayama, the daughter of a rival *keiretsu*'s bank branch. Because he was a devout Catholic, Miku's parents opposed the relationship to the point Miku disowned herself and converted to Catholicism to be with Daisuke.

After that, Daisuke opted to change the public face of Hoshikawa Group. Rather than continue running the *keiretsu* in nearby Kobe, Daisuke opted to create a newer headquarters for Hoshikawa Group, now located in the southwest portion of what used to be Osaka. He decided on this to help with the reconstruction of portions of Japan that had yet to be rebuilt after the war but for a personal reason—to spend more time with his family.

The route from the current headquarters of his *keiretsu* to his mansion in Kamiishikiricho was to remind Daisuke why he's the President of Hoshikawa Group—to always help in building a better future. Yet Daisuke's trip to a location only he knows was what made this night different from past Sunday nights where he would tell Ugaki to go to the mansion only.

#

Hotel Soleil, Higashiosaka Ward. 0058 hours

Daisuke reached a room in Hotel Soleil. He immediately knocked on the door and footsteps from the room were heard.

"So you came," "Fred Smith" said as he opened the door.

"I did," Daisuke sternly replied.

"Then come in."

"Smith" opened the door further to let Daisuke inside. Once the latter was inside the room of the former, he closed the door.

"Why did you ask me to come here?" Daisuke asked.

"Your daughter," "Smith" answered.

"What does this have to do with Maria?"

"Before I answer that, why don't you sit down first?"

Without saying anything, Daisuke sat down on one of the chairs in the room. "Smith" then grabbed a bottle of water from the room's mini-refrigerator and offered it to Daisuke.

"I could have given you a beer but I know you'd rather come home sober," "Smith" said upon giving Daisuke the bottle.

"Now what about Maria?" Daisuke asked.

"I cannot say much. Let's just say certain organizations are after Maria and it all boiled down to the day you found her."

"I should have known. So, what do you need from me?"

"We've hired a mercenary group named Iron Dutchman Services who'll serve as monitors for your daughter. One member of Iron Dutchman Services is a teenage boy named Tarou Ganji and he offered to act out as a transfer student at Nishi High School. We need your help in getting Ganji enrolled. Right now, he's learning the ways of the Japanese teenager and next month, he'll come here with another member, a doctor named Anita Hamilton, who'll be acting as his guardian."

"Anything else?"

"He asked for an apartment and we offered Dr. Hamilton a small clinic."

"I'll see what I can do, but don't rush me. As for the apartment, why don't I provide a condominium for this Tarou Ganji? If I'm to fake sponsoring his settlement into Japan, I should at least have a hand in where he lives?"

"Fair enough. As for rushing you, there's no need because I was told to make sure you take your time. Here's who you'll be dealing with."

"Smith" found an envelope and gave it to Daisuke. "That will be all for now. Once you've finished everything, come back here next Sunday."

"Before I go, I have one question: is this threat against my daughter real?"

"That's my mission: to determine that."

Without saying anything else, Daisuke left the room.

#

Hoshikawa Group Headquarters, Suminoe Ward. March 11, 2030; 1350 hours

The following day, Daisuke opened the envelope "Smith" gave to him earlier that morning in Hotel Soleil. He only had ten minutes to read what the envelope contained, as there were only ten minutes of liberty for him before he had to resume his work.

As the envelope was open, Daisuke widened the hole he made. Naturally, he found papers inside the envelope and Daisuke began to get all of them. After that, he raised them up and the first paper he saw was that of the *Iron Dutchman.*

These papers must contain information the FIS collected on those mercenaries Fred talked about, Daisuke thought as he looked at the papers. *This first one is about the Iron Dutchman, the namesake of the mercenary unit's name. Why exactly is it a cruise ship? I'll have to read that later. I don't have time to go over every file so I need to skip to the document on Tarou Ganji.*

Daisuke began flipping papers one at a time. The previous paper was moved to the rear in order to make it start from the paper on the Iron Dutchman. After skipping documents, including those that respectively pertained to every other member of Iron Dutchman Services, Daisuke reached the document on Tarou Ganji. Unbeknownst to Daisuke, the document on Tatev Mirzoyan was next, but that wasn't of his concern.

So this is Tarou Ganji? Daisuke thought as he looked at the paper. *He's as old as Maria. I see why Fred wants him to infiltrate Nishi High School as a student.*

Daisuke continued reading the document. His eyes widened as he continued to read. This was natural because of how old Tarou was and how long had he been in Iron Dutchman Services.

Says here he was recruited in Libya, Daisuke thought as he continued to read the document. *Wait, I remember this incident. Someone I met from Egypt Oil spoke of an attack on one of their oil rigs in Libya and that they hired a small group of mercenaries to defend it. They were saved by a teenage boy because he stole one of the bandit's Walgears and turned the tide against them. If this Tarou Ganji is the same boy, then I should be careful with him.*

#

Iron Dutchman; Naval Station Pearl Harbor, United States of America. March 13, 2030; 1150 hours (Hawaii-Aleutian Time)

"Tarou, lunch is ready," Anita Hamilton said as she approached a room in the *Iron Dutchman.*

She caught Tarou Ganji writing on a piece of paper. On his right was an open book and on his left were unused pieces of paper.

"Hold on, Doctor, I'm just about finishing the katakana that start with a 'g'," Tarou replied as he continued to write without looking at Hamilton.

Tarou currently wrote the *katakana* "ge". After that, he moved his head toward the book on his left and looked at the other *katakana.* He saw the *katakana* "go" in how it was written. After that, he resumed writing. Hamilton then walked up to the room to look at Tarou as he worked.

"I see you're writing down the katakana," Hamilton said as she saw Tarou finished writing "go".

"After this is the katakana that start with an 's'," Tarou replied just as he wrote the romanization of "go".

"Like I said, it's lunch."

"I guess I can stop for now."

#

1219 hours

Every member of Iron Dutchman Services gathered at the dining hall for lunch. Tarou sat and ate in the same table as Hamilton and Tatev Mirzoyan.

"Ganji, how goes your Japanese?" Jason Luke Crawley asked as he turned his head to Tarou while seated at a separate table with Wouter Vos, Sunan Wattana, and Federico Díaz.

"I've gotten past hiragana and I'm currently in the middle of katakana," Tarou replied after chewing and swallowing his meal. "I do admit it can be confusing that kana that start in "k" and "g" appear to be similar whether it's hiragana or katakana."

"You're going to have to keep remembering the differences," Vos added. "Remember, you need to make sure you can blend in."

"Roger that," Tarou said before resuming his meal.

We can't afford to mess up on this, Vos thought as he also resumed his meal.

FIS Headquarters, McLean, Fairfax County, Commonwealth of Virginia; United States of America. 1743 hours (Eastern Standard Time)

A woman came inside Alberto Pérez's office, and her name was Alicia Caguiat. Twenty-nine years old, Caguiat had long black hair tied in a ponytail, dark brown eyes, and dark intermediate skin.

Whenever the New United Nations needed mercenaries, responsibility for making sure mercenary groups obeyed contracts offered by NUN fell upon the Intelligence Collective's Foreign Intelligence Service with individuals within the FIS assigned to working with these mercenaries are called "coordinators". Caguiat herself was a coordinator assigned to work with Iron Dutchman Services.

"How goes your studies on Iron Dutchman Services, Caguiat?" Pérez asked.

"It's going well, sir," Caguiat replied.

"Might I quiz you on how much you know so far? It's making sure you can do your job."

"Of course, sir. I'm ready."

"First question: when and how was Iron Dutchman Services formed?"

"It was because of an incident in former Zaire three years ago where the unit Sunan Wattana and Jake Crawley once belonged to was ambushed and that Wouter Vos, serving in the South African Marine Corps at the time, led his unit into saving our forces from that ambush. For that, Vos was discharged, while Wattana and Crawley opted for a discharge. The three met again in Angola and, after a card game, acquired the ship we now know as the *Iron Dutchman*, hence their name 'Iron Dutchman Services'."

"Next question: what do you know about the other members of Iron Dutchman Services?"

"After their first contract for us in the United Nigerian States, they took in one Bartolemeu Moura, a former soldier from the Angolan Army, a former South American Union Ground Force mechanic named Federico Díaz, and a wandering doctor named Anita Hamilton. Their next contract a year later was with the African Federation, where they took in two other mechanics, Semir Bosić from the Commonwealth of Euro-African States and Vikas Mistry from the South Asian Confederation. After that, they took another contract with Egypt Oil, which had to be vetted by the Commonwealth of Euro-African States. There, it is reported they took in a new member."

"Who do you think that new member is?"

"I would say Tarou Ganji."

"Correct. Also, I was told that there was another teenager living with these mercenaries; a girl this time. When do you suppose they took her in?"

"Two years ago when Iron Dutchman Services took another contract from the African Federation to assist the National Police of the Republic of Somalia in dismantling a human trafficking ring and it is believed that Iron Dutchman Services took in a teenage girl as she was the only one who hadn't been sold."

"Last question: when contacting these mercenaries, what name will you use?"

"Maria Clara."

"Good. You're dismissed for now. I'll notify you as to when you're to contact these mercenaries."

#

Iron Dutchman; Naval Station Pearl Harbor, City and County of Honolulu, State of Hawaii. March 14, 2030; 1925 hours (Hawaii-Aleutian Time)

Every member of Iron Dutchman Services ate their dinner in their namesake's main deck dining hall. Tarou Ganji went over notes while chewing his food.

"Are you sure you can eat and review at the same time?" Anita Hamilton asked as she and Tatev Mirzoyan looked at Tarou since all three shared a table.

He then swallowed his food and looked at Hamilton and Tatev, putting down his notes. "Sorry, wanted to review this one kanji. I'll stop for now."

"Nice for you to take this seriously, but ease it up," Wouter Vos warned.

"Wouter, I must ask: did you imagine yourself doing this?" Jake Crawley asked Vos as they sat in the same table.

"Doing what?" Vos asked before he turned to Crawley.

"Taking up this contract. Don't get me wrong, we're mercenaries. I, for one, do find it suspicious that because we have teenagers amongst us that one of them has to infiltrate a high school."

"You're right. I do, however, hope we don't have to go through any more pay cuts."

"Oh… sorry about that."

"It's alright. I needed such a question anyway."

"Gochi sou sama deshita," Tarou said as he finished his meal. He then bowed, stood up, and left.

Vos, Crawley, and Sunan Wattana saw Tarou leave the table he shared with Tatev and Hamilton. "He got that pronunciation right," Crawley remarked.

"What does that mean again?" Wattana asked.

"Thank you for this meal."

"You know Japanese?" Vos asked as he faced Crawley.

"I enjoy anime and manga, Wouter. Haven't you forgotten?"

"Why don't you help Ganji out?" Wattana asked Crawley.

"There's a difference between learning Japanese normally and getting it from anime and manga."

"And you never bothered to learn Japanese properly?" Vos asked.

"Never had the time to," Crawley answered.

Everyone then resumed their meals. Bartolomeu Moura then appeared with his own meal and joined Tatev and Hamilton at their table.

#

1959 hours

Tarou returned to his room in the *Iron Dutchman*. Once he was inside, Tarou proceeded to his nightstand and opened its drawer.

Finding his personal sidearm, a P226 semi-automatic pistol, Tarou grabbed its magazine, separated from it, with his right hand. Using his left hand, Tarou also reached for a nearby box and opened it.

Inside the box were 9x19mm bullets. Tarou grabbed one bullet and loaded it into the P226's magazine. After loading nine rounds into the magazine, Tarou placed the magazine in his left hand and used his right hand to pick up the P226 itself. Once he loaded the magazine into the P226, Tarou left the room.

#

2044 hours

In what used to be the disco of the ship that now bore the name *Iron Dutchman*, Tarou Ganji fired at a sofa with red paint sprayed on it. The red paint consisted of circles that surrounded each other, making a target.

Tarou had covered his eyes with goggles and ears with a protective headset as he fired his pistol, a P226. He fired until he had depleted his entire magazine.

Taking off his goggles, Tarou found that he wasn't able to hit the smallest circle. Despite that, he put down his gun, goggles, and headset. It was then that Sunan Wattana approached him from behind and he noticed.

"Figured you would be here," Wattana said.

"Felt like fire a few rounds to relax a little," Tarou replied as he turned to Wattana.

"Feel like sparring?"

"Sure. I need to wait until it's safe to clean up my pistol anyway. But before that… "

Tarou began to use his pistol's safety. Then he found a nearby sticky pad, grabbed a piece and the nearest pencil, wrote "Do Not Touch. Will clean up later", and placed the note beside the P226 before joining Wattana.

Preparations

Charmshahr, Tehran Province, Region 1; Islamic Republic of Iran. August 28, 2023; 17:10 hours (Iran Standard Time)

"Die in the name of God!" a ten-year-old boy shouted as he fired an assault rifle.

The boy had very light skin, black hair underneath his M1 helmet, and brown eyes. However, his facial shape wasn't that of those in Iran. He carried a Type 56 assault rifle and fired at a giant made of metal.

The "giant" was a machine that was three meters in height with arms and legs like those of a human being. Its head was shaped like a dome with a red-colored dot that glowed in a dark gap. It carried a rifle that resembled the AKS-74U carbine with brass knuckles attached to both of its wrists. On the legs of the machine were two wheels each.

After the 7.62x39mm bullets hit the machine, the latter turned and moved its left arm forward, putting aside its rifle. The machine faced the boy with the latter himself moving away and in time as the machine fired a machine gun located at its chest. The boy miraculously survived and just as he reloaded his Type 56 by loading another magazine, the machine was hit in the head, falling into the ground.

The boy turned to find a teenager of the same gender hiding at a house that wasn't destroyed yet carrying an RPG-7 rocket-propelled grenade launcher. He looked more like a native of Iran than the boy and he didn't wear a helmet.

"Get in, quickly!" the teenager shouted.

The boy with the Type 56 rushed to the house. However, the teenager heard the sound of helicopter rotors, a sound he and the boy with the assault rifle were familiar with, being louder.

"Quickly!" the teenager repeated.

The boy was only an inch near the house when an attack helicopter appeared. The pilot of the helicopter, spotting the children, fired the helicopter's 30x165mm autocannon.

Iron Dutchman; Naval Station Pearl Harbor, City and County of Honolulu, State of Hawaii; United States of Liberion. March 16, 2030; 0604 hours (Hawaii-Aleutian Time)

As if he was forced to, Tarou Ganji woke up. He breathed fast but quietly while gripping his bedsheet firmly.

That dream again, Tarou thought as he stopped his fast breathing.

Letting go of his bedsheet and pushing it away, Tarou got out of his bed. He put on his green pants and a white shirt, then left the room.

Before proceeding further, he stopped as he saw Tatev Mirzoyan coming his way. "You're up early," Tarou said.

"I volunteered to get clothes today," Tatev replied. "Mr. Vos knows about this. Now, may I please go into your room?"

"Sure."

#

0645 hours

Tarou was now at the pools of the cruise ship that the *Iron Dutchman* used to be. As the mercenaries saw no need for swimming pools with the limited funds they had, the pools remained empty. Instead, they turned the area surrounding the pools into their personal running track.

I've been having that dream since I left Iran, Tarou thought as he jogged. *When the Eurasian Tsardom invaded Iran, I left that refugee camp because I thought fighting would allow me to find out who I really am.*

During that time, I met Vahid Farahani. He took care of me as if we were family. To my surprise, we were joined by someone from the same refugee camp where I came from—Shireen Baloch. Ever since that battle in Charmshahr, I haven't seem Farahani nor Shireen. I assumed them dead, which I should be as well, and left Iran. After five years of wandering the desert, I wound up in Libya and meeting Iron Dutchman Services. I joined them hoping to attract the attention of those who knew my real past.

Unbeknownst to Tarou, Tatev had followed to the pool area and watched. *The way he talked to me earlier must mean he had that dream again,* Tatev thought. *Is it worth taking this mission just to find out about your past?*

Tarou, to Tatev's surprised, stopped his jogging. Tatev immediately hid to make sure Tarou didn't see her.

"I know you're out there, Tatev," Tarou said.

After a slight giggle, Tatev came out to face Tarou. "H… How did you know I was here?" Tatev asked.

"I can smell you because you've been collecting our laundry," Tarou answered.

"I see."

"Whatever it is you came to see me for, what is it?"

"I… Can you ask you something?"

"What is it?"

"What will you do when you ever come into close contact with Miss Hoshikawa?"

"I… honestly don't know, but regardless, keeping an eye on her is the mission. Now, if you excuse me."

Tarou began to leave the pool area with Tatev stepping out of his way.

#

0658 hours

Tarou then reached the one amenity of the cruise ship that the *Iron Dutchman* used to be had to offer—its spa. However, to the current owners of the ship, the spa wasn't to be treated as an amenity.

Naturally, a washroom was needed. For these mercenaries, the spa was most suited for that task. Tarou used it as if it was a normal washroom and, like everyone else on board the ship, Tarou didn't care what the washroom used to be.

I'm surprised Tatev followed me to the pool area, Tarou thought as he washed himself. *She never acted this way before.*

Tarou then finished washing himself. After putting on the clothes he took from his earlier, he began to exit the washroom. Upon reaching the door and opening it, however, he found Jason Luke Crawley waiting outside.

"Were you waiting long?" Tarou asked.

"Yes, but it was worth it," Crawley answered.

"What are you talking about?"

"Saw you and Tatev at the pool area earlier. *What did you do*?"

"What on Earth are you talking about?"

"Come on, Ganji, tell me! You must have done *something*?"

"No. Now if you please excuse me… "

Tarou continued moving out of the washroom, with Crawley getting out of the way. As Tarou continued moving, Crawley remained where he stood and watched.

I do wonder what's going to happen once Ganji is enrolled in that high school, Crawley thought. *This contract ought to be fun at least.*

#

Hoshikawa Condominiums, Higashiosaka Ward, Kansai City, Kansai Prefecture; State of Japan. 1300 hours (Japan Standard Time)

You're starting to amaze me, Daisuke, "Fred Smith" thought as he looked upon a condominium complex in the Toriicho neighborhood of Kansai City's Higashiosaka ward.

One member of Hoshikawa Group was Hoshikawa Real Estate, dedicated to housing. This arm of Hoshikawa Group was crucial in the reconstruction of Japan following the Third World War, with modern-day Kansai City as a stepping stone. Among what was considered a memorial to Hoshikawa's contributions for Kansai City was Hoshikawa Condominiums.

"So you're Preston Turner?" a woman asked as she approached "Smith".

The FIS agent turned to see the woman approach him. "Hai desu," "Smith" replied.

"Fujioka Hana desu. Kochira e douzo."

"Wakatta."

Hotel Soleil. March 17, 2030; 0128 hours

"How was the condominium?" Daisuke Hoshikawa asked "Smith" at the room of the latter in Hotel Soleil.

"It's perfect," "Smith" replied. "The paperwork?"

"We're to see a contact of mine in the Ministry of Justice tomorrow. He wishes to see Ganji-kun himself next month."

"Of course, though after that, I need to leave for Hawaii."

"What for?"

"I need to make sure Ganji-kun is actually learning Japanese. On the first day of the following month, I'll test him myself."

"You're serious about this?"

"I have to be. It's an order."

"Why did you join the FIS?"

"Smith" gulped slightly and widened his eyes at the same time. "Do I have to answer that?"

"You don't have to. I didn't think you, Frederick Dirks, would be the type to join an intelligence agency?"

"You're the only one to call me Frederick Dirks since I joined the FIS. Let's just say I joined to see the world."

"I see." Daisuke then stood up. "I must get going. I'll upset my wife if I stay any longer."

"Then good night."

"You too."

#

Off Rebun Island; State of Japan. November 3, 2013; 0610 hours (Japan Standard Time)

Daisuke and Miku Hoshikawa sat on a boat off Rebun Island, known for hosting hiking expeditions. The island contained a mountain also named Rebun, a *chashi*, and excavated remains of dead aquatic mammals.

The couple rented the boat they're riding on, as this trip was the only time they can afford as a married couple. Daisuke naturally moved the boat with its motor engine.

"Daisuke, there's something I want to ask?" Miku asked.

"Hai?" Daisuke asked.

"What do you think about having children?"

"W... What made you bring that up?"

"I don't know? Maybe it would feel lonely if it's just the two of us? I know we're together now, but once we go back to Kansai City, I'll be alone again waiting for you to come back two hours after midnight at most."

"I apologize for that."

"You don't have to."

Suddenly, despite the wind and the ocean tides, Daisuke and Miku began to hear black-tailed gulls making a particular sound. It was too tempting to ignore that the couple used their ears to direct them to where they can find the source of the gulls' sounds. What didn't help was that Daisuke and Miku heard another sound that was unique, despite the sound of the gulls silencing it.

"I found it," Daisuke declared as he saw the gulls, with Miku also turning to his gaze.

The Hoshikawas found another boat, yet there wasn't a single person on board. The gulls surrounded it and the ability to resist the temptation of knowing why vanished from the couple.

"We should see what's going on, right?" Miku asked.

"Agreed," Daisuke replied.

Daisuke moved the boat toward the other boat. As the Hoshikawas got closer, the gulls left the other boat. Upon getting closer, the Hoshikawas found an infant crying.

"What's a baby doing in this boat all alone?" Miku asked.

Hoshikawa Mansion, Higashiosaka Ward, Kansai City, Kansai Prefecture; State of Japan. March 18, 2030; 0558 hours (Japan Standard Time)

Miku Hoshikawa (née Sayama), in the present, woke up to find her husband sitting at a chair by their bedroom's window. She stood up, but because her vision wasn't complete as she had just woken up, Miku first went to the bathroom.

While Miku wet her face to help her eyes wake up, Daisuke paid little attention. After wiping her face with the nearest facial towel, Miku joined her husband.

"What are you looking at?" Miku asked, only to see that what Daisuke was looking at was something that gave her pause. It was a letter written by someone with the initials "SET":

To whosoever finds this letter and the infant,

The infant's name is Maria, a girl. If anyone has found her and this letter, I must be dead. I ask that you take care of her and should she ask about her past, tell her that everything about her is in a microchip that I inserted into the same envelope as this letter.

I also ask to tell Maria that she was loved.

SET.

"Why did you bring out that letter, Daisuke?" Miku asked, as if she saw Daisuke commit a crime.

"I get the feeling we must prepare for the day we show Maria her past," Daisuke answered as if he was ready to die.

"But this doesn't change that Maria is our daughter."

"I know. I also want to know who she really is because there are people out there who know and may intend to hurt her."

"Is that why you've been coming home late as of recently?"

"The one who wrote that letter Maria found in a coffee bottle when we left the church last week has been investigating her?"

"Why?"

"I want to know, too. At this point, I can't say. He only asked for me because we served in the same unit in the military."

"And will you be seeing him again?"

"Later. I intend on my own half-day because 'Smith'-san and I need to see someone I know from the Ministry of Justice. And that's all I have to say."

"Come on. We must dress up and join Maria for breakfast."

"Agreed."

Daisuke stood up and put the letter on the chair he sat on. While he went on to their bathroom first, Miku put the letter back into the very envelope that they found in 2013.

#

Daniel K. Inouye International Airport, Honolulu, City and County of Honolulu, State of Hawaii; United States of America. March 20, 2030; 0536 hours (Hawaii-Aleutian Time)

Outside Daniel K. Inouye International Airport, the FIS agent "Fred Smith" raised his right thumb to attract a taxi. On his left hand was a suitcase while his wheel bag stood beside him.

"Smith's" patience rubbed off on him as a taxi appear. The driver, a man, opened the right front mirror.

"Where to?" the taxi driver asked.

"Pacific Inn, please," the FIS agent answered.

#

Naval Station Pearl Harbor. 0959 hours

Hours later, "Smith" returned to Naval Station Pearl Harbor with his suitcase. After the routine checks, "Smith" was taken to the *Iron Dutchman* by one NUNMF guard. After they made it to the docked ship, "Smith" got off the vehicle and walked up to the *Iron Dutchman*. He then rang a bell placed near the gangway.

"Smith" waited until someone found him. His waiting didn't last long as Tarou Ganji appeared.

"You need to come inside, Mr. Smith?" Tarou asked.

"Yes, please," "Smith" replied.

"Hold on."

#

Iron Dutchman. 1038 hours

"So, why did you come back?" Wouter Vos asked "Smith" as he and all of his subordinates gathered at the Iron Dutchman's dining hall.

"I've already secured the paperwork needed for Mr. Ganji, "Smith" answered. "Before we prepare to go to Japan, I have to test Mr. Ganji on his Japanese."

"Alright. I assume you intend on doing this with Ganji alone?"

"Yes. Know a good location for me and Mr. Ganji?"

"Use the library," Tatev Mirzoyan suggested.

"You still have a library?" "Smith" asked as he turned to Tatev.

"It was left alone when we first got this ship," Sunan Wattana answered.

"Good," "Smith" replied before turning to Tarou. "Mr. Ganji, go on to the library. I'll join you soon."

"Yes, sir," Tarou replied.

#

1110 hours

At the library of the *Iron Dutchman*, an amenity of the cruise ship it used to be that was preserved, Tarou Ganji sat alone. It wasn't for long as "Smith" came inside with his suitcase. As he joined Tarou at the same table, he laid his suitcase between them on the table and opened it.

"As I said earlier at your dining hall, I have to test you on your written Japanese," "Smith" repeated to Tarou. "The first part of this test is oral. I am going to act out as a shopkeeper, a teacher, and any role of my choosing.

"I will be speaking in Japanese and you are to respond in Japanese. Is that understood?"

"Hai," Tarou replied.

"Yoshi. Sate, hajimemashou."

"Smith" moved his right hand toward a metallic device inside his suitcase. After pressing the device's button, he grabbed a paper from his suitcase. Naturally, he made sure Tarou didn't look at what it contained.

"Namae?" "Smith" asked as the first question of this oral test.

"Ganji Tarou desu."

"Oikutsu desu ka?"

"Jyu-nana sai desu."

"I see you got those right," "Smith" commented in English. "Now then, this part of the oral test is identifying what the word or phrase is in Japanese. Here's the first one I got: Good morning?"

"Ohayou gozaimasu," Tarou answered.

He's answered instantly to every question, "Smith" thought. *Thank goodness I'm having this recorded.*

#

Pacific Inn, Honolulu. 1950 hours

At his room in the Pacific Inn, located near Daniel K. Inouye International Airport, "Smith" used an application in his laptop computer named "IntMail". He used IntMail to not only send a file that was titled "Oral Test" but also a file named "03-19-2030 Report". He did this by putting the files in the same message he was about to send.

Next, he began to write the following as a text message:

In this message are my report from my activities in Japan and the oral test I gave to Tarou Ganji. I will spend the rest of the week composing a written test for Mr. Ganji.

"Smith".

"Smith" then pointed the arrow on his computer's screen, using his mouse button in the center of the laptop's keyboard to the "Send" button in IntMail. Upon pressing the left button in the bottom-center of the keyboard, a line appeared in IntMail with a blue-colored rectangle that appeared. It kept on increasing until it filled the entire line. After that, another rectangle appeared; this time it contained the words "Message sent".

Now I have to wait, "Smith" thought.

#

FIS Headquarters, Langley, Commonwealth of Virginia. March 21, 2030; 0054 hours (Eastern Standard Time)

In her desk in FIS Headquarters, Alicia Caguiat received "Smith's" message on her desktop computer's IntMail. Using her mouse, a separate device connected to her computer, she pointed the arrow representing the mouse to the message and after pressing the mouse's left button, she saw the text of the message and the two files he added to the message.

Caguiat then directed the arrow toward the two files. Going first for "Oral Test", she placed the arrow and pressed the mouse's left button. As a result, a large square appeared, blocking almost all of IntMail.

On top of the square were the words "Where to Direct Download". Caguiat moved the mouse, and by extension, the arrow to the word "Courier" and pressed the left button. After she pressed the left button, the line with the blue rectangle appeared. After the line vanished as soon as it was filled by the blue rectangle, Caguiat moved to "03-19-2030 Report" and after pressing the left button again, the same square appeared again and like with "Oral Report", Caguiat moved the arrow to "Courier" and pressed the left button. The line with the blue rectangle appeared again, but for the rectangle to fill the entire line, it didn't take long as contrast to when Caguiat downloaded "Oral Report" to "Courier".

That should do it, Caguiat thought. *Now, I need to take this to Deputy Director McAllister.*

Caguiat moved her mouse to the bottom left of the computer's screen. Finding a triangle, Caguiat pressed it by pressing the mouse's left button. A square with more icons appeared, but Caguiat directed the arrow toward an icon based on a USB device. This time, she pressed the mouse's right button and a small rectangle appeared with the words "Open All Devices and Printers" on top of the rectangle. She moved the arrow to the words "Eject Courier". Pressing it with the left button of the mouse,

Caguiat waited, albeit for one second, until a square appeared. In the square was the message "This USB storage device can now be removed".

Caguiat let go of her right hand from the mouse and placed it on a green-colored USB device connected to the computer that had a small strip of masking tape on it with the word "Courier". Because of the message, she can remove the USB from the computer. After that, she stood up, used her left hand to get the USB, used her right hand to exit IntMail, and leave her desk to find the Deputy Director of Covert Action.

#

0105 hours

Caguiat arrived at Stanley McAlister's office. The latter moved his head to face his face.

"You have something for me, Miss Caguiat?" McAllister asked.

"I do," Caguiat answered before showing the USB device to McAllister. "Inside are Mr. 'Smith's' report and an audio file named 'Oral Report'."

"Anyone else know of this?"

"No. I downloaded the files into my USB only after that. I rushed here."

"What about IntMail?"

"I exited it".

"Where else did you download these files?"

"Just into the USB. That's it. Nowhere else."

"Good. Please give it to me, but you can't leave just yet. I just need to cut and paste the files into my computer, copy it into my USB for the Director to see, then I can give you back your USB and dismiss you. You can sit down while waiting."

"Yes, sir, and thank you."

After giving the USB device to McAllister, Caguiat sat down on the nearest chair while waiting for McAllister to get the files from her USB. After plugging in Caguiat's USB into his computer, McAllister used his mouse to direct the arrow to the square that appeared after connecting Caguiat's USB as the square had the word "Courier" at the top with the two files she downloaded from "Fred Smith's" message inside. One-by-one, McAllister pressed the files and downloaded them into the computer but he pressed them again to download the files onto his gray-colored USB, which was indicated in the computer with the name "My USB".

McAllister continued looking at this computer to see if his file transfer to his USB was finished. *Come on, come on,* McAllister thought just as the blue rectangle in the line that represented the file transfer progress continued to fill the line, albeit slowly.

After two minutes, the speed at which the blue rectangle filled the line increased. After one more second, the rectangle now filled the line, finishing the copying of the file. McAllister again pressed "03-19-2030 Report" and downloaded it onto his USB, represented by a USB icon on the square with the name "My USB". Unlike "Oral Report", the transfer wasn't long. After that, he disconnected Caguiat's USB from his computer and, after physically removing the USB, he stood up and walked up to Caguiat.

"I apologize for the long wait," McAllister said upon giving Caguiat her USB back. "Now you're dismissed."

"Thank you, sir," Caguiat replied upon getting her USB and standing up.

#

McAllister Residence, McLean. 0320 hours

Using his private laptop computer in his house in McLean, McAllister plugged his USB into the laptop. He then opened an application named "GOKMail" which functioned like IntMail.

First, he typed a message:

Dear Gatekeeper of Intelligence,

Here are the recent reports from 'Fred Smith'. I send these to you as an update on FIS activity concerning Maria Hoshikawa.

Devotee-Infiltrator Stanley McAllister.

McAllister then used his laptop's mouse button to move the arrow into an icon in GOKMail based on an envelope. Pressing the left button in the bottom-center of the laptop's keyboard, a square with the words "Select File to Upload" appeared. McAllister then moved the arrow to "My USB" and clicked on "Oral Report". Like before, he had to wait until the upload was finished. Once the upload the finished, he clicked on "03-19-2030" and waited only three seconds for this upload to be complete.

After that, McAllister moved the arrow to an icon with the word "Send" and once he pressed the left button, McAllister waited again for his message to be sent. After it was confirmed that the message was sent, McAllister exited GOKMail, disconnected the USB, removed it, and turned off his laptop.

It was then that his wife Cynthia came out of their bathroom. McAllister then diverted his attention to his wife.

"Bathroom's ready, dear," Cynthia said.

"Thank you," McAllister replied.

#

Unknown Location; Enlightenment Point. 1411 hours (EP Time Zone)

"Grand Gatekeeper, I come with a new report from our Devotee-Infiltrator in the Intelligence Collective," the hooded man said to Grand Gatekeeper of Knowledge Sergei Akulov.

"What is it?" Akulov asked.

"The FIS agent calling himself 'Fred Smith' is already preparing for a written examination to test Tarou Ganji's Japanese?"

"I assume this relates to Maria Hoshikawa?"

"It does as the Devotee-Infiltrator says."

"And who is this Tarou Ganji?"

"A member of Iron Dutchman Services. Seventeen years old, he joined the mercenary group after a contract they had with the Euro-African Alliance's Egypt Oil two years ago."

"And I assume he'll be the one assuming the cover of a transfer student to Nishi High School to keep an eye on Hoshikawa?"

"Yes, Grand Gatekeeper."

"How long will it take for this 'Fred Smith' to finish this test?"

"He claims that he will not start until he receives permission to start composing the test. Tarou Ganji was told to continue his studies."

"I can imagine 'Smith' will get his authorization soon. For now, we wait until Ganji takes this test. Tell our Devotee-Infiltrator to convince the Director of Foreign Intelligence to say yes and to not provide another update until next week."

"By your will, Grand Gatekeeper."

#

McAllister Residence, McLean, Fairfax County, Commonwealth of Virginia; United States of America. 0900 hours (Eastern Standard Time)

Stanley McAllister woke up ahead of his wife after four hours of sleep; an occupation hazard for the Deputy Director of Covert Action. Quietly, he went to his bathroom and slowly turned on the sink to make sure his wife didn't wake up. Regardless, the sink was turned on, allowing McAllister the water he needed to make sure his eyes wake up.

After wetting his face and drying it with a towel, McAllister returned to his laptop computer that he used to contact the Gatekeepers of Knowledge. After that, he turned on GOKMail again and found a new message:

Dear Devotee-Infiltrator McAllister,

The Grand Gatekeeper has given you the order to tell your Director of Foreign Intelligence to say yes to allowing "Fred Smith" to make his examination for the mercenary Tarou Ganji. He also asks that you cease your reports until next week.

Gatekeeper of Intelligence.

As it was hours before, McAllister turned off GOKMail and the computer. He rushed back to the bathroom to take a bath.

#

FIS Headquarters, Langley. 1107 hours

"He has my permission," Alberto Pérez declared to McAllister and a woman as old as McAllister in his office. "I'll also arrange for transport to take him, Ganji, and Hamilton to Japan."

The woman was named Yanin Saetang. She had a body with an inverted triangle shape and average height, long black hair tied in a bun, dark brown eyes, and dark skin. She served as the Deputy Director of Foreign Intelligence.

"With all due respect, Director, I don't think we should start getting this Tarou Ganji to settle in Japan just yet," Saetang argued. "From that recording 'Smith' made, Ganji was able to memorize his Japanese flawlessly. He never had a proper education and yet he's able to converse as if he were a native. I recommend that we continue studying Ganji's behavior and how he can learn anything fast."

"We don't have time for that," McAllister refuted. "The paperwork is already being prepared by the Japanese government as we speak. 'Smith' needs to have Ganji prepared for the trip to Japan."

"Exactly," Pérez replied just before he turned to Saetang. "I understand your argument, Yanin, but if we don't act fast, whoever's after Maria Hoshikawa will act if assuming they haven't at this point."

"Can I at least be given all the information we have on Hoshikawa, Ganji, and every report 'Smith' has sent?"

"Consider it done," McAllister replied.

"You two are dismissed," Pérez ordered.

Update Part 1

Hoshikawa Group Headquarters, Taisho Ward, Kansai City, Kansai Prefecture; State of Japan. March 22, 2030; 2340 hours (Japan Standard Time)

Alone in his office, Daisuke Hoshikawa looked at a series of documents. These contained the insignia of the Japanese government's Ministry of Justice. It consisted of a *kirimon* with the initials "MOJ" below.

I hope we really are doing this to protect Maria? Daisuke pondered while he looked at the documents.

"Shachou, I have Nishikoyama-san waiting outside," a female voice said over a small PA system installed on Daisuke's desk. "Shall I let him in?"

"Hai," Daisuke replied.

Daisuke grouped the documents together and hid them. The man named Nishikoyama came into the office.

#

Iron Dutchman; Naval Station Pearl Harbor, City and County of Honolulu, State of Hawaii; United States of America. March 25, 2030; 1000 hours (Hawaii-Aleutian Time)

Every member of Iron Dutchman Services was now at their dining hall. "Fred Smith" also came to the ship with the same suitcase he brought with him four days before.

"I assume this is it?" Wouter Vos asked.

"Yes," "Smith" answered. "Mr. Ganji must pass this test. After that, we must prepare him and Dr. Hamilton for settling into Japan."

"And I assume the Japanese government and Daisuke Hoshikawa know of this?" Anita Hamilton asked.

"Yes."

"Ganji, you know where to go," Vos said as he faced Tarou Ganji.

"Yes, Mr. Vos," Tarou replied.

#

1109 hours

Like it was four days before, Tarou waited at the ship's library. "Smith" then arrived with his suitcase and like before, he sat opposite of Tarou in the same desk. Before sitting down, he laid his suitcase in front of Tarou.

Upon sitting down, he opened the suitcase, and it contained stacks of paper that were stapled together. He then gave the papers to Tarou.

"This here is the test," "Smith" explained. "The rest are in the directions, which have been romanized and translated into English. Answers must also be written thrice; in the original Japanese, romanized, then in English."

"Hai," Tarou replied.

"Then good luck."

#

1200 hours

While Tarou answered the test, "Smith" looked at his watch. He found that it was 1200 hours and faced Tarou next.

"Mr. Ganji, think you could please stop?" "Smith" requested to Tarou.

Without saying in response, Tarou stopped and gave the papers to "Smith". The latter looked at the answers so far, then faced Tarou again.

"You can take a break by having lunch," "Smith" said. "Come back when you finished."

"Yes, sir," Tarou responded before standing up and leaving the library.

1240 hours

"Look who's here," Jason Luke Crawley said as he and every other member of Iron Dutchman Services see Tarou enter the dining hall.

"Why are you here?" Wouter Vos asked just as Tarou joined Tatev Mirzoyan, Anita Hamilton, and Bartolomeu Moura.

"Mr. 'Smith' allowed me to take a break," Tarou answered.

"Figures," Crawley replied. "How was the test so far?"

"Hard," Tarou replied. "Remembering spoken language is one thing, but remembering written language is another."

"That's how it is," Hamilton replied. "You best eat now. Better not keep Mr. 'Smith' waiting."

"Got it."

#

1310 hours

"I've finished, Mr. 'Smith'," Tarou said at the library upon finishing the last question of the last page of the Japanese language test "Smith" gave him.

"Really?" "Smith" asked.

Tarou gave the test papers to "Smith". The latter looked at every page and found all questions answered. Portions with questions entirely using words and sentences mixed with *kanji*, *hiragana*, and *katakana* were answered in both romnaized Japanese and English. Portions with questions written in romanized Japanese were in written Japanese with English translations provided. Portions whose questions were in English were answered in both written and romanized Japanese.

I can't say if he passed or failed just yet, but Ganji managed to answer every question as instructed, "Smith" thought. *Not even one mistake.*

"Very well, Mr. Ganji. I will go back to my hotel for now to see if you passed or failed this test," "Smith" announced. "You'll have to wait until tomorrow for what I have to say."

"Smith" then put the test inside his suitcase and closed the latter. After that, he stood up and began to leave the library and, by extension, the ship.

#

Pacific Inn, Honolulu. 1950 hours

"Smith" had returned to his room in the Pacific Inn. Again he wrote a message in IntMail that read:

I've finished grading the written Japanese test I prepared for Tarou Ganji. I can say for certain he passed. I took photos of the written test and they are in this message along with today's report. At this point, I'll need non-civilian transportation to Japan because I intend to return to Japan with Ganji and Dr. Hamilton. I also intend on contacting Daisuke Hoshikawa so that he and Meiko Narumi from the Japanese Ministry of Justice can prepare to receive Ganji and Hamilton and until the meeting is arranged, I'll use the safehouse at Yao. However, we must immediately notify Deputy Director Saetang of this.

"Smith".

"Smith" pressed the "Send" button in IntMail. After waiting, he was shown "Message sent".

#

FIS Headquarters, McLean, Fairfax County, Commonwealth of Virginia. March 26, 2030; 0117 hours (Eastern Standard Time)

"Excellent work, Caguiat," Stanley McAllister said as he found the files from Caguiat's USB device and copied them onto his desktop computer and his USB device connected to it. "Before you go, there's something I need you to do."

"What is it?" Caguiat asked.

"I need you to contact Deputy Director Saetang. Please tell her to go to the museum because I will be there."

"I'm not allowed to know why you're meeting her, aren't I?"

"No. You're dismissed."

"Yes, sir." McAllister watched Caguiat leave his office. Unbeknownst to her, McAllister had another USB device plugged into his desktop computer and once Caguiat left, he copied the same files into that USB.

#

0240 hours

Yanin Saetang waited alone at the entrance of the Museum of Intelligence Collection with a cigarette between her right index and middle fingers. Only was the museum open on Saturdays to the general public—making this museum the only section of the complex open to the public—with declassified material allowed to be exhibited. This included material from the old Central Intelligence Agency that once operated the complex.

In front of both Saetang and the museum's entrance was a statue of Witold Pilecki, who was the current namesake of the entire FIS Headquarters complex. There were two notable reasons for naming the complex after the Polish resistance fighter from the Second World War. One reason was that Pilecki had infiltrated the Auschwitz concentration camp to gather intelligence about what happened inside, where Pilecki witnessed and reported on the mass executions of people called "sub-humans" by Poland's Nazi occupiers for two years until he escaped to prevent being compromised. Another reason was to show to the world that the New United Nations will not tolerate genocide with the Foreign Intelligence Service as an instrument of that policy.

Saetang then heard footsteps. Although the museum was closed, there were no guards and Saetang's presence, along with the individual who was the source of the footsteps, was the reason why the guards were absent. The Deputy Director of Intelligence turned to find Stanley McAllister, the Deputy Director of the Covert Action Center, joining Saetang.

"Why are we meeting here?" Saetang asked.

"You wanted up-to-date information about Tarou Ganji," McAllister answered as he brought out his USB. "Here you go."

"Thank you." Saetang grabbed the USB and placed it in her longcoat's right pocket. As she attempted to leave, she turned her head ninety degrees to her left and stopped walking. "I must ask: did you not consider any other mercenary group for this?"

"They were the first ones to pick up this job offer," McAllister answered before Saetang left.

#

1000 hours

Later, McAllister and Saetang entered Alberto Pérez's office. "Good, you two made it," Pérez said. "Allow me to cut to the chase: have you two sorted out your differences about Tarou Ganji?"

"We have," Saetang answered.

"Good. Stanley?"

"I can contact 'Smith' to have him tell Ganji that he passed, but he's asking for non-civilian transport to pick them up at Hickam," McAllister answered.

"I'll ask Blanchard if he can arrange something with ASFSOC," Pérez replied. "However, Deputy Director Saetang must send in one of her analysts to supervise your return to Japan with Ganji and McAllister."

"Who?"

#

1022 hours

John Vue reached the door to Pérez's office. Thirty-four years old, Vue descended from Hmongs who fled Laos, a third of former French Indochina, after it was taken by its Communist Phatet Lao movement. He had a body of average height and weight, lightly dark skin, dark brown eyes, and black hair in an undercut. Although the Foreign Intelligence Service was filled with people from across the New United Nations, for Vue, it felt that he lived in a new world because he had been used to living with fellow Hmongs in the same community. Despite that, Vue made a career in the FIS.

He entered the waiting room of Pérez's office with his secretary, Marjorie Thiam. Forty-five years old, Thiam had dark skin, black hair tied in a bun, and dark brown eyes. Like Vue, she too felt that the FIS was a world one wouldn't have lasted long as she came from a community of Senegalese immigrants who settled in the United States of America. Yet she was able to stay for twenty years.

"Morning, John," Thiam said upon receiving Vue.

"Morning to you too, Jorie," Vue replied. "Director Pérez wishes to see me?"

"Hold on, I'll let him know you're here."

After the buzz from a button Thiam pressed was heard, Vue continued on toward Pérez's office. He found not only the Director of Foreign Intelligence but also superior, Deputy Director of Intelligence Yanin Saetang and Deputy Director of the Covert Action Center Stanley McAllister.

"Glad you made it, John," Saetang said.

"Thank you, Deputy Director Saetang," Vue replied before he faced Pérez. "You called for me, Director Pérez?"

#

Pacific Inn, Honolulu, City and County of Honolulu, State of Hawaii. 0730 hours (Hawaii-Aleutian Time)

"Fred Smith" woke up due to his smartphone's alarm and turned the alarm off. After gaining the energy to remain awake, "Smith" used that energy to go to the bathroom and wash his face. After that, he opened his laptop computer and found that a message was sent to him through IntMail.

Opening IntMail, he found that the message came from Alicia Caguiat, which read:

After your trip to the Iron Dutchman, you're to receive one John Vue. Deputy Director Saetang has assigned him to oversee Tarou Ganji and Anita Hamilton's settlement into the State of Japan. Currently, he is availing for tickets to see you tomorrow and he will acquire funds to buy his own plane ticket for your trip to Japan with Ganji and Hamilton. I ask that you give him the courtesy of respecting him as a colleague in the Foreign Intelligence Service and to assist him in matters concerning talks with the Japanese government and Daisuke Hoshikawa.

Deputy Director of the Covert Action Center, Stanley McAllister.

Great, a desk weenie, "Smith" thought. *I can understand why Saetang would do this because I too want to know as well and the last thing I need from her or anyone directly answering to her is a human rights lecture.*

#

FIS Headquarters, McLean, Fairfax County, State of Virginia. 1334 hours (Eastern Standard Time)

Maurice Blanchard arrived at Alberto Pérez's office. Sixty-two years old, Blanchard hailed from Canada and served in its air force despite Canada escaping the Third World War mostly unharmed. Despite that, he joined the New United Nations Air and Space Force (NUNASF) after the Canadian Armed Forces downsized itself. Eventually, he became the Associate Director of Military Support, where he was to assist the Intelligence Collective by serving as a middleman between the IC and the New United Nations Defense Forces as a whole.

"So, why did you interrupt my lunch plans, Al?" Blanchard asked Pérez.

"I apologize for that, Maurice," Pérez replied. "I need your help with something."

"With what?"

"Transport. One of my agents is handling a couple of assets, and they need a plane. Preferably from ASFSOC."

"And if I do get you this plane from ASFSOC, where are your assets needed?"

"Japan. Actually, the assets are in Hawaii. My agent is with them now and that they need to be picked up by this plane which will take them to Japan"

"And I suppose I don't have a need to know?"

"At this point, not yet."

"… Fine. I'll call up Darshi and see if he can spare a Commando from Comox. But you owe me for how much I'm spending with this call."

"Sure."

Iron Dutchman, Naval Station Pearl Harbor, City and County of Honolulu, State of Hawaii. 1100 hours (Hawaii-Aleutian Time)

As it had become the norm for Iron Dutchman Services, every member of the mercenary group gathered at their dining hall after "Smith" arrived. He had his suitcase beside him and once Tarou Ganji came inside, he put down the suitcase on the desk he sat close to and stood up.

"Thank you for coming," "Smith" said. "I've finished grading the test I gave to Tarou Ganji, thus you know what I've come here to do."

"Smith" ceased to speak as he needed to open his suitcase. After getting what he stored in the suitcase—the written Japanese test he made Tarou answer the previous day, "Smith" resumed standing before the mercenaries but hid his face with the papers.

"I can now say for certain that Tarou Ganji has passed this test." "Smith" showed the paper he looked, showing the test but with the grade he gave, a 100.

"Sugoi," Jake Crawley said in awe.

"Is that it?" Wouter Vos skeptically asked.

"No," "Smith" answered as he put down the paper and faced Vos. "Now that Mr. Ganji has passed his test, we need to prepare for the trip to Japan. As was discussed before, Dr. Hamilton must act as his guardian."

"When do we get tickets?" Jake Crawley asked.

"No need for that. My superiors have already arranged transport. For Mr. Ganji and Dr. Hamilton, whatever belongings you have with you, I suggest packing up now. Except for firearms, that is."

"And what about the rest of us?" Vos asked again. "When do we make preparations for this ship to leave for Japan? We don't have enough fuel and going at maximum speed will waste even more of it."

"Not only that, we need more food because we're almost out," Bartolomeu Moura added.

"I've already arranged for additional fuel and nourishment to be delivered to this ship. However, this ship will only leave after those supplies arrive.

"For now, I have these to provide."

"Smith" returned the test to his suitcase. However, he brought out a smartphone similar to his out of the suitcase and showed them to the Iron Dutchman Services members.

"You are to use these smartphones to not only receive calls and messages from the Foreign Intelligence Service but to contact each other," "Smith" explained. "I've only brought three for the time being. Dr. Hamilton, Mr. Vos, and Mr. Ganji will be the only ones receiving these smartphones because Dr. Hamilton and Mr. Vos must be in contact while the former and Mr. Ganji are being settled."

"And how will our calls not be intercepted?" Tatev Mirzoyan asked.

"I will explain that now," "Smith" answered, but not before giving the smartphone he held to Tarou. This was followed by the former bringing out his smartphone.

"To turn on your smartphone, press the smaller button on the right below the bigger button."

"Got it," Tarou replied. As he did as "Smith" instructed, light began to appear on the smartphone's screen.

"Good," "Smith" complimented. "Now-"

"Why don't I teach Ganji here how to use one?" Sunan Wattana asked. "Most of us here do use but money has been tight that we never did utilize our earlier ones."

"Alright, you win this one. I'll come back tomorrow to teach you how to use the programs that make this smartphone applicable for FIS personnel only."

"Smith" returned to his suitcase, closed it, and began to leave the *Iron Dutchman.* However, as he began to exit the dining hall, he reared his head toward Tarou.

"One last thing: just because you passed doesn't mean you can get complacent with your Japanese," "Smith" warned. "Keep practicing."

The FIS agent continued to leave the ship. Everyone in Iron Dutchman Services looked at each other.

"Now then, let me continue where 'Smith' left off," Wattana announced to Tarou.

Comox Air Force Base, Comox, Comox Valley Regional District, British Columbia; Canada. 1650 hours (Pacific Standard Time)

After the Third World War, the United States of America suffered a secession crisis in the 1990s. Responsible for this was a movement to recreate the Confederate States of America, which was destroyed in 1865, was resurrected as the former Confederacy was hit the hardest during the Third World War. This fueled ethnic tensions due to what the New Confederacy stood for.

Northwestern Florida fell to these rebels in the as a result. Among their spoils was Eglin Air Force Base, which hosted the headquarters of the United States Air Force Special Operations Command (USASFSOC). This was around the time the New United Nations Defense Forces was conceived and that the US government was reluctant to participate in this concept as it involved downscaling its military. Even the idea of downscaling the US Armed Forces and giving most of its equipment to the nascent NUNDF encouraged a sizeable number of the Armed Forces to defect to the New Confederates. Due to the loss of Eglin, the NUNDF needed a headquarters for their own Air and Space Force's branch of Special Operations Command (SOCOM). The Royal Canadian Air Force base in Comox was found to be suitable as a headquarters for the New United Nations Air and Space Force Special Operations Command (NUNASFSOC).

A woman in her mid-thirties with short red hair, a body with average height and weight, very light skin, and green eyes arrived at the office of Colonel Emilio Gregorio, commander of the NUNAF's 1st Special Operations Wing. Both saluted after Gregorio stood up with the former standing firm and placing her arms backward and crossing their respective hands.

"At ease, Captain O'Leary," Gregorio ordered, with his female subordinate responding non-verbally. "Now then, I've gotten a request from the Director of the Foreign Intelligence Service relayed to me by Major General Blanchard."

"If I may, sir, what are the orders?" the woman named O'Leary asked.

"I was asked to provide one of our Commandos because an FIS agent has assets with him and they need a transport to take them to Japan.

They'll be waiting in Hickam Field, so I need you and your Commando to go there, pick up this agent and his assets, and drop them off at Japan."

"Yes, sir." O'Leary saluted to add as an acknowledgment to the order.

Good for you to not complain about this, Gregorio thought.

#

Unknown Location; Enlightenment Point. March 27, 2030; 1411 hours (EP Time Zone)

"Is that all from our Devotee-Infiltrator?" Sergei Akulov asked his hooded subordinate.

"Yes, Grand Gatekeeper," the hooded man answered. "Tarou Ganji was able to pass that Japanese examination prepared by 'Fred Smith' and now they'll be going to Japan to meet Daisuke Hoshikawa and his contact from the Japanese Ministry of Justice.

We're clearly dealing with no ordinary human if he's able to pass a written Japanese test, Akulov thought be resuming his discussion with his subordinate. "What is it you suggest?"

"We inform the OVR about this. We can also make arrangements for them to hire Serdar Muhadow to assist in watching Maria Hoshikawa."

"Do it."

"By your will, Grand Gatekeeper."

#

OVR Safehouse, Nishinari Ward, Kansai City, Kansai Prefecture; State of Japan. 2044 hours (Japan Standard Time)

Facing the Kizu River was a building. Secretly, it served as a safehouse for the Eurasian Tsardom's external intelligence agency, the OVR.

In charge of this safehouse was Tatiana Ioannovna Tsulukidze. At her den, she heard her smartphone, placed by the wall below the window as the window was used to tie down a satellite dish as it was connected to the phone below by a wire.

Tatiana then grabbed her phone and found that she received a message through an application named "SatCom". She found that the message came from "Nizhny".

What do you have for me, Vyacheslav? Tatiana pondered as she realized who "Nizhny" is. The message Tatiana read:

"Elizaveta",

I've received information about Iron Dutchman Services. Two of its members will be delivered by the Foreign Intelligence Service and the New United Nations Air Force to Japan in order for the former two to get settled as they're to meet Daisuke Hoshikawa and Meiko Narumi from the Japanese Ministry of Justice. For now, wait until you receive further instructions.

"Nizhny".

I best do as Vyacheslav says, Tatiana thought after reading Puzanov's letter. *We're outnumbered and outgunned to do anything.*

#

Pacific Inn, Honolulu, City and County of Honolulu, State of Hawaii; United States of America. 1333 hours (Hawaii-Aleutian Time)

"Smith" returned to the Pacific Inn. However, he found John Vue waiting in his room.

"I take it you're Vue?" "Smith" asked.

"I am," Vue answered.

"Then wait for me to open my door. You can come in after."

Vue then stepped out of "Smith's" way as the latter used his room's keycard to unlock the door. After the latter got inside his room, the former followed and closed the door.

"So, you were sent here by Saetang?" "Smith" asked as he sat on one of the two chairs facing his room's window.

"I was," Vue answered before he saw the chair opposite "Smith's". "Mind if I sit down?"

"Smith" gave no answer. After a gulp, Vue knew that was an answer in of itself and simply sat down next to "Smith".

"I know why Saetang sent you, but why did it have to be you?" "Smith" asked as a continuation of their discussion before Vue sat down.

"From how Deputy Director Saetang phrased it, I'm supposed to inspect your planned trip to Japan and your meeting with Daisuke Hoshikawa and Meiko Narumi," Vue answered.

"Good. I assume you have money for your trip to Japan?"

"I do. Though I have to ask my wife to intercede for me when talking to her father."

"What's the story there?"

"Father-in-law doesn't like me. He was once my boss at his manufacturing company."

"And what company is this?"

"United American."

"Wait, you married Cecil Boettger's daughter?!"

"Met her in high school. Boettger insisted on working for him so that I can marry his daughter. While working there, I didn't enjoy what I saw there and thus, I quit, angering him. My wife stuck with but around that time, I got her pregnant. Deputy Director Saetang heard of what happened and offered a job at the FIS. Naturally, I took it just in time for my daughter to be born."

"My turn to tell why I joined the FIS, though before you do: have you heard of Frederick Dirks?"

"No."

"That's my past life. I was once with the Special Operations Brigade of the Ground Force."

"The Green Berets?"

"Yes, the Green Berets. I met Daisuke Hoshikawa there, hence why I was able to approach him. After our service was up, I got myself embroiled in a diplomatic matter that nearly led to the current civil war in America becoming nuclear."

"What happened?"

Naval Station Pearl Harbor. 1948 hours

"Smith", or rather Frederick Dirks, approached the office of Naval Station Pearl Harbor's commander, Đỗ Văn Diệm. Fifty years old, Đỗ was a naval aviator and was promoted to Captain before given the assignment of Naval Station Pearl Harbor's garrison commander.

"What brings you to my office, 'Smith'?" Đỗ asked.

"I've come to tell you that Iron Dutchman Services, as well as myself, will be leaving soon," Dirks answered. "In my case tonight. However, I must warn you that a Commando II from Comox Air Force Base should be on its way here, and I'll be riding on that one with two members of Iron Dutchman Services when it shows up."

"And why are you telling me this?"

"Because I need your permission to notify the control tower that the Commando II is coming."

"Very well, I'll grant it."

"Thank you." "Smith" began to leave the office.

Finally, Đỗ thought.

#

March 28, 2030; 0405 hours

All members of Iron Dutchman Services were gathered outside their namesake ship. While Tarou had his duffel bag, Hamilton wore a backpack. A Joint Light Tactical Vehicle (JLTV), or "Jolt-Vee" as it's commonly called, approached the mercenaries.

The JLTV stopped in front of the Iron Dutchman Services members. The right front window opened with Dirks seated inside and turning his head to face the mercenaries.

"Good, you woke up on time," Dirks said. "Mr. Ganji, Dr. Hamilton, please get on through the back."

"Got it," Hamilton replied.

"Good luck for now," Wouter Vos said to Hamilton and Tarou.

"Thank you Wouter," Hamilton replied as she reared her head to face Vos.

Both Hamilton and Tarou entered the JLTV through the right rear door. Tarou, however, entered first, with Hamilton following. Once Hamilton closed the door, the driver began to make the JLTV move, but Dirks stopped them. Dirks then faced Vos.

"I must tell this to you now: you'll be receiving your first paycheck along with the supplies you need for your voyage to Japan?"

"Why now?" Vos asked.

"You'll need to exchange those UN dollars for Japanese yen."

"Got it."

It was then that Dirks allowed the driver to start up the JLTV. Once that was finished, the JLTV left for Hickam Field.

Update Part 2

Unknown Location; Enlightenment Point. March 28, 2030; 1837 hours (EP Time Zone)

Serdar Muhadow returned to the throne room of Sergei Akulov, the Grand Gatekeeper of Knowledge. The former clenched his right hand into a fist, placed it toward his chest, and bowed.

"Glad you returned, Muhadow," Akulov said.

"I live to serve, Grand Gatekeeper," Muhadow replied.

"Before I explain why I called for you, how familiar are you with Iron Dutchman Services?"

"As a recently created mercenary outfit, they've caused the expected amount of trouble you can see with newly created mercenary outfits. In short, I am not impressed."

"What I'm about to say will shock you. Are you ready?"

"I am, Grand Gatekeeper."

"Iron Dutchman Services will be getting themselves involved with Maria Hoshikawa."

"… Why them?"

"The FIS was the one to provide a contract for any mercenary group willing to accept it to protect Hoshikawa. Iron Dutchman Services took the contract, and now, two of their members are currently leaving for Japan with transportation provided by the FIS and the New United Nations Air and Space Force Special Operations Command."

"So who's going to Japan now?"

"An FIS agent calling himself 'Fred Smith' and two members of Iron Dutchman Services named Anita Hamilton and Tarou Ganji."

Tarou Ganji!? Muhadow incredulously pondered. *Impossible! I thought he died with those riffraffs in Charmshahr? This is quite the surprise, and I didn't think the Grand Gatekeeper himself would tell me about this.*

"Is something the matter?"

"... Sorry!" Muhadow replied before bowing to add as part of his apology. "I seemingly know who Tarou Ganji is."

"Do you? Please enlighten me."

"A weird child to say the least. He managed to learn how to fight and learned a little Russian. I know this because he was a part of the unit I commanded in Iran when the Eurasians invaded."

"And why are you telling me this now?"

"Because I assumed him dead."

"And what will you do when you see him?"

"Kill him. We're enemies now at this point."

"Good. Now, I need you to return to Turkestan because soon, I'll have the Gatekeeper of Intelligence use our Devotee-Infiltrator in the Tsardom's OVR to get them to work with a cell they inserted into Kansai City."

"I'm to work with the OVR?"

"That's right. Operating the cell in Kansai City is Grand Duchess Tatiana Ioannovna Tsulukidze."

"The daughter of Tsar Ivan is a spy!?"

"Surprising, isn't it? The Tsar opposed this, but he ultimately allowed her to join. She's obsessed with figuring out Tsesarevich Viktor's daughter that she thinks Maria Hoshikawa is the Tsesarevich's daughter."

"And why does she think that?"

"From what our Devotee-Infiltrator in the OVR told us, Grand Duchess Tatiana was able to retrieve a strand of Hoshikawa's hair by mistake and compared it to Tsesarevich Viktor's widow Svetlana Sonina. The Tsar seemed skeptical about it, ordering the Grand Duchess to remain in Japan and to continue monitoring Hoshikawa."

"And how am I supposed to work with the Grand Duchess?"

"Do what she tells you to do. However, you must always report to the Gatekeeper of Intelligence. As to what interest we have with Hoshikawa, we need you to capture her and deliver her to a laboratory we own in Sakhalin Island."

"And how am I supposed to capture Hoshikawa without the Grand Duchess noticing?"

"You'll have to figure that one out on your own. Once you've found a way to do so, we can send in your unit to assist you."

"Thank you, Grand Gatekeeper."

"In addition, you must make sure no one, especially Iron Dutchman Services or the FIS, knows about you nor the OVR cell."

"Yes, Grand Gatekeeper."

"For the time being, please return to Turkestan. All the information we so far will be sent to Gatekeeper Turkestan by the Gatekeeper of Intelligence."

"By your will, Grand Gatekeeper." Unbeknownst to Muhadow, the female hooded subordinate watched the whole conversation as was the order given three weeks before.

#

Hickam Air Base, Honolulu, City and County of Honolulu, State of Hawaii; United States of America. 0456 hours (Hawaii-Aleutian Time)

The JLTV "Fred Smith" (Frederick Dirks), Tarou Ganji, and Anita Hamilton rode on reached Hickam Field, a former United States Army Air Force base built in 1938. Three years prior, it was named Hickam Field after one Horace Hickam, who died in an accident on November 5, 1934 in Galveston, Texas. Now, the New United Nations Air Force used the airbase, and it shared a runaway with Daniel K. Inouye International Airport.

The JLTV stopped near an MC-130J Commando II special operations military transport aircraft. Dirks, Tarou, and Hamilton then exited the JLTV and proceeded to the Commando II. Reaching the laid ramp, they find the loadmasters; a dark-skinned man with dark brown eyes whose uniform and a woman with very light skin and blue eyes. The male loadmaster's hair, or lack of, was hidden by his helmet while the female loadmaster's had some of her blonde hair sticking out.

"You're 'Smith'?" the female loadmaster asked.

"That's me," Dirks answered.

"Technical Sergeant Andrew Singleton," the male loadmaster said.

"Master Sergeant Grace Norton," the female loadmaster said before turning to Tarou and Hamilton. "Are they the mercenaries?"

"We are," Hamilton answered.

"Then follow us inside," Singleton added before gesturing to the Commando II. Dirks, Tarou, and Hamilton followed the loadmasters to the Commando II.

Once inside the Commando II, Dirks, Tarou, and Hamilton gave their respective belongings to Singleton and Norton. After that, Norton begins unfolding the jump seats for Dirks, Tarou, and Hamilton to sit down on. After that, the latter three sit down and are belted by the former.

Because they didn't get enough sleep, the mercenaries and Dirks began falling asleep. Norton smiled at the sight that the FIS agent and his assets opted to sleep upon sitting down until she returned to work.

#

Pacific Inn, Honolulu, City and County of Honolulu, State of Hawaii; United States of America. March 27, 2030; 1350 hours (Hawaii-Aleutian Time)

"What happened?" John Vue asked "Fred Smith", who told of his real name to the former earlier, at his room in the Pacific Inn.

"You see, I'm from North Carolina," Frederick Dirks answered. "Any slave attempting to flee the New Confederacy manages to go to North Carolina, but that attracts Covert Service agents to North Carolina. I don't need to tell you who they are and why they pursue slaves. In any case, my family took in this free slave named Monique Wexler. You can guess where this was headed. Unfortunately, CS agents bribed a policeman my family knew into where Wexler was taken. My parents wind up dead as a result of Monique being taken in by them. I pursued those guys into South Carolina. Luckily, they didn't go far enough because they needed to figure out which plantation Monique escaped from and, through that, I was able to get her. However, as we neared free North Carolina, Monique died in the process. By the time I made to free North Carolina, I was arrested, and seeing that I lost everything in that debacle, I explained everything and pleaded guilty. Somehow, I was released and you can guess *who* pulled those strings."

"I'm sorry to hear that."

"*They* gave me a choice: I join or I go back to prison. I had nothing left to lose, so I took the first choice. I wouldn't call it a happy ending just yet, but taking up that offer allowed me to meet my wife. She gave me twin daughters as a result."

"That's good. Alright, enough of the past. I must ask you this: what do you think of Tarou Ganji?"

"Strange kid, I must say. He was able to learn Japanese as if he was a robot. I can see why Deputy Director Saetang sent you here."

"I am to do my own evaluation of this Tarou Ganji and deliver it to Deputy Director Saetang."

"Anything else you need from me?"

"When will you be leaving for Japan?"

"Tomorrow, with Hamilton and Ganji. I need to notify Hoshikawa first, who in turn will notify Narumi. Then it will be up to them to arrange the meeting. If you're going to be a part of this meeting, I must tell them about you and you'll need to make hotel arrangements."

"That I can do on my own at this point. What about Ganji and Dr. Anita Hamilton?"

"They should be packing up now. Until the meeting is arranged, I'll be having them stay at a safehouse in Yao that I've used in the past"

"Speaking of which, I was told that transport will be provided by ASFSOC."

"Good. I can notify Hickam about that."

"As for me, I can get my own ticket. Thank you."

New United Nations Air and Space Force Special Operations Command MC-130J; Above the Pacific Ocean. March 28, 2030; 0850 hours (Chomorro Standard Time)

Frederick Dirks, Tarou Ganji, and Anita Hamilton began to wake up. They found Andrew Singleton approaching them with a black bag.

"Enjoyed your sleep?" Singleton asked.

"Thank you, Sergeant," Hamilton replied.

"For now, call me Andy. We got rations. Before you say anything, we're not an airliner."

"It's alright," Dirks added before he turned to Tarou and Hamilton. "That we agree on?"

"Of course," Hamilton answered.

"Same here," Tarou added.

"Here you go," Singleton said before he began handing over rations to Dirks and his "assets".

After each receiving their rations, Dirks, Tarou, and Hamilton began to eat. While eating, Tarou began to think back to the previous day like Dirks did, but this time, he was awake.

#

Iron Dutchman; Naval Station Pearl Harbor, City and County of Honolulu, State of Hawaii; United States of America. March 27, 2030; 2109 hours (Hawaii-Aleutian Time)

In his room at the *Iron Dutchman*, Tarou Ganji looked at the only things he could take with him to Japan. Because he couldn't take his gun with him, he had only his spare clothes. He then heard a knock.

"Who is it?" Tarou asked.

"Tatev. Mind if I come in?"

"Hold on." Tarou walked to the door and as he opened it, he found Tatev Mirzoyan outside. "Come in."

Tarou stepped out of Tatev's way as she entered. He then closed the door and joined her in looking at his only luggage.

"This is all you're taking?" Tatev asked.

"I also have to take my Japanese learning materials and the smartphone Mr. 'Smith' gave me."

"Unlike me, you never asked for anything that wasn't food nor clothing."

"Why are you here?"

"Do I have to answer that?"

"Up to you."

"Well… I came because I want to ask you something."

"What is it?"

"What's it like… going to a country that hasn't seen war since the 20th century?"

"I don't know yet. While watching Japanese anime with Mr. Crawley, Japanese schools require uniforms. In Iran, that unit I belonged to didn't have uniforms."

"Did you have any friends when you fought against the Eurasian Tsardom?"

"There were two people I only knew that I could call friend… One was my commander, Vahid Farahani. He ran away from his home to fight and because he had more experience fighting, he was made the commander. The other was someone I knew from the Baloch community I was raised in… Shireen Baloch.

"I didn't know it at the time, but Shireen followed me when I left to fight. She proved her worth."

"And what happened to these people?"

"After Tehran fell, our unit was tasked with sabotaging the Eurasian advance. However, our numbers dwindled that I could only find Farahani. A Eurasian attack helicopter spotted us and fired. I don't know what happened next, but somehow, I survived, but I wasn't able to find Farahani nor anyone else. Since then, I traveled across the Middle East on foot in a trance until I encountered Iron Dutchman Services in what used to be Libya."

Another knock was heard. "Tarou, are you done sorting out your luggage for tomorrow?" Anita Hamilton asked from outside the room. "Remember, we have to wake up early for tomorrow."

"Got it," Tarou replied.

"I best get going," Tatev replied.

"Tatev, is that you? Why are you with Tarou?"

"I was just leaving," Tatev replied, after turning her head to face the door. After that, she resumed facing Tarou. "Good night."

"You too." Tatev began to leave the room. Upon opening the door, she found Hamilton getting out of the way.

"Excuse me," Tatev said to Hamilton before turning to her left. Hamilton then came inside the room.

"Is that all your taking with you other than your Japanese materials and the smartphone?" Hamilton asked.

"It is." Tarou answered.

"Then you should pack them up and get to sleep already."

"Got it."

Hamilton then left the room just as Tatev did. Tarou then packed up the clothes into a white-colored duffel bag.

#

New United Nations Air and Space Force Special Operations Command MC-130J; Above the Pacific Ocean. March 28, 2030; 0915 hours (Chomorro Standard Time)

That's the first time I ever brought up my unit to anyone, Tarou Ganji thought in the present as he finished his meal.

"You done?" Singleton asked.

".. Sorry," Tarou replied before giving his empty ration container, now filled with trash that once acted as containers for what the ration pack offered to Singleton.

Frederick Dirks removed his jump seat's seatbelts and walked up to Singleton, giving him his ration container. "Sergeant, if you don't mind, I need to talk to the crew," Dirks said. "I need to see who's in charge of this plane."

"That will be me." Dirks turned to find two women. One was Grace Norton, and the other had red hair as a contrast to Norton. Singleton saluted the two women.

"Captain Joanne O'Leary," the red-haired woman said. "You're 'Fred Smith?'

"I am."

O'Leary turned to Tarou and Hamilton. "And they're your assets?"

"I'm Dr. Anita Hamilton," said the woman seated down. "Beside me is Tarou Ganji."

Tarou simply nodded. O'Leary turned back to Dirks. "And where in Japan are we exactly going?"

"Yao," Dirks answered. "I have a safehouse there and that will be where Dr. Hamilton and Mr. Ganji will be staying at. As to why they're going to Japan in the first place, that's need to know."

"Okay, but how will you get to your safehouse?"

"I was about to find you on that. I need to notify the Japanese government that we're on a covert mission that involves asking for permission to land at Yao Airport."

"Fair enough. Follow me."

#

Japan Ground Self-Defense Force Camp Yao, Yao, Kansai Prefecture; State of Japan. 0839 hours (Japan Standard Time)

In the control tower of Japan Ground Self-Defense Force (JGSDF) Camp Yao, connected to Yao Airport, a woman anxiously but dutifully switched from one radio frequency to another. As a member of the New United Nations, the State of Japan was allowed to it keep its Self-Defense Forces, albeit downscaled. Camp Yao was one such installation the Japan Self-Defense Forces (JSDF) as a whole was allowed to keep with most installations now used and owned by the New United Nations Defense Forces.

"Yao Control, this is Nagoya Control," a male voice said over the radio. "We've been ordered to allow a transport from the New UN Air Force to land at Camp Yao. I say again, permission has been given to allow a transport from the New UN Air Force to land at Camp Yao."

"This is Yao Control," a male JGSDF soldier replied as he appeared to use the radio. "Order acknowledged."

#

New United Nations Air and Space Force Special Operations Command MC-130J; Above the Pacific Ocean. 0945 hours (Chomorro Standard Time)

"Sanzu 2-3, this is Yao Control," the male JGSDF soldier said over the radio of the MC-130J Commando II. "Authorization to land at Camp Yao approved. Please acknowledge."

"Yao Control, this is Sanzu 2-3," Joanne O'Leary replied. "Acknowledged."

"What will be your ETA?"

"1400 hours, Japan Standard Time. Currently, it's 0946 hours, Chomorro Standard Time."

"Acknowledged."

O'Leary then gave the headset she used earlier to talk to JGSDF Camp Yao to Frederick Dirks. "Yao Control, I am Package 1. I'm sure you've been told that three individuals are on board Sanzu 2-3 with Yao as their destination. Might I please request that you direct me to your superior officer?"

"Sanzu 2-3, this is Colonel Izubuchi, 1st Air Group," another male voice said over the radio. "What might be the reason for you to go to Camp Yao??"

"Colonel Izubuchi, I'm afraid that's on need to know. I can provide a few details, but only after Sanzu-2-3 drops us off."

"Understood. I look forward to what you have to say."

Japan Ground Self-Defense Force Camp Yao, Yao, Kansai Prefecture; State of Japan. 1359 hours (Japan Standard Time)

The Commando II ultimately reached JGSDF Camp Yao. Before reaching Camp Yao, however, the Commando II had to land at the civilian runaway used by Yao Airport.

Civilians watched as a New United Nations Air and Space Force plane landed on their runaway. Lest a military *otaku* was among those watching what was unfolding, no one knew that this military plane was a part of a covert operation.

Upon landing, the Commando II used its landing gear to push toward Camp Yao. Once it reached the JGSDF base, the Commando II stopped. Two LAVs (Light Armored Vehicle) arrived near the Commando II.

"Ladies and gentlemen, welcome to Camp Yao," a male voice said over the Commando II's PA system. "Local time is 1407 hours, and the temperature is 36 degrees celsius.

"For your safety and comfort, please wait until the loadmasters have removed your seatbelts. This is until the ramp is lowered and once it is lowered, you're free to move about. In addition, your respective luggage will be given to you after the seatbelts have been removed.

"On behalf of the New United Nations Air and Space Force and the entire crew, I'd like to thank you for joining us on this trip and we are looking forward to seeing you on board again in the near future. Have a nice day!"

"Show off," Grace Norton softly muttered while she and Andrew Singleton approached Dirks, Tarou Ganji, and Anita Hamilton.

Norton attended to Dirks while Singleton attended to Tarou and Hamilton. After that, the loadmasters began to reach for the respective luggage of the passengers. After that, Dirks, Tarou, and Hamilton stood up with O'Leary joining them.

"Follow you as we step out of the plane," O'Leary instructed to Dirks, Tarou, and Hamilton. "Izubuchi sent welcome wagons for us."

As O'Leary, Dirks, Tarou, and Hamilton exited the Commando II through the ramp, they were approached by four JGSDF soldiers. Their uniform consisted of a blouse-trousers combination using a camouflage pattern they called *Nishiki* (Type 2), black-colored boots as called *Nishiki*, and the *Hachi-jyu hachi* (Type 88) helmet; a local replication of the Personnel Armor System for Ground Troops (PASGT) helmet.

The JGSDF infantrymen carried the Hachi-jyu kyu (Type 89) assault rifle, which was nicknamed "Buddy". The rifle had been in service with the JGSDF since 1989, but despite that, the JGSDF still used the rifle. Such was the result of member-states of the New United Nations asked to downscale their respective militarys which led to the cessation of arms procurement updates for these militaries as many assumed that having NUNDF bases was more than enough for their defense.

Another JGSDF soldier joined the four confronting O'Leary, Dirks, Tarou, and Ganji. Unlike the former four, he didn't wear a Type 88 helmet but a patrol cap. Dirks looked at the man and assumed he knew who he was and rapidly prepared what to say when addressed to. This was while the JGSDF soldier with the patrol cap and O'Leary saluted each other.

"I'm Colonel Juzo Izubuchi," the JGSDF soldier with the patrol cap said.

"Captain Joanne O' Leary," the NUNASF officer replied.

"I assume you won't be staying long?"

"My work here is done. My crew and I will go to Iruma and refuel before returning to Hickam, in which we'll refuel again before returning to Comox."

"I see." Izubuchi turned to Dirks, Tarou, and Hamilton. "And you're the 'Packages'?"

"Hai desu," Dirks replied. "Namae wa Sumisu Fuderikku desu." Dirks then turned to Tarou and Hamilton. "Kochira wa Hamiruton Anita-sensei to Ganji Tarou desu."

"Yoroshiku onegai shimasu," Tarou replied with a bow.

"Dewa, shitagatte kudasai."

#

1517 hours

Dirks, without his luggage, was brought to Izubuchi's office by one JGSDF soldier. After the soldier and Izubuchi saluted each other, the former left.

"Suwatte kudasai," Izubuchi said as he offered the chair facing him for Dirks to sit on.

Dirks then sat down. "You speak Japanese awfully well," Izubuchi complimented.

"Thank you," Dirks replied.

"I assume you're with the FIS?"

"I can neither confirm nor deny that."

"And those two you brought with you, it's need to know?"

"That's right."

"When we talked prior to your arrival, you said you were willing to tell me a few details as to why you're here."

"I have a safehouse here in Yao. All I need now is a ride."

"And where is this safehouse?"

Before Dirks could answer, the sound of the Commando II that brought Dirks, Tarou, and Hamilton to Japan was heard lifting off. As Joanne O'Leary said, her job was done.

"Takasagocho," Dirks answered to resume his conversation with Izubuchi.

"I'll see what I can do," Izubuchi replied. "For now, you three must remain here in the base."

"Wakarimashita."

#

FIS Safehouse. 1622 hours

An LAV provided by Izubuchi brought Dirks, Tarou, and Hamilton to a public bathhouse in Yao's Takasagocho neighborhood. As the LAV was a military vehicle in the middle of a dense neighborhood, it had to be parked in front of an abandoned shack in the middle of the street.

"If you don't mind me asking, sir, this is the safehouse?" the LAV driver asked Dirks.

"That's need to know at this point," Dirks answered. "Thank you for this."

Dirks then joined Tarou and Hamilton. They moved toward the bathhouse in order for the LAV driver to get out of the street. Once the LAV was no longer seen, Dirks knocked on the door. Answering the door was a woman in her fifties.

"Ara, it's been a long time since you've been here, Preston-san," the woman said.

"Glad to see you're well, Miyako-san," Dirks replied.

"And who are they?" the woman named Miyako asked upon seeing Tarou and Hamilton.

"They're with me, but can we please take this conversation inside?"

"Mochiron desu."

#

1634 hours

"So you intend on settling here in Japan after escaping a war zone?" Miyako asked Hamilton and Tarou at the top floor of the bathhouse with Dirks sitting with them.

"Sou desu," Tarou replied.

"And you even learned Japanese before coming here."

"I taught him Japanese," Dirks added.

"And where will you be staying?"

"Miyako-san, mind if we talk about that by ourselves? You're on need to know at this point."

"Wakarimashita."

Both Dirks and Miyako stood up and left the room. They then reached the corridor of the top floor.

"Those two are a part of a mission I'm currently undertaking," Dirks continued. "I've already made arrangements as to where they're staying at but I need to make contact with Hoshikawa Daisuke because he knows someone from the Ministry of Justice who can help."

"You know Hoshikawa Daisuke?"

"We're acquainted, to say the least. However, I cannot make contact with him until this Sunday. For the time being, could you please allow Hamilton-sensei and Ganji-kun to stay with you? I'll pay for all of it."

"If they need to use my bathhouse, there's no need to pay for that. Food, on the other hand… "

"I can pay for that."

"Also, they cannot use the baths if there are customers."

"I'll tell them that."

#

March 29, 2030; 0649 hours

At the room he shared with Tarou in the bathhouse, Dirks woke up. After waiting to gather strength, he got his laptop computer and after turning it on, he began to use IntMail. He typed the following:

We've already settled in Japan, specifically in Miyako Horikawa's bathhouse. Right now, I need to figure out a way to make contact with Daisuke Hoshikawa. While I can attempt to contact him when he and his family hear Mass this Sunday, it will compromise me. Expect another update by the end of this week.

"Fred Smith".

#

0800 hours

Later, Dirks, Miyako Horikawa, Tarou, and Hamilton were gathered at the table at the top floor of the bathhouse. "Until I make contact with Hoshikawa regarding the meeting with his contact in the Ministry of Justice, you two are to remain here until then."

"Understood," Tarou and Hamilton replied in unison.

"Now, as for food and drinks, we'll need money for that. Today, I'll find a bank to turn my UN dollars into Japanese yen. After that, we can find food to eat for today."

"Acknowledged."

"Good. Stay here until I come back."

Unknown Location; Enlightenment Point. 1349 hours (EP Time Zone)

"Thank you for notifying me of this new update, Gatekeeper Int Frühling," Sergei Akulov said to his hooded subordinate.

"I can arrange for something to get Puzanov to hire Gatekeeper-Major Muhadow," the hooded man named Frühling replied.

"Not yet. Relay everything we have on Iron Dutchman Services and our recent updates to our Devotee-Infiltrator in the OVR. *She'll* be the one to tell Puzanov as to why he'll need Muhadow."

"By your will, Grand Gatekeeper."

#

Askarova Apartment, Nizhegorodsky District, Imperial City of Nizhny Novgorod; Eurasian Tsardom. March 30, 2030; 0334 hours (Novgorod Time)

One Aigul Askarova parked her car in front of an apartment building in Nizhny Novgorod, located near the Nikolai Ivanovich Lobachevsky University. Forty-nine years old, Askarova had long black hair in a Dutch braid, and light skin. Despite her age, she served as the Deputy Director of the OVR which would make Stanley McAllister her equivalent in the New United Nations' Foreign Intelligence Service.

The apartment complex where Askarova lived at was near the Nikolai Ivanovich Lobachevsky University. This part of Nizhny Novgorod was a remnant of the Soviet period, as the city wasn't harmed during the Third World War. Although turned into a battlefield during the subsequent Unification War that created the Tsardom, the damage was repaired. The apartment building was one such building that was repaired despite it being a *khrushchyovka*, itself a relic of the Soviet era.

After parking her car, Askarova reached her apartment and after bringing out the key but before using it on the door's lock, she knocked twice; one lightly and one loudly.

She must be asleep, Askarova thought before unlocking her door.

After coming inside, she placed an empty can of *baikal* by the sink in the apartment's kitchen but after she had pressed a red button below. She then brought out two smartphones; one with a red cover and another with a green cover. She placed the latter beside the supposed *baikal* can and began to use the former.

"You're home," a female voice said, surprising Askarova.

Askarova reared her head to find the woman that appeared and faced her. A year older than Askarova, the woman had dark brown hair like her eyes.

"Sorry about that," Askarova replied while she desperately stood in front of the *baikal* can and her smartphone in red cover and placing the smartphone with a green cover on top of it. "I also apologize for waking you up."

"It's alright. How long will you be standing there?"

"There's just something I need to see before I go to bed. I'll join you soon."

"Then good night, Ai."

"You too, Pati."

Relaying Messages

Askarova Apartment, Nizhegorodsky District, Imperial Capital of Nizhny Novgorod; Eurasian Tsardom. March 30, 2030; 0851 hours (Novgorod Time)

Wearing but a bathrobe, the woman named Pati found Aigul Askarova cooking their breakfast. Another girl was seated at the dinner table eating a simple loaf of bread with butter on it.

"You're awake, Pati," Askarova said as she saw Pati. "Go on, sit down."

"Spasibo."

Although they were women, Askarova and Pati, whose real name was Patigül Aytmatova, were married though this is simply referred to as a "civil union". The younger girl eating their bread was their adoptive daughter Yulia. One notable difference between the Eurasian Tsardom and the past Eurasian empires before it was that civil unions for same-sex couples were legal and that they were to be given the same rights as opposite-sex couples. This was conceived by Tsar Ivan Vladimirovich Tsulukidze because he found no good reason to continue the policies practiced against homosexuals. Some continued to oppose this, some have sung praises ever since but most didn't care as Tsulukidze brought peace and order across Eurasia because that was preferable to constant war that would have seen no end in sight. Aigul Askarova and Patigül Aytmatova had benefited from this, especially having grown up in the former Kyrgyz Soviet Socialist Republic, where their love wouldn't have been accepted by their friends and respective families.

Askarova then joined her civil partner at the table with their breakfast. "I'm surprised you chose to cook today," Pati said.

"I felt that I've been taking you for granted for weeks," Askarova replied.

"I see. You haven't forgotten right?"

"Forgot what?"

Pati sighed. "We have plans for tomorrow."

"Oh right! Thank you for reminding me. Speaking of which, I best hurry before I'm late."

#

OVR Headquarters. 1156 hours

After being alerted by his secretary, Vyacheslav Leonidovich Puzanov received Aigul Askarova into his office. "So, what brings you to my office before I'm to leave for my lunch?" Puzanov asked his Deputy Director.

"I've received information about the FIS's movements concerning Maria Hoshikawa," Askarova answered.

"And I suppose you can't tell me where you get your information?"

"Net."

"I see."

Askarova handed over the envelope to Puzanov. After removing the sticker lock, Puzanov removed all the papers and before reading them, he put on the appropriate eye glasses and started reading.

As he read through each file on Iron Dutchman Services' members, Puzanov stopped as soon as he reached the file on Tarou Ganji.

"Not exactly surprised that we have an Iranian as a part of this band of mercenaries but… " Puzanov said before hesitating to continue. "He's only a boy! I don't care if he may have joined willingly, but why would he be our enemy?"

"I'd like to say revenge, given that he's Iranian, but the file stated that he claims to find out who he really is," Askarova answered.

"I see." Askarova then proceeded to the next file: Tatev Mirzoyan. "Says here this Ta-"

Puzanov said nothing else, opting to continue reading without saying anything else. Askarova knew what that entailed.

"Is… something the matter?" Askarova asked.

"This girl was a victim of Anton Kravchenko's sex slavery ring. It shouldn't be surprising that a mercenary group would take her in, but I'm surprised she's not the one they're sending on this mission to spy on Maria

Hoshikawa. Regardless, I must continue reading about these mercenaries."

"One last thing, Director, I was given a file on someone I recommend to assist Grand Du- I mean, Gospazitza Tsulukidze."

"And who is this mercenary?"

"Serdar Muhadow."

"I've heard of him. The 'Butcher of Godana', as they called him for laying a well-organized trap that ended with the destruction of a Mongolian motor rifle battalion."

"And why does your 'contact' wish for me to hire Muhadow?"

"He speaks multiple languages and should he fail, he can easily be disposed of as a result."

"I see. Let me talk this over with the Tsar. Of course, I need my lunch first."

"Again, I apologize for having asked for this."

"Nonsense. Speaking of which, why don't you eat lunch with me? It can get lonely."

"Spasibo."

#

1240 hours

Both Puzanov and Askarova began eating chicken Kiev. For many across the Eurasian Tsardom, it was a miracle recipes for this dish, which originated in the Russian Empire that preceded the Union of Soviet Socialist Republics, survived both the Third World War and the Unification War.

"Tell me, how's Pati?" Puzanov asked before chewing and swallowing his piece of chicken Kiev.

"She's well," Askarova answered after swallowing her meal. "I cooked for her this morning to make up for her always cooking for me."

"And what about your adoptive daughter, Yulia?"

"Finishing her high school. She intends to enlist to avoid making us pay for university."

"That's good to know. Speaking of which, I must say this in advance: Happy birthday."

"Spasibo."

"When you do see Pati again, give her my regards."

"Spasibo."

#

Nizhny Novgorod Kremlin. 1630 hours

Puzanov was alone in the waiting room leading to the throne room of the Nizhny Novgorod Kremlin. As it survived the Unification War, Tsar Ivan Vladimirovich Tsulukidze made the fortress, built in the 16th century during the reign of Tsar Ivan III of the Romanov Dynasty, his seat of power.

"The Tsar is ready to see you now," a female member of the squad of the Imperial Eurasian Army's Lifeguard Regiment said. She had light intermediate skin, brown hair underneath her *shako*, and dark brown eyes. She had an AK-2000 assault rifle slung across her back.

"Spasibo," Puzanov replied.

Puzanov and the Lifeguard Regiment soldier proceeded inside the throne room. Both knelt and bowed before Tsar Ivan Vladimirovich Tsulukidze.

Seventy-three years old, Ivan still showed the character that stemmed from his physique. Light-skinned, Ivan had gray hair that was once brown and gray eyes. A descendant of Georgian aristocracy, Ivan Vladimirovich Tsulukidze dreamed of living as if the Russian Empire hadn't collapsed in 1917 but kept this to himself, especially when he became an officer in the Soviet Army. That changed while he was stationed at the Democratic Republic of Afghanistan when an alien ship crash-landed in 1985. Miraculously, Ivan survived, but kept it secret for a while, but that too changed when a nuclear weapon struck the USSR's capital of Moscow in the year 1989. When Ivan returned, he found his country ruined after three years of war and divided, yet he found hope as his wife, Yekaterina and their twin sons, Viktor and Iosif, alive.

Seeing an opportunity that would never come to him had he not acted upon it, Ivan gathered like-minded soldiers, officers, and civilians tired of the armed factions killing each other across the former USSR, Ivan began the Unification War, creating the Eurasian Tsardom in the process with himself as Tsar.

"You two may stand," Ivan ordered to Puzanov and the female soldier.

Both stood up, with Ivan turning to the latter. "You may return to your position, Serzhánt Borasanova."

"Da, Vashe Velichestvo," the woman named Borasanova replied before standing to the right of the Tsar.

Ivan then turned to Puzanov. "Slava, what brings you here?"

"Your Majesty, I've received a report that the New United Nations' Foreign Intelligence Service has begun its mission to monitor Maria Hoshikawa. I believe you've been told as to who she is?"

"I see." Ivan then saw the same envelope he was given by Aigul Askarova hours before. "Why don't we resume this discussion in my office?"

#

OVR Headquarters. 1855 hours

Askarova returned to Puzanov's office. "I assume the Tsar has approved of my recommendation?" Askarova asked.

"Da," Puzanov answered. "However, the Tsar asks that Muhadow see him. If you can contact who sent you that information, please let them know of this request."

"Zametano. Odnako… "

"Chto eto takoye?"

"I would prefer that I contact my source at my apartment. I feel safer that way."

"You're not using this as an opportunity to dine with your partner, are you?"

"Partially that… "

"Fine. Once you've received a reply, return here immediately!"

"Spasibo."

#

Askarova Apartment. 1914 hours

Askarova immediately entered her apartment after unlocking the door. Upon proceeding inside, she found Patigül Aytmatova cooking.

"Ai, you're home!?" Pati asked incredulously upon seeing her civil partner return. "What are you doing here!?"

"Work-related reasons," Askarova answered.

"Did you not know I cook dinner at this time?"

"I do."

Pati sighed. "It will take me an hour to cook for you. Yulia will be home soon and I just assumed it would just be us two."

"Then don't bother. I was told not to come back until my business here is done. I can eat there."

Pati sighed. "I apologize for that. I didn't think you would come home this early for once. Do you want me to cook for you?"

"I apologize myself. Do what you have to do. I'll just be in our room."

Askarova then stormed off to their bedroom. After closing the door, Askarova removed her empty *baikal* can from her bag and placed it on the left nightstand. After pressing the button at the bottom of the can, Askarova brought out her smartphone with the green cover and began using the smartphone's GOKMail, typing the following:

On using Gatekeeper-Colonel Serdar Muhadow on the mission to capture Maria Hoshikawa, permission has been granted by the Tsar and Director Puzanov in acquiring Muhadow's services. However, both the Tsar and Director Puzanov have requested that they must see Muhadow before making a final decision.

Devotee-Infiltrator Askarova.

Once finished, Askarova used her right thumb to press the "Send" button in GOKMail. After waiting for the message to be sent, Askarova laid on the bed while hiding her phone underneath the pillow behind her.

And now, it's a waiting game, Askarova thought. *Problem is, what will happen first? I get a response from Gatekeeper Int or Pati finishes making dinner for me?*

Unknown Location; Enlightenment Point. 2114 hours (EP Time Zone)

Frühling, the Gatekeepers of Knowledge's intelligence chief, barged into the throne room of Sergei Akulov. As a result, Frühling was too exhausted to do the Gatekeepers' salute.

"I assume that by rushing in here without saluting me means we have an update from out Devotee-Infiltrator in the OVR?" Akulov asked.

"... Yes, Grand Gatekeeper?" Frühling answered.

"I'll let this go for now, so what does she have to say?"

"She's... been... given permission to have Devotee-Colonel Muhadow assist in watching Maria Hoshikawa. However, the Tsar and Director Puzanov ask that they see Muhadow."

"Then contact Gatekeeper Turkestan and have him relay to Muhadow that he must go to the Tsardom."

It was then that Frühling now had the strength to salute his Grand Gatekeeper. "By your will, Grand Gatekeeper."

#

Askarova Apartment, Nizhegorodsky District, Imperial Capital of Nizhny Novogorod; Eurasian Tsardom. 2045 hours (Novgorod Time)

Aigul Askravora returned to the bedroom she and Patigül Aytmatova used. Remembering which pillow she used to hide it, the former extracted the phone with the red cover. Opening GOKMail, she found the reply that read:

Thank you for the recent information you sent, Devotee-Infiltrator Askarova. I've notified the Grand Gatekeeper of this and he has consented to sending Devotee-Colonel Muhadow to meet Director Puzanov and the Tsar. Currently, we're in the middle of contacting him.

After that, we'll inform you as to when he will arrive. You are to deliver him to Director Puzanov first and from there, he'll inform the Tsar. That will enable an audience between the Tsar and Devotee-Colonel Puzanov.

Gatekeeper of Intelligence.

Finally, Askarova thought. *Now, I just need to type in "Acknowledged" and we're done for now.*

Askarova began typing her reply. Once she finished and pressed "Send", she turned off the smartphone and hid it in her bag. After that, she returned to the empty *baikal* can and pressed its button again.

And now I can go back to the office, Askarova thought.

#

Turkestan Tachyon Particle Receiver; Turkestani Republic. March 31, 2030; 0150 hours (Turkestan Time)

Serdar Muhadow arrived at the office of Gatekeeper Turkestan. Both men did the clenched fist salute of the Gatekeepers.

"I assume the Grand Gatekeeper has new information about the FIS agent and his mercenary assets going to Japan?" Muhadow asked.

"They're now in Japan," Gatekeeper Turkestan answered. "I have a message from Gatekeeper Int. I'll be sending it to your GOKMail account."

Gatekeeper Turkestan began to use his GOKMail to send the message he received from the Gatekeeper of Intelligence to Muhadow's account. Muhadow then received the message in his smartphone's GOKMail. It read:

To Gatekeeper Turkestan.

I've been told that the Foreign Intelligence Service agent "Fred Smith" and his assets from Iron Dutchman Services, Dr. Anita Hamilton and Tarou Ganji, have arrived in Japan. I have been given authorization by the Grand Gatekeeper himself to have Devotee-Colonel Muhadow sent to the State of Japan. However, the Tsar and Director Puzanov of the OVR have asked to see him in order to see if he can be sent to Japan to be inserted as part of the OVR cell led by Grand Duchess Tatiana Ioannovna Tsulukidze. Therefore, the Grand Gatekeeper has given the order for a transport plane to be sent to the Turkestani Republic to pick up Gatekeeper-Major Muhadow and transport him to the Eurasian Tsardom, specifically to Nizhny Novgorod. This plane will be carrying medical supplies as cover to deliver Muhadow.

If the Tsar and Director Puzanov recruit Devotee-Colonel Muhadow, he will im mediately return to the transport plane and it will take him to Japan, From there, Muhadow will answer to her until he finds a good opportunity to get a hold of Maria

Hoshikawa. If the Tsar and the Director of the OVR refuse to recruit Muhadow, he is to be returned to Turkestan. Once you've received this message, please relay this to Devotee-Colonel Muhadow.

Gatekeeper of Intelligence.

"I should have known recommending me would invite suspicion," Muhadow remarked.

"Either way, you're to pack up before the plane arrives," Gatekeeper Turkestan ordered. "For the time being, you'll have to work alone."

"Acknowledged."

"You're dismissed."

Muhadow began to leave the room. *Suddenly, I get the feeling I'm going to be the evil dragon tasked in taking the princess and that I'll be pursued by the knight in shining armor.*

#

Turkestan City International Airport, Turkestan City. 0900 hours

Muhadow now arrived at Turkestan City International Airport. A C-141 Starlifter strategic transport bearing the insignia of the Gatekeepers of Knowledge's air force, the Wings of the Defenders, had already landed at Turkestan City International Airport.

Although a neutral organization, the Gatekeepers were allowed to own a military to at least provide security with the former United States Air Force's fleet of Starlifters used for delivering supplies for natural disasters across the world.

Muhadow then approached the Starlifter. The two loadmasters, both of whom were women, approached Muhadow, and both parties saluted each other.

"You're Devotee-Cōlonel Muhadow?" one loadmaster asked.

"I am," Muhadow answered.

"Follow us," the other loadmaster replied.

Strigino International Airport, Aztozavodsky District, Imperial Capital of Nizhny Novgorod; Eurasian Tsardom. 1352 hours (Novogorod Time)

Muhadow then disembarked from the Starlifter after it arrived at Strigino International Airport, which served Nizhny Novgorod. He then sharply dressed men, covering their eyes with sunglasses in his way.

"Vy Serdar Mukhadov?" one man asked.

"Da?" Muhadow asked in response.

"The Tsar has ordered us to take you to him," the other man answered. "Please follow us."

#

Nizhny Novgorod Kremlin. 1500 hours

Muhadow then arrived at the throne room of the Nizhny Novgorod Kremlin. Vyacheslav Puzanov stood beside Tsar Ivan Vladimirovich Tsulukidze, seated on his throne on a suit of armor as if he were in the 16th century, while Muhadow bowed to the two of them.

"I apologize for not having informed you sooner that I was coming, Your Majesty," Muhadow said, while he continued to kneel before the Tsar. "I assume you know why I've come?"

"You may stand," Ivan ordered with Muhadow complying. "As you can see, the Director of the OVR stands beside me and he has asked that I hire you for a mission that will require your set of skills."

"What do you ask of me?"

"Why don't we answer that in my office?"

#

1511 hours

Ivan, Puzanov, and Muhadow arrived at the office connected to the throne room. Ivan then sat down.

"Gospodin Mukhadov, naturally I would have the Ministry of Defense explain what you're to do and how much you're to be paid, but because this is an OVR operation, I must personally oversee this. Shall we discuss payment?"

"Da," Muhadow answered. "One million rubles."

"Consider it done. Now, I'll have Director Puzanov explain what you're supposed to do."

"You're to assist a cell we've inserted into Japan because for the past three months,, we've been observing a girl named Maria Hoshikawa," Puzanov explained before giving a file to Muhadow.

The Turkmen mercenary feigned ignorance by receiving the file and reading it. *Quite the irony that my real client is also in the dark as to who Hoshikawa really is,* Muhadow thought.

Muhadow continued reading the file. He found a page in the file pertaining to Kansai City, with a red dot near the Kizu River. *This must be the safehouse they're talking about and it's run by someone they call "Elizaveta". Interesting.*

Muhadow then returned the file to Puzanov. "I assume you're done reading?"

"I am," Muhadow answered. "Has 'Elizaveta' been notified that she is to receive me?"

"I'll contact her on that matter. The contract was also in the file and I must warn you in advance that should you accept it, you must follow orders given by 'Elizaveta'."

"Understood."

"Good," Ivan added before facing Puzanov. "Director Puzanov, show he the contract."

Puzanov opened the file but flipped to the contract. He then gave it back to Muhadow.

"I have a pen here for you to sign with," Ivan said as he offered a ballpen for Muhadow to use.

"Spasibo, Vashe Velichestvo," Muhadow replied as he received the pen.

Muhadow read the contract before signing it. *There must be a fine print in here because they can't be stupid to not anticipate treachery,* Muhadow thought. *The Tsar is even wearing the armor that helped him create this polity in the first place.*

"Your Majesty, forgive me for this request, but might I be allowed some time to think about this contract before signing it?" Muhadow asked.

"I understand," Ivan answered. "You can stay at the New Hotel Ukraina until then. I'll have Agents Vovk and Zhukovsky accompany you and help get you settled. After you decide to sign it, give the file to either agent."

"Spasibo, Vashe Velichestvo."

"One last thing: how exactly did you come here through a Gatekeepers of Knowledge transport?" Puzanov asked as Muhadow began to leave.

"I do some work for them on occasion," Muhadow asked. "Transport is payment enough, and the plane isn't to leave until I decide to leave."

#

New Hotel Ukraina. 1749 hours

Muhadow was now at his room in the New Hotel Ukraina. Built after the Unification War ended, the hotel was named after the original Hotel Ukraina, one of the "Seven Sisters" that dominated Moscow's skyline during the Soviet era; all of which were destroyed when the city, harmed in a nuclear attack that started the Third World War, became a battlefield in the Unification War.

Such a hotel was built near the Kremlin to receive foreign dignitaries and the occasional businessman doing his or her part for the Tsardom. It was a rarity for a man like Serdar Muhadow to stay in the hotel, even for one night. Such was the work of the two Ohkrana agents, Vovk and Zhukovsky, standing outside his room.

Immediately upon settling in, Muhadow began to search for the contract's fine print. He brought out two belongings: a magnifying glass and an "eraser". He pressed a button on the latter and began to use the former to scan the contract.

Now, where's that fine print? Muhadow pondered as he looked for the fine print.

Again, Muhadow read the entire contract from the beginning. Unlike the contract he received years before from the Tsardom's Ministry of Defense, which led to his involvement in the war of independence that created the Turkestani Republic, a contract from the OVR was written differently and Muhadow knew that fine prints for mercenary contracts related to what a mercenary could or couldn't do.

As he reached the last paragraph of the contract, Muhadow moved his right arm slowly. He knew that fine prints were found IN the last paragraph.

There you are, Muhadow had in his mind as he found the fine print. *It says "Any form of suspicious activity as reported by your supervisor will warrant a punishment wholly decided by the supervisor. As to what we define as suspicious activity that will depend on the supervisor."*

Damn it. Either way, if I don't accept this contract, I'll make the Tsar look like a fool. If I do sign it, I'll have to find a way to enact a plan to grab Hoshikawa without alerting 'Elizaveta'. I guess I have no choice.

Muhadow began to use the pen. He wrote in both Turkmen and in Cyrillic. After that, he stood up, carrying the file, and knocked on the door.

"Da?" one Ohkrana agent asked.

"I've signed the contract," Muhadow answered.

Muhadow then opened the door. He then gave the file and the pen to one of the two agents.

"Spasibo, Gospodin Mukhadov. I must ask how long you intend to stay here because we need to arrange your departure from this hotel?"

"Tomorrow morning."

"Spasibo, Gospodin Mukhadov. Agent Vovk will go to the Kremlin and notify the Tsar. He's authorized us to allow you to use the amenities here in this hotel."

"Spasibo."

#

Turkestan City International Airport, Turkestan City; Turkestani Republic. April 1, 2030; 0900 hours (Turkestan Time)

The Starlifter returned to the Turkestani Republic. Upon exiting the transport plane, Muhadow found three armed men waiting for him; two hiding their entire heads while one approached him while wearing a sky blue beret. Both Muhadow and the man in the beret saluted each other.

"Welcome back, Commander," the man with the beret said.

"Hawa, Ghaemi," Muhadow replied. "I assume you're here to pick me up?"

"Yes, sir."

"Good. I could use the rest."

#

Turkestan Tachyon Particle Receiver. 2035 hours

Damn it! Serdar Muhadow cursed in his mind at his bedroom in the TPR complex while looked at all of his forged visas. *Not once have I ever infiltrated a NUN member-state. I knew it was going to be hard, but I'll need a visa to avoid suspicion from the authorities. Made worse is that between here and Japan are the Asian Pact. Neither the ECS nor the Asian Pact have good relations with NUN and the one time I've infiltrated the CEAS not only got my real identity exposed to them but also to NUN. Think, what country can I go to Japan from that wouldn't arouse suspicion?*

Muhadow then looked at the map of the world in his room. His head turned to the South Asian Confederation, then the South American Union; respectively colored orange and yellow.

I could claim to be from the Turkmen community in India, but that would require too much money for flight transfers. The SAU is also out of the question because there aren't Turkic groups that live there.

Muhadow then walked across his room to continue his thinking. For him, traveling and using multiple languages wasn't a problem, but it was if it meant infiltrating the New United Nations, which received the least amount of refugees from Iran following its annexation by the Eurasian Tsardom and that Turkic groups, which included Turkmen, would have been among those who fled.

A knock was heard on the door, interrupting Muhadow. He answered it to find a man in outside.

"What is it, Ghaemi?"

"You haven't left your room in an hour, Commander," the man named Ghaemi said. "The men haven't left because we need your authorization."

"Then go. Most of you are just eating, right?"

"Hawa."

"Just come back before 0930 hours."

After the salutes and the closing of the door, Muhadow resumed his thinking, yet Ghaemi's interruption made it harder for him to concentrate.

Damn you, Ghaemi, Muhadow cursed again in his mind. *Thanks to you, I ca- That's it!*

Muhadow rushed back to his map. His eyes were focused on the Middle Eastern League, marked in green. It was as if a light bulb that wasn't working now worked.

I can pretend to be an Iraqi Turkmen, Muhadow thought. *It's only until recently that NUN and MEL are working together to the point people from NUN can travel to the MEL without a visa and vice versa. All I have to do is find records of babies who died on my birthday, alter my appearance for a passport, and speak in English.*

Laying Foundations

Nishi High School, Higashiosaka Ward, Kansai City, Kansai Prefecture; State of Japan. April 8, 2030; 0840 hours (Japan Standard Time)

Tarou Ganji was now at the auditorium of Nishi High School, in a sea of teenagers. Most were within the age range of fifteen to sixteen years while those closer to Tarou were within the age range of sixteen to seventeen years.

The principal of the school, a woman already in her early sixties, gave a speech welcoming the new students with Tarou as one of them. Although he listened, he had different thoughts in mind.

I made it, Tarou thought. *A week ago, I was able to go through Miss Narumi.*

Now, Tarou was about to listen less to the principal's speech as he now thought of what happened almost the week before.

#

Horikawa Bathhouse, Yao. April 1, 2030; 0850 hours

Tarou, Hamilton, and Frederick Dirks waited outside the bathhouse. All had their belongings with them as yesterday was the last day they were to stay at the bathhouse.

To the surprise of the three, a limousine appeared to pick them up. The driver, Ugaki, opened his window and faced the FIS agent and his mercenary assets.

"Get in," Ugaki ordered.

Tarou and Hamilton got inside. After the latter closed the door behind her, Ugaki moved the limousine.

Hoshikawa Condominiums, Higashiosaka Ward, Kansai City. 0922 hours

Ugaki then reached Hoshikawa Condominiums. Dirks, Hamilton, and Tarou then exited the limousine and found Hana Fujioka waiting for them.

"You're back, Turner-san," Fujioka said.

"Hai desu," Dirks replied.

"And these two are the ones who wish to buy the condominium?"

"Hai."

"Dewa, kochira e douzo."

#

0934 hours

Dirks, Hamilton, and Tarou reached the condominium. The latter two looked in awe that this was where they would be staying at until they found Daisuke Hoshikawa and a woman half a decade Hoshikawa's junior sitting at one of the two sofas in the condominium. The woman hid her dark brown eyes with glasses and carried a clipboard carrying yellow-colored pad paper. Seated on the other sofa was John Vue, also carrying a ballpen and notepad.

"Glad you like this condominium," Daisuke said, making Hamilton and Tarou stop looking around.

"Thank you," Hamilton replied. "I'm Dr. Anita Hamilton."

"And you must be Tarou Ganji?" Daisuke asked Tarou upon facing him.

"H… Hai desu," Tarou replied before bowing.

"And I'm Meiko Narumi of the Ministry of Justice," the woman at the sofa added as she stood up. "Shall we begin?"

"And you?" Hamilton asked as she faced John Vue.

"John Vue," Dirks answered. "He's also FIS, but he's only here to record everything for our superiors. Though he does have a few questions himself and those can wait to later. That's all there is to it for him being here."

"Please don't mind me," Vue said as he turned to the two mercenaries yet he continued looking at Tarou. *Not that I was ever lied to, but it is still surprising that a child soldier will be doing this mission.*

"Can we please start already?" Dirks asked.

"Of course," Daisuke replied before he turned to Hamilton and Tarou. "Please sit beside Mr. Vue."

Tarou, Hamilton, and Narumi sat down. Narumi brought out a purple-colored ballpen and pointed it at her yellow pad.

"I've already been told as to who you really are and why you wish to settle into Japan," Narumi admitted to the two mercenaries. "However, the Minister of Justice cannot approve of a passport for Mr. Ganji, a passport registration and a clinic for Dr. Hamilton, arrangements for Mr. Ganji to be enrolled into Nishi High School, nor this condominium for the both of you until you answer questions I've been instructed to ask to the both of you. Are you ready?"

"Yes, we are," Tarou and Hamilton answered in unison.

"Here's my first one: none of you lived in any country prior to going to Japan?"

"No. We simply stayed in the *Iron Dutchman* during missions," Hamilton answered, with Narumi and Vue writing down Hamilton's answer.

"Now this question is for you, Dr. Hamilton: when was the last time you had your passport updated?"

"Last year." Narumi wrote down the answer before turning to Tarou. "Next question is for Mr. Ganji. What were you doing in Egypt?"

"I honestly don't know. After Iran, I wandered across the Middle East until I found myself in another battle. I simply lent my assistance, and I was only told that I ended up in Egypt after the battle."

"It's true," Hamilton added.

"You intend on enrolling at Nishi High School, yet Mr. Ganji never had a proper education. What makes you think you can succeed in pretending to be a transfer student?"

"I am certain I will not jeopardize this," Tarou answered. "I've been practicing my Japanese enough to make sure that I blend in."

"Care for a test?"

"Hai."

#

Nishi High School. April 8, 2030; 0850 hours

I was able to pass Miss Narumi's test that Dr. Hamilton and I got everything we needed, Tarou thought in the present.

"And now, I will give the stand to our Student Council President," the principal of Nishi High School announced.

The principal then made her exit. Tarou, however, paid no attention to the Student Council President of the school approaching the stage because he noticed students with red armbands approaching.

Mr. Crawley warned me that in Japanese high schools, students with armbands are most likely members of a school's discipline committee who make sure students obey the rules of the school, Tarou thought. *That means I best listen to this Student Council President's speech.*

#

Hamilton Clinic, Taisho Ward. 0850 hours

Anita Hamilton and Daisuke Hoshikawa arrived at the clinic the former asked for. Located in front of Hoshikawa Group headquarters, this allowed people who worked there to get immediate medical attention should it be needed.

"Thank you again for this, Mr. Hoshikawa," Hamilton said.

"Think nothing of it," Daisuke replied. "You've been given my number, so call me if there's anything you need. Now, I must get to my office."

"Of course."

Hoshikawa began to leave the clinic. Hamilton then settled herself in the clinic's office.

Finally, something I can do other than be a medic for mercenaries, Hamilton thought. *It isn't a bad thing, but I'd prefer to be a doctor for civilians now and then. I'm even surprised Tarou passed that test imposed on us by Miss Narumi.*

Hoshikawa Condominiums, Higashiosaka Ward. April 1, 2030; 1021 hours

"That was impressive," Meiko Narumi said as she and John Vue wrote down all of Tarou Ganji's answers to all the questions she answered. "Now then, if you have questions, feel free to ask, but nothing involving Nishi High School nor your clinic for the time being."

"I assume the Minister of Justice knows who we really are to tell you about us?" Anita Hamilton asked with Vue writing by himself this time.

"I told him and gave him everything Mr. 'Smith' has given me," Daisuke answered. "Other than us, only the Minister and Miss Narumi here know."

"And the people responsible for making the passports will simply make one?"

"They have to if they wish to keep their jobs," Narumi answered with cynicism in her tone.

"I have to ask this: why you?" Tarou Ganji asked.

"I wasn't busy when the Minister of Justice was contacted by Mr. Hoshikawa. Therefore, I was asked by the Minister of Justice to deal with this matter."

"I have another question: do you have a list of anything that can threaten Maria Hoshikawa and how to counter those threats?"

"What kind of threats?"

"I was told teenage women might be prone to incidents involving older men."

Everyone froze upon hearing Tarou's answer. Hamilton slammed her right palm onto her face as she knew how and why Tarou asked such a question. Hamilton regained her composure to cough in order to break the silence.

"I can understand why you ask such a question," Narumi replied. "If that worries you, you can take your gun with you, but you'll need a hiding place where no one can find it and you have to hide it before going to school. If the Minister of Justice approves of you getting a passport, that is."

"One of my colleagues asked about part-time work for additional money," Hamilton said with Narumi, knowing this led to another question. "If we do find a part-time job because we need the additional money, how will Tarou's absence be handled?"

"That depends on the excuse you can come up as Mr. Ganji's guardian. I've already been told that a coordinator from the FIS will always update you, so contact your coordinator and he or she will contact me. I, in turn, will notify the Minister of Justice, who will notify the school."

Narumi finished writing her answer, then stood up and Vue doing the same. "Thank you for this. Expect the passports by two days at most." Narumi then began to exit the condominium, with Daisuke following.

#

Hamilton Clinic. Taisho Ward. April 8, 2030; 0905 hours

And after two days, we got those passports, Hamilton thought in the present. Just as her reminiscing ended, she heard someone knock on her door.

"Hai?" Hamilton asked, miraculously managing to figure out what "Yes" meant in Japanese.

#

Iron Dutchman; Hoshikawa Shipyards. 0916 hours

The *Iron Dutchman* was now docked at Hoshikawa Shipyards. Once owned by the Hitachi Group as Hitachi Shipbuilding, the latter was acquired by Daisuke Hoshikawa after the Third World as Tokyo, where Hitachi Group was headquartered at, was hit during the war.

Since then, Daisuke made Hoshikawa Shipyards one of the main shipbuilding giants across Japan, if not the entire New United Nations. As a result, the *Iron Dutchman* was able to dock at Hoshikawa Shipyards.

In her room, Tatev Mirzoyan used her computer. The application she used functioned like a record book, a necessity for mercenaries to act like a business.

As soon as we got the money from Mr. "Smith", we start spending it as if we find water after a perilous journey in the desert, Tatev thought. *Not only that, this type of job allows us to act like normal people because it's up to the FIS to tell us when we leave. That or if we really fail.*

Tatev then stopped using her computer and, after putting on a pair of slippers, stepped out of the room. She wandered across the Iron Dutchman until arriving at the 11th deck of the ship. Upon stopping, she turned to Kansai City.

Why did I not ask to volunteer? Tatev lamented in her mind. *I can understand Tarou volunteering, but he might just mess it up. Of course, I wouldn't have been able to adjust easily. It was a miracle I managed to learn English by the time Iron Dutchman Services saved me, but Japanese would have been difficult than learning how to interact with everyone else. Somehow, Tarou managed to blend in when he and Dr. Hamilton welcomed us to Japan, along with Mr. Hoshikawa.*

#

April 7, 2030. 1800 hours

The *Iron Dutchman* had arrived at Hoshikawa Shipyards. After the gangway was connected to the ship, Wouter Vos and Sunan Wattana stepped out and, upon nearing Japanese soil, they found Frederick Dirks, Daisuke Hoshikawa, Tarou Ganji, and Anita Hamilton waiting for them.

"Glad you made it," Dirks said to Vos. "Allow me to introduce to you Daisuke Hoshikawa."

"So you're the commanding officer, for lack of a better term, of Mr. Ganji and Dr. Hamilton," Daisuke remarked.

"That's right. I assume you have questions for us, so follow us into the ship."

#

1835 hours

By the time Vos, Wattana, Dirks, Tarou, and Hamilton reached the briefing room of the *Iron Dutchman*, every other member of Iron Dutchman Services was gathered at the briefing room. *I still find it baffling that Iron Dutchman Services is small enough because they manage to operate this ship,* Daisuke thought as he looked at the rest of Vos' subordinates.

Wattana, Tarou, and Hamilton then sat in their usual chairs in the briefing room. Tatev Mirzoyan, meanwhile, used her laptop computer to open the picture of the map of Kansai City with the location of Hoshikawa Mansion, marked by a red circle. With the computer connected to the projector, the map was now shown on the projection screen.

"Everyone here has already been told about your mansion's location," Dirks explained to Daisuke. "We've thought of having the surrounding area scouted every day with one member of Iron Dutchman Services assigned to patrol the area and that the following day, another member will take over. Do you consent to this idea?"

"Before I answer that, I must ask this: are any of you experienced in matters such as this?" Daisuke asked.

"To be frank, no," Vos answered. "We only took this job because we were that desperate for the money."

"And how do you expect me to entrust my daughter's safety to you?"

"I've got that covered," Dirks answered. "In addition, that's why we needed Mr. Ganji to act out as a transfer student. He'll be our eyes and eyes inside Nishi High School. He'll only be assigned on patrols around Kamiishikiricho on Sundays."

"So who'll patrol Kamiishikiricho tomorrow?"

"I'll do it," Vos answered.

"Will this rotation be permanent?"

"I'll leave that to Mr. Vos and his subordinates," Dirks answered. "After that, I'll notify you."

"I see. All I can say at this point is good luck."

#

Hamilton-Ganji Condominium, Hoshikawa Condominiums. April 9, 2030; 0059 hours

Tarou began to go to sleep. This time, it was now at the condominium where he and Hamilton will be staying at.

This does feel different compared to my room in the Iron Dutchman, Tarou thought. *After Miss Narumi and Mr. Hoshikawa left, John Vue stayed to ask me and Dr. Hamilton those questions. Why?*

Tarou then closed his eyes. He thought of what happened the week before.

April 1, 2030; 1023 hours

"And why aren't you leaving yet?" Frederick Dirks asked John Vue after Meiko Narumi and Daisuke Hoshikawa left the condominium.

"Because I have a few questions I wish to ask Dr. Hamilton and Mr. Ganji," John Vue answered.

"Suit yourself." Dirks returned to the corner he stood by earlier with Vue, Tarou Ganji, and Anita Hamilton sitting down again.

"I'll ask Dr. Hamilton first," Vue announced before turning to Dr. Hamilton. "Doctor, wh why did you join Iron Dutchman Services?"

"I joined because my boyfriend left me five years ago," Hamilton answered. "As you know, I worked in varying refugee camps and when the refugee camp in the United Nigerian States I worked at came under attack, Wouter Vos, Jake Crawley, and Sunan Wattana saved me and the camp. I, alongside Federico Díaz and Bartolomeu Moura, joined Mr. Vos, Mr. Crawley, and Miss Wattana."

"I see." Vue wrote down Hamilton's answer below the question he asked, already written on his notepad, then faced her. "Now, why did you volunteer to act out as Mr. Ganji's guardian?"

"Because I wish to help Mr. Ganji fit in and… because I feel guilty for not preventing him away from fighting."

Not much else was said. Vue looked at Tarou, assuming he would respond to Hamilton's answer, but nothing came out of Tarou's mouth. Vue continued to write but unbeknownst to everyone but Dirks, he wrote "Ganji didn't respond to this answer" below the answer in parenthesis.

"Last question: why do you think you should have prevented him from fighting?"

"He's only a child. If at all possible, I hope he can learn to live a normal life as teenagers ought to with this mission."

"I see," Vue repeated as he wrote down the answer but before writing "...as teenagers ought to with this mission", Vue looked at Tarou before resuming. *He didn't respond to what Dr. Hamilton said again.*

Like before, Vue wrote "Ganji didn't respond to this answer" in parenthesis below after he finished writing "...with this mission".

"Thank you for your answers, Dr. Hamilton." Vue then turned to Tarou. "Mr. Ganji, do you mind if I can ask you some questions?"

"Depends on what they are?" Tarou answered.

"Here's one I hope you can answer easily: how were given the name 'Tarou Ganji'?"

"All I was told by the Baloch community that took me in was that the name 'Tarou' was written on a small piece of paper on top of my forehead when they took me in."

"Wait, you said a Baloch community?"

"Yes, I did. I was told that they're survivors of when the *Revelator* crashed into Afghanistan in 1985."

"And that's all you know, other than what Mr. 'Smith' has told me?"

"That's right."

"Because they managed to feed me despite with little they had. I explained who I was, where I came from, and why I ended up in Libya. Mr. Vos suggested that I stay with them as a way to find out as to who I really am."

Vue simply wrote down Tarou's answer. "Here's my next question: Have you been told as to how things work in a Japanese high school?"

"Mr. Crawley was able to tell me as such."

"And Mr. Crawley is qualified to have taught you about Japanese society as a whole?"

"No. However, I will do my best to act as a transfer student as to avoid the wrong kind of attention."

"But you might have to follow Miss Hoshikawa, right?"

"Mr. Vos plans on dividing such a responsibility amongst everyone in Iron Dutchman Services."

"I see," Vue ultimately said as he finished writing Tarou's answer. *Dr. Hamilton's right. This boy shouldn't be partaking in such a mission, yet it will help him find a path beyond that of the gun. And I say this as a father.*

"I believe that will be all," Vue declared before standing up. "I'll be going now. Tomorrow, I intend to return to Deputy Director Saetang."

"Good luck," Dirks said as he, Tarou, and Hamilton saw Vue leave.

Dirks then turned to the mercenaries and, after approaching them, he brought out an envelope and opened it, giving it to Hamilton.

"What's this?" Hamilton asked.

"Get your hand in there," Dirks answered.

Hamilton did and found that there was a check inside in her name. The amount offered was one hundred and eighty thousand UN dollars.

"T… This is… " Hamilton said, despite being overwhelmed by how much was in the check.

"I'm making sure you and Ganji get your money now," Dirks explained. "However, since Ganji is a minor and you're acting out as your guardian, I decided to combine your respective cuts into one check."

"What about Tatev?" Tarou asked.

"Vos' check is also to the amount of one hundred eighty thousand. Let me know if there's anything you wish to spend that money on. Also, you can have these converted to Japanese yen. I assume you know how much you will get once you do?"

"I've been to Japan before," Hamilton answered. "If assuming much hasn't changed, I think that the Japanese yen we'll get will be more than enough after we converted our UN dollars to Japanese yen."

"There is one thing… " Tarou said as he thought about Dirks' earlier offer before he mentioned conversion between UN dollars and Japanese yen.

"What is it?"

#

April 9, 2030; 0114 hours

I didn't think I would be questioned like that, Tarou thought in the present. *Though regardless, I must do this mission.*

Tarou allowed himself to sleep. He had to wake up early enough to go to school in five hours for a task only he could do around the school if he was early enough.

Qatar Tachyon Particle Receiver; Off Doha, Al-Dawhah; State of Qatar. April 9, 2030; 1915 hours (Arabia Standard Time)

Among the supernational unions created after the Third World War was the Middle Eastern League (MEL). An evolution of the Gulf Cooperation Council (GCC), created in 1981, this supernational union was created due to the collapse of the original United Nations and as a result, there was no need for them to join the New United Nations.

Two of its member-states, the States of Kuwait and Qatar, were small peninsulas while the Kingdom of Bahrain was an island. All three member-states faced the Persian Gulf, so as a result, their respective Tachyon Particle Receivers were built on artificial islands. Qatar's TPR was built on an artificial island near Hamad International Airport, which served the capital city of Doha. This made it convenient for Serdar Muhadow, who was given a room to stay at.

In his room, a cleanly shaven Muhadow looked at a passport for Qatari citizens. The second page of the passport contained a photograph of Muhadow's cleanly shaved face with tags for certain information written in both Arabic and their respective translations. Under "Forename" with its Arabic equivalent in a parenthesis was the name "Mansur" and under "Surname" with its Arabic equivalent also in a parenthesis was "Fahri".

You are a handsome devil, Muhadow thought as he looked at his passport. *However, it was risky coming here to make this passport so I can't use it for long.*

Muhadow then put the passport down. "But for now, I need some food," Muhadow declared before he left his room.

#

Unknown Location; Enlightenment Point. April 2, 2030; 1410 hours (EP Time Zone)

Muhadow, back when he had a beard, appeared at the office of Frühling, the Gatekeeper of Intelligence. Both men saluted each other after the former entered the office of the latter.

"Rare for you to call me here," Muhadow remarked.

"Please sit," Frühling ordered.

Muhadow sat down. "Now, I've heard from Gatekeeper Turkestan that you wish to acquire papers proving that you're an Iraqi Turkman that was believed to have died as an infant the day you were born?"

"That is correct. I get the papers from Gatekeeper Turkestan, then I travel to the Middle Eastern League's headquarters in Doha to find a particular passport forger with the information from the dead infant to be used for my passport. After that, I avail for a flight to Japan."

"I assume you'll be looking for Omar Mahmud?"

"That's right. Mercenaries I've worked with used him to create new identities when they needed to flee from the law."

"Very well, I'll contact our hideout in the Caliphate and get them to arrange for you to acquire papers proving that you are an infant that died on February 27, 1984. However, you'll have to wait for Gatekeeper Turkestan to hear from me about that."

#

Turkestan Tachyon Particle Receiver; Turkestani Republic. April 3, 2030; 1639 hours (Turkestan Time)

Muhadow was now summoned to the office of Gatekeeper Turkestan. The former then sat down.

"You called for me?" Muhadow asked.

"I've heard from Gatekeeper Int," Gatekeeper Turkestan said. "I have the papers you need. Please stand up and receive them."

Muhadow stood up and walked closer to Gatekeeper Turkestan. The latter picked up the documents on the table in front of the desktop computer and gave them to Muhadow.

"Thank you," Muhadow replied. As he left Gatekeeper Turkestan's office, Muhadow thought of the time he met Omar Mahmud.

Port Café, Doha Port, Doha, Al-Dawhah; State of Qatar. April 4, 2030; 2239 hours (Arabia Standard Time)

Muhadow arrived at a particular café in the Doha Port neighborhood of Doha. Once the commercial port of Doha, commercial operations ended when Hamad Port was completed in 2016.

Only tourist attractions such as the Doha Corniche and the Souq Waqif gave Doha Port notoriety. The Port Café existed to cater to those frequenting the Corniche. However, it hosted another business, and Muhadow came to the café for that reason.

Although he saw a man leaving the café and placing a sign that said "Closed" in both English and Arabic, Muhadow tapped the man's right shoulder with his right index finger.

"Are you Omar Mahmud?" Muhadow asked.

"I am but as you see I've clo-" the man named Omar Mahmud said.

"I'm not here for a drink. Well, maybe later and I have money for that. For now, I wish to purchase a 'ticket'."

"Did you say a *ticket*?"

"Yes."

"Come inside."

Muhadow followed Mahmud into Port Café. The latter took the former to the café's pantry.

"Do you have papers I can use to make a passport?" Mahmud asked.

"Of course," Muhadow replied before giving to him the application form for passports, which was a legitimate government form as a contrast to the fake passport, he filled out hours before. Mahmud examined the application form as if his eyes were magnifying glasses. He then faced Muhadow as he finished.

"You managed to fake an imam's signature," Mahmud remarked. "Tell me, are you really this 'Mansur Fahri'?"

"Not really. Let's just say I have something to do and it involves traveling to a New United Nations member-state and that NUN's Intelligence

Collective is already familiar with a cover identity I used because they were warned about it by CEAS' Intelligence Committee."

"And you need this passport to travel to one NUN country?"

"That's right."

"Come back here tomorrow and I'll give you the passport application form. However, you'll have to sign here and after that, wait four days for the passport. After those four days, come back here again and I'll give you the passport."

"How much will you charge me for this?"

"Depends. Who are you?"

"Just a mercenary. That's all you need to know?"

"Asked to be paid in half?"

"I have."

"I'll tell you my price in five days. Now go."

"Can I at least buy that bottle of water first?"

#

Qatar Tachyon Particle Receiver; Off Doha, Al-Dawhah. April 9, 2030; 2009 hours (Arabia Standard Time)

In the present, Muhadow returned to his room. He then laid on his bed, but managed to glance at his passport.

That passport might have cost me a bit of my savings, Muhadow thought. *Either way, I best get to sleep because I have a flight tomorrow.*

Unknown Location, Enlightenment Point. 2340 hours (EP Time Zone)

"Good," Sergei Akulov said as he spoke to his Gatekeeper of Intelligence in his throne room. "However, I do not like how much that Omar Mahmud charged for that passport."

"What do you wish to be done?" Frühling asked.

"When will Muhadow leave for Japan?"

"Tomorrow morning in Arabia Standard Time."

"Tell him to ask Grand Duchess Tatiana of a contingency plan if in the event he is compromised."

"By your will, Grand Gatekeeper."

"And notify our Devotee-Infiltrator in the OVR to have her Director contact his cell in Kansai City to receive Muhadow."

#

OVR Safehouse, Nishinari Ward, Kansai City, Kansai Prefecture; State of Japan. April 9, 2030; 0600 hours (Japan Standard Time)

"Zametano," Tatiana Ioannovna Tsulukidze said while using her smartphone's SatCom before turning it off. She then heard a knock on her door.

"Come in," Tatiana ordered.

A man with blond hair in a crew cut, light skin, and brown eyes came into the room. "I assume that was the Director?" the man asked.

"Da," Tatiana answered. "He's given us instructions."

"What are they?"

First Day

Hamilton-Ganji Condominium, Hoshikawa Condominiums, Higashiosaka Ward, Kansai City, Kansai Prefecture; State of Japan. April 8, 2030; 0700 hours (Japan Standard Time)

Anita Hamilton woke up to hear the door open. Upon getting out of her bed, she began to proceed to the sinks in front of her room in the condominium she and Tarou Ganji were allowed to use a week before to wash her face, which was to help her wake up, but upon leaving her room, she saw Tarou entering the condominium. Tarou had returned with bags filled with food and drinks while wearing a white shirt underneath a green leather jacket, blue pants bound by a black leather belt, and black rubber shoes.

"Tarou, is that you?" Hamilton asked as she was barely able to see Tarou.

"Need help going to the sinks?" Tarou asked.

"Where were you?"

"Went out exercising."

"I see. Please lead me to the sinks."

Tarou then led Hamilton to the condominium's sinks. As they reached the sinks, Hamilton washed herself. After drying her face with the nearest towel, she faced Tarou.

"Shall we make breakfast?" Hamilton asked Tarou.

"Can I please take a bath first?" Tarou requested. "I exercised a little after my scooter practice, and it involved dragging the scooter back to the condominium parking lot."

Hamilton giggled upon hearing Tarou's explanation for why he needed a bath. "Sure."

"Will do."

Tarou then proceeded to the bathroom, but before that, he needed to get clothes found in his room, which was closer to the bathroom than Hamilton's room. Hamilton then proceeded to the kitchen.

#

0736 hours

Tarou had finished his bath. Now he wore the uniform of Nishi High School, which consisted of consisted of a button-up shirt that was colored white, a tie and trousers that were colored jet black, a brown-colored leather belt that tied up the trousers, and black-colored leather shoes.

He then arrived at the dining table located between the kitchen and the living room at sat down. Hamilton joined Tarou with a plate with four loaves of croissants and a metal container with butter inside. Hamilton, however, had yet to sit down, as she needed to get something from their refrigerator: a jar of orange marmalade. Once she got the marmalade, she sat down and got her croissant and used a knife to cut it open and filling the croissant with marmalade. Tarou, by contrast, filled his croissant with butter.

"Tarou, I must ask you: how do you feel about being with people your age?" Hamilton asked after biting and chewing the last piece of the croissant with marmalade.

"I… honestly don't know," Tarou answered after eating from his butter-filled croissant. "Thanks to our discussion with Mr. Vue, I can imagine everything that Mr. Crawley said wouldn't work in making sure I'm seen as suspicious."

"Keep your head down when needed. Also, you have your gun with you, right?"

"No. It's still in my room." Both Tarou and Hamilton immediately finished their respective croissants.

"If you have to take it with you, just keep it on your scooter. Also, please go to the vault as to where we keep our money. You'll need some for food and other necessities. We're running out, so I'll go grocery shopping later."

"Understood." Both Tarou and Hamilton drank from their respective glasses filled with milk.

"Now finish your other croissant and brush your teeth before leaving for school."

Tarou and Hamilton each grabbed the last two croissants. After filling them with butter and orange marmalade respectively, they ate the croissants. After that, they finished their milk, licked their respective index fingers and thumbs, and stood up. Tarou moved to the sinks first to brush his teeth while Hamilton began to wash the dishes and knives.

Once he finished brushing his teeth, Tarou returned to his room to get what belonged to him. The first thing he got was the smartphone he received from Frederick Dirks almost a month before in Hawaii. Tarou then turned on the smartphone and used his right thumb to find the phone's IntMail application. He pressed the IntMail icon firmly until a white box with writing in black appeared with the question "What do you wish to do with the application" at the top with the choices "Delete" and "Hide" below.

Tarou then pressed "Hide". This caused the IntMail icon to turn into a simple gray-colored square. After that, Tarou placed the smartphone in a white-colored duffel bag. He began to place equipment needed for school, including certain papers needed for assistance, into the duffel bag. Lastly, Tarou opened the drawer of his nightstand.

Inside the drawer was his P226 semi-automatic pistol. Tarou then grabbed the P226 and placed it on the nightstand proper as he needed to fill one empty magazine with 9x19mm rounds. After that, he loaded the magazine into the P226. As it was already in safety, Tarou simply placed the P226 into his bag.

Tarou then stepped out of his room with Hamilton brushing her teeth. He passed by the vault Hamilton spoke of earlier and, remembering the combination, Tarou opened it and took ten thousand yen from the vault.

"Is ten thousand yen enough?" Tarou asked.

Upon hearing the question, Hamilton spat out the toothpaste from the sink. "Take eight thousand," Hamilton answered. "I also that money."

"Got it." Tarou then loaded the eight thousand yen into his bag and proceeded to the door.

"I'll be leaving now," Tarou said as he was one inch away from the door.

"Good luck," Hamilton replied.

0759 hours

Tarou reached the parking lot of Hoshikawa Condominiums. Finding his motor scooter, a PCX, Tarou put his duffel bag down in order to open the scooter's seat, as it hosted the compartment where the helmet he must wear was kept.

Before getting the helmet, Tarou opened the duffel bag and got his P226. Upon placing the P226 inside the helmet compartment, Tarou got the helmet and closed the compartment. Tying up the duffel bag, Tarou put on the helmet and after getting the duffel bag, he sat on the PCX. He strapped the duffel bag behind him in order for it to not fall off, and after that, he started up the scooter. With the scooter started up, Tarou left for Nishi High School.

#

Nishi High School. 0807 hours

Tarou reached Nishi High School, located in the Takadonocho neighborhood beside the Toriicho neighborhood where Hoshikawa Condominiums was located at. Combined with his scooter, this made it convenient for Tarou.

However, he remembered that he had to take the scooter into the school complex, even if it meant going through those also going inside the school.

Some of these people have bikes with them, Tarou thought as he looked around. *However, I can't simply follow them inside with my scooter.*

"Nani ka tasuke ga hitsuyou desu ka?" a teenage girl asked behind Tarou.

Tarou turned and found a girl his age with long blonde hair that went past her shoulders, blue eyes and light skin standing behind him. Tarou then realized who the girl was as she wore the female uniform of Nishi High School students, which included brown leather shoes.

Of all the things to happen to me today, I have Maria Hoshikawa standing in front of me, Tarou thought. *Her Japanese is better than mine. I guess it's natural because she's lived in Japan for practically her entire life. I best play along.*

"H… Hai," Tarou answered nervously in Japanese. "Kono… sukuutaa… "

"I can tell you're having difficulty speaking English," Maria Hoshikawa said in English. "Do you at least know English?"

"Yes, I do," Tarou replied in the same language. "I apologize for this."

"I understand. There's a section in the bicycle rack for scooters."

"Thank you very much."

"We best hurry. We can't miss the welcoming ceremony."

"Thank you again for this."

Tarou proceeded ahead to the school proper. Maria looked on at the boy with suspicion in her mind.

That's most likely a PCX, Maria thought. *How could an exchange student get one unless-*

"Maria-chan, what are you standing there for?" another girl asked as she approached Maria. She had short brown hair and dark brown eyes with her uniform hiding her athletic build.

"Oh, good morning, Misa-chan," Maria said to the girl approaching her.

"Come on, we're going to be late," the girl named Misa said.

"Right." Both Maria and Misa continued toward the school. *That boy possessing a PCX before his first day here is something to look into, but not now,* Maria thought.

#

0830 hours

Tarou then reached the auditorium of Nishi High School where the welcoming ceremony was held. He didn't have his duffel bag as he gave it earlier upon entering the main hall of the school. Miraculously for him, he was able to find an empty seat, as many have yet to fill the auditorium.

After Tarou sat down, Maria Hoshikawa and her friend Misa appeared at the auditorium. However, there weren't that many chairs left, yet they found two empty chairs beside each other. Naturally, they took those seats and sat down.

Those coffee bottles we found twice at Hamada Church. Then there was Father receiving a crate only to have it delivered to Hoshikawa Condominiums… could they be related? Maria pondered.

#

Hamada Church, Higashiosaka Ward. March 31, 2030; 1008 hours

As they finished hearing Mass, the Hoshikawas neared their limousine parked near the Hamada Church. However, their driver, Ugaki, rushed toward them and bowed, perplexing the family of three.

"What's the matter, Ugaki?" Daisuke Hoshikawa asked.

"*He… He…* came and gave me this," Ugaki replied as he saw a ghost while he gave a seemingly empty bottle of iced coffee to Daisuke. "*He* said there's a message for you."

He can't possibly be- Miku Hoshikawa (née Sayama) thought as she looked at the bottle.

"We're returning home now," Daisuke declared before he turned to his daughter Maria. "Now. Also, I intend to come with you while you're dropped off at school."

"But Fa-" Maria attempted to say.

"That is final, Maria!" Daisuke's tone was stern yet soft enough for many to ignore.

"Hontou ni gomen nasai," Maria added with a bow.

#

Outside Hotel Soleil. April 3, 2030; 1900 hours

The limousine owned by the Hoshikawa family stopped in front of Hotel Soleil. This was because of a truck that appeared far from the hotel, yet its appearance made Ugaki stop.

"Doushita no, Ugaki-san?" Maria asked.

"A truck came from our route into the mansion," Ugaki answered. "Either way, we can proceed further now."

Hoshikawa Mansion. 1916 hours

Ugaki then arrived at the Hoshikawa Mansion, located in the Yamatecho neighborhood. The route Ugaki and Maria used involved driving past Hotel Soleil in the Kamishikiricho neighborhood beside Yamatecho. As a result, the mansion's location was seen by many to symbolize the Hoshikawa family's affluence, with a truck coming out of the route Maria and Ugaki used to leave the mansion.

The truck, however, became the least of their concerns as both Maria and Ugaki saw that Daisuke Hoshikawa, whom they knew wasn't home around this time, was at the mansion's foyer. As soon as Ugaki stopped, Maria stepped out and rushed to her father.

"Tadaima, Otou-sama," Maria said, but with suspicion in her tone.

"Okaerinasai, Maria," Daisuke replied, but his tone now showed that he suspected that Maria saw something she shouldn't have. "From the way you greeted me, it seems that you have something to ask."

"Father, Ugaki-san and I saw a truck use the route we used to enter and exit the mansion. I didn't look like it came from our neighbors. I assume you have something to do with it?"

Daisuke sighed, as if he anticipated Maria's inquiry. "Why don't we talk about it inside while waiting for dinner to be prepared?"

"Wakarimashita, Otou-sama."

#

Nishi High School. April 8, 2030; 0859 hours

"Maria-chan, come on, stand up!" Misa said to Maria.

Maria was then brought back to the present. She then saw that Misa and everyone else surrounding them were standing. This forced her to stand up.

0916 hours

At the classroom that belonged to class 2 for the second-year students, Tarou Ganji was led inside the room by a thirty-year-old woman with short black hair and dark brown eyes. She wore a white dress shirt, a red-colored pencil skirt over black tights, and black-colored heeled shoes. Everyone in the class stood in attention.

The woman bringing me to this room must be their teacher, Tarou thought.

"Everyone, I ask that you pay attention as we have a new transfer student," the woman announced, proving Tarou's assumption that she is the class' teacher. "Please sit down."

As the students sat down, the teacher then faced Tarou. "Go on. Please introduce yourself."

"Hai, Hasegawa-sensei," Tarou replied before he faced his classmates. "Hajimemashite," Tarou said to the class before bowing. "Namae wa Ganji Tarou desu. Yosushiku onegaishimasu."

"Anyone have questions for Ganji-san here?" the woman named Hasegawa asked to her students. "I've told him to speak in English, so I will interpret."

"Where are you from?" a female student asked.

Hasegawa interpreted the question to Tarou. "I was once a child soldier from Iran until I met a non-governmental organization or NGO for short," Tarou answered, while managing to tell only half of the truth about his past. "One of the NGO members, Dr. Anita Hamilton, took me and she opted to run a private clinic, hence why I'm studying here."

Hasegawa then interpreted what Tarou had said as he spoke in English. Everyone made no reaction to it, but some closed their eyes in silence as they grew up hearing stories about Iranians having fled their homes due to the Eurasian Tsardom's invasion of Iran in 2023.

"I was told beforehand that you and Dr. Hamilton lived in South Africa?" Hasegawa asked.

Most likely that was engineered by Mr. 'Smith', Tarou thought while anxiously thinking of an answer to Hasegawa's question. "Yes," Tarou ultimately answered with Hasegawa interpreting it as "Hai" to her students

"Do you have any hobbies?"

Can't tell them I use guns, Tarou thought. *I'm supposed to act out as a* ***former*** *child soldier.*

"I practice Muay Thai," Tarou answered. "I also do some reading."

"What books?"

"*The Circassian Slave*, *That Hagen Girl*, and *What the Day Owes the Night*; the last one being translated from French."

"That's enough," Hasegawa declared. "Ganji-san, please sit beside Todoh-kun."

Hasegawa then turned to a boy a year younger than Tarou. He had short brown hair with fringes on the left side of his head and eyeglasses covering his dark brown eyes. "Todoh-kun, please raise your hand to direct Ganji-san."

"Hai," the boy, named Todoh, replied as he raised his hand. Tarou then moved to the table and chair beside Todoh's.

As Tarou put down his bag and sat down, Todoh leaned toward him. "Todoh Riku desu. Douzou yorushiku."

"Arigatou," Tarou replied.

"We're beginning homeroom now," Hasegawa declared. Please pay attention."

#

Iron Dutchman; Hoshikawa Shipyards, Taisho Ward. 0925 hours

Mr. Vos is currently around Yamatecho, Tatev thought in the present. *I just hope he spends his money well enough because we're not getting another nine hundred thousand until next month.*

"What are you doing, Mirzoyan?" Tatev turned to find Sunan Wattana behind her.

"I apologize for this, Miss Wattana," Tatev replied. "I needed air after counting how much was spent so far."

"I see. Since we all got our share of the salary from 'Smith', why don't you come with to get some clothes?"

"Sure." Wattana, however, sensed that Tatev's answer wasn't enthusiastic.

"Why are you out here?" Wattana asked with a serious tone.

"I… " Tatev answered incompletely.

"Let me guess, it has something to do with Ganji, right?"

"I'm ashamed to admit it, but yes." Tatev bowed after his answer.

Wattana sighed as she watched Tatev bow in shame. "Why is Ganji eating at you?"

"It's my own fault. I should have volunteered to infiltrate Nishi High School."

"But you hardly go out of this ship. No one blames you, but are you going to be that upset that Ganji gets to be surrounded by other girls as old as you are?"

"It's not that. It's Tarou's belief that if he can do his mission, he can figure out who he really is."

"Look, worrying about Ganji is nice and all. We all are, but for different reasons, but just trust in him like we all have."

"You're right."

"So, do you still want to come with me or not?"

"Of course. I could use more than what I'm wearing right now."

"Atta girl. Come on."

#

Nishi High School. 1216 hours

Tarou Ganji arrived at a particular room at Nishi High School where certain items were sold. Using his eight thousand Japanese yen, Tarou bought a cutlet sandwich, a bottle of water, and two textbooks needed for the last two classes of the day.

After acquiring what he purchased, Tarou began to make his way back to Class 2-2's room. However, as the room where he was before and the classroom he was going to was three floors apart, Tarou found it difficult to travel through one set of stairs with everything he bought, yet he pressed on. By the time Tarou reached the second staircase, he began to fear his chances of an accident should he continue as he looked at everything he bought.

"Need some help?"

Tarou moved his head as he found Maria Hoshikawa in front of him.

"I… I guess," Tarou weakly answered.

Maria then joined Tarou. "You can keep the sandwich and water with you," Maria said. "I'll take care of the books."

"Are you sure about this?" Tarou asked.

"I can handle two books."

"Forgive me for this." Tarou said before lowering his head again.

"Come on. We have to get you to you room for as long as lunch break lasts. Speaking of which, which class are you in?"

"Class 2-2."

"Then follow me and we can make it before the break ends."

"Understood."

Maria then entered the staircase. Once Tarou gave Maria the books, he took the cutlet sandwich and water bottle and while carrying the former, Tarou forced the latter into his right elbow. After that, they moved upstairs. Upon reaching the fourth floor, Maria and Tarou exited the staircase.

"Why did you buy from the store?" Maria asked.

"Dr. Hamilton and I weren't able to devise a plan for food preparation because we had to focus on getting adjusted here," Tarou asked.

"I never got your name."

"Oh, I apologize. My name is Tarou Ganji."

"I'm Maria Hoshikawa. Where are you from?"

"Iran. I don't know how, but somehow, I'm half-Japanese and half-Iranian, hence my first name."

"And why are you here in Japan?"

"After I was taken in by Dr. Anita Hamilton, a member of an NGO that found me in Iran, she opted to go to Japan to start anew and hoped that I can rebuild my life."

"How old are you?"

"Seventeen."

"Same. You being a second-year was to be expected as you transferred here. Where did you come from before this?"

"The NGO was based in South Africa, so I studied there first."

"Well, we're here," Maria said as she and Tarou came across Class 2-2's room.

"Thanks again for this."

"Maybe you can tell me more about yourself when we're free?" Maria asked while offeringTarou back his books.

"Same here." Tarou put his sandwich above the books and gained the books with the sandwich on top. Maria then opened the door, attracting the attention of every boy and girl from Class 2-2.

"Then take care," Maria said before leaving.

Using his left foot, Tarou slowly moved into the room while making sure he didn't drop everything he carried. Miraculously, he succeeded, but the rest of the classroom staring at him, for reasons he couldn't fathom, made it hard for him to focus.

Despite that, Tarou returned to his table. After putting the books on the floor, Tarou took the sandwich away from the books and into his desk then joining it with his water. However, he couldn't start eating his sandwich because his seatmate, Riku Todoh, faced Tarou with suspicion bordering on envy evident in his face, confusing Tarou.

"Can… I help you?" Tarou asked in English as he was unable to concentrate enough to use Japanese.

"How did you get Hoshikawa-senpai to help you?" Riku asked in English.

Didn't expect him to use English flawlessly, Tarou thought. "I… really don't know myself."

"You must have the luck of the Devil to get Maria Hoshikawa to help you out since you're new here."

"Is she famous?"

"Famous doesn't even begin to describe it. She's the daughter of Daisuke Hoshikawa, one of the biggest names in the Japanese corporate world. In every test, she gets the highest score, and she's the president of our Judo club. It's like we've been granted the opportunity to have a goddess study alongside us."

Is all of that enough to warrant interest by intelligence agencies other than surviving cold ocean water as an infant? Tarou incredulously pondered while opening the container of his cutlet sandwich and chewing on it. *I wonder if it's worth asking him about Hoshikawa?*

"By the way, your English is good," Tarou said to change the subject after swallowing.

"Thanks," Todoh replied. "My mother insisted on that because she works as a tour guide. My father owns a karate dojo, but my mother insisted that my older sister and I know more than the usual lessons."

"If it's okay with you, mind if I ask some questions about Miss Hoshikawa?"

"Before I answer that, you translate '-san' as 'Miss'?"

"I apologize. I referred to everyone in the NGO that found me, with the exception of Dr. Hamilton, as either 'Mister' or 'Miss'."

"I guess that's a reasonable equivalent in English. As for your questions about Miss Hoshikawa, sure. Though you'll have to answer one particular question in return."

"You have my word." Tarou said before chewing on his cutlet sandwich again and swallowing it. "Now, how much do you know about Miss Hoshikawa's past?"

"That's a bold question to ask."

"I apologize for even asking."

"It's alright. Luckily, I've been around Miss Hoshikawa for years because my older sister has been friends with her since late elementary."

"Interesting." Tarou resumed eating his cutlet sandwich, as lunch break almost ended.

"If you're wondering where she's actually from, it's a complete mystery. Even her adoptive parents wouldn't know from what I imagine. Because of that, Miss Hoshikawa didn't have much friends until she met my older sister Misa."

And answering that question is why I'm here, Tarou thought as he continued eating his sandwich. "Is that all you have to ask?" Riku asked.

Tarou gulped upon hearing Riku's question, making him swallow his sandwich piece fast. "... Yes," Tarou answered despite rushing his swallowing.

"Sorry about that. Drink your water first before answering my question."

Tarou then opened his bottle of water and drank. "Ready," Tarou declared.

"You said you came from Iran, right?" Riku asked.

"Yes... " Tarou answered with suspicion in his tone. *Should have known he would ask me about that.*

"Did you ever come across the Eurasian Tsardom's Donian IIs?"

Walgears were called Aswārān by the Iranian forces when they first heard about them because they were the revival of old Persian cavalry units, Tarou thought. *As Japan is part of the New United Nations, Todoh would have heard the reporting name "Donian" when the Eurasians unveiled the first bipedal Walgear, the SH-5, and when the Eurasians made the SH-6, it was given the reporting name "Donian II". He's already told me enough about Hoshikawa. I best repay him for that.*

"Yes," Tarou answered. "They're intimidating, to say the least."

"I know, right? Though they make mecha anime boring to watch these days."

"Mecha anime?"

"Japanese animation. 'Mecha' simply means 'mechanical' but it's easy to use for anime with giant robots. Walgers seem to subscribe to 'mini-mecha' as they've been called to differentiate from those whose height range from seven meters at minimum."

"Why 'seven meters by minimum'?"

"Can we please resume this discussion another time?" Riku asked as he looked at his watch. "Lunch break is almost over."

"Agreed." Tarou immediately resumed eating his sandwich.

Nukata Station/Nukata Sushi. 1345 hours

Wouter Vos then came out of Nukata Station in the Yamatecho neighborhood. As he told Daisuke Hoshikawa the previous day, he would travel to his mansion in Kamiishikiricho, but it required a train trip. Because the *Iron Dutchman* was located on the other side of the city, Vos' train ride required a walk to the station nearest Hoshikawa Shipyards and after that, he had to walk to another station and after that, there was the need to transfer to yet another line. As it was the afternoon, the crowds delayed the trip for Vos.

Now, it was only a quarter to fourteen hundred hours. Vos now had food in his mind as he left Nukata Station. Luckily for Vos, there was a *sushi* restaurant nearby.

Finally, Vos thought upon finding the sushi restaurant.

After coming inside, Vos sat down, was greeted by a waitress, and given a menu. As the items had English translations, Vos had no problem reading the menu. Once he stated to the waitress his orders, the latter noted them down and left, but not before she was given the menu by Vos.

While waiting, Vos opted to think about the past. Despite how much Japan changed after the Third World War to acquire the help of foreigners such as Vos, the mercenary still thought of the Republic of South Africa as his home.

Prior to being a mercenary, Wouter Vos was once in the South African Marine Corps as a protest against his father Reinier Vos, an officer in the South African Army. At first, the older Vos ceased his opposition to his son's choice of service branch within the South African Defence Force as Wouter mastered the art of piloting a Walgear. That changed in 2027 when the younger Vos, whose unit was stationed in the Congo Federation as this nation-state and South Africa were both members of the African Federation (AF), saw a New United Nations Ground Force unit coming under attack but choosing to be human, Vos took his unit into the New United Nations-aligned Democratic Republic of Congo and saved that NUNGF unit. This led to Wouter being discharged from the South African Marine Corps, making Reinier disown him.

When two of the NUNGF soldiers he saved, Sunan Wattana and Jason Luke Crawley, traveled to South Africa to thank and apologize to Vos, the latter invited the former two into creating a mercenary unit for people like them. This was the beginning of Iron Dutchman Services.

In the present, the waitress returned with everything Vos ordered. Vos began his meal before he resumed his work.

#

Kamiishikiri Park No. 1. 1529 hours

Vos ultimately reached Kamiishikirocho. Remembering that a park was nearby, Vos stopped there. This park was designated "No. 1" as there were three parts throughout Kamiishikiricho alone.

Vos had an objective upon being assigned to go to Kamiishikiricho, and he had to complete as fast as he could because he could be seen doing something suspicious. Finding some grass, Vos immediately dug with his bare hands and once he finished, he took out a small stick with a glass orb on it. He planted the object into the hole he made and almost buried it.

After that, he began to leave the park and by extension, Kamiishikirocho. Despite his dirty right hand, Vos began to use his smartphone's IntMail application and contacted Sunan Wattana. He typed in "Proximity Sensor planted", pressed "Send", and pocketed the phone.

First Challenge Part 1

Nishi High School, Higashiosaka Ward, Kansai City, Kansai Prefecture; State of Japan. April 8, 2030; 1600 hours (Japan Standard Time)

Tarou Ganji began to exit from Nishi High School. However, as he stepped outside, he heard footsteps approaching him.

Tarou then reared his head to find Maria Hoshikawa. "You needed something, Hoshikawa-senpai?"

"I've just heard that you've already gotten a couple of invitations for clubs," Maria said as a preface to her explanation of why she followed Tarou outside. "Have you thought about which one you'll be joining?"

"Not yet." Tarou fully turned his body to face Maria after his answer. "Other than that, I have to consult Dr. Hamilton on the matter."

"I see. I apologize for doing this, but how about the Judo club? Not that I'm going to force you or anything… "

"Like I said, I need to think about this. If that is all you needed to talk about, I must get going."

"Agreed. I'll be late for Judo club. Please take care."

"Thank you." Tarou bowed, then continued moving toward his PCX scooter.

#

Hamilton-Ganji Condominium, Hoshikawa Condominiums. 1845 hours

Having returned to his condominium and removed his button-up shirt, Tarou had studied. However, that was interrupted by his smartphone. Tarou then found that it was an audio message from Anita Hamilton. After picking up the phone, he pressed the button that was needed to be pressed in order to respond to the call.

"This is Ganji," Tarou said.

"Tarou, I've closed the clinic for the night," Hamilton said on her end. "Since it's been a day since Wouter and the others arrived in Japan, we have to report to them. Naturally, this is because Barto has a new recipe with the ingredients he bought today. It's considered an order."

"Understood," Tarou thought as his message to type. He then put the phone down.

Immediately after that, he began to take only his smartphone and his P226 semi-automatic pistol. Like before, he hid the P226 underneath the PCX's seat and removed the helmet to put it on his head. After closing the seat and pocketing his smartphone, Tarou sat down and started up his scooter.

#

Iron Dutchman/Hoshikawa Shipyards, Taisho Ward. 1939 hours

Tarou reached Hoshikawa Shipyards. After parking his PCX, he raced to the gangway connected to the *Iron Dutchman* and, upon getting on the ship, he found Hamilton waiting for him.

"Come on, everyone's waiting for us," Hamilton ordered to Tarou.

#

1955 hours

Tarou and Hamilton then reached the dining hall they're familiar with. Their usual table was occupied only by Tatev Mirzoyan and Federico Diáz.

"Ganji, Doc, you made it," Wouter Vos said upon seeing Tarou and Hamilton. "You came just in time. Sit down already. Barto's almost done."

"It's ready!" Bartolomeu Moura as he appeared with a tray filled with food; a repeat of the evening when Tatev picked up the contract offered by the Foreign Intelligence Service that led them to Japan.

As Tarou and Hamilton sat with Tatev and Diáz, Moura began distributing each plate to everyone sitting down. This time, it was chicken *teriyaki* with a cup of rice and stir-fry lettuce. As soon as each member of Iron Dutchman Services received their meal, they began to eat.

2049 hours

After they finished their dinner, everyone gathered in the briefing room. Vos then stepped onto the stage.

"So, everyone, how was your first day in Japan?" Vos asked. "Of course, Ganji and Doc already had settled in Japan before we did. Tonight, we must discuss everything we found while acting out as immigrants. Ganji will have to be the last one.

"I'll start first. I managed to install the proximity sensor 'Smith' gave us around Kamiishikiricho. Mirzoyan will be able to detect any sort of activity around Kamiishikiricho as a result.

"Now then, who aside from Ganji and Barto wish to talk next?"

"I do," Jason Luke Crawley said as he raised his hand. "I've started looking for a van to use as 'Smith' recommended."

"Found one at a good price?" Vos inquired.

"Not yet. Will resume tomorrow."

"Mind if I come next?" Sunan Wattana asked.

"Sure, Wattana," Vos replied.

"I went to this bar. While I got a cold one, some guy sat beside me. He's clearly the same as us but I noticed that while he managed to speak Japanese fluently, his 'domo' seemed accented. His 'do' sounded like 'dugh'."

"Really? Did you ask where he came from as small talk?"

"I did. His English was good but like his Japanese, it's accented. He claimed to be a refugee that fled from the Russian Soviet Federative Socialist Republic."

"Doesn't seem out of the ordinary, but if you go to that bar tomorrow, follow that man, but make sure he doesn't see you. Use your phone to take a picture of where he lives."

"Roger that."

"What about you, Mirzoyan?" Vos asked as he turned to Tatev.

"Installed and learned the program Mr. 'Smith' asked me to install," Tatev answered.

"Good." Vos then turned to Diáz. "Fed, what about you?"

"Sem, Vikas, and I simply went to get soap and other bathroom supplies," Diáz answered.

"Now it's your turn, Doc," Vos said to Hamilton.

"Other than a sprained ankle, nothing else happened," Hamilton answered. "Mr. Hoshikawa even paid me as if I were a normal employee."

"Then use that money to support yourself and Ganji." Vos turned to Tarou. "Now you may speak."

"I ran into Maria Hoshikawa three times," Tarou answered.

Everyone made no effort to hide that they were surprised by what Tarou said. Crawley opened his mouth as if he was shot, and that blood began to flow out of his mouth.

"Y… You're joking, right?" Vos asked.

"No. I could hardly believe myself. Mr. Crawley did warn me that I wouldn't be accepted so easily because I'm a transfer student. Yet Miss Hoshikawa helped me out when I needed to park my PCX."

"But she could suspect that her father got that scooter for you," Wattana warned.

"I know. Maybe that could be it."

"And how do your new classmates take the idea that the most popular student in Nishi High School ran into you thrice?" Crawley asked.

"I don't think they know I ran into her three times. The first time was that everyone was worried about being late for the welcoming ceremony. They only noticed during lunch break and I doubt we were interrupted after that when I started leaving."

"Just be careful, Tarou," Hamilton warned. "Especially if Miss Hoshikawa finds time to ask you some more about your past."

"I understand."

A loud sound, however, interrupted the discussion. Everyone now saw that it came from Tatev's smartphone as she accessed an application called "Sensor Control".

"Picked up something?" Vos asked.

"Yes," Tatev answered. "Someone's at the Hoshikawa Mansion."

"That early?" Crawley incredulously asked. "Whoever this bloke or sheila is, he or she must be very bold to do this."

"Ganji, you have the scooter," Vos said as he turned to Tarou. "Head on over there, now."

"Roger," Tarou replied before standing up and saluting.

#

Kamiishikiri Park No. 1, Higashiosaka Ward. 2137 hours

Tarou then arrived at Kamiishikiricho. Because he remembered the proximity sensor placed at Kamishikiri Park No. 1, Tarou stopped at the park and parked his PCX scooter.

After that, Tarou got off the scooter and opened the seat. He removed the helmet and placed it at the compartment the seat hid while getting his P226 pistol. After that, Tarou closed the seat and pocketed the pistol as he brought out his smartphone and used IntMail to contact Tatev.

"At the park where Mr. Vos planted the proximity sensor," Tarou typed in IntMail before pressing "Send".

Tarou then waited for Tatev's reply. Such was the consequence of an application that's explicitly electronic mail. However, Tarou's wait ended as Tatev managed to reply.

"The red dot representing the intruder hasn't moved since you reached Kamiichikirocho," Tatev typed in response. "He or she entered the road leading to the Hoshikawa Mansion but hasn't moved since."

"Acknowledged," Tarou typed in return before pocketing the smartphone and rushing toward the road leading to the mansion.

#

Near the Hoshikawa Mansion. 2201 hours

Tarou walked slowly across the road leading to the Hoshikawa Mansion. Although it was dark, Tarou slowly walked toward the individual he could see.

Despite that, Tarou aimed his pistol while moving toward the intruder. Out of all the battles he survived, he never imagined himself having to start using his pistol in Japan.

"Dare da?" a male voice asked, which made Tarou stop.

That voice… Tarou thought as he heard the voice, making him pocket his pistol.

After hiding his P226, Tarou used his smartphone's flashlight and used it to identify the person he heard. Only when Tarou got closer did he identify the person whose voice he recognized—Riku Todoh.

"You're Tarou Ganji, right?" Riku asked.

"Hai," Tarou answered. "What are you doing here?"

"And what are *you* doing here?"

"I suggest we leave before any of us get into trouble."

Riku sighed and briefly faced the road. "… Right."

#

Kamiishikiri Park No. 1. 2229 hours

Both Tarou and Riku returned to the park where Tarou parked his PCX. Upon reaching the scooter, Tarou sat on the seat, doing his best to hide his P226.

"So, what are you doing here?" Tarou asked.

"You sound like a policeman," Riku commented.

"I really do?"

"How did you find me?"

"I didn't."

"Then why did you come out here?"

"I'm still trying to adjust, so I like to familiar myself with where I'll be living."

"I see. Remember our discussion this afternoon at school?"

"About mecha?"

"You see, I like to travel to Yao to take pictures of the Ground Self-Defense Force base at Yao Airport. Hours before, some guys from Class 2-3 ganged up on me and took my camera, filled with the photos from Yao Airport."

"And what does this have to do with you being here?"

"Two guys from Class 2-3 wanted me to use my phone to infiltrate Hoshiawa-senpai's mansion and take photos of her dressing up. I show them the photos and they'll give me back your camera."

"Why would they do that?"

"I honestly don't know?"

"What are their names?"

"… Why do you want to know?"

"I'm not sure if you've been told of this, but I was once a child soldier. Dr. Hamilton brought me here to Japan to learn to live like a normal human, but in that unit, we took care of each other. You were the first to approach me today, so please, allow me to help."

"Just like that?"

"Trust me, I think I can think of something. But first, we need to get you home."

"Funnily enough, I live nearby, so I can just walk back."

That's surprising, Tarou thought. "Before I ask again about those names, why do you take pictures of the base in Yao Airport?"

"Because they occasionally drop off Walgears there. The last time I took photos was last week."

"I take it you like mecha as a whole?"

"Who doesn't? I consider Walgears the greatest invention of mankind, and I thank *Revelator* for crashing in 1985. Without that ship, we wouldn't have Walgears."

Figures he would say that, Tarou thought while managing to keep his emotions in check. "Anyway, I best leave."

Tarou then properly sat down on his scooter then turns it on. "Wait," Riku blurted. "Will you really help me with those boys from Class 2-3?"

Iron Dutchman, Taisho Ward. 2324 hours

"So, what did you say?" Sunan Wattana asked Tarou after the latter returned to the *Iron Dutchman*'s briefing room.

"I told him yes," Tarou answered.

"Why did you do that?" Jake Crawley asked.

"Before I answer that," Tarou said before turning to Wouter Vos. "Mr. Vos, have you talked to Mr. 'Smith' yet?"

"Not yet," Vos answered. "Seems to me you want 'Smith' to know about this plan of yours. Before he asks why, I want to know why you're sticking up for this Todoh kid?"

"I feel that it's best that I'm his friend because I'm still new at acting out as a normal teenager and that he can still tell me more about Miss Hoshikawa."

"I suppose those are good reasons," Anita Hamilton replied.

"Alright," Vos added. "What's your plan?"

#

OVR Safehouse. Nishinari Ward. April 9, 2030; 0540 hours

Tatiana Ioannovna Tsulukidze arrived at her office in the OVR safehouse she commanded. Once she connected her smartphone to the dish she placed on the window, she activated SatCom. She found a message from Vyacheslav Leonidovich Puzanov and responded.

"So you're awake, now?" Puzanov asked on the other side of the smartphone.

"Da," Tatiana replied. "I imagine you have new information?"

"Your fa- I mean, the Tsar hired a mercenary on the advice of Deputy Director Askarova."

"Why a mercenary?"

"He can easily pose as a tourist and if in the event he will make a mistake, he can easily be eliminated."

"What's his name?"

"Serdar Muhadow."

"The Butcher of Godana?"

"Da."

"I think that's a terrible idea. You know what he did to those women after the Turkestani rebels took Korla?"

"I know. Please, do it for the Tsar."

"When will he arrive?"

"From what I've heard from Askarova, He's already moving toward Hamad International Airport."

"He's coming from the Middle Eastern League."

"His current alias is 'Mansur Fahri'. You'll need to tell either Chadov or Zhakiyanov that because you'll need either of them to pick him up."

"Zametano," Tatiana replied before turning off the smartphone. She then heard a knock on her door.

"Come in," Tatiana ordered.

A man with blond hair in a crew cut, light skin, and brown eyes came into the room. "I assume that was the Director?" the man asked.

"Da," Tatiana answered. "He's given us instructions."

"What are they?"

#

Nishi High School, Higashiosaka Ward. 1239 hours

In between two classrooms, both for second-year students at Nishi High School, Tarou Ganji stood while eating an apple strudel.

"Still haven't talked with Dr. Hamilton about proper food?" Maria Hoshikawa asked as she appeared beside Tarou.

Because he was startled, Tarou swallowed the piece of struddel despite not having finished chewing it. "… What can I do for you today, Hoshikawa-senpai?" Tarou asked.

"What are you doing here?"

"Showing some concern for Todoh."

Both Tarou and Maria saw Riku Todoh leave the classroom of Class 2-3 to return to his classroom. "You mean Riku-kun, I can see why."

"You know anything?"

"Nothing concrete. I could imagine that it has something to do with Todoh's obsession with mecha anime."

"He really seems to like mecha anime, especially with how Walgears were the result of *Revelator* crashing into Afghanistan in 1985."

"Figures he would make you humor his tastes. I'm glad you did anyway."

"Tell me, what do you know about Atsushi Nakagawa and Seiji Uminari?"

"They're a part of the Judo club. Why do you ask?"

"Nothing. Caught those names while conversing with Todoh."

"Thank you for being a friend for Riku-kun. I guess it's kind of me and Misa-chan's fault for focusing more on our studies."

"I see. I best return to the classroom."

"I understand. I'm under Class 3-1 so my room is a little father and not to mention that I'm floor above."

#

Nagoya International Airport, Toyoyama/Nishikugai District, Aichi Prefecture. 1359 hours

Serdar Muhadow had stepped out of Nagoya International Airport. After using his alias "Mansur Fahri" to go through customs, he stepped out of the airport. He then found a man in a suit approaching him.

"Are you Mansur Fahri?" the man asked.

"Who's to know?" Muhadow answered as he knew that the man would address him with that name for one particular reason.

"Please follow me. We're to see Gatekeeper Japan."

Japan Tachyon Particle Receiver, Seto. 1450 hours

Muhadow was then brought to the Japan Tachyon Particle Receiver complex in the city of Seto, also in the Aichi Prefecture. Like the TPR in the Turkestani Republic, the TPR for Japan was built near the capital of Nagoya.

For countries that recovered after the Third World War, they had to allow the Gatekeepers to maintain branches in order for them to operate the TPRs. However, this gave many the impression that they control the world as a country, if not a supernational union provided a country was a member of one, would suffer if they dared to defy the Gatekeepers.

After granted entry, Muhadow and the man who picked him up parked their car and proceeded inside. They reached the office of Gatekeeper Japan.

Once it was explained to the Gatekeeper's secretary, Muhadow alone approached the office of Gatekeeper Japan, a man hiding his face with a hood as with all Gatekeepers of Knowledge personnel. Both men clenched their fists and saluted.

"So you're Serdar Muhadow?" Gatekeeper Japan asked. "Please sit."

Muhadow then sat down. "I've heard as to why you're here. Now, please answer this: what is your plan now to get Maria Hoshikawa?"

"What I intend to do first is find a hotel in Kansai City, then meet up with Grand Duchess Tatiana's cell. From there, I am to obey her but while I do so, I will do my own monitoring of the Hoshikawa family but once I find an event where they have to leave Kansai City, I will plan out what to do from there though I will need your help."

"About that… our Devotee-Infiltrator in the OVR needs to know that you're here in Japan. Therefore, you must stay here for the time being so that the OVR cell in Kansai City can send in one of their agents to pick you up. Then you'll be taken to 'Elizaveta', whom you're to report to. After that, they'll allow you to find a room."

"I understand."

"Once all of that is sorted out, you can find your hotel, but once you do, contact me when you'll need my help. Type in 'GJYS' in GOKMail and use that to establish a conversation between the both of us. In fact, when you do reach Kansai City, I must be notified first. That way, I can notify Gatekeeper Int in turn who will use his contact in the Eurasian OVR and from there, she'll notify the Director. The OVR cell in Kansai City will be informed of this and of their agents will pick you up."

"Will do, Gatekeeper Japan."

#

Iron Dutchman, Taisho Ward, Kansai City, Kansai Prefecture. 1509 hours

Unbeknownst to Muhadow, Frederick Dirks also arrived in Japan, albeit his destination was Kansai City. After arriving at the Iron Dutchman, he was brought inside the ship by Wouter Vos. Vos then brought Dirks to the ship's library, the same library where Dirks tested Tarou Ganji in his Japanese. There, Tatev Mirzoyan was using the same chair and table Dirks and Tarou used while she had her laptop computer with her.

"I've read all the information you sent me about those two kids Ganji wishes to 'deal' with," Dirks said. "I think Ganji's plan can work, though he cannot move yet unless I give the word."

"He knows that," Vos replied. "For now, all he has are names."

"What are they?"

"Atsushi Nakagawa and Seiji Uminari."

"You'll need this." Dirks brought out a USB device and gave it to Tatev. Tatev then plugged the USB onto her computer and found an icon named "Records".

"What's in here?" Tatev asked with regard to the icon.

"I'd rather explain when Ganji comes," Dirks answered.

"I'll have Doc tell Ganji to come here once they both return to their condominium," Vos added.

#

1739 hours

At the same time, Sunan Wattana returned to the *Iron Dutchman*. However, she didn't find Wouter Vos receiving her. Instead, she found Jake Crawley receiving her.

"Jake, where's Wouter?" Wattana asked.

"Heard from Fed that he's with Tatev and 'Smith' at the library," Crawley answered.

"The spook's here?"

"Apparently."

"I need face time with him."

"I need to know why 'Smith' came, so I'm coming with you."

Both Crawley and Wattana reached the library door with the former knocking. On the other side, Wouter Vos, Tatev Mirzoyan, and Frederick Dirks heard the knocking.

"Who's there?" Vos asked.

"It's Wattana," the female mercenary answered. "Jake and I wish to come in."

"You may." After Vos' permission, Wattana opened the door, and she entered, with Crawley following.

"What are you doing?" Wattana asked.

"Making a presentation for later," Tatev answered.

"A presentation?" Crawley asked.

Both Wattana and Crawley joined Vos and Dirks in looking at Tatev was doing. The former two found Tatev reading files pertaining to Nishi High School and summarizing them into the program needed for presentations.

"What's this about?" Crawley asked.

"I had 'Maria Clara' hack into the smartphone message history of both Seiji Uminari and Atsushi Nakagawa," Dirks explained. "They're giving a somewhat vital asset trouble, and Ganji wishes to make sure we keep that asset."

"Really?"

"Nakagawa and Uminari had bullied Riku Todoh into trespassing in the Hoshikawa Mansion to take racy photos of Maria Hoshikawa. Normally, this shouldn't be within the FIS's jurisdiction, but Ganji does have a point in making sure Todoh will provide information Ganji will need."

"And this information will help how?"

"We'll discuss that later," Vos answered. "However, we need to wait for Doc to tell Ganji to come here."

"About that, there's something I need to bring up and now's a good time," Wattama added.

"What is it?" Dirks asked.

#

Hamilton-Ganji Condominium, Hoshikawa Condominiums, Higashiosaka Ward. 1700 hours

While Tarou Ganji studied, his smartphone rang. He answered and found that it was Anita Hamilton contacting him through IntMail. Upon opening IntMail, Tarou found Hamilton's message:

Closed up for today, but Wouter just contacted me. We're needed at the Iron Dutchman. Please pick me up first because I've just closed up the clinic and I need to ride to Hoshikawa Shipyards.

Tarou nodded and stopped his studies. Shutting down what could be turned off in the condominium, Tarou raced out of the condominium.

#

Iron Dutchman/Hoshikawa Shipyards, Taisho Ward. 2039 hours

Meanwhile, Tarou and Hamilton arrived at Hoshikawa Shipyards with the latter riding behind the former as he used the PCX scooter. After Tarou parked the PCX, he and Hamilton continued toward the *Iron Dutchman.*

Upon boarding the *Iron Dutchman*, Tarou and Hamilton were received by Sunan Wattana. She led them to the briefing room. Once they sat down, Wouter Vos and Frederick Dirks took to the stage.

"Now that Ganji's here, I'll have 'Smith' explain how we'll do this plan Ganji wishes to enact," Vos announced before stepping aside and allowing Dirks to continue.

"I've reviewed Ganji's plan, but I insisted that we find useful information to use," Dirks added. "Ganji, what's the status on Todoh?"

"He hasn't made a move," Tarou answered. "Luckily, Nakagawa nor Uminari haven't forced him to continue. Seemingly, they just want those photos and don't really care how or when to get them."

"Kinda smart for a couple of bullies," Jake Crawley remarked.

"Before we resume, I have a personal opinion about this idea," Dirks added. "I do think this is a waste of time and resources, mainly because I do not believe that a boy your age makes for a vital source of information."

"Forgive me for speaking above my station, but having someone like Todoh wouldn't be vital to make sure I blend in?" Tarou retorted, yet unbeknownst to him, Hamilton saw through Tarou's supposed reason for helping Riku Todoh.

"I guess. That's why I'm here. I had 'Maria Clara' look up on what else we can use against Nakagawa and Uminari."

Dirks then turned to the direction of the projector room, where Tatev Mirzoyan already connected the projector and the USB she received from Dirks hours before to her laptop. "Start up the presentation, Mirzoyan," Dirks ordered.

"Acknowledged," Tatev replied.

The projection screen now showed a series of text messages. Everyone was surprised that this was what Dirks had in mind.

"We intercepted a series of text messages made between Atsushi Nakagawa and Seiji Uminari," Dirks explained. "As you can see, they were dumb enough to plan everything and explain those plans by text."

"And how exactly will this help?" Vos asked.

"Whenever Ganji decides to confront Nakagawa and Uminari alone, he'll threaten them with his gun," Dirks answered. "Of course, those two will not take it seriously. You should know Ganji wouldn't be the type to let them take him lightly."

"I see. So the copy of the text messages will be blackmail if in the event those two refuse to let sleeping dogs lie?"

"Correct, but as Vos told me, Ganji plans on intimidating Nakagawa and Uminari into giving back Todoh's camera."

"So, when will you issue the challenge?" Hamilton asked as she turned to Tarou.

"Tomorrow," Tarou answered. "As I told everyone last night, I intend to infiltrate the Hoshikawa Mansion and take those photos. I show those photos to Nakagawa and Uminari. However, I will suggest to them that the hand-off be at a secluded location."

"At the Morinomiya Station," Dirks said. "Because it's a part of Crater Shore, makes for a good spot that's secluded to make sure there will be witnesses, save for us."

"That's right. There, I threaten those two with my gun because I plan on deleting the photos upon showing them to Nakagawa and Uminari. With these text messages, I can ensure their silence should they threaten to tell anyone that I have a gun after I threaten them with it."

"And that's also why I'm here," Dirks added. "I need to tell Daisuke Hoshikawa about this so that he can help out with this."

"You better come up with a good reason to make him help perverts take photos of his daughter in her lingerie," Sunan Wattana warned.

"Trust me, I think I can appeal to Daisuke on the matter," Dirks replied.

"Good luck with that," Vos murmured while turning his head away and saying it softly to make sure Dirks didn't hear it.

"Anything else to discuss?" Dirks asked.

"None," every member of Iron Dutchman Services answered in unison, except for Tatev.

"Then we call it a night, except for Ganji. He must resume his studies before he goes to bed. Before we launch the operation, we gather here at 2000 hours," Vos ordered before he turned to Tarou. "Ganji, have a message for Nakagawa and Uminari telling them to meet at Crater Shore tomorrow at 2100 hours. Other than that, we're dismissed."

First Challenge Part 2

Ishikiri Station, Higashiosaka Ward, Kansai City, Kansai Prefecture; State of Japan. April 10, 1845 hours (Japan Standard Time)

Serdar Muhadow, after a car ride from the Japan TPR to Nagoya Station, followed by the train ride from Nagoya Station to Kyoto Station, which led to a line change, reached Kansai City. After surrendering his last train ticket, Muhadow stepped out of Ishikiri Station. He then found a man in a long coat waiting by a car.

"Are you 'Mansur Fahri'?" the man asked to Muhadow.

"Yes?" Muhadow asked.

"I've been ordered by 'Elizaveta' to take you with me."

"By all means, take me to her."

#

OVR Safehouse, Nishinari Ward. 1939 hours

Muhadow was then taken to the OVR cell's safehouse that he was told about. The man who drove him then took him to the room of the cell's leader, 'Elizaveta', whom both knew as Tatiana Ioannovna Tsulukidze.

"So you're Serdar Muhadow?" Tatiana asked.

"Hail, Your Highness," Muhadow replied before kneeling.

"Thank you, but you may stand now." Muhadow did as Tatiana commanded. "Now, I assume you know that you must do everything in your power to make sure you do not expose your real identity much less us for this assignment the Tsar recruited you for?"

"Of course."

"I also assume you're hungry. Pyotr here can take you to where you wish to eat. I only ask that you get us dinner as well."

"Zametano."

2030 hours

Both Serdar Muhadow and the man named Pyotr returned to the OVR safehouse. As they entered, both Tatiana Ioannovna Tsulukidze and another man who had the same haircut and eye color as Pyotr but with black hair and light skin bordering on light intermediate received the former.

"I see you got us dinner," Tatiana deduced. "What is it?"

"Chicken curry."

"Öte jaqsı!" the man beside Tatiana declared.

"Before we eat, I'd like to speak with Gospodin Mukhadov in my office."

"Zametano," Muhadow replied.

#

2039 hours

Both Muhadow and Tatiana reached the office of the latter. "I assume you're *real* objective is different from me and my men?" Tatiana asked.

"Who's to say? I have my orders and I have to obey them to get my money." Muhadow answered.

"And I assume you've reserved a room for yourself?"

"Not yet."

"I must ask: what will you do after this?"

"Find another job or go back to training the Turkestani Army."

"Then wait until Chadov finishes his meal. I'll have him take you to your hotel of choice."

"Spasibo."

"As we've been stationed here, we can avail to you all the information we've gather."

"Thank you, but I will only avail of such information tomorrow at the earliest."

Hoshikawa Group Headquarters, Taisho Ward. April 10, 2030; 1219 hours

"Shachou, I've been told someone named 'Preston Turner' is here to see you," a female voice over a small PA system installed on Daisuke Hoshikawa's desk, interrupting the President of Hoshikawa Group. "Shall I let him in?"

Daisuke slightly gulped upon hearing the name "Preston Turner" as he knew that the name was an alias. "… Let him in," Daisuke answered.

"Kashikorimashita."

"Preston Turner" then approached Daisuke's office once he was let inside. The latter, however, knew the former by his real name—Frederick Dirks.

"So, Mr. 'Turner', what can I do for you?" Daisuke asked in English.

"Tasuke ga hitsuyou desu," Dirks answered in Japanese.

Figures he would use Japanese to make sure that his plea is something serious, Daisuke thought. "Very well. But we discuss this elsewhere and after I've gotten my lunch."

"And I know just the place."

#

Nishi High School, Higashiosaka Ward. 1219 hours

Tarou Ganji entered the room belonging to Class 2-3. Riku Todoh then led him to the table belonging to one Seiji Uminari with Atsushi Nakagawa beside him. As old as Tarou and Riku, Uminari and Nakagawa had dark brown eyes, but the former had a shaved head while the latter had black hair dyed into blond.

"So, you're Ganji?" Uminari asked.

"I am," Tarou answered.

"Todoh says you can get us those photos of Hoshikawa-senpai," Nakagawa said.

"I can, but in exchange, you give Todoh his camera back."

"Whatever."

"In addition, I also ask that we do the exchange at the Morinomiya Station ruins, nine in the evening."

"Just get us those photos," Uminari demanded.

And now, all I have to do is wait for Mr. Vos' message to proceed, Tarou thought.

#

Iron Dutchman, Suminoe Ward. 1320 hours

Both Daisuke and Dirks arrived at the *Iron Dutchman*'s library, with Wouter Vos waiting for them. The former two then occupied the same table Dirks used in testing Tarou Ganji's Japanese.

"So what is it you need help with?" Daisuke answered.

"It concerns your daughter and two of her charges from Nishi High School's Judo club."

After his answer, Dirks explained everything Tarou Ganji planned out and his reason for helping Riku Todoh. "I see," Daisuke said after Dirks finished his stories. "Though why does this story need Maria in her lingerie?"

"Normally, I'd rather just tell Nakagawa and Uminari's respective parents, but that would cause some trouble for Todoh," Dirks answered. "With those photos, we can make Nakagawa and Uminari let their guard down, allowing Ganji to use his *coup de grâce*."

"Very well. I'll see to it Mr. Ganji is allowed inside the mansion once you've told him of this."

"Thank you."

"But in exchange, I must tell Maria something. She's already voiced her suspicions."

"What suspicions?" Vos asked.

"Other than the PCX, we've intercepted empty coffee bottles with handwritten messages by Fre- I mean, Mr. 'Smith'."

"Understood. I'll remind Ganji."

"Now, if you excuse me, I must return to my company." Daisuke stood up and, as he began to leave the library, Vos joined him in order to escort him out of the ship.

#

Nishi High School, Higashiosaka Ward. 1549 hours

As he arrived at the bicycle rack, Tarou reached his PCX scooter. Before turning it on, however, he brought out his smartphone. He found that Vos had sent a message to him through IntMail that read:

Hoshikawa's given permission to let you into his mansion.

Tarou then put away his smartphone and began to leave the school. Unbeknownst to him, Maria Hoshikawa watched from the entrance.

He still hasn't picked a club yet, Maria thought.

"There you are, Maria-chan."

As she was interrupted by her name being called out, Maria turned to find her friend with the short brown hair. This girl was Misa Todoh, Riku Todoh's older sister.

"Why you are you here?" Misa asked. "Judo club's about to begin."

"Right," Maria replied. "Sorry about that."

#

Hoshikawa Mansion. 1645 hours

Tarou then reached the Hoshikawa Mansion. Once the gate opened, Tarou hid the PCX in the trees to his left and proceeded into the mansion by foot. As he reached the front door, it was opened by Miku Hoshikawa (née Sayama).

"I assume you're Tarou Ganji?" Miku asked.

"I am," Tarou replied before bowing. "I apologize for doing this."

"I've been told by my husband why, so I can understand, but I'd prefer it that you make sure you're not detected. Maria will be home in less than fifteen minutes."

"Wakarimashita."

"Please follow me. I'll take you to Maria's room."

Miku then let Tarou throughout the mansion. Eventually, they reached Maria's room, with Miku opening the door. As they approached the room, Tarou looked around as if curiosity overrode his brain. It was to be expected, considering where Tarou came from and his living circumstances since.

At the mansion's second floor were five windows in the side rooms. In Maria's bedroom, there were three. The bed was located left of the door, between two of the three windows. To the right of the door was the desk where Maria's computer was located at. Beside that was a bookshelf filled with external HDDs (hard disk drives) that could be only connected to the computer by way of a USB-C cable; the standard USB "head" toward the computer while the C "head" to the HDD.

"I honestly don't know how you'll get those photos," Miku said. "Just get them and once Maria comes back, hide. I also suggest that you leave only when she leaves this room."

"And does Maria-san ever leave this room after coming back from school?"

"She joins me for Rosary once she finishes washing up."

Didn't think she would be the religious type, Tarou thought. "Very well. I best get into position."

"All I can say at this point, even if it's horrible to say as a mother, but good luck."

As soon as Miku left the room, Tarou started establishing what he needed. First, he rushed to the clothes cabinet and wardrobe found at the left end of the room. He brought out a device that contained a fiberscope called a "snakecam" and placed it below the wardrobe.

I just hope Maria doesn't find this, Tarou thought.

After the snakecam was installed, Tarou activated the snakecam using his smartphone through an application called "CamControl". However, Tarou heard an engine, and remembering Miku's warning, he immediately fled the wardrobe.

Thank goodness her bed is big, Tarou thought as he saw Maria's bed. After rushing to it, he crawled underneath it. While prone, Tarou slowly and carefully had to switch his position to prevent his limbs from being detected by Maria as she opened the door.

As a result, Tarou was unable to move his head, as that would alert his presence to Maria. The wait wasn't long as Maria entered her bathroom to take a bath as she came from Judo club.

Hearing the shower, Tarou now moved his head. Seeing that the door was closed, Tarou used this opportunity to escape the bed, but upon standing up, he had to walk slowly toward the door and open it slowly to avoid catching Maria's attention. Managing to slowly open the door, Tarou quickly exited the room without making a sound.

Once outside, Tarou slowly closed the door. Immediately after that, he began to use his smartphone. Going to CamControl, Tarou was now able to see the room from the bottom of the wardrobe. Tarou then tested what else CamControl had to offer by using his left index finger to move across the screen. This caused the snakecam's lens "head" to move like an actual snake.

While not taking his eyes off CamControl, Tarou left the phone and snakecam alone, as he needed to wait for Maria to finish taking a bath. To Tarou's relief, he saw the bathroom door open.

Good, Tarou thought as he now saw Maria in a towel move toward her wardrobe.

While unaware that she was being spied on, Maria proceeded to her wardrobe. After Maria opened her wardrobe, Tarou now saw what men shouldn't see out of women as he moved the snakecam's lens head. Remembering that neither Nakagawa nor Uminari asked for a specific amount of photographs, Tarou opted to only take two photographs. Once he had gotten those two photographs, Tarou hid at the room beside Maria's bedroom until she left the room to pray the Rosary with Miku.

After closing the door, Tarou found that he was now in a personal gym. At this point, it didn't matter what room Tarou was in, as long as Maria didn't notice he was in the house taking pictures of her in her lingerie. Upon stopping, Tarou moved the snakecam again to see what changed after he took his second photograph. Now, Maria wore a white button-up shirt with a blue ribbon and a skirt of the same color that stopped before the ankles. Her footwear was none other than her white socks and black shoes.

As she was clothed again, Maria began to leave her room, still unaware of what was below her wardrobe. Tarou waited until Maria was no longer seen from the snakecam. As she was unaware that the person who installed a snakecam below her wardrobe was not only in the mansion but also hiding in the gym beside her room, Maria continued going downstairs.

Tarou slowly opened the door to see if Maria was gone. He looked at his left and right, but found no one or anything approaching him. He now saw this opportunity to return to Maria's room.

As he entered Maria's room again, the first thing Tarou did was retrieve the snakecam. After turning it off and pocketing it away, Tarou then rushed to the nearest window and opened it. Assured that Maria didnn't know that he was in the mansion, Tarou jumped out of the room.

Rolling once while falling, Tarou was able to land without injury. He kneeled with his right knee and his right palm touched the pavement surrounding the mansion.

Now, I have to get out of here, Tarou reminded himself in his mind while standing up.

#

Iron Dutchman, Suminoe Ward. 1919 hours

"Yep, you are a real pervert," Jason Luke Crawley said as he looked at the two photographs Tarou made hours before of Maria in her lingerie on Tarou's smartphone just as they and the rest of Iron Dutchman Services, save for Bartolomeu Moura, were gathered at their namesake's dining hall.

"How did you even make sure Miss Hoshikawa didn't spot you?" Tatev Mirzoyan asked with suspicion in her tone.

"And you really intend on getting rid of these photos after you show them to Uminari and Nakagawa?" Wouter Vos asked skeptically.

"I do," Tarou answered.

"Either way, we don't move out until 2000 hours. 'Smith's' already going to Morinomiya after he finishes his dinner."

"Roger," all members replied in unison just as Moura arrived with tonight's dinner.

Hoshikawa Shipyards. 2000 hours

Every member of Iron Dutchman Services stepped out of their namesake and approached Tarou's PCX. "Now, does anyone wish to accompany Ganji?" Vos asked.

"I do," Wattana answered.

"Then good luck to the both of you."

Tarou then opened the seat of the PCX and gave Wattana the helmet. The former then closed the seat and sat on it, with the latter joining him after putting on the helmet. After starting up the PCX, Tarou and Wattana left.

#

Near Morinomiya Station Ruins, Higashinari Ward. 2056 hours

Tarou and Wattana arrived near Morinomiya Station. After parking the PCX, both got off the scooter.

"I'll find somewhere to hide," Wattana said. "I'll give myself five minutes, then I make my way to the station ruins to monitor the situation."

"Got it," Tarou replied.

#

Morinomiya Station Ruins. 2104 hours

Both Atsushi Nakagawa and Seiji Uminari waited at the ruins of the entrance of Morinomiya Station. Nearby were the ruins of Osaka Castle.

The area both Morinomiya Station and Osaka Castle occupied was the easternmost end of Crater Shore, the result of Osaka being struck by a nuclear warhead during the Third World War. This made the area a suitable location for a shady exchange for Tarou Ganji, which Frederick Dirks understood as he hid near the abandoned trainyard nearby while using night-vision binoculars to watch the exchange.

Tarou himself then approached the station's entrance. Both Uminari and Nakagawa turned to see him. Unbeknownst to the latter two, Sunan Wattana also appeared, but hid herself.

"Took you long enough," Nakagawa said. "The photos?"

"First, the camera," Tarou demanded.

Uminari brought out the camera, a COOLPIX L320. Dirks briefly looked at the camera moreso than those participating in the exchange.

That Todoh kid's got good taste in cameras, Dirks thought. *Ganji better handle this smoothly because there's no telling what Uminari and Nakagawa would do with that camera.*

"Fine, fine," Nakagawa said. "Seiji, give it to him."

Uminari gave the L320 to Tarou. It had a strap, which made it easy for Tarou to keep with him. The fact that Tarou was familiar with a rifle's sling before putting on Nishi High School's uniform helped with Tarou putting on the camera around him.

"The photos, now!" Uminari reminded Tarou.

Tarou then brought out his smartphone. Accessing the application called "Photos", Tarou found the photographs he took hours ago on Maria Hoshikawa putting on her brassiere and panties, both of which were colored lavender.

"How did you even get these photos?" Nakagawa asked.

"I have my ways," Tarou answered.

"Signal's good," Uminari said as he looked at his smartphone. "Just give us your e-mail address."

"I'm sorry, what?" Tarou asked.

"You don't know what an e-mail address is?" Nakagawa asked. "Have you been living under a rock?"

"Yes," Tarou bluntly answered. "This kind of rock."

Tarou again showed his smartphone. A white box with writing was found below the photograph with the question "Delete Photo" and the choices "Yes" and "No" below. Tarou positioned his right thumb on "No" and immediately pressed it.

As the next photograph appeared, Tarou made the phone look at him and pressed the icon for deleting, based on a garbage can. As the choices appeared again, Tarou chose the same one.

"Why did you do that!?" Nakagawa screamed.

"I will not dishonor Miss Hoshikawa in this fashion," Tarou defiantly answered.

"What are you, some sort of a knight in shining armor?"

"I leave that to you to answer that question."

"Don't you mess with me!" Nakagawa shouted as he charged at Tarou with his right hand now clenched into a fist.

Tarou, however, brought out his P226 semi-automatic pistol, making Nakagawa stop. "… Is that a real gun?" Uminari asked.

"Yes," Tarou answered. "Let me walk away with this camera and I will not shoot you."

"You think that gun's real?" Nakagawa arrogantly asked.

Tarou pointed the gun at Uminari, then diverted it beside his left foot, albeit far. He pulled the trigger, scaring the latter and Nakagawa. As the former intended, the bullet instead made a hole beside Uminari, as the latter found.

"We'll tell on you for this!" Uminari warned as Tarou pocketed his P226.

"Really?" Tarou nonchalantly asked. "Because I've been given these text messages."

Tarou walked up to Nakagawa and Uminari. Opening his smartphone, he showed them the copy of their text messages.

"Look familiar?" Tarou asked rhetorically before he resumed.

"W… Where… did you get those?"

"I told you. *I have my ways.* Tell anyone of this and I'll tell about these messages."

"P… Please don't… " Nakagawa shamelessly requested.

"You should have thought of that before bullying Todoh into this."

"You're doing this for him?" Uminari asked.

"He's the only one who approached me two days ago. I'm not in the mood for continuing this any longer, so I'll be on my way. Leave Todoh alone from now on and I promise you, these messages will not be made public."

"You win! We'll leave Todoh alone!"

"And now I'll be leaving, but before that… "

Tarou walked toward the hole he made. Unbeknownst to him, Uminari got behind Tarou in an attempt to steal the camera. He moved his arms as soon as Tarou retrieved the shell, but after that, he quickly got up and used his right leg to hit Uminari's left leg, forcing him into the ground.

"Did you really think that would work?" Tarou asked.

"You'll pay for that!" Nakagawa shouted as he made another attempt to punch Tarou. However, Tarou stood there as if he wanted the punch, not bringing out his pistol.

"Fine for me to not use your gun," Nakagawa said as he got close to Tarou.

Nakagawa's right fist neared Tarou's face. Tarou continued to stand still. As the fist of the former was only a meter before the face of the latter, it stopped.

Sunan Wattana just arrived near the entrance of the station. If she planned on helping Tarou, she was too late. Upon arriving, she found that Tarou was able to punch Nakagawa at his belly with his left fist.

"Is that all you got?" Tarou asked.

Nakagawa was unable to respond. He then fell to the ground. Uminari, already getting back up, rushed to help Nakagawa.

"Cease this at once and I will not reveal those text messages," Tarou warned.

"Fine, fine, you win!" Uminari replied.

"And I will be going now." Tarou began to leave the station with both Uminari and Nakagawa watching, but not before picking up the shell casing that fell out of the P226 earlier.

"With his gun and how fast he put us into the ground, he's no mere transfer student," Uminari warned Nakagawa.

As Tarou exited the station entrance, Wattana and Frederick Dirks joined him. "I really have taught you well," Wattana complimented.

"Thanks," Tarou replied.

"Now you best return to the condominium," Dirks warned. "You still have to study."

"Acknowledged," Tarou replied. 'But I need to drop off Miss Wattana at the *Iron Dutchman*."

"Speaking of which, I must warn you about something Wattana warned everyone but you and Dr. Hamilton about earlier."

"What is it?"

"Remember that guy Wouter told me to follow?" Wattana rhetorically asked to remind Tarou. "I took this photo."

"Wait," Dirks interjected, forcing Wattana and Tarou to stop. He reared his head toward Morinomiya Station.

"What is it?" Wattana asked.

"We better continue this discussion at the trainyard. Nakagwa and Uminari will hear us."

"Agreed," Tarou replied.

#

Trainyard near Osaka Castle Ruins. 2200 hours

Dirks, Tarou, and Wattana reached the old trainyard. Picking up from where they left off, Wattana brought out her smartphone and, accessing the Pictures application, Wattana found the photograph she showed to Dirks and the rest of Iron Dutchman Services the previous night. The photograph was that of the man Wattana claimed to have met the previous day, whom they didn't know bore the name Pyotr Chadov, coming inside the building that was the OVR's safehouse in Kansai City. There, Chadov went inside with a man who didn't show his face, yet this man was none other than Serdar Muhadow.

"The man I met yesterday brought someone over," Wattana explained. "As soon as I took this photo, I bailed because had I stayed longer, they would have noticed me."

"And where is this building?" Tarou asked.

"Also in Suminoe Ward," Dirks answered. "Near the Sembom Matsu Bridge."

"What do we do?"

"For now, nothing. We don't know who this man is other than his accent. As Wattana said, he could be from the Russian Soviet Federative Socialist Republic, but the fact he let someone inside the building is something that cannot be ignored. I'll have to inform Mr. Hoshikawa and, speaking of which… his daughter Maria started inquiring to her father about that PCX of yours."

"She did that?"

"That was smart of her to deduce that," Wattana remarked.

"Kind of my fault," Dirks added. "In the two times I contacted Hoshikawa before this, I used messages inside empty coffee bottles. His daughter must have noticed those bottles because I always made sure her father found those bottles while he and his family heard Mass and she must have connected it to the PCX."

"What will happen now?"

"If you run into her tomorrow, at the earliest, I suggest you act normal."

"Understood."

"We best get out of here," Wattana said. "Ganji has to study and sleep for tomorrow."

"Agreed," Dirks replied.

#

Suminoe Hostel, Suminoe Ward. 2300 hours

Serdar Muhadow had found a room at the Suminoe Hostel. It was the best he was able to afford with his budget, as it was limited for a week in Japan until he devised a way to capture Maria Hoshikawa. There, he had gone over intelligence provided to him by Tatiana Ioannovna Tsulukidize's OVR cell.

Based on what they've given me, they've managed to act out as refugees from the Soviet Remnant, Muhadow thought. *I'd like to know how they got that piece of hair that convinces "Elizaveta", or should I say Tatiana Ioannovna Tsulukidze to investigate as to who Maria Hoshikawa really is, but they make it clear they won't tell me. Whatever. I best devise something and gain more intelligence myself before coming up with something.*

OVR Safehouse, Nishinari Ward. 2300 hours

At the same time, Tatiana Ionanovna Tsulukidze spent time alone in her thoughts. She had instructed her subordinates to not disturb her lest it was urgent at times like these. Although her assignment to Japan was an order, she knew that she was only assigned there because of her family.

Yet Tatiana had done enough to earn such an assignment and these times by herself were when she could think about her past. Because she was the only daughter of Tsar Ivan Vladimirovich Tsulukidze, she was sheltered most of the time compared to her older twin brothers Viktor and Iosif. That didn't last as Tatiana opted to join any of the branches within the Imperial Eurasian Armed Forces, much to the surprise of her entire family. Reluctantly, her father allowed it as by this time, he reformed the military education system of the Eurasian Tsardom to be different as a contrast to how it was in the days of the Tsarist Russian Empire and the Union of Soviet Socialist Republics. In territories under his domain during the Unification War, Ivan had Viktor and Iosif study at the Tver Suvorov Military School as they became adolescents.

By the time Tatiana asked to join the military, she was seventeen years old, but unlike her brothers, she wasn't a student at any of the Suvorov schools for adolescent males. It was only around this time Ivan had finished his reforms, where the Suvorov schools were to act as universities for those who've finished upper secondary education for those who wished to join the Imperial Eurasian Armed Forces as officers.

Reluctantly, Ivan agreed to allow Tatiana into the military, but she had to obtain higher education at a Suvorov school. Tatiana then chose the Kiev Suvorov Military School and after four years, she graduated as a *Mládshiy Leytenánt.* Unlike her brothers, Tatiana applied to be an officer for the Imperial Airborne Division of the Imperial Air Force, itself a separate service branch from the Imperial Eurasian Army and the Imperial Eurasian Navy, which Viktor and Iosif respectively served at. While assigned to the 2nd Brigade, Tatiana heard news that would change her life forever.

On January 2, 2013, Viktor was found dead. As a result, Iosif was made the *Tsesarevich*, as Viktor was the older twin. This was of grave concern for Tatiana as not only was she close to her brother but she feared what would happen should Iosif become Tsar. She wasn't alone with this fear as she was approached by a family friend—Vyacheslav Leonidovich Puzanov. He came to Tatiana with an invitation to join the *Otdeleniye Vneshney Razvedi* as a way to figure out how Viktor died and what became of his bride Svetlana Eduardovich Sonina. Naturally, Puzanov and Tatiana asked for Ivan's blessing, which he reluctantly gave. After two years of foreign language studies, Tatiana joined the OVR. After assignments in the Asian Pact's Russian Soviet Federative Socialist Republic and the Federative Republic of Moldova in the Commonwealth of Euro-African States, Tatiana was given the assignment of operating a safehouse in Kansai City. This was where two men, Pyotr Stepanovich Chadov and Karim Olegovich Zhakiyanov, were assigned to her.

Tatiana then stopped her reminiscing. She stood up and left her office.

Invitation

Cheri Café/Kitakagaya Station, Suminoe Ward, Kansai City, Kansai Prefecture; State of Japan. April 11, 2030; 0800 hours (Japan Standard Time)

Serdar Muhadow began his first day as a "tourist" at a café attached to Suminoe Hostel called Cheri Café. After his meal, he left and walked to his next destination, which required five turns.

After those five turns, the last one involving crossing the Nanko-dori that started from Suminoe Ward up until the Hirano Ward, Muhadow reached the Kitakagaya Station. The station was a part of the Yotsubashi Line of the Osaka Metro, the underground rail transit system that served Osaka.

While the rail transit system survived the destruction of Osaka during the Third World War, many lines that were a part of the system were split apart due to the city becoming a flooded crater while some were rendered extinct. The Yotsubashi Line was one example as it started from the Suminoekoen Station up until the Nishi-Umeda Station; the latter now underneath the crater created by the nuclear warhead. Now, the Yotsubashi Line started from Suminoekoen up until the Hanazonocho Station.

After buying his ticket, Muhadow increased the speed of his walking as he needed to reach the train. Miraculously, he made it just as the train arrived. As soon as the doors opened, Muhadow boarded the train.

#

Kishinosato Station, Nishinari Ward. 0825 hours

Muhadow's train reached Kishinosato Station at the Nishinari Ward. Upon handing over his ticket after leaving the train, Muhadow began to exit the station.

Once he did, he found Pyotr Stepanovich Chadov waiting for him with a van. "Spasibo," Muhadow said upon seeing the OVR agent.

"Get in," Chadov ordered.

OVR Safehouse. 0844 hours

Both Chadov and Muhadow reached the OVR safehouse near the Sembom Matsu Bridge. After Karim Olegovich Zhakiyanov let them inside, he took them to the office of Tatiana Ioannovna Tsulukidze.

"How was your first morning here in Japan?" Tatiana asked.

"Got breakfast at the café beside the hostel," Muhadow answered.

"Now that you're here, what can you do for us?"

"Going over the information I've been given, you intend to capture Maria Hoshikawa?"

"Da. We need to engineer an opportunity to get her."

"I think I can help with that but I need to do things my way."

"How so?"

"We need to test how good are the mercenaries the FIS hired to protect Gospatzitza Hoshikawa."

"And how will you do that?"

"I just need to find some boorish idiots willing to help… for a price."

"I leave that to you."

"Spasibo."

#

Nishi High School, Higashiosaka Ward. 1218 hours

At his table in Class 2-2's room at Nishi High School, Tarou Ganji ate his usual lunch. However, this lunch wasn't to be a normal one.

"What's she doing here?" Tarou stopped eating at that question with similar ones asked as he saw the subject of the questions, Maria Hoshikawa, outside the room.

He knew why Maria would come to Class 2-2 and walked up to her, much to the puzzlement of the class. "I assume you're here for me?" Tarou asked.

"Sou desu," Maria answered. "Please follow me."

"Hai."

As Maria began to leave, Tarou left the room. Everyone, mostly the boys, barely hid their envy that a transfer student like Tarou Ganji would be sought out by Maria Hoshikawa, seen as the school's idol.

#

1239 hours

Both Tarou and Maria reached the bicycle rack. Upon reaching Tarou's PCX scooter, they stopped.

"You needed to discuss something with me?" Tarou asked upon biting the apple strudel he carried with him.

"I know my father got you this scooter," Maria admitted as she pointed at the PCX.

If you run into her tomorrow, at the earliest, I suggest you act normal, Tarou thought as he remembered the order Frederick Dirks gave to him the previous night. "I admit it. Your father had a hand with why I transferred here."

"I see. I confronted my father about it this morning. In any case, my father wishes to invite you and Hamilton-sensei to have lunch with us this Sunday. Do you accept this invitation?"

"I do," Tarou answered without hesitation.

"Domo arigatou gozaimasu," Maria replied before bowing. "You can return to your room now. I do apologize for this."

"I apologize for not mentioning your father."

"I understand. We best return before lunch break ends."

#

1254 hours

Upon returning to Class 2-2's room, Tarou found himself stared by most boys in the room. As he reached his desk and sat down, Riku Todoh leaned on him with his jealously bare on his face.

"What's with you?" Tarou asked.

"You got to be with Hoshikawa-senpai," Riku answered. "Do you know *lucky* you are?"

"Does it matter? She knew I was being sponsored by her father and, for some reason, she wants to invite me and my guardian to have lunch with her and her family this weekend."

"*Many* will deprive themselves of an eye and an arm to be with Hoshikawa-senpai."

"Is she that important?"

"Do you not remember what we discussed when we first met!?"

"Look, I don't know why she's taking an interest in me. I'll go along with it because it would be rude otherwise. Now please prepare yourself because lunch break is about to end."

"Kiritsu!" a female voice, presumably Class 2-2's representative, ordered. Everyone then stood up, as this was the end of lunch break.

#

Near Hoshikawa Group Headquarters, Taisho Ward. 1300 hours

Near Hoshikawa Group Headquarters, a bus reached a stop in front of an *izakaya.* One man stepped out of the bus and his name was Serdar Muhadow.

Now, from what I was told by Grand Duchess Tatiana, Daisuke Hoshikawa's secretary tends to go out for lunch around this area, Muhadow thought as he began walking. *She told me the secretary has-*

Muhaodw stopped walking and thinking because he saw a woman with long brown hair in a high ponytail crossing the street. *That's her!* Muhadow thought. *That must be Hoshikawa's secretary. Just stand and watch. Only follow after the cars are gone.*

Once the woman finished crossing the street, Muhadow paid attention to her movements. As Muhadow predicted, the cars began to move as soon as the woman left the street. Luckily for Muhadow, the wait wasn't long as after the cars passed, the next ones to appear weren't able to reach the crossing before the street light turned red. That allowed Muhadow to cross the street.

Now, if I remember, that secretary likes to eat at a Chinese restaurant, Muhadow thought before bringing out his smartphone.

Accessing the "Maps" application, Muhadow zoomed in to go over the map of Kansai City. Finding where he was, Muhadow found the Chinese restaurant nearby and put away his phone to continue moving.

As he reached the restaurant, he found the secretary leaving with a bag of what she had bought inside. Sensing an opportunity, Muhadow wisely remained where he stood, but as soon as a container carried by the woman began to fall, Muhadow seized the opportunity by rushing to her and getting the container before it fell on the ground.

"A… Arigatou," the woman replied.

"Mondai nai," Muhadow replied in flawless Japanese. "Eigo ga hanasemasu ka?"

"I do," the woman answered.

"I apologize for this, but I'm still not good enough to keep a full conversation in Japanese."

"Where are you from?"

"Qatar."

"Good to know, but could we please resume this discussion elsewhere? I'll be late."

"Before we leave, I actually came here to Japan because I'm a businessman wishing to do business with Hoshikawa Group."

"For what purpose?"

"That I can only discuss where these containers are going."

#

Hoshikawa Group Headquarters. 1339 hours

Muhadow and Daisuke's secretary reached Hoshikawa Group Headquarters. After explaining to the guard that Muhadow was a businessman, he was allowed to follow the secretary inside.

Both then reached the mess hall. Many men came around the woman as she handed them the food she bought from the Chinese restaurant. After the last colleague left, Muhadow and the woman began to resume their conversation outside the restaurant.

"So why did you come here to Japan to seek us out?" the secretary asked.

"I wish to ask Mr. Hoshikawa to invest for a newly established company I'm a part of."

"What's its name?"

"Doha E-Logistics. The 'E' means 'Electronics'."

"I take it you're into electronics distribution?"

"That's right."

"Now, what's your name?"

"Mansur Fahri."

"My name's Kirika Nonaka. I work as Mr. Hoshikawa's personal secretary"

"I don't suppose you can try to convince Mr. Hoshikawa to seek me out."

"I'll see what I can do. Do you have any contact information?"

"Hold on." Muhadow began to dig through his pockets. Luckily, he had a business card and gave it to Nonaka.

"Thank you. I assume that's all you wish to do here as soon as we came inside?"

"That's right."

"Before you leave, you can help yourself to the food here if you're interested. I only bought that Chinese food for myself and those I owed favors to."

"Thank you."

"Now I must return to my desk," Nonaka said before standing up and bowing.

After bowing, Nonaka took her container and left Muhadow. Muhadow then opted to buy from the mess hall and although he wasn't an employee, Muhadow was able to buy his meal. After eating and drinking what he bought, he returned the tray with the used containers and left.

OVR Safehouse, Nishinari Ward. 1526 hours

"How was your trip?" Tatiana Ioannovna Tsulukidze asked as Muhadow entered her office in the OVR Safehouse.

"Good," Muhadow answered. "When Kirika Nonaka asked for a business card, she doesn't know what it really is."

"What is it?"

"A hacking module. I'll be able to figure out what's on her computer because she's Daisuke Hoshikawa's secretary and she must know events that we can use to get her daughter."

"Then use this hacking module already."

"Hold on." Muhadow brought out his smartphone and, accessing an application named "CardHack", he found that the "business card" he gave to Nonaka detected a computer that was turned on.

Finding the option "Hack Computer", Muhadow pressed it. As he did, a meter appeared, with a small blue square increasing its length to show progress on the hacking.

"As soon as you get everything from that application, you copy it and cease," Tatiana ordered.

"Zametano," Muhadow replied.

Both Muhadow and Tatiana resumed paying attention to the hacking. Miraculously, the length of the square, now a rectangle, increased its length at a favorable rate. That meant the hacking was almost done.

"I'll get us water to drink," Tatiana declared. "Please sit down."

"Spasibo," Muhadow replied as Tatiana left the room.

Once Muhadow sat down on the office's sofa, he resumed looking at the meter. Now, the speed as to which the rectangle increased its length was slow, which meant that sensitive files were next to be hacked.

Muhadow then opted to go to another application, as he can be notified if the hacking was finished. The application Muhadow traveled to was named "News" and it provided what it was named after: news on the world.

The article Muhadow opened concerned another attack in the Eurasian Tsardom's Iran Governorate. However, Tatiana had just returned to her office with two bottles of water.

"I got us water," Tatiana announced, making Muhadow stand up to face her. "Now, anything new on the hacking?"

Just then, an announcement appeared on Muhadow's smartphone, saying "Hacking complete. Files are ready to view".

"It's finished, but let me see what we got before we copy the files," Muhadow announced in response.

Muhadow now saw the files that he hacked from Nonaka's computer. He then began to make sure all the files were to be copied to his e-mail address. Both knew that they have to wait, yet they feared that the files wouldn't be copied fast enough because the hack will be noticed by Japan's domestic intelligence apparatus and the Foreign Intelligence Service.

Despite that, both knew that they needed to calm their respective minds. They opted to drink the water Tatiana got.

As Muhadow joined Tatiana at her desk, the latter gave the former a bottle. Before opening the bottle, Muhadow put down his smartphone, as he knew the copying of the files from Nonaka's computer wouldn't be fast. After putting down the phone, he opened his bottle and drank like a cat.

Only after drinking half the bottle did Muhadow check on how much was copied. Upon opening the smartphone, he found that only fifty percent of the files have been copied.

It was then that Pyotr Stepanovich Chadov appeared. "You're back," Chadov said upon seeing Muhadow.

"I am," Muhadow replied upon turning to Chadov.

"Anything you have to report, Pytor?" Tatiana asked.

"Da," Pyotr answered upon facing Tatiana. "Not much has changed with Maria Hoshikawa, but… "

"But what?"

"She's been talking to a male student that appears to be a transfer student. Didn't catch his name, but he owns a PCX scooter."

How could a transfer student already own a PCX? Muhadow pondered before he resumed looking at his phone on the progress of the files he hacked from Nonaka's computer being copied to his e-mail address. *Either way, at least I know now how Tatiana got that piece of hair she claimed to have received.*

"Mukhadov, how goes the progress of those files being copied?" Tatiana asked upon turning to Muhadow.

"Going well," Muhadow answered. "It's almost done and I've not been notified that anyone's noticed the computer being hacked."

"That's good. Once those files are copied, please send copies to me."

"I'll need your e-mail address, though."

"You're dismissed for now. Just send us copies when you return to Suminoe Hostel. As usual, Pyotr will take you to Kishinosato Station."

"Zametano."

#

Kitakagaya Station/Kitakagaya Café, Suminoe Ward. 1609 hours

Muhadow then exited Kitakagaya Station. He then brought out his smartphone to see how much of the files he hacked from Kirika Nonaka's computer have been copied to hius e-mail address.

It's finished, Muhadow thought as he found that all files had been copied. *I best turn off the hacking tool because it must have become a blip in the radar of Japanese intelligence, but I can't stand around for long. I need somewhere to do this and to send copies to Tatiana.*

Muhadow used the Maps application yet again. Going to the area around Kitakagaya Station, he found many restaurants nearby and to Muhadow, one restaurant was what he needed as a place to do what he needed to do.

It's too early for dinner, so I need a café to do my business. Luckily, there's one really close that all I have to do is look left while walking.

Muhadow continued walking and reaching the intersection past the pedestrian crossing he took earlier, managing to remember the name of the café and how to find it. He stopped upon seeing the café's sign with its name, "Kitakagaya Café".

Muhadow then stepped inside. After the "Irasshaimase" greeting, Muhadow then sat down. Normally, the café, like many, would accept adolescent students, but many were a part of a club, so Muhadow had no trouble finding a table.

After receiving the menu from a waitress that was as old as his target, Muhadow opted to forward the copies of the files he hacked from Nonaka's computer to Tatiana's e-mail address, which he received before leaving the OVR safehouse in Nishinari Ward.

"Excuse me, have you decided on an order yet?" the same waitress who gave Muhadow the menu asked as she appeared.

"Yes," Muhadow hesitantly asked. "I'll have your toast with egg and a cup of coffee, please. The coffee must be sweetened, of course."

"Domo- I mean, thank you."

"It's alright. I'm only here for business so I had some mistakes with Japanese myself. Might I know your name, please?"

"Akagi Ryoka desu."

"Mansur Fahri."

"Thank you for your order."

Once Akagi left, Muhadow resumed with what he really came to Café Kitakagaya for. While he had the files he hacked from Nonaka copied, Muhadow turned off his CardHack application.

Good, Muhadow thought. *Not only was I not detected, but with the hacking module disabled, I don't have to fear being detected and I copied every file I took from Nonaka's computer. All I have to do now is enjoy the meal I ordered, then return to the hostel to look at those files.*

#

Suminoe Hostel. 1645 hours

Muhadow then returned to his room in the Suminoe Hostel. Now that he was alone, Muhadow began to access the files he got from Nonaka's computer.

As Nonaka was Daisuke Hoshikawa's secretary, this allowed her access to private matters within the Hoshikawa family. This was useful to Muhadow, as he can formulate a plan to capture Daisuke's daughter Maria.

Look what we have here, Muhadow thought as he found a folder with the name "Schedule of Hoshikawa Family".

Pressing the folder, Muhadow found more folders. One folder read "Schedules" and pressed it. Inside this folder were documents and a particular document bore the name "Schedule for Hoshikawa Nemuro Hotel Opening".

A hotel opening? Muhadow pondered. *What's this about?*

Muhadow pressed the file. He found that the document was dated April 21. *This is it!* Muhadow thought. *An event like this is what I needed. All I need are my men, material to start a fire with, and a way to travel to the Gatekeepers' facility in Sakhalin Island without being detected.*

Muhadow then began to use GOKMail. Typing in "GJYS" in the search bar "Find Contacts", he was shown a rectangle with the words "You've started a conversation with GJYS". Muhadow typed where he stayed at and that he acquired the information he needed to capture Maria.

After pressing "Send", Muhadow then uploaded the document named "Hoshikawa Nemuro Hotel Opening" into another message and pressed "Send" again.

The wait for the reply wasn't long as Gatekeeper Japan replied:

Thank you for this information. Please give me time to read this schedule, then I'll listen to what your plan is and what you need.

Thank you Gatekeeper Japan, Muhadow thought, which he also wrote as a reply in GOKMail.

Once Muhadow finished typing in the reply, he pressed "Send". *And now, I'm going back to that news story. I don't want to eat just yet, so I got plenty of time.*

Muhadow returned to the News application and patiently digging through the stories that had been added ever since he left the application hours before, Muhadow found the article he intended on reading in the OVR safehouse had Tatiana Ioannovna Tsulukidze not interrupted him.

As Muhadow read the article concerning the rebellion in Iran, Muhadow reflected on how Iran was conquered by the Eurasian Tsardom because he had a hand with how the war started. This also made Muhadow think back on his past.

Born on February 27, 1984 to Turkmens living in the Democratic Republic of Afghanistan, Muhadow was only an infant when the alien ship that was given the name *Revelator* crashed into Afghanistan. He and his family survived as they lived in the northeast near the border with the Turkmen Soviet Socialist Republic and while he and his family cheated death yet again throughout the Third World War, their luck vanished like a glass of water when someone drank it because he or she was thirsty.

Muhadow's family became victims of the Unification War when it started. As a result, he was abducted by one Soviet officer, who opted to create his own nation-state as a result of the USSR's collapse in the world war. Eventually, this warlord's faction was destroyed by Eurasian Tsardom forces as they began their conquest of the former Soviet republics in Central Asia and Muhadow would be taken in by the Gatekeepers of Knowledge.

This was both a blessing and a curse for Muhadow. While he learned many languages, history, and some mathematics, Muhadow, however, never escaped the loss of his innocence. This was what the Gatekeepers intended as they built their own military and that Muhadow was recruited into this military.

Other than defending possessions of the Gatekeepers, which the Gatekeepers swore to do with its military yet had secret purposes for their military, Muhadow was given an additional order: operate as a mercenary leader. This was to gather intelligence for the Gatekeepers, and Muhadow had no such problem obeying this order.

Due to his experience, he became a Gatekeeper-Colonel and one example of a mercenary contract being an opportunity to spy for the Gatekeepers was with the Islamic Republic of Iran. The Eurasian Tsardom's invasion of Iran in 2023 was the result of the Iranian government, offered assistance by the Gatekeepers in reconstruction, argued with them over how it was to be done. This led to the Gatekeepers scheming for the destruction of Iran and they did this by engineering a war with the Eurasian Tsardom.

As he was a Turkmen and that Iran hosted a noteworthy population of Turkmens, Muhadow was tasked in making the war. He and his mercenary outfit offered their services to the Iranian government, which allowed them weapons and uniforms. Their plan was to raid an Imperial Eurasian Army border post with those weapons and uniforms. While they did this, the Gatekeepers infiltrated teams to established bombs across Iranian government offices. When Muhadow launched his attack, the bombs were detonated.

This began an eight-month war between the Eurasian Tsardom and Iran. The new government then kept Muhadow and his unit, as there was a need for additional manpower. Like in the war Iran had with the Iraqi Republic that was ruled by Saddam Hussein from 1980 until 1988, Iran made soldiers out of children as young as eight. Muhadow's unit was tasked with training these children into being soldiers.

Despite that, the war ended in victory for the Tsardom because they were willing to utilize nuclear weapons against a country that lacked them. Muhadow was then ordered to abandon the Iranians and, since then, continued serving the Gatekeepers in this fashion.

In the present, Muhadow finished reading his story and found that evening had come. For him, it was time to get dinner and that meant leaving the hostel.

#

Mamekan. 1800 hours

Muhadow then arrived at an *izakaya* that was near Suminoe Hostel named Mamekan. After finding a seat and table, receiving the menu, and telling what his orders were, Muhadow found that Gatekeeper Japan sent another message on GOKMail that read:

I've read that file. Now I wish to know about your plan.

Muhadow then typed his response:

Currently eating dinner. I apologize for this, but I will tell you after my dinner.

Once Muhadow finished his message, he pressed "Send". After that, he hid his phone. At that point, the wait had ended as Muhadow's order, *yakitori* and *goma-ae,* along with a glass of *sake.*

Although a foreigner, the people in charge of Mamekan paid no attention to what Muhadow would do upon receiving his meal, and the latter knew this. As a result, he immediately started on his meal without saying "Itadakimasu".

#

Suminoe Hostel. 1950 hours

Muhadow then returned to Suminoe Hostel. He then brought out his smartphone and used his GOKMail.

Picking up where he left off with Gatekeeper Japan, Muhadow began to type in his message that read:

Finished my dinner. I'm ready to discuss my plan with you.

Muhadow then pressed "Send". Now, he waited for Gatekeeper Japan's reply.

#

Iron Dutchman, Taisho Ward. 2019 hours

"You mean to tell me Maria Hoshikawa invited you and Doc to have with her and her family this Sunday?" Wouter Vos asked Tarou Ganji after the latter informed him about Maria Hoshikawa's invitation while they were in the briefing room of the *Iron Dutchman.*

"I confirm it," Tarou answered.

"You *really* have the luck of the Devil for that to happen," Jason Luke Crawley remarked.

"Do you think we should do it?" Anita Hamilton asked.

"I, for one, say yes," Frederick Dirks answered. "I didn't think she would tell her father about her suspicions this quickly."

"But won't this require fancy attire that we can't afford?" Sunan Wattana asked.

"I'll take care of that," Dirks answered upon turning to Tarou. "Ganji, just tell Maria you accept the invitation and ask if formal attire is needed."

"Got it," Tarou replied.

OVR Safehouse, Nishinari Ward. April 12, 2030; 0930 hours

"So that's your plan?" Tatiana Ioannova Tsulukidze asked after Serdar Muhadow came to her safehouse's office and explained to her the plan he devised, which he told Gatekeeper Japan the previous evening. Both Pyotr Stepanovich Chadov and Karim Olegovich Zhakiyanov were also in the office and had listened to Muhadov's plan.

"Da," Muhadov answered. "Of course, I'll need a way to join my subordinates."

"I know of a way. I always use it whenever I'm needed at the capital to report to the Director."

"Do tell. I might need it at any time for any contingencies."

#

Nishi High School, Higashiosaka Ward. 1215 hours

Tarou Ganji, with the cutlet sandwich and apple strudel for lunch as usual, returned to the floor in Nishi High School where Class 2-2's room was located at. However, as he neared the room, he saw Maria Hoshikawa waiting by the room's door.

"Have you thought of an answer to the invitation I offered yesterday?" Maria asked.

"I have," Tarou answered. "Dr. Hamilton and I accept."

"We made reservations at the restaurant named Demeter, located at the Cosmo Square Building. Come before two in the afternoon."

"Will we need formal attire?"

"Up to you. My father won't be wearing a blazer."

"Thank you."

"There you are, Maria-chan." Both Maria and Tarou turned to find Misa Todoh approaching them, only for her to stop.

"Misa-chan, what are you doing here?" Maria asked upon turning to Misa.

"I could ask you the same thing."

"So it's true," Misa said as she turned to Tarou. "So you're the transfer student I've heard about."

"I apologize for how I'll ask, but who are you?" Tarou asked warily.

"Misa Todoh. Yorushiku."

"Again, I apologize if I've wasted your time along with Hoshikawa-senpai." Tarou bowed after his second apology. "I must go inside then."

Tarou continued toward Class 2-2's room. Due to how the situation evolved, Maria was unable to say anything.

"Now why are you here?" Misa asked.

"Nothing really," Maria answered.

"Doesn't look like it's 'nothing'. That transfer student's the reason why you've been frequenting this floor, right?"

"If that's all it takes to end this, yes."

"Then can we please return to our room?"

"Fine."

#

Port Café, Doha Port, Doha, Al-Dawhah; State of Qatar. 0619 hours (Arabia Standard Time)

Omar Mahmud arrived at the café he owned at the Doha Corniche. Just as he brought out the key for the lock used to make sure no one entered Port Café while it was closed, another finger touched his left shoulder.

"Again," Mahmud complained while rearing his head only for his eyes to widen and for his mouth to be slightly open with his teeth clenched, as if he saw a ghost.

"Omar Mahmud, you're under arrest," a woman in uniform said. She belonged to one of the State of Qatar's three law enforcement agencies, the Rescue Police Department.

Adjustment Part 1

Iron Dutchman, Taisho Ward, Kansai City, Kansai Prefecture; State of Japan. April 14, 1340 hours (Japan Standard Time)

At his room in the *Iron Dutchman*, Tarou Ganji was in the middle of putting on a suit. However, he had no such experience because of how he grew up and as a result, Frederick Dirks was also in the room assisting in putting on the suit.

"I must ask, Mr. 'Smith', how did you get this suit?" Tarou asked as Dirks put on a red tie with blue dots around the neck of the former.

"It's all rental," Dirks answered. "That means you can't keep this with you after this business."

"I understand."

"After this, you will have to finish up on your own because we need to leave as soon as possible."

"Roger."

"You really don't seem nervous about having to wear a suit?"

"It's part of the mission. If I am nervous, I won't be able to fulfill the mission."

"You're right about that. Now get in your blazer."

There was no reply from Tarou. Getting the blazer on his bed, which was colored onyx like his trousers, Tarou put it around the bright turquoise button-up shirt he wore while Dirks put the red tie around his neck.

"Now I just need to tighten the tie a little," Dirks declared. "Please stand still."

Tarou said nothing again, only complied. Dirks used his right hand to hold the red tie firmly and his left hand to tighten the knot. Having worn ties before, Dirks knew how tight the knot ought to be and thus, when he stopped, he stopped.

"There," Dirks said. "Now I suggest waiting somewhere that's cold. You'll sweat if you stay here for long."

"I'll go to the dining hall. We use a fan there to cool ourselves."

"Good idea. You best hurry because it's preferable that we go there before the Hoshikawa's notice we'll be late."

"Aren't they the ones who invited me and Dr. Hamilton? So wouldn't it be a problem that the people invited show up before those who invited them."

"That's a good possibility, but I'd rather that you and Dr. Hamilton leave as soon as she finishes."

"One last thing: I remember Mr. Crawley telling me that women need make-up for events like this. Where did you get the make-up?"

"I got it from my wife. Like that suit you're wearing, the make-up has to be returned. Now please go to the dining hall."

"Roger that." Tarou then left his room. He noticed Wouter Vos waiting outside as he left.

"Nice suit," Vos complimented.

"Thank you, Mr. Vos," Tarou replied. "I'll be at the dining hall."

Tarou continued to move to the dining hall. As soon as he exited the room of the former, Dirks joined Vos.

"How did you even rent that suit?" Vos asked.

"Had to ask Vue," Dirks answered.

"Who?"

"He's also FIS. That's all you need to know. Surprisingly, Ganji fits in that suit."

"I just hope Ganji doesn't say or do anything stupid there."

"That's where Dr. Hamilton comes in."

"Fair enough. Now let's join Ganji until we hear from Doc."

"Good. I forgot to give Ganji this." Dirks then brought out a spider that was made of metal.

"What's that?" Vos asked upon seeing the metal spider.

"It's a tracking device delivery system," Dirks answered. "I figured this would be a good time to have this inserted as close as possible to Miss Hoshikawa."

"Should have known you would resort to that trick. How will you insert that thing?"

"We'll tell Ganji that now. Let's move."

"I'll tell Sunan first. I'll follow afterward."

#

1346 hours

Tarou then reached the dining hall. He found that the electric fan used to cool the room when its occupied was already turned on because Tatev Mirzoyan was already inside using her laptop computer.

Upon hearing the door, Tatev turned to find Tarou. She stood as she saw Tarou arrive in his suit. Unlike the normal clothes he wears, Tatev saw Tarou differently and was filled with many emotions.

"Tatev, what's wrong?" Tarou asked, with a combination of confusion and concern in his tone.

I can't believe he asked what's wrong with me. Tatev pondered while desperately hiding her emotions as she continuously looked at Tarou in his suit. Jason Luke Crawley appeared and noticed what happened but couldn't help that he smiled upon seeing Tatev reacting to Tarou in his suit.

"Mr. Crawley, what's going on?" Tarou asked.

"It's simple, my friend," Crawley happily answered. "Tatev's gushing that you're in a suit."

"Gushing?"

"She's a girl and you're a boy. Both of you are of the same age and you're in a suit. Naturally, a girl like Tatev would react this way."

"Please stop… " Tatev pleaded, as it was clear she was having trouble concentrating.

"Tatev, please, if there's something you're doing here, calm down," Tarou pleaded.

"… Right." Tatev then returned to her computer. She was now using the application for utilizing the proximity sensor Vos planted earlier that week near the Hoshikawa Mansion. "The Hoshikawas have begun to move."

"What?"

"What did you find, Mirzoyan?" Frederick Dirks asked as he and Wouter Vos appeared.

Both Tarou and Crawley forced themselves inside to let Dirks and Vos follow them. All moved toward Tatev and her computer.

On the computer screen was the map of Kansai City enlarged to show the area surrounding the Hoshikawa Mansion. Four blue dots appeared with three close to each other, with one joining the fourth one. This was until all four blue dots were close together.

"Those must be the Hoshikawas about to move to the restaurant," Dirks deduced. "Mirzoyan, what time is it?"

"Already two in the afternoon," Tatev answered as she looked at the time shown at the lower-right of the computer's screen.

"Damn it," Vos lamented. "Aren't Sunan and Doc finished yet?"

"Yeah, yeah, we're here."

Everyone turned to find Sunan Wattana and Anita Hamilton arriving at the dining hall. The latter wore a white sleeveless dress that almost reached the knees. Her footwear consisted of brown flat slip-on shoes and she carried a purse of the same color.

Everyone but Wattana was now surprised by what Hamilton wore. Ever since she joined Iron Dutchman Services, it was either her usual attire as a doctor or the most casual of clothes. This made it hard to reconcile that Hamilton was forty-nine years old.

"Well, what are you lot waiting for?" Wattana asked. "Don't we have to get to Bay Hotel?"

"… Right," Dirks answered. "Speaking of which… "

Dirks then brought out the metal spider and gave it to Tarou. "Place this beneath your chair when you reach Demeter," Dirks instructed to Tarou. "I'll control it from here."

"What is it?" Tarou asked.

"A tracking device delivery system. It'll do what it's called, but I'll control it. Just take it with you and place it underneath your table."

"Roger that."

"Now get going," Vos commanded to Tarou and Wattana.

In front of the INTEX Center, Suminoe Ward. 1421 hours

Both Tarou and Hamilton reached the Nankokita neighborhood of Suminoe Ward. This part of Kansai City was built to accommodate foreign tourists and investors. This part of Kansai City hosted the International Exhibition (INTEX) Center.

Tarou stopped the PCX scooter to look for where they were to go. Both then found a particular tower to their left and Hamilton brought out her smartphone. Going to the application named "Pictures", Hamilton found the same building in a picture and that picture is named "Cosmo Square Building".

"Doc, what is it?" Tarou asked.

"I found the Cosmo Square Building," Hamilton answered before pointing at the tower named the Bay Hotel for Tarou to find.

"Nearby is a parking lot. I'll see if we can use it."

Tarou continued moving the PCX toward the parking lot he spotted to his and Hamilton's right. After waiting at the stoplight, Tarou had to turn back to enter the parking lot and miraculously, he was allowed inside and given a parking space because scooters had to be parked differently. After parking the PCX, Tarou and Hamilton exited the parking lot and moved as fast as they could to the Cosmo Square Building.

#

Demeter/Bay Hotel, Cosmo Square Building. 1429 hours

Both Tarou and Hamilton made it to the Cosmo Square Building, which hosted the Bay Hotel; named as such because it faced Osaka Bay. Going to the nearest concierge, Tarou and Hamilton asked where the Demeter restaurant was, claiming they were invited by the Hoshikawa family.

After being directed as to where the hotel's three restaurants were, Tarou and Hamilton thanked the concierge and went to the elevator. Reaching the three restaurants located at the hotel's first floor, the two mercenaries were able to find Demeter because of the directions.

Once they repeated who invited them to the restaurant, the waiter allowed Tarou and Hamilton inside. The latter two were able to find the table the Hoshikawas were seated at, with two chairs already prepared for them.

"Glad you could make it," Daisuke Hoshikawa said to Tarou and Hamilton.

"Thank you, Mr. Hoshikawa," Hamilton replied.

"So you're Dr. Hamilton," Miku Hoshikawa (née Sayama) said. "My husband told me about you."

Miku offered her right hand, with Hamilton accepting it. "Nice to meet you."

"And this is Tarou Ganji, I presume?" Miku asked upon turning to Tarou.

"Hajimemashite," Tarou replied before bowing.

"Now now, that will be enough pleasantries," Daisuke interrupted. "Please sit down."

"Right," Hamilton replied before she and Tarou sat down.

A waitress appeared with five menus and gave them to each individual occupying the table. Once they got the menus, the occupants began to read their respective menus for what they want and although the menus were also written in English alongside Japanese, their curiosity delayed what they wish to order.

I've never eaten anything offered on this menu before, Hamilton thought. *I'd rather not ask too much out of Mr. Hoshikawa, so I think I'll go for the cheapest one.*

"I'll have the sausages and mashed potatoes," Hamilton told the waitress after the Hoshikawas have given their respective orders.

"For me, I'll try your… " Tarou paused to look at the menu again as he forgot the name of the item he wished to have. "Filet… mignon?"

"It's pronounced 'filay minyon'," Miku answered as the proper pronunciation for the meat dish Tarou ordered.

"Thank you," Tarou replied to Miku.

"Thank you for your orders," the waitress replied to the occupants of the table. "Please wait."

As the waitress left, the Hoshikawas faced Tarou and Hamilton. "I apologize for having you to correct me," Tarou said as he faced Miku again.

"It's alright," Miku replied. "Filet mignon is a French term in origin, so it's natural you would get the pronunciation wrong on your first try."

"Speaking of which, Dr. Hamilton, why did you order the sausages and mashed potatoes?" Daisuke asked Hamilton.

"Because it reminded me of home," Hamilton answered. "For those wondering, it's called 'bangers and mash' there."

"You're from the United Kingdom?" Miku asked.

"Haworth, to be specific. My parents owned a clinic there."

"And you didn't stay?" Maria asked.

"For a time, I did. At that time, I was in a relationship with a man named Thomas Porter, a solicitor. Unfortunately, he saw another woman when I had to accompany my parents to see a relative of ours living in Cambridge so we ended the relationship and I became a wandering doctor to not only take my mind out of what happened but I found helping many was my true calling."

"And that's where you met Tarou?"

"At a refugee camp. We then moved to South Africa because of the NGO I worked for having its headquarters there."

"Now then, I must explain to you the real reason why I invited the both of you to lunch," Daisuke announced to Hamilton and Tarou. "As my daughter discovered, I've helped Dr. Hamilton and Tarou settle in Japan and to make it easier on Tarou to travel to Nishi High School, I got him a PCX scooter."

"Father, forgive me for interrupting but that does remind me, how are you able to learn how to use that scooter?" Maria asked to Tarou.

"I taught Tarou how to do so," Hamilton answered. "In fact, he learned awfully quickly."

"Thank you," Maria replied before facing her father. "Father, you may continue."

"As I was about to say," Daisuke continued. "Because my daughter confronted me about what I was doing, I've talked it over with her and my wife. We all agreed to make my sponsorship official."

"And might we please know what that means?" Tarou inquired.

"That means that if there's anything else you need, we can make sure it's delivered to you without having it done in secret," Maria answered. "First of, we hope to make sure you have proper meals at school."

"I apologize for that," Hamilton replied. "I've been too busy in my work that I never found time to cook for Tarou."

"It's alright," Miku said. "I can understand, but having your ward rely on cutlet sandwiches and apple strudels isn't healthy."

"Other than that, I've heard from my daughter that you have yet to join a club," Daisuke said as he resumed his announcement. "It's not really required, but it will help you with future job prospects. Speaking of which, do you know what you want to do after school?"

"If I may be honest, I don't know," Tarou answered and while it was mostly a lie, there was honesty in his tone. "Moving here to Japan with Dr. Hamilton made it hard for me to decide instantly."

"I understand. My daughter does have a recommendation."

"Judo," Tarou deduced.

"That's right. You don't have to say yes, though."

"As I told Maria, I'll think about it."

"If you have a club in mind, just come to my office and tell me."

"We'll do that," Hamilton replied just as Tarou remembered to take the tracking device delivery system out of his pocket and, after making sure no one was looking, he placed it on the floor beneath his feet.

#

Iron Dutchman, Taisho Ward. 1444 hours

"Ganji's already planted the tracking device delivery system," Frederick Dirks announced at the *Iron Dutchman*'s dining hall with Wouter Vos, Sunan Wattana, Jake Crawley, and Tatev Mirzoyan, who had remained after Tarou and Hamilton had left, hearing and watching Dirks use his smartphone.

"Then get it moving," Vos demanded. "Though where will you plant the tracking device anyway, and how will you monitor it?"

"That's need to know now. Preparing to move delivery system."

Dirks firmly pressed his right thumb on the smartphone's screen. This made the tracking device delivery system move as he moved the thumb on the screen in various directions. He then pressed a button on the screen that made the delivery system summon a ray of green light against the first pair of legs it saw. He found that Maria Hoshikawa herself owned those legs.

"And now we got Maria," Dirks announced. "Now I just need to know if she brought a purse."

Dirks moved his thumb across the smartphone's screen, making the delivery system move. He then pressed his left thumb on the same screen, allowing a tube with a lens to launch out of the delivery system and extend as far as the chair Maria sat on. This allowed Dirks to see that Maria has a purse.

"And we have our ride," Dirks declared. "Now we wait until they're done with their lunch."

#

Demeter/Bay Hotel, Cosmo Square Building, Suminoe Ward. 1519 hours

At Demeter, a waiter filled the glasses of the Hoshikawas, Tarou, and Hamilton with water. After that, he left. All immediately drank.

"I've been wondering, why did you have lunch at this time?" Hamilton asked.

"At Nishi High School, clubs hold special sessions on Sundays and today is a Sunday," Daisuke answered. "Naturally, Maria has to go, but before that, we make sure to go to Mass because it's a Sunday."

"You don't go to church?" Miku asked. "No offense. I was just asking."

"I wasn't able to find time to ever since I left the UK," Hamilton answered. "Which denomination are you with?"

"Roman Catholic," Daisuke answered. "Not only is it a Sunday, it's Palm Sunday today. We even had palms to use."

"I'm surprised you're devout."

"It's what sets me apart from those in Japan's corporate world. Not to brag, but I like to remind others that my faith is why I run my *keiretsu.* A lot of those in the corporate world forget where they came from and my faith is to remind myself of where I came from. It also reminds me to do right by those who buy my *keiretsu*'s products."

"And I willingly converted to Roman Catholicism to marry Daisuke," Miku added.

"Tarou, if you don't mind me asking, but what hobbies do you have?" Maria asked Tarou. "Forgive me if you've been asked this on the first day of this year, but I never did ask much about you every time we ran into each other at school."

"I practice Muay Thai and I read?" Tarou answered.

"You read?" Miku asked. "What books?"

"*The Circassian Slave*, *That Hagen Girl*, and *What the Day Owes the Night*; the last one being translated from French."

"How did you come across *That Hagen Girl*?" Daisuke asked. "That book's a rarity."

"We knew someone back in South Africa who collects such books," Hamilton answered.

Unbeknownst to the Hoshikawas, Dirks made the tracking device delivery system move toward the salmon pink purse Maria owned that she tied to her chair by using its strap. As the delivery system was basically a metallic *Latrodectus*, commonly called a black widow, it was small enough for no one to notice.

The delivery system was able to jump into the purse. Although it was a spider made of metal, the delivery system only moved on four legs as the two frontmost "legs" were used to open anything. Finding the former, Dirks used the delivery system to slightly open the purse's main compartment by pushing the flap forward enough to get in, as an open flap would have alerted the Hoshikawas.

After a minute of pushing, Dirks found the opening he needed. As a result, he stopped pushing the flap and moved the delivery system into the purse. By this time, the respective orders of the Hoshikawas, Hamilton, and Tarou had arrived.

#

1640 hours

After finishing their lunch, the Hoshikawas, Hamilton, and Tarou left Demeter and, by extension, Bay Hotel. "Thank you again for this meal," Hamilton said to the Hoshikawas before bowing, with Tarou doing the same.

"Think nothing of it," Daisuke replied. "Now, if you do have an answer, I suggest you contact Maria first then we talk it over at my office."

"Understood. We best leave now."

"Thank you again," Tarou repeated.

"I'll see you tomorrow," Maria replied before Tarou and Hamilton separated from the Hoshikawas.

I hope you say yes, Daisuke thought. *It would help that you can keep an eye on Maria by joining the Judo club.*

#

Iron Dutchman, Taisho Ward. 2007 hours

"So, how did it go?" Frederick Dirks asked Tarou and Hamilton as every member of Iron Dutchman Services was gathered at their briefing room in their namesake. The latter two were now in their usual attire.

"It went well," Hamilton answered. "If Tarou wished to join a club, Mr. Hoshikawa offered to make sure Tarou does join."

"He and his daughter recommended the Judo club, didn't they?"

"They did," Tarou answered.

"I suggest you take them up on their offer. It would be easier on Ganji to keep an eye on Maria if he was in the same club as her."

"But wouldn't it be difficult for Ganji to reconcile his Muay Thai with Judo?" Jake Crawley questioned.

"Not really," Dirks answered. "Judo does allow striking, but it's not permitted in professional competition."

"I say go for it." Wouter Vos suggested. "It wouldn't hurt to learn more than one martial art."

"Very well, I'll go to the Judo club and approach Miss Hoshikawa for my answer tomorrow when classes are dismissed," Tarou declared.

"Anything else?" Dirks asked for every other member of Iron Dutchman Services. He heard no from all members. "Then we're dismissed for the night."

#

Nishi High School, Higashiosaka Ward. April 15, 2030; 1640 hours

Tarou approached the room where the Judo club was held at for Nishi High School. As it was the end of extracurricular activities for the school, Tarou found that the entrance became a river of boys and girls in white *judogi*.

After that test of patience, Maria Hoshikawa began to step out, still in her *judogi*. She then found Tarou outside.

"You're here?" Maria asked.

"I am," Tarou answered.

"I take it you wish to take my father up on his offer?"

"Hai desu."

"Your Japanese is improving."

"Domo arigatou."

"Sure, I'll talk to my father. You and Dr. Hamilton best be ready for when my father asks for the two of you."

"Wakarimashita."

"You may go now." Both Tarou and Maria went their separate ways and in the case of the latter, she found Misa Todoh standing in her way.

"Is it a problem that I invited Ta- I mean, Ganji-kun to our club?" Maria asked.

"Not only did you almost call him by his first name, but suddenly, you're doing all of this for the transfer student?" Misa asked.

"My father's sponsoring him. Therefore, I must help him too."

"So that's what it is. Fair enough. Now, could you please assist me with cleaning up?"

"I apologize for that."

#

Hamilton Clinic, Taisho Ward. 1920 hours

Tarou then arrived at the Hamilton Clinic near Hoshikawa Group Headquarters to pick up the owner of the clinic. He found Daisuke Hoshikawa's limousine outside with its driver, Ugaki, waiting outside the clinic as he stood beside the clinic door.

Tarou then stood opposite of where Ugaki stood. "Konbanwa, Ugaki-san," Tarou said to the driver before bowing.

"Have you approached Maria ojou-sama with your answer?" Ugaki asked.

"I have. I said yes."

"You best Hoshikawa-san of that. Just knock."

"Hai." Tarou approached the door while Daisuke and Hamilton continued talking. He then knocked. The knock was loud enough for both Daisuke and Hamilton to hear.

"Come in," Hamilton said, followed by Tarou opening the door.

"Glad you made it, Ganji-kun," Daisuke said as he turned to Tarou. "You approached my daughter, yes?"

"I did," Tarou answered after his bow. "I said yes."

"Then please come with me to my office." Daisuke turned to Hamilton. "You too, Hamilton-sensei."

"Wakarimashita," Hamilton replied in flawless Japanese.

Hoshikawa Group Headquarters. 1935 hours

Daisuke, followed by Tarou and Hamilton, reached his office. As the former sat down, the latter two were confused as to whether they should stand or sit down since only one chair stood facing Daisuke's desk.

"I apologize for not having an additional chair prepared," Daisuke said to Tarou and Hamilton.

"I see a couch," Tarou replied. "I can sit there while Dr. Hamilton can sit in the chair in front of you."

"Tarou-"

"I insist, Doc. You're my guardian, after all."

"That's fair."

As Hamilton sat down at the chair facing Daisuke's desk, Tarou sat on the couch. "Now that Ganji-kun has told my daughter that he said yes, I've prepared this document."

Daisuke handed a piece of paper to Hamilton. The latter found the English translation that read:

I, ____________________, allow my ward ____________________ to be officially sponsored by Daisuke Hoshikawa for the purpose of living and studying in the State of Japan. This will allow ______________ to be provided with food and other means to assist in his education. Should he commit a serious offense, this sponsorship will be terminated.

"You'll contact Narumi-san for this?" Hamilton asked with Daisuke nodding as his answer.

"Before I sign this, might I please consult this with everyone in Iron Dutchman Services?"

"I understand. I'll come to you tomorrow night and if you've signed by then, please give it to me."

"Domo arigatou."

"You may leave now. I do look forward to your answer tomorrow."

Iron Dutchman. 2019 hours

"Seems something worth signing," Dirks declared at the Iron Dutchman's briefing room with all of his subordinates gathered, and that Frederick Dirks had joined them.

"Ja, but what about the mention of 'serious offenses'?" Wouter Vos asked.

"I'm sure Ganji can do his best." Dirks then turned to Tarou. "Right?"

"Yes, sir," Tarou replied.

"So, what are we waiting for?" Jake Crawley asked. "Get Doc to sign already."

"I need a pen first," Hamilton requested.

#

OVR Safehouse, Nishinari Ward. April 16, 2030; 0845 hours

"Glad you made it," Tatiana Ioannovna Tsulukidze said as Serdar Muhadow came to her office in the OVR safehouse. "I've just come across this."

Tatiana gave Muhadow an envelope. The latter opened it and found a document inside. Although written in Cyrillic, Muhadow knew Cyrillic and it read:

To "Elizaveta",

I've been told by the source the Deputy Director has within the New United Nations' Foreign Intelligence Service that Daisuke Hoshikawa has officially opted to sponsor Tarou Ganji. As he is the member of Iron Dutchman Services assigned to monitor Maria Hoshikawa, this is bound to make any attempt to capture Hoshikawa complicated.

"Nizhny".

"It seems I wasn't dreaming when I first read that Tarou Ganji is a member of Iron Dutchman Services," Muhadow said after reading the document.

"You seem to know who this Tarou Ganji is," Tatiana remarked.

"I trained him," Muhadow replied. "I can assume you know where."

"The past is the past. Now, how do you suppose we deal with this Tarou Ganji?"

"About that... I have an idea, but you won't like it."

"Tell me."

Adjustment Part 2

OVR Safehouse, Nishinari Ward, Kansai City, Kansai Prefecture; State of Japan. April 16, 2030; 0845 hours (Japan Standard Time)

"Tell me," Tatiana Ioannovna Tsulukidze ordered after Serdar Muhadow made a suggestion as to what to do with Tarou Ganji.

"I need to test if Ganji's a threat," Muhadow answered.

"Why?"

"Try something and he will respond. Believe me, I've seen it happen before."

"Very well. I leave it to you. I can avail to you Chadov and Zhakiyanov."

"Spasibo. Takzhe… "

"Chto eto takoye?"

"I need to borrow some money."

"Pochemu?"

#

Nishi High School, Higashiosaka Ward. 1225 hours

Tarou Ganji again bought a cutlet sandwich and apple strudel for lunch. As he neared Class 2-2's room, he saw Maria Hoshikawa waiting outside again. "So, have you signed it?" Maria asked.

"The document?" Tarou asked in response as he assumed Maria knew about the document Anita Hamilton had to sign to guarantee that Maria's father, Daisuke Hoshikawa, will sponsor Tarou. "She did. She'll give it to your father tonight."

"Good. Hopefully, you can start eating healthy starting tomorrow."

Maria made it clear to Tarou that she was referring to his sandwiches. "Who knows," Tarou replied. "I best get inside. You ought to go back to your room because Todoh-senpai is watching us."

Maria then found her friend Misa Todoh hiding behind the lockers in-between the two doors of Class-2-2's room. Tarou then took that opportunity to go inside his classroom.

Once Tarou went inside, Misa then joined Maria. "You really have to stop doing that," Maria warned Misa.

"Gomen, Maria-chan," Misa replied. "He comes off too suspicious to ignore. I mean, why is your father sponsoring him?"

"My father's always been like that. He must be seeing something in Ta- I mean, Ganji-kun. In any case, he's right. *We* must return to our room."

"Hai."

#

Hamilton Clinic, Taisho Ward. 1850 hours

Tarou then arrived at the Hamilton Clinic. After he parked his PCX scooter, he entered the clinic, much to the surprise of Anita Hamilton.

"Tarou, you're here early!" Hamilton exclaimed. "Why?"

"Mr. Hoshikawa always goes here to hand over your paycheck, right?" Tarou asked, ignoring Hamilton's question.

"… Yes?"

"Then I'm here to see that you give him that signed document. Do you have it with you?"

"Of course." Hamilton rushed to her office and after two minutes, she rushed back to Tarou with the same paper. As he received it, Tarou saw that the paper now read:

I, Anita Hamilton, allow my ward Tarou Ganji to be officially sponsored by Daisuke Hoshikawa for the purpose of living and studying in the State of Japan. This will allow Tarou Ganji to be provided with food and other means to assist in his education. Should he commit a serious offense, this sponsorship will be terminated.

It was then that Daisuke Hoshikawa appeared. Both Tarou and Hamilton bowed.

"You're early this time, Ganji-kun," Daisuke said upon seeing Tarou.

"I came to see this through," Tarou answered.

"Did you?" Daisuke then saw that Tarou carried the document he gave to Hamilton the previous evening. "I can see why you *really* came. In any case, are you ready to hand over that document?"

Tarou immediately turned to Hamilton. "You do the honors, Tarou," Hamilton said before Tarou said anything. He obliged by walking up to Daisuke and using both of his hands to give to him the signed document.

Daisuke took the document and looked at it. He nodded before facing Tarou and Hamilton. "Before I allow the both of you to leave, I need to do something."

"What might that be?" Hamilton asked.

"Mind if I measure Ganji-kun?"

"If by measure, you mean my body?" Tarou inquired.

"That's right. I'd like to help Maria prepare a *judogi* for you once you join the Judo club. Just take off your shirt." Daisuke then turned to Hamilton. "Dr. Hamilton, I assume you have measuring tape?"

"I do. Please wait until I get it."

"I'll start removing my shirt," Tarou added.

As Hamilton returned to her clinic, Tarou began to remove his button-up shirt. Daisuke slightly gulped as he saw the scars on Tarou's body, a reminder that the teenage boy was a child soldier.

"I have the tape," Hamilton announced as she left her office and walked up to Daisuke and Tarou.

"... Yes," Daisuke replied as he was reminded of what to focus on. "Please raise your arms sideward."

Tarou complied without making a single sound. Daisuke took the measuring tape and began to use it on Tarou.

Mamekan, Suminoe Ward. 1910 hours

Serdar Muhadow returned to Mamekan. Like in the previous week, he made the same order. He then noticed that a man sitting beside him having drunk three cans of beer.

I think I found my scout, Muhadow thought.

OVR Safehouse, Nishinari Ward. April 17, 2030; 0844 hours

"Found someone to use?" Tatiana asked Muhadow when the latter came to the OVR safehouse.

"Da," Muhadow answered. "He's simply named 'Harada'."

"What can he do for us?"

"Have a hangover at Nishi High School. That money I asked for will be needed to buy enough to get him intoxicated."

"And then what?"

"One of your subordinates and I will have that drunk delivered to Nishi High School. Tomorrow, he will then cause trouble."

"That's a very devious plan. How will we get the result of what we'll do if we leave him at the school?"

"I'll infiltrate the school to see for it myself. I'll get out as soon as I can."

"Fine. Like I said, if you slip up, we will dispose of you in any way *we* see fit."

"I understand."

#

Nishi High School, Higashiosaka Ward. 1219 hours

Tarou Ganji again bought an apple strudel. Just as he neared Class 2-2's room, he found Maria Hoshikawa waiting by the lockers carrying a *judogi* folder into a square while tied by a white belt, with Maria carrying the *judogi* through the belt.

"Still buying lunch?" Maria asked.

"Just an apple strudel," Tarou answered. "Dr. Hamilton actually got me a *bento* box and a utensil set for my lunch."

"That's good. I have your *judogi*." Maria lifted the *judogi* to show it to Tarou.

"Arigatou."

"I need your help in placing it in your locker."

"Sure."

#

1240 hours

Maria then returned to her room, which belonged to class 1 of the third-years. Once she entered the room, she found her table with a *bento* set and utensils prepared. Misa Todoh, who sat at the table behind Maria's, saw that her friend returned.

"You're back earlier than usual," Misa said to Maria.

"I just have to give Ganji-kun his *judogi*," Maria answered as she sat down and prepared to eat her lunch.

"Run that by me again?"

"Ganji-kun will be receiving his judogi. He finally chose a club, and it's the Judo club."

"Really? I mean, did you put him up to this?"

"I gave him the suggestion. He chose to join on his own volition." Maria placed her food, a piece of chicken *teriyaki* and rice inside her spoon and the spoon with its contents, into her mouth, and began chewing.

"Something must be up with him?"

Maria then finished chewing, followed by swallowing her food. "Is there a problem with him choosing to join our club?"

"Don't you think it's too fast for the transfer student to join our club because you invited him?"

"I consider it my duty as his *senpai* to help him fit in." Maria continued her meal.

"Fine. If he's joining today, mind if I test him out?"

Maria stopped chewing upon hearing Misa's question. Despite that, she resumed chewing, albeit slowly. After swallowing, she faced Misa.

"You really need to stop suspecting him," Maria warned.

"I don't know. It's just that… it feels like it's too suspicious. Your father suddenly decided to sponsor this boy from Iran. And now he opted to join the Judo club at your invitation. Has he practiced Judo before?"

"No, but he practiced Muay Thai."

"*Really*? How did you find that out?" Maria now felt Misa's tone that was filled with suspicion. She then sighed in defeat.

"My family and I… invited Ganji-kun and his guardian Hamilton-sensei for lunch last Sunday."

Many gasped as they heard what Maria had said. As Riku Todoh warned Tarou the week before, many found it that someone in the school, especially a transfer student in a lower year, to have been with Maria, to be a Herculean task who was seen as an idol to the school.

"You're not lying, right?"

"No! And it's not what you think!"

"And why did you think it was a good idea?"

"Lunch was my father's idea. I just simply made him admit he was sponsoring Ganji-kun. He used the lunch trip to make the sponsorship official."

"And I take it your father's the reason Ganji-kun will be getting a *gi*?"

"Sou desu."

"That's all I need to know… for now. We best finish our lunch before the bell rings."

"Hai."

#

1536 hours

At Nishi High School's Judo club, all members were gathered. "Hoshikawa, I leave today's announcement to you," the club's instructor, a man with tanned skin, ordered to Maria.

"Hai," Maria replied as she stepped forward and turned to face the rest of the club. "Today, we have a new member." Maria then faced the club's changing room. "Please come out."

Tarou Ganji did as Maria instructed. He now wore the *judogi* and stopped just beside Maria. He then repeated the introduction he gave the week before.

"Arigatou, Ganji-kun," Maria replied, with Tarou turning to bow to her. The former then faced the rest of the club. "We'll begin with fifty round trips. Since Ganji-kun only joined today, I must show him how to do a round trip."

"If I may, Hoshikawa-senpai, but I'm familiar with the round trip."

"Then you can join today's hundred laps."

"Hai, Hoshikawa-senpai."

"Get into your positions, everyone!" the club captain barked.

#

Mamekan, Suminoe Ward. 1910 hours

Serdar Muhadow and Pyotr Stepanovich Chadov arrived at Mamekan. Once stopping, the former faced the latter. "Wait right here," Muhadow ordered.

"Zametano," Chadov replied just as Muhadow proceeded inside Mamekan.

#

OVR Safehouse, Nishinari Ward. 2130 hours

"Why did you bring home this drunk?" Tatiana asked after Muhadow and Chadov brought the man Muhadow knew as Harada with them to the OVR safehouse, the consequence of their trip to Mamekan.

"He'll be crucial in what I wish to do tomorrow," Muhadow answered.

"And you think that will work?"

"All that needs to be done is to deliver this drunk to a situation where he'll bump into Maria Hoshikawa. Then we can see what Tarou Ganji is capable of."

"And how will you do that?"

"I'm going to need either Chadov or Zhakiyanov's help for that tomorrow."

"Fair enough. How long do you suppose that drunk will remain intoxicated?"

"I gave him enough *sake* to make it that his hangover will make it hard for him to be lucid again. I'd say six hours from now we attempt to drop his ass off at Nishi High School and let him cause trouble."

"What about watching the whole thing?"

"I might have to stay longer to scout for a possible escape route."

"Now I suggest you get to sleep already if you wish to get this drunk to the school at 0300 hours. I'll have Zhakiyanov wake up an hour before to pick you up, then the two of you are to return here and pick up our guest before you go to the school to leave him there."

"Zametano."

#

Hamilton-Ganji Condominium, Hoshikawa Condominiums, Higashiosaka Ward. April 18, 2030; 0550 hours

As a result of now being a member of Nishi High School's Judo club, Tarou Ganji woke up earlier than usual. In addition, he carried food with him for lunch because Daisuke Hoshikawa's sponsorship, now official, allowed Anita Hamilton to purchase the packaging for homemade lunch.

Tarou then reached his PCX scooter. Once he opened the storage compartment underneath the scooter's seat, he placed his lunch inside, followed by his P226 semi-automatic pistol.

After that, Tarou closed the compartment, boarded the PCX, and started it before moving to the school.

Nishi High School. 0600 hours

At the same time, Tarou had arrived. Because he was at the school's front gate, he stepped out of the scooter and walked while dragging it with him.

Reaching the bicycle rack, unaware that his former commander in Iran, Serdar Muhadow, hid in the nearby bush, Tarou parked his scooter and got his lunch. He then left the scooter, yet he didn't notice Harada's body in the middle of the entrance of the school's main building.

Once Tarou was no longer to be seen, Muhadow then stepped out of the bush and walked up to the scooter. He then opened the storage compartment and found Tarou's P226.

You picked quite a good gun, Ganji, Muhadow thought. *I best return to the bush.*

Tarou then reached the entrance of the school again. This time, he simply stood to the wall on his left while carrying his lunch and his judogi. The teachers who entered paid no attention, and those who did were simply greeted by Tarou.

It was then that a certain limousine arrived. Its sole passenger, Maria Hoshikawa, stepped out with her lunch, bag, and her *judogi.* Once she exited the vehicle, it left. Maria then continued toward the school until she saw Tarou and walked up to him.

"You're early," Maria remarked as she saw Tarou.

"You told me to be early," Tarou answered.

"Either way, we wait for the rest of the Judo club."

"You always do this by yourself?"

"That's right."

At lease she has me now to guard her, even if she may not know it.

"Ara, you're here early, Ganji-kun," Yumi Hasegawa, the homeroom teacher of Class 2-2, said as she entered the school and saw Tarou and Maria.

"Ohayou gozaimasu, Hasegawa-sensei," Tarou replied before he and Maria bowed.

Hasegawa then noticed Tarou's *judogi.* "I see you joined the Judo club."

"I did."

"That also explains why you're here with Hoshikawa-san."

"I'll admit to that," Maria replied.

"I assume you're waiting for the rest of the club?"

"Sou desu."

"Well then, I must get going myself." Hasegawa then turned to Tarou. "Ganji-kun, I'll see you later in class."

"Wakarimashita."

Suddenly, Tarou, Maria, and Hasegawa heard commotion and naturally, they went to where it came from: the front entrance to the school's main building. As they were around, they found the first teachers who arrived surrounding Harada, who was no longer inebriated.

The common questioned asked was why was he in the school. No one knew Harada, yet he laid on the ground. He was awake, and it was evident he's suffering from a hangover from how much alcoholic beverages Serdar Muhadow, who secretly watched, made him drink the previous night.

"Excuse me, sir, but we request that you have to lea-" Hasegawa attempted to say as she approached Harada before he pushed her aside as he was unable to comprehend where he was and who approached him.

He mistakenly touched Maria at her left breast. Everyone was horrified as to what happened. Some students who arrived early, which included those in the Judo club, witnessed this. Among those students was Misa Todoh.. Suddenly, Tarou appeared, no longer carrying neither his lunch nor his *judogi*, and used his right leg to forcibly make Harada stop.

You really haven't changed in seven years, Ganji, Muhadow thought as he watched. *That about settles it. I best leave before I'm noticed.*

He did that for Maria-chan without any second thought, Misa thought as she watched Tarou kick Harada.

Muhadow then escaped from the bush. Because of what Tarou did, no one noticed Muhadow, and he used that to his advantage. Returning to the fence he used to enter, Muhadow made another jump to escape and, like before, he succeeded in his jump. He then walked slowly to make sure no one noticed he was around.

0610 hours

Tarou and Hasegawa were in their room. Maria waited outside because their presence on the second floor was a consequence of what Tarou did to Harada.

"Ganji-kun, do you have any idea of what you did earlier?" Hasegawa asked.

"I kicked that man after he touched Hoshikawa-senpai at her left breast," Tarou answered.

"It isn't that simple. You caused trouble for our school's good name by doing that. However, that man was intoxicated to comprehend what he did. And I suppose what you did was the best course of action. That doesn't mean you will be excused. For now, I must report to a meeting with the staff. You can join Hasegawa-san now."

"Arigatou, Hasegawa-sensei."

#

Unknown Location; Enlightenment Point. 0255 hours (EP Time Zone)

"Are you sure this information is accurate?" Sergei Akulov asked after hearing from Reinhard Frühling, his Gatekeeper of Intelligence.

"It's true, Grand Gatekeeper," Frühling replied. "Omar Mahmud gave away Gatekeeper-Colonel Muhadow's alias in exchange for a lesser sentence."

"Will Gatekeeper-Colonel Muhadow be in danger?"

"That depends on how fast the FIS hear of this. However, he asked for two of his subordinates and that they're from the troops he requested that they be brought to our facility in Sakhalin Island. He'll be going to the TPR in Japan to meet up with those two subordinates of his because he asked for our help in getting them to Japan."

"What about the OVR's contact within the FIA?"

"Most likely *he* has heard of this."

"Get our Devotee-Infiltrator in the OVR to warn Director Puzanov and get him to warn Grand Duchess Tatiana."

"What about Gatekeeper-Colonel Muhadow?"

"I have an idea."

#

OVR Safehouse, Nishinari Ward, Kansai City, Kansai Prefecture; State of Japan. 1400 hours (Japan Standard Time)

At her office, Tatiana heard her smartphone's SatCom make a sound. She then rushed to her phone, already connected to the dish needed for the phone to receive the signal needed for SatCom. Once she opened her phone, she placed it on her right ear.

"This is 'Elizaveta'," Tatiana said.

"Good, you responded," Vyacheslav Puzanov replied on the other end of the smartphone. "Where's Mukhadov now?"

"He left to pick up two additional men who will help him with his plan to get us Maria Hoshikawa. Why do you ask?"

#

FIS Headquarters, McLean, Fairfax County, Commonwealth of Virginia; United States of America. 0019 hours (Eastern Standard Time)

At her office in FIS Headquarters, Deputy Director of Intelligence Yanin Saetang received her subordinate John Vue. Also in the office was Deputy Director of Covert Action Stanley McAllister, whom Vue noticed as he entered. McAllister carried a file.

"I assume Deputy Director McAllister's presence is related to why I was summoned?" Vue asked.

"Correct," Saetang answered before she signaled to McAllister to give to Vue the file he carried.

"What's this?" Vue asked as he received the file.

"Our contact in the Middle Eastern League's FIA has just informed us that an identity forger named Omar Mahmud has been arrested," McAllister explained. "If you're wondering how we got that information, the FIA gave it to us. As to why, it's because Mahmud's last client before the Qatari Rescue Police arrested him went by the name 'Mansur Fahri' and used the passport Mahmud provided with false information Fahri provided in order to travel to Japan."

"Naturally, we need you to figure out who this "Fahri' is and why he needed to go to Japan," Saetang added. "I suggest you go home and go over that file there. Once you finish, you'll need to get enough rest because Director Pérez would want to hear what you say."

"Understood," Vue replied.

#

Nishi High School, Higashiosaka Ward, Kansai City, Kansai Prefecture; State of Japan. 1531 hours (Japan Standard Time)

The day had ended for Class 2-2 in Nishi High School as everyone in the classroom stood up. Tarou Ganji began to leave the room like everyone else, but when Yumi Hasegawa looked at Tarou, the latter wasn't going to be leaving.

"Ganji-kun, please stay for a while," Hasegawa commanded with Ganji obeying.

As a result, every other student left. Now it was just Tarou and Hasegawa.

"I talked to the principal about what happened this morning," Hasegawa continued. "While I warned you that what you did would be bad for the school's image, a drunk appearing in our school is equally bad. Therefore, I was told to let you off with a warning. Only this time, do you understand?"

"Wakarimashita," Tarou replied.

"Now you're dismissed. If you arrive at Judo club late, please explain it to the captain that I simply needed your help with my belongings."

#

Vue Residence, Alexandria, Commonwealth of Virginia; United States of America. 0200 hours (Eastern Time Zone)

As soon as he received the file from McAllister, Vue rushed back to his house in the Arlington neighborhood of Glencarlyn. He then parked his car, a PT Cruiser, behind an Odyssey van. Although he worked for the

Foreign Intelligence Service, an analyst's salary wouldn't be able to afford a house in Glencarlyn, despite the size of the house and that's if Vue didn't have two cars.

Once Vue parked the PT Cruiser, he got the file and got out of the car. After he locked the car, Vue proceeded to his house's front door, but not only did he find it open, he found his wife Annerose standing with the door behind her. A year younger than Vue, Annerose had very light skin, auburn hair in a lob, and blue eyes. Her original full name was Annerose Boettger, as her father was Cecil Boettger, the corporate executive officer (CEO) of United American, the largest manufacturing conglomerate for the entire New United Nations. The house and the two cars were the result of Vue's earlier career in United American and playing the stock market. Although he left United American, Cecil still sent money to provide for Annerose and her daughter only.

"I was warned to go home early tonight," Vue replied to his wife. "After I finish reading the file I'm carrying, I need to rest because something big's come up and, considering why I'm here now, it must be big."

"Have you eaten?"

"I have. How's Mary?"

"Already asleep."

"Then could you please let me in?"

"Promise me you'll ask for time off after this 'big' event."

"I'll try." Although doubtful by the sincerity of her husband's word, Annerose simply moved to hold the doorknob, keeping the door open. Vue then proceeded inside his house.

#

OVR Safehouse, Nishinari Ward, Kansai City, Kansai Prefecture; State of Japan. 1810 hours (Japan Standard Time)

Serdar Muhadow had ultimately returned to the OVR safehouse in Kansai City. He wasn't alone as he brought two men with him into Tatiana Ioannovna Tsulukidze's office. Both were Turkmen like he was. One of them was his second-in-command, Raşit Ghaemi.

"So these are your men?" Tatiana asked.

"Da," Muhadow answered.

"Good, but we have bad news."

"What is it?"

"The Director contacted me while you were gone. He heard from our source in the Middle Eastern League's Foreign Intelligence Agency that Omar Mahmud, who helped with that passport of yours, was arrested by the Qatari Rescue Police. They could have notified the FIS, who, in turn, will notify the Japanese government."

"Not good. I got all I need to commence my plan to get Maria Hoshikawa and now this happens!"

"I suggest you three make your escape now. I can-"

"We can't end it like this! Look, I doubt the FIS will be fast enough in alerting my falsified information so I should still at least have time to still get Maria Hoshikawa."

"And what is your plan!?"

"First, I got my men here, and we even brought weapons and black clothing. Chadov and Zhakiyanov are having them brought in now."

A knock was heard. Ghaemi opened the door and found both Pyotr Stepanovich Chadov and Karim Olegovich Zhakiyanov carrying one crate. Ghaemi kept the door open while moving aside, allowing the two OVR agents to continue to the room. Once they stopped and put down the box, Ghaemi closed the door.

Tatiana then stood up and got a crowbar. Using the crowbar, she opened the box. To everyone's amazement but the Turkmen mercenaries, the crate contained ski masks, shirts, and trousers all colored black. In addition, AK-2000 assault rifles and a blonde wig were among those spotted inside the box. Chadov and Zhakiyanov's evident exhaustion showed that there was more to the box that Muhadow had told them.

"H… How did you get these into Japan?" Tatiana asked.

"Sadly, that's need to know," Muhadow answered. "Other than those, my plan will need the cooperation of your men and resources."

"Tell me!" Tatiana screamed as she turned to Muhadow.

"First, I need your help in abducting a girl named Ryoka Akagi."

FIS Headquarters, McLean, Fairfax County, Commonwealth of Virginia; United States of America. 0800 hours (Eastern Standard Time)

Vue then returned to FIS headquarters. This time, he headed straight for Alberto Pérez's office. Both Yanin Saetang and Stanley McAllister already arrived before Vue.

"You're made it in time," Saetang said as a compliment to her subordinate.

"Thank you, ma'am," Vue replied.

"I assume you read that file Deputy Director McAllister gave to you?" Pérez asked.

"I have, sir," Vue replied as he turned to Pérez. "This Mansur Fahri could be bad news if he needed a fake passport to travel to Japan. He could be the man that entered that building with the man 'Fred Smith' mentioned in one of his reports."

"Excuse me, who?"

"He was a man 'Smith' mentioned in his report dated April 8. He learned of this man from the mercenary Sunan Wattana. Two days after that, he heard from Wattana that he came back to the building he resided in with another man. Based on what I read about Mahmud being paid by Fahri, the latter could have arrived at Japan the same time."

"I see." Pérez then turned to his Deputy Directors. "Yanin, Stan, what do you propose should be done?"

"I advocate for Mr. Vue here to be sent to Japan to assess the situation," Saetang answered. "This Mansur Fahri must have come to Japan for a reason and while we can have 'Smith' investigate, we need quicker delivery on everything he reports and Vue is the right man for this job."

"To be honest, gentlemen and lady, I don't oppose such an idea, but I also read those reports," McAllister added. "There's a good chance the man Miss Wattana ran into could be an OVR or KGB infiltrator. Knowing why Fahri came to Japan and why the man Wattana identified helped him is what we need to know, but what happens when we get that answer."

"What do you think Fahri is here for?" Saetang argued to McAllister.

"Regardless, Fahri must have come for Maria Hoshikawa."

"We'll take your concerns into consideration, Stan." Pérez then turned to Vue. "John, go to Japan and talk with 'Smith' on this."

"Will do, but… there's something I wish to discuss."

Final Preparations

OVR Safehouse, Nishinari Ward, Kansai City, Kansai Prefecture; State of Japan. April 18, 2030; 1817 hours (Japan Standard Time)

"Tell me!" Tatiana Ioannovna Tsulukidze screamed as she turned to Serdar Muhadow because the latter argued with the former about his refusal to stop in his mission to abduct Maria Hoshikawa.

"First, I need your help in abducting a girl named Ryoka Akagi," Muhadow replied.

"Who?"

"A teenage girl working at the Kitakagaya Café. She may be working there, but it must be altered to balance with schoolwork. Normally, most Japanese teenagers ought to be in a club once classes finish, yet this girl chose a café. She could be struggling with family finances."

"And why abduct her?"

"We need a fake Maria. That box will carry her while I take the real Maria with me through that escape route of yours."

"And where does the girl you need our help in kidnapping relate to this?" Pyotr Stepanovich Chadov inquired.

"We abduct Akagi tomorrow and then go after Hoshikawa the next day. Ghaemi, Gurdov, and I will get Hoshikawa two days from now. I even brought a sedative to inject her with to knock her unconscious, in which I'll throw her into the crate. I'll bring Akagi with us, hooded. After that, it will involve a car chase throughout Kansai City that will end with us plummeting into Osaka Bay. I'll get out and get Hoshikawa out of the crate in order to use your 'escape route'."

"But what about your men?" Tatiana asked.

"We're ready to die as long as Commander Muhadow achieves his objective," Ghaemi answered in Russian.

"Your Russian's good," Tatiana replied as she faced Ghaemi.

"Spasibo," Ghaemi replied in return.

"What about the car?" Tatiana asked after facing Muhadow again.

"I'll use half of what remains of my money, but that will be in two days. I still need enough for eating and paying to end my reservation at Suminoe Hostel."

"So, when will you check out?"

"Tomorrow. I'll stay here if you don't mind."

Tatiana nor her men gave an answer. Muhadow took it as their answer. "So when do we abduct this Ryoka Akagi?" Karim Olegovich Zhakiyanov asked.

"Tomorrow evening after her shift ends. I'll give you the signal to follow because what I intend to do is offer her an escort to the station nearby. I'll also carry that sedative agent with me because it will only take half to knock someone unconscious once injected."

"Then what?"

"We keep her here until this Saturday. After we get her, I'll put an end to my reservations, get the car, then we make our move against Hoshikawa."

"Do you even know where she will be this Saturday?"

"I do. I even made things easier for us then."

"How?"

"Let's just say in two days, Daisuke Hoshikawa will not be there. Maria and her mother might hear Mass then, giving us a good opportunity to strike?"

"But what about those mercenaries?"

"Only one member will keep an eye on the Hoshikawa women. And I doubt he or she will go after us because it will compromise his or her position."

"And what about your men here?"

"Think you can keep them here until this Saturday?"

"Fine. Let us know when you intend on getting Akagi."

"I'll let you know tomorrow."

Hoshikawa Group Headquarters, Taisho Ward. April 19, 2030; 0814 hours (Japan Standard Time)

At his office, Daisuke Hoshikawa had received a business card from his secretary, Kirika Nonaka. The name on the business card was that of "Mansur Fahri" and that the company is named "E-Logistics".

Although he didn't know the information on that business card was falsified, Hoshikawa made his calls. "I'm sorry, this number appears to not be in service," a female voice replied on the other end of the phone Daisuke used, immediately repeated in Arabic by a male voice.

That's strange, Daisuke thought. *Maybe Aziz can help get me to one of his clients from the past.*

Hoshikawa then made another call, this time using the calling code of the United Arab Emirates. After pressing the buttons for the number he is seeking out, Hoshikawa immediately heard a male voice ask "Good Morning, this is Siraj Aziz, how may I help you?"

"Hello again, Siraj, it's me," Daisuke answered.

"Daisuke Hoshikawa? Do you know what time it is here in the Emirates?" the man named Siraj Aziz asked; his tone showing that he intended on sleeping had Daisuke not called him.

"I apologize for that, old friend. I need your help but I will make it short: have you done business with companies in Qatar because there's a company named E-Logistics that piqued my interest because of my secretary but I can't get through to them and I'm hoping to ask someone from Qatar, preferably a past client of yours, to see if he or she knows."

"Please wait."

Daisuke then played the game of patience. Luckily for him, the wait wasn't long as he heard another male voice on the phone asking "Mr. Hoshikawa, what is it that you need?"

"And who might this be?" Daisuke asked.

"I'm Rashid Zaman, President and CEO of QatarEnergy."

"Thank you for your time, Mr. Zaman. I need your help because of a company named E-Logistics that was said to be headquartered in Doha.

The one who told me of this company is my secretary because she was given a business card by someone named Mansur Fahri."

"Wait, did you say Mansur Fahri?"

"Yes?" Daisuke now knew there was trouble coming from Zaman's tone.

#

Vue Residence, Alexandria, Commonwealth of Virginia; United States of America. April 18, 2030; 1840 hours (Eastern Standard Time)

Annerose Vue (née Boettger) returned to her house with her house with her five-year-old daughter, Mary. However, she found her husband's PT Cruiser parked where it should be parked. For Annerose, that was the tip of the iceberg as she knew her husband John wouldn't be home at that time.

Despite that, Annerose parked the Odyssey where it belonged. "Mary, we're home," Annerose said to her daughter. "Please remove your seatbelt."

"Yes, Mommy," Mary replied. She had her father's lightly dark skin, dark brown eyes, and black hair, but it was in twintails

Once Annerose got out after removing her seatbelt, so did Mary. The latter got out after the former opened the left side door for her just as she got her backpack. As soon as Mary got out, she and her mother proceeded to the front door.

"That's Daddy's car, right?" Mary asked. "Why is it here?"

"I like to know that too," Annerose replied as she got the keys for the front door.

Unlocking the front door, Annerose proceeded inside her house, with Mary following. Both found John in the dining room having prepared the table and the food he bought.

"John, you're home," Annerose said.

"Daddy!" Mary shouted as she ran up to John.

"How are you?" John replied as he got Mary with both of his arms and raised.

"I showed my tooth at Show and Tell today!"

"Do you still have it?"

"It's in my bag."

"Then please allow me to bring you down so that you can remove your backpack and get that tooth. I want to talk to Mommy."

"Got it."

Once Vue put his daughter down, Mary ran off to the living room. "Why are you home at this time?" Annerose inquired.

"There's something crucial I have to talk to you about," Vue answered. "But it will have to wait until we finish dinner, though Mary will have to wait until we tell her."

"And that's why you bought food for tonight?"

"You and Mary like that brand."

"You know I'm on a diet."

"You can walk off a fair amount once you listen to what I have to say."

"Daddy, here's the tooth!" Mary reappeared with a tooth and showed it to her parents.

Annerose then took the tooth and showed it to her husband. Vue then brought out his wallet and got a hundred-UN dollar bill and gave it to Mary.

"Aren't we going to have the tooth fairy get my tooth?" Mary asked as she got the bill.

"This is your first tooth that fell out of you," Vue explained. "If you lose another tooth, sure. Though I doubt her reimbursement will match mine."

"In any case, we should start eating already," Annerose reminded.

#

1930 hours

Everyone in the Vue household finished their meals. "Mary, why don't you brush your teeth already and start studying," Annerose said to her daughter. "Allow Dad to help with the dishes tonight."

"Are you sure?" Mary asked.

"I'll handle it," Vue replied. "Now please get going."

Mary then left the dining room. "Mary's gone," Annerose said as she turned to her husband. "What is it that made you come home this early?"

"Remember how you wanted me to take some time off?" Vue asked rhetorically. "I managed to eke it out of my superiors but… "

"What?" Annerose's tone when she asked made Vue give a face filled with guilt. He gulped which indicated to Annerose that whatever suspicion she had when Vue claimed he got a day off was correct.

"It's a paid vacation," Vue answered. "Meaning, we go somewhere, but I have to do something."

"Should have known," Annerose replied. "When are we leaving?"

"Tomorrow evening at the earliest. The deadline as to when I have to convince you was in two days. Otherwise they'll assign someone else, but I get a pay cut."

"What is it that you have to do, anyway?"

"Go to Japan to meet someone. That's need to know, in case you're wondering."

"Japan? If I were to say yes to this, how long will we be gone?"

"Hopefully, the entire weekend. Everything will be provided by my superiors, and knowing them, they plan on doing something to Mary's school that will make it easier for us to be in Japan for who knows how long. Even transport, though that will take us to a military airbase as opposed to a civilian airport. That way, we don't have to deal with visas."

"Shall we tell Mary of this?"

"Of course. I'll get her. One last thing, though. My meeting's in Kansai City."

#

Hamilton-Ganji Condominium, Hoshikawa Condominiums, Higashiosaka Ward, Kansai City, Kansai Prefecture; State of Japan. April 19, 2030; 1235 hours (Japan Standard Time)

Tarou Ganji had returned to his condominium after having lunch at the closest restaurant. He returned to resume his studying as today wasn't the day where he was to keep an eye on Maria Hoshikawa and that it was Good Friday.

Although secular, the State of Japan made many changes after the Third World War. In particular, it had to make Good Friday a national holiday to make it easier for immigrant workers from the Republic of the Philippines needed to help rebuild after the war, as most were Roman Catholic. Students who weren't religious, much less Catholic, continued their students with Tarou as one of those students.

However, as he got inside, Tarou felt his smartphone and removed it from the right pocket of his trousers. He found a message from Anita Hamilton in IntMail that read:

Tarou, all members are needed at the Iron Dutchman. Mr. Hoshikawa himself is on board.

Tarou then put the phone back in the pocket where it came from and rushed outside.

#

Iron Dutchman, Taisho Ward. 1240 hours

Tarou managed to reach the *Iron Dutchman*. He was then escorted to the briefing room by Hamilton and other than everyone else in Iron Dutchman Services, both Daisuke Hoshikawa and Frederick Dirks were inside as well.

"Glad you made, Ganji," Dirks said before he turned to Daisuke. "Daisuke, you take it from here."

"Ladies and gentlemen, it's come to my attention that a man named Mansur Fahri might have come here to Japan in relation to not only me, but my daughter. He gave my secretary a business card filled with false information that I verified through a contact of mine in Qatar."

"I've also been given the same warning by my superiors," Dirks added. "John Vue from the FIS will join us with additional information.

"For now, we need to keep our eyes open. Everyone is to patrol various portions of Kansai City." He then turned to Tarou. "Ganji, I need you to go to Kamiishikiricho."

"Yes, sir. But mind if I get my pistol first?"

"Do what you have to do."

"You're all dismissed," Wouter Vos ordered.

#

Kamiishikiri Park No. 1. 1339 hours

Tarou then arrived at Kamiishikiri Park No. 1, where the proximity beacon used to track Maria's movements was installed by Vos. After he parked his PCX scooter, he brought out his smartphone and turned on his IntMail.

"Ganji-kun, is that you?" Tarou moved his head as to where the question came from. He found it was Misa Todoh who asked, prompting him to hide his smartphone.

"Konichiwa, Todoh-senpai," Tarou replied before bowing.

"What are you doing here?"

"Wandering around the city to relax myself."

"Same here. Or… you came here to try to enter the Hoshikawa Mansion."

Damn it, Tarou cursed in his mind. *I best come up with a good lie.*

"No. I just wanted to explore this part of the city first. Though I do know Hoshikawa-senpai lives nearby."

"So you were with my brother?"

"Todoh Riku?"

"Sou da. Although we're a year apart in the school, we're still siblings and I did have a suspicion something was up when I didn't see Riku around with his camera. Somehow, he has it again. Do *you* have anything about it?"

"Not really."

"I'll leave it at that. Now that I'm here, there is something I want to say."

"And what is that?"

"Arigatou gozaimasu." Misa bowed after what she said, perplexing Tarou. "Although you had to answer for what you did, you saved Hoshikawa-senpai yesterday morning."

"You're referring to that? I didn't think kicking that drunkard to make him stop was that noteworthy."

"Sure it is. You just went out of your way to do it and you weren't asking for anything in return. You should be lucky Hasegawa-senpai let you off with a warning."

"Thank you for the compliment."

"I must ask you: why did Mr. Hoshikawa sponsor you?"

"I honestly don't know myself. I can imagine Mr. Hoshikawa felt sorry for how I was raised.

"Now then, what do you think of Hoshikawa-senpai?"

"Why ask such a question?"

"You're being sponsored by her father. You might spend a lot of time with her, regardless of *your* feelings. If I hear something that happened to Maria-chan and that you might have some involvement in it, you will regret it after this conversation."

"And I welcome what will happen *when* that happens. For now, I must go."

Tarou returns to boarding his PCX and starts it up. He then left Kamiishikirocho.

#

Kansai Mart, Suminoe Ward. 1809 hours

Serdar Muhadow, upon leaving the Kitakagaya Café, reached the van used by the OVR cell as it was parked in front of Kansai Mart, a supermarket located in front of Kitakagaya Café. This was one of many Kansai Marts as there are more across the entire Kansai Prefecture if not the historic region that is the namesake of the prefecture.

Just as Muhadow reached the van with the unconscious Ryoka Akagi, so did Pyotr Stepanovich Chadov, himself carrying groceries. "Back already?" Chadov asked.

"Da," Muhadow answered. "Please help me get this girl inside."

"I need to put down my supplies first."

OVR Safehouse, Nishinari Ward. 1825 hours

"So what happens next?" Tatiana Ioannovna Tsulukidze asked as she looked to Muhadow while they, Pyotr Stepanovich Chadov, Karim Olegovich Zhakiyanov, Raşit Ghaemi, and Gurdov watched the unconscious Ryoka Akagi. Her head was now covered in a black big with her limbs tied to the chair was had to sit on.

"I need to go back to Suminoe Hostel to finalize my check-out, then come back here and ask my operative if she has all the necessary equipment needed to set Nemuro Hotel on fire."

"Wait, you had another subordinate of yours infiltrate Nemuro?"

"Having Nemuro Hotel on fire, which is already complete and that its grand opening will be this Sunday, is a good way to keep Daisuke Hoshikawa out of Kansai City. He'll have to leave tomorrow morning and while his wife and daughter attend Mass, we can go after the daughter then."

"How do you know all of this?"

"I have my ways."

"And what do we do with this girl when she regains consciousness?"

"I'll deal with her."

"And where will you stay once you check out of Suminoe Hostel?"

"Here, if you don't mind?"

"I'm already sheltering your subordinates. When will you find that car to use in your kidnapping?"

"Tomorrow morning at the earliest. For now, I have a hostel to check out of."

"Chadov, take him to Suminoe Hostel," Tatiana ordered as she turned to Chadov.

"Da," Chadov replied.

1901 hours

Both Chadov and Muhadow then returned to the safehouse. They both heard screaming and knew where it came from, immediately walking there.

Reaching the room where they left Akagi, they found her struggling and screaming. Tatiana, Zhakiyanov, Ghaemi, and Gurdov surrounded her with Ghaemi covering her mouth to make sure no one nearby heard what was happening.

"She came to?" Muhadow asked.

"Da," Tatiana answered. "What took you so long?"

"Traffic between here and Suminoe Hostel. Luckily, I have money for the car and when I need food."

"Now do something about her! I'll be at my office." Tatiana then turned to her and Muhadow's respective subordinates. "Everyone, back to your posts."

"Da," Zhakiyanov, Chadov, Ghaemi, and Gurdov replied in unison. They, along with Tatiana, left. Now, it was just Muhadow and Akagi.

"What is it that you want!?" Akagi asked despite not seeing anything.

"Your help," Muhadow answered.

"Fahri-san, is that you?"

"Yes. What I'm about to tell you is the truth, but I need your help. If you do help, I promise you will be a free woman. You can even tell all about me because I intend to make sure the police will find you."

#

FIS Headquarters, McLean, Fairfax County, Commonwealth of Virginia; United States of America. 0830 hours (Eastern Standard Time)

"So, what did your wife and daughter say about the 'paid vacation' you told them about?" Yanin Saetang asked to Vue after the latter entered her office in FIS headquarters.

"They agreed to it," Vue answered. "Though my wife does need to know one detail: how will we go to Japan on such short notice?"

"The Director already made calls for a C-5 to come to Andrews. I'll have someone take you and your family there tonight."

"Thank you so much for this, Deputy Director."

"What time does your wife come home?"

"Six PM. She picks up Mary first."

"Go home at the same time and start packing. Traffic should be bad come this evening because the weekend's coming, so we'll send a taxi then to your house and as soon as you finish packing up, rush to the taxi because you're to go to Andrews at nine PM."

"Yes, Deputy Director."

#

Nemuro Hotel, Nemuro, Nemuro Subprefecture, Hokkaido Prefecture; State of Japan. 2300 hours (Japan Standard Time)

Facing Tomoshiri Bay was the recently finished Nemuro Hotel. Part of the Hoshikawa Resorts chain that was a subsidiary of Hoshikawa Group, this was conceived by Daisuke Hoshikawa in a way to vitalize Nemuro's economy by encouraging foreign guests to go there with the amenities provided by the hotel to serve as a way to provide their expectations as an equivalent to what they should do while in Nemuro. Another reason was to provide work for the immigrant communities in Nemuro, the byproduct of the Third World War, work to allow them to feed themselves.

Although finished, the hotel wasn't to be opened in two days. Because he acquired information about it from Kirika Nonaka, Serdar Muhadow had sent an agent named "SB" to the hotel. "SB" was a girl who covered her entire body in a black raincoat and boots of the same color as footwear. She covered her mouth with a surgical mask.

Carefully, she gathered what she needed for a fire, as Muhadow ordered. Inside a wagon were six wine bottles filled with gasoline and "SB" approached from the beach to be used as part of the hotel, "SB" neared the hotel.

Avoiding the guards, "SB" was able to go to a spot where the fire was about to start. Before commencing, she brought out her smartphone and began to use its GOKMail. Finding the conversation with the name "SM", she typed:

Commander Muhadow,

I've gathered all that I needed for the fire. I apologize for bothering you at this time but do I have permission to start the fire?

SB.

After pressing "Send", SB looked around to see if anyone approached. There wasn't and now she felt that her reply had come, which simply read:

Do it.

Serdar Muhadow.

Putting away the smartphone, "SB" began to pick the first wine bottle she had in the wagon. She hurled it toward the hotel as far as she could see. She continued to do so until the wagon was empty. After that, she brought out a pistol with a grappling hook attached to and firing it at the wall above her, she used it to climb. Once in the resort proper, she brought out a box of matches and after getting one, she lit it on fire and threw it at where she had thrown all six of the wine bottles filled with gasoline.

#

FIS Headquarters, McLean, Fairfax County, Commonwealth of Virginia; United States of America. 1059 hours (Eastern Standard Time)

Alicia Caguiat then approached Vue's office while carrying a file. She faked a cough to get Vue's attention.

As Vue turned, he found Caguiat behind him. "Excuse me, Mr. Vue, but I need to tell you something," Caguiat said.

"You didn't have to fake a cough to get my attention," Vue replied.

"You knew that was faked?"

"Learned it while I was in the US Army. What is it that you need?"

"I had someone review the information we received from the FIA on Mansur Fahri. It's all in here."

Caguiat offered Vue the file. As soon as he received it, Vue opened it and began to read but he found papers that referred to "Fahri" by another name: Serdar Muhadow. He was unable to read as a result, with Caguiat worried.

"Mr. Vue… are you alright?" Caguiat asked.

"I must report this to Deputy Director Saetang," Vue ultimately replied. "Please… please warn Deputy Director McAllister!"

"Will do."

#

1130 hours

Stanley McAllister then barged into Yanin Saetang's office. He already found Vue with Saetang.

"I apologize for barging in like this, but I assume Vue here told you?" McAllister asked Saetang.

"He did," Saetang answered.

"We need to tell the Director now," Vue warned.

"Not a chance. He's still talking to Blanchard about getting that Galaxy to Andrews."

"Damn it! Smith and those mercenaries need to know that it's Serdar Muhadow we're dealing with."

"What would the Butcher of Godana be doing in Japan?"

"Most likely he was hired to get to Maria Hoshikawa," McAllister guessed. "He must be assisted by that man Sunan Wattana described."

"John, how much are you taking with you to Japan?" Saetang asked Vue."

"Ignoring my laptop, my phone, and my wallet, I'm just taking this suit, an additional button-up shirt, two additional shirts, socks, and jocks," Vue answered. "Rose and Mary know not to pack up too much. She also intends to close her clinic early and get Mary before we meet."

"And we can't rush you out of here. We still have to wait for the Director and Blanchard."

"I suggest you get lunch now," McAllister said to Vuc.

"Thanks," Vue replied.

1507 hours

Vue was now at the office of Alberto Pérez. In a case of *déjà vu*, both Saetang and McAllister were also at the office.

"Any update of the Galaxy?" Vue asked.

"Yes," Alberto Pérez happily answered. "Blanchard managed to pull through because a Galaxy is on its way to Andrews. The Galaxy will fuel up while waiting for you, so once you arrive, it'll launch immediately to Japan."

"Good."

"However, we can't have you leave just yet," Saetang warned. "We need you to take two certain app installers with you once you meet up with Smith and Iron Dutchman Services."

"Which apps?"

#

Abenobashi Car Rental, Abeno Ward, Kansai City, Kansai Prefecture; State of Japan. April 20, 2030; 0705 hours (Japan Standard Time)

Serdar Muhadow approached a car rental service named Abenobashi Car Rental, named as such because it was near the Abenobashi Station. He had waited for the employees to come inside as he knew the rental service wouldn't be open until 0600 hours, which made him go an hour later.

Now all I have to do is get the car and return to the safehouse, Muhadow thought. *After that, we put Akagi into that blonde wig and into the crate, then me, Ghaemi, and Gurdov move to Hamada Church.*

#

Andrews Air Force Base/Joint Base Andrews, Camp Springs, Prince George's County, State of Maryland; United States of America. April 19, 2030; 1950 hours (Eastern Standard Time)

A taxi then arrived at the entrance of Andrews Air Force Base. This was one of the few military installations still used by the United States Armed Forces as a whole upon the creation of the New United Nations Defense

Forces, where most US military installations had to be turned over to the NUNDF. Since 2009, Andrews AFB was merged with the Washington Naval Air Facility, now used by the United States Coast Guard, into Joint Base Andrews. This air base was where the two VC-25 airliners, specialized 747s, were kept that were used to transport the President of the United States with the call sign "Air Force One". It was for that reason that the US Armed Forces were still allowed to keep the base in order to assure the US President he or she still had troops that answered to him or her.

After exiting the taxi, the Vues approached the guard at the entrance. Once John showed his identification card that reminded the guard that he's with the FIS, the guard made a call. Thankfully for the Vues, the wait wasn't too long as a truck appeared. Once the gate opened, the Vues rushed to the truck.

Abduction

OVR Safehouse, Nishinari Ward, Kansai City, Kansai Prefecture; State of Japan. April 20, 2030; 0806 hours (Japan Standard Time)

Why did I have to meet that man? Ryoka Akagi pondered while she was still tied to her chair and her head covered in a black bag.

Suddenly, the sound of a car's engines was heard. Because she couldn't see anything, Akagi was unable to know who appeared. Yet she thought of one answer and *he* came inside.

"It's time we ended this!" Serdar Muhadow loudly announced.

#

Kitakagaya Café, Suminoe Ward. April 19, 2030; 1650 hours

Serdar Muhadow returned to Kitakagaya Café. In a stroke of good fortune, the table Muhadow sat on the week before was vacant and sat there.

"Here's your menu," Ryoka Akagi as she appeared to Muhadow's table and gave him the menu. "Wait, you wouldn't be Fahri-san by any chance, would you?"

"Why yes, I am," Muhadow answered as he turned to find his target serving him again; a coincidental replay of what happened last week.

"I'm glad you came here you again."

"You should be. I'll be leaving tomorrow."

"Why?"

"Something happened at my company. In any case, I have my order."

Muhadow explained what he wanted to Akagi. Once she finished writing it in her notepad, Muhadow then gave her the menu and she left.

1754 hours

Akagi then returned to Muhadow's table now carrying a folder bill. As she stopped, she gave Muhadow the folder but was unaware of the glass already close to the edge of the table.

Muhadow then filled the folder with yen bills. As Akagi got the folder after Muhadow folded it, she then hit the glass, forcing it to fall. Akagi, however, was fast enough to stop the glass from falling. Unbeknownst to Akagi, Muhadow struck her right hand, which carried the folder, with a syringe filled with a lime green liquid. When Akagi got the glass, Muhadow pressed the needle but stopped as she saw Akagi move her to him and hid the syringe.

"I apologize for that," Muhadow said while immediately hiding his syringe.

"Why was the glass there?" Akagi asked.

"I needed space to get my money. My arms are awfully long that big spaces are needed for stuff like that and I forgot to get the glass further into the table by the time you arrived."

"In any case, please wait for the receipt and change."

Akagi then left again. As she walked to the cashier, her walking speed had decreased in a split second, attracting the cashier's attention. The eyes of the former then began to close her eyes yet she resisted.

I… What's happeni… Akagi thought before she ultimately lost consciousness, shocking everyone in the café.

#

OVR Safehouse, Nishinari Ward. April 20, 2030; 0822 hours

Akagi, while still wearing her hood, was brought to an Odyssey van that Muhadow purchased. At the rear trunk of the van was the crate Raşit Ghaemi, and Gurdov brought with them, now empty of its original contents.

Using one of the AK-2000 assault rifles that once inhabited the crate, Ghaemi forced Akagi into the box. "… Is that a gun?" Akagi fearfully asked in accented but flawless English.

"Yes!" Ghaemi replied, also in English, before he removed the bag. "Now put this on."

He then gave Akagi the blonde wig that also came in the box. Akagi wore the wig while managing to avoid looking at her captors. "Now get in the box!" Ghaemi demanded.

Akagi attempted to look back only for Ghaemi to face his rifle at her head. Knowing that the metal touching the rear of her head will kill her, Akagi moved one leg into the open crate, then her body by pressing her arms onto the box. Briefly facing her body sideway, Akagi became the sole content of the box.

She then closed her eyes as she was now inside the box. Gurdov then returned the piece that was needed to open and close the box followed by Karim Olegovich Zhakiyanov appearing with two nails and a hammer. Giving one nail to Gurdov, Zhakiyanov hammered one nail onto the box to seal it. He then got the other nail from Zhakiyanov to seal it entirely.

Tatiana Ioannovna Tsulukidze joined her subordinates and the Turkmen mercenaries. "I assume this is it?" Tatiana asked.

"Da," Serdar Muhadow answered. "Ghaemi, Gurdov, and I are to go to Hamada Church and hopefully, once Mass is finished, we get Maria Hoshikawa in the process."

"The submarine is waiting in Osaka Bay. You'll have to swim to get to it, though. How will you get the real Maria with you?"

"That's where the other half of the sedative in the syringe comes in. I inject her with it as soon as we get her at Hamada Church. After that, we rush to Osaka Bay and once we're near enough, we'll open the rear trunk to allow the crate with Akagi inside to fall off. If we're chased, our pursuers will be more focused on her as she will be wearing the wig that came with the rifles and they'll think she's Maria because she and Maria are of the same age."

"I guess this is goodbye?"

"More or less."

"I hope to never work with you again since we helped kidnap an innocent girl."

"Don't push your luck." Muhadow then faced his subordinates. "Gideli!"

The Turkmens then got into the Odyssey. Muhadow occupied the left front seat while Ghaemi sat behind him. Gurdov occupied the driver's seat. All three then put on ski masks before Gurdov started up the Odyssey. After that, Gurdov gave his AK-2000 to Muhadow and moved it out of the safehouse.

#

Iron Dutchman, Taisho Ward. 0730 hours

All members of Iron Dutchman Services were gathered in their briefing room. That included Tarou Ganji and Anita Hamilton, who managed to attend because it was Black Saturday. Like Good Friday, Black Saturday was also made into a national holiday in Japan to appease foreign workers from the Philippines that practiced Roman Catholic Christianity. Schools were closed as a result, allowing Tarou to partake in this briefing, while Hamilton was to come later to her clinic near Hoshikawa Group Headquarters.

Dirks then walked up the stage of the briefing room. "Listen everyone, we're to go to Hamada Church and we're to provide overwatch for the Hoshikawa women today and only that. Daisuke Hoshikawa left to attend to his hotel in Nemuro catching fire hours before, so we are to make sure his wife and daughter are safe.

"For this, I need Ganji and Wattana to provide overwatch. I will go to the nearby Olive House café to keep track on the phones used by the Hoshikawa women. I also need volunteers to wait somewhere in the event something does go wrong. For those willing, raise their hands."

"I'll go," Jason Luke Crawley said as he raised his right hand. "I finally got the van we need and I want to make sure it's well spent."

"I'll go as well," Wouter Vos, who stood beside Dirks, added.

"Then we launch," Dirks ordered.

"Wait, don't we need somewhere if Ganji and I are to provide overwatch?" Sunan Wattana asked after she raised her hand in order to add to the attention she needed from Dirks for him to answer her question.

"You and Ganji will climb above Olive House," Dirks answered. "I'll distract the owner."

"And we have a ladder from the days this ship used to be a cruise liner," Vos added. "I'll plant it and you two will use it to climb. Once the both of you are at the roof, I'll take it away to make sure no one is the wiser."

"Any more questions?" Dirks asked.

"What about weapons?" Tarou asked. "If something goes wrong, should we respond in kind?"

"Preferably not. Hopefully, the Hoshikawas ought to be there for only an hour. It may be Black Saturday but school clubs hold special meetings and Maria intends to go there straight after Mass. But I will permit pistols only."

"Understood."

"No more questions, people. We launch now."

#

Olive House/Near Hamada Church, Higashiosaka Ward. 0849 hours

Crawley, Vos, and Dirks arrived at Olive House. Dirks, wearing a beige jacket despite the summer heat, was the first to get off the van Crawley had purchased: a Townace. As soon as Dirks was inside Olive House, Vos got out of the Townace and rushed to the rear trunk, where the latter was located at.

As Dirks was seated and looking at the menu as he did a month before, Vos began to move with the ladder, but seeing that the proprietress was also looking outside, Dirks then declared what he wished to order, allowing the proprietress to be distracted. Vos then planted the ladder.

Suddenly, Tarou Ganji, not wearing his uniform despite schools being open on Black Saturday, arrived while using his PCX scooter with Sunan Wattana behind him. By now, the proprietress moved to her kitchen to prepare Dirks' orders, and that Vos had finished planting the ladder. Both Tarou and Wattana rushed to join Vos.

"You took your time getting here," Vos said to his subordinates.

"Sorry about that," Wattana replied.

"You best hurry now. The owner of the café will notice us."

"I'll go first," Tarou said.

Tarou then rushed to use the ladder. Vos resumed looking at the inside of the café to see if the proprietress was still inside her kitchen. To his luck, she was. It was then that Tarou had finished climbing up the rooftop of the café.

"Sunan, you're up," Vos said to Wattana.

"Roger," Wattana replied before she used the ladder to join Tarou.

Vos again looked at the inside of the café. However, the proprietress had come out with what Dirks had ordered. Vos anxiously looked at Wattana and she was almost to the roof, yet she only had seconds to reach the roof.

Vos resumed looking at the café, but in one split second, he stopped because that too would attract attention. Dirks, however, saw the former and faced the proprietress before eating what he ordered.

"Mizu mou ippai onegaishimasu," Dirks requested.

"Wakarimashita," the proprietress replied, making her leave.

It was then that Wattana finished climbing onto the roof. Vos then took away the ladder and rushed back to the Townace and returned it to the rear trunk. He then took the PCX with him and walked to the pedestrian crossing in front of him and Crawley, but he stopped just before touching the first white rectangle that made up the pedestrian crossing. Crawley then opted to go to the nearest parking lot that was in front of Hamada Church.

Tarou and Wattana, now standing on the rooftop of Olive House, ran until they reached the house facing the pedestrian crossing. Once they stopped, they pointed themselves to their respective upper-right and began to crawl on the roof they're currently standing on. Other than his P226 pistol, now holstered in his left armpit, Tarou had his scooter's helmet strapped onto his back until he removed it and put it on his head. Wattana, by contrast, simply had her P5 holstered at her right hip. She then brought out a pair of binoculars and began to watch the street. Tarou then brought out his smartphone and used IntMail to contact Vos. He typed:

Miss Wattana and I are in position.

After Tarou pressed "Send", he resumed looking at what he could look at as he and Wattana, although on top of the house closest to the Hamada Church, had to make sure they wouldn't be seen from below. Only Wattana was able to see across the street because she possessed binoculars. It was then that Vos responded with his message that read:

Standing below you and Sunan. Jake's in the parking lot. "Smith's" at that café monitoring on activity from the Hoshikawa's end. Don't know how he pulled that off and I do not want to know.

"I see a limousine," Wattana warned with Tarou writing another message that read:

Miss Wattana spotted a limousine. She and I will take a closer look.

After pressing "Send", Tarou crawled a little further across the roof to see the limousine Wattana claimed to have spotted. Below, Vos also saw the limousine, but because he was below Tarou and Wattana, as well as wearing something that made inconspicuous, he was able to determine that it was a limousine. Now outside the Townace, Crawley also saw the limousine, but as he was closer to the limousine, he saw the driver and the passengers. Yet it was still too far for him to identify those in the limousine.

Once Tarou was able to see the street without making it easy for those below to spot him, he, Wattana, Crawley, and Vos now saw who came out of the limousine: Maria Hoshikawa and her mother Miku. Once they were inside, the limousine's driver, Ugaki, began to move the vehicle backward, then to its upper-left. Crawley promptly rushed to the left side of the Townace, as he knew that Ugaki was going to use the same parking lot. His assumption was right as Ugaki then entered the limousine into the parking lot and because not that many people are Catholic, much less willing to use a personal vehicle to travel to Hamada Church, Ugaki chose somewhere far from Crawley and the Townace; to the relief of the former.

However, as Ugaki parked the limousine, he saw Crawley and the Townace. He then got out of the limousine and, after locking it, he began to walk up to the latter. Crawley began to make more assumptions as to why the Hoshikawa's personal driver would approach him, but it didn't matter when Ugaki reached Crawley.

"You're one of those mercenaries, aren't you?" Ugaki inquired in English that still had a trace of his Japanese accent.

"… Yes?" Crawley fearfully answered but kept his mouth slightly open as he thought of something that then made him close his mouth before opening it again. "Your English is good though it still has that accent"

"Thank you. I learn in whatever free time I do have because it'll help me deal with my employers."

"Now I must ask you this: what do you think I'm here for?"

"Keeping an eye on Miss Maria."

"Good answer, as far as I can tell you."

Neither Ugaki nor Crawley had anything else to say yet, both struggled to stay silent. The former quickly moved his mouth, which made him willing to resume the conversation.

"Do you mind me asking you something?" Ugaki asked.

"What is it?" Crawley asked in kind.

"Knowing that you can't mention much of your mercenary career so far, I can at least ask this: what made you become a soldier?"

"That's an interesting question. Let's see… I'm from Australia. Tasmania to be specific. My father owned a vineyard, but I didn't want to inherit it. Therefore, I joined the New United Nations Ground Force, and I opted for an honorable discharge after watching a display of political stupidity between the New United Nations and the African Federation because my unit was involved in an ambush that would have dragged both supernational unions into a war had it not been for the one responsible accepting what he did. That's all I can tell you."

"I see. I too was once a solider."

"New United Nations Defense Forces?"

"Japan Ground Self-Defense Force. Seemed awfully brief due to what happened next… "

"Something tells me the next part of this story is something that no one's going to like."

"And you're not wrong. Found that my wife saw another man behind my back while I was in the Ground Self-Defense Force. I lost my… "patiencc", for lack of a better term. I ended up losing the benefits that came with my time in the Ground Self-Defense Force and no one, friends nor family, was willing to talk to me. Only Mr. Hoshikawa took pity on me."

"So that's why you're his driver?"

"Since then, I've done what I can to atone for that."

Suddenly, an Odyssey van appeared. Both Crawley and Ugaki saw the van; each filled with their own questions in their respective minds. Unbeknownst to the former two, the men in the van were Serdar Muhadow, Raşit Ghaemi, and Gurdov.

"Are they friends of yours?" Ugaki asked.

"Nope," Crawley answered.

"And they can't be parishioners. By now, it must be past today's Gospel reading. Other than that, Mr. Hoshikawa and his family are the only parishioners who travel by limousine with me as the driver. Every other parishioner walks."

"Not only that, I bet these guys are up to no good."

"What do you mean?"

"They're wearing ski masks." Crawley then pointed at the man seated at the left chair in the front of the Odyssey and another man seated behind. Crawley then touched Ugaki and pointed to his rear with the latter managing to know that the former was urging him to hide. Ugaki then stepped back with Crawley also stepping back. Crawley, however, moved his head forward as far as his neck would allow him to and he found that the man he pointed at was now facing his opposite side, presumably talking to another occupant of the Odyssey. Crawley immediately hid again and brought out his smartphone.

"What is it?" Ugaki asked as he saw Crawley use his smartphone's IntMail.

"This could be trouble," Crawley answered as he typed:

Wouter, you're seeing that Odyssey, right?

As soon as he finished writing his question to Vos, Crawley pressed "Send". Crawley then saw "WV is typing" below his message. After a minute, the "WV is typing" vanished. In its place was Vos' reply that read:

I am now. I'm seeing two guys in the front. Presumably there's another guy behind the one on the left seat.

Crawley then typed "I can confirm the third guy" and pressed "Send".

Again, "WV is typing" appeared. While waiting, Crawley pocketed his smartphone and brought out his P5 pistol, the same as Wattana's. *Thank God he brought a pistol with him,* Ugaki thought before facing Crawley.

"Is that all you brought with you?" Ugaki asked to Crawley.

"Apparently, yes," Crawley answered grimly. "Could you please hold on to it? I need to see if Wouter got back to me and I need both of my hands for this."

"Is it on safety?"

"Yes." Both stopped talking as Crawley gave the P5 to Ugaki. The former brought out his smartphone again and found in IntMail Vos' reply that read:

I'm contacting "Smith". Don't be a hero.

Crawley then wrote "How can I" followed by pressing send. After that, he hid his smartphone again and took back his P5.

#

Olive House. 0949 hours

At Olive House, Frederick Dirks received Vos' message in IntMail that read:

We got big trouble. An Odyssey appeared with three men (Crawley spotted the third guy) and it's plain as day they're not parishioners. They even covered their faces with ski masks. Most likely Wattana and Ganji have spotted the van. Do you have any bright ideas if these guys are armed?

Dirks then wrote his reply. Taking almost two minutes, the FIS agent finished his message and pressed "Send". After that, he asked the proprietress for the bill.

#

Outside Hamada Church. 0956 hours

At the parking lot in front of Hamada Church, Crawley felt his smartphone. He pocketed his P5 and got his smartphone. Finding that

Vos sent him another message in IntMail, Crawley opened IntMail and found Vos' new message that read:

"Smith" got back to me. He's ordered us not to do anything yet, but he's also concerned our new friends must have brought automatic weapons with them. Hide if fired upon.

Automatic weapons?! Crawley thought exasperatedly. *Bloody hell!*

#

Hamada Church. 0958 hours

Mass had ended for the day. As the parishioners began to leave, the priest approached the Hoshikawa women as they were also exiting the church. "Excuse me," the priest said to Miku and Maria, making them turn to him.

"Yes, Father Afable?" Miku asked.

"I didn't see your husband today."

"He had to leave for Nemuro because a fire struck the hotel one of his subsidiaries finished. The hotel is to open tomorrow."

"I see. I'm sure the Lord understands, even if it's Black Saturday. Thank you for entertaining my question and I apologize for delaying your leave."

"It's alrig-"

Maria was interrupted by shouting and screaming. She, her mother, and Father Afable rushed outside.

#

Outside Hamada Church. 1001 hours

The Hoshikawa women and Father Afable found the three men that the Iron Dutchman Services members spotted. Raşit Ghaemi and Gurdov aimed AK-2000s while Serdar Muhadow PM-01 semi-automatic pistol.

"Where's Maria Hoshikawa?" Muhadow PM-01 asked.

Father Afable walked up to the armed men. "Please leave. Don't bring violence into the house of God."

"Give her to us or you will all die!" The man with the pistol walked up to the priest and aimed the pistol between his eyes. "Starting with you, Father."

"Wait!" shouted Maria Hoshikawa as she walked out of the fearful crowd. "What is it that you want with me?"

"So you're Maria Hoshikawa." Muhadow stopped aiming his pistol at Father Afable and holstered it as he approached the teenage girl. "You're awfully brave to approach us. Do you know *why* we want you?"

"No, but I anticipate that I am of extremely high value that you're willing to kill these innocent people. Do you promise to leave them alone if you take me?"

Unbeknownst to everyone, Tarou Ganji and Sunan Wattana watched everything unfold. *Damn it,* Tarou cursed in his mind when he saw Miku rush to Maria after she approached the armed men in black. *If I'm to go down there, I need to use Japanese. Think… think… what's "Put your guns down" in Japanese?*

"Maria, do you even know what you're doing?" Miku asked to her daughter.

"Mother, it's alright," Maria assured Miku before she faced the man with the PM-01. "Do you promise to spare my mother and everyone else here if I go with you?"

"If you're so willing… " the man said before he brought out his syringe and stabbed Maria near her left acromion. As a result, she lost consciousness. The man then grabbed Maria, opened the rear right door, and shoved Maria inside.

"You best not follow because this little princess bartered her life for yours," Muhadow warned as he brought out his PM-01 and aimed it and Miku and the other parishioners.

Suddenly, Tarou jumped out of the roof and upon landing, got up and aimed his P226 at the gunmen. This caused many to run in panic as the Turkmen mercenaries aimed their AK-2000s at Tarou.

"Sugu ni juu o oroshite kudasai!" Tarou shouted at the gunmen.

You idiot! Vos shouted in his mind as he saw what happened just as Frederick Dirks joined him.

Suddenly, Jason Luke Crawley appeared and shot one of the Turkmen mercenaries. The other Turkmen with the AK fired upon Crawley, who then hid at his Townace.

"Get the van ready!" Muhadow ordered to his subordinate. "I'll distract them."

Muhadow then challenged the Iron Dutchman Services members while the surviving gunman with the AK rushed inside the Odyssey. Muhadow was able to fire at both Crawley and Tarou but had no intention of killing them, even if Crawley killed one of his subordinates. This continued, allowing the Turkmen to succeed in getting inside the Odyssey and with the key still in the ignition switch, he immediately used it to start up the van.

With the van's engine turned on, the gunman with the AK-2000 began driving backward, with Muhadow following and firing to stop Tarou and Crawley from pursuing. Once far enough, Muhadow opened the rear right door again and jumped inside. The former immediately increased speed and after backing far enough from Tarou, Crawley, Vos, and Dirks, the gunman with the AK-2000 opted to move forward as he was now at a route where he could easily escape. Once he turned onto that street, he moved. This forced Dirks and the Iron Dutchman Services members to stop at the man Tarou killed. Wattana then joined them.

"You idiot!" Vos shouted at Tarou. "That was reckless of you!"

"They took Maria!" Tarou shouted in response. "I did warn everyone that something like this would happen!"

"Knock it off!" Dirks shouted to stop the argument. "Ganji's right. We even got ourselves a corpse but we need to take it with us."

"Where?" Wattana asked.

"We need to split into two groups. One group goes on to pursue those men in black who made off with Hoshikawa. The rest must go to Camp Yao and acquire the JGSDF's assitance."

"How do we do that?" Crawley asked.

"Hold on." Dirks then brought out his smartphone, followed by turning to Vos. "Vos, bring out your phone. There's a file I need you to receive from me by IntMail."

"Sure," Vos replied before bringing out this phone. He and Dirks put on their respective phones' IntMail, with the latter going through his phone's files. After selecting a particular file, he had it delivered to Vos' IntMail address. Vos then received the file and, to his surprised, the file bore the name "FIS Document".

"What sort of file is this?" Vos asked.

"Just open it when you go to Camp Yao," Dirks answered. "Ganji and I will pursue that van but we can't make it obvious because the police will catch us too."

"And what about the rest of us?" Crawley asked as he referred to himself, Vos, and Wattana.

"You're to go to Camp Yao. Now get this corpse and go!"

"You heard the man," Vos ordered. "Let's move!" Vos and Crawley immediately got the corpse of the dead gunman while Wattana got the AK-2000 of the latter.

The one with the PM-01, he sounded familiar, Tarou thought as he and Dirks rushed back to the PCX parked in front of Olive House.

#

Japan Ground Self-Defense Force Camp Yao, Yao. 1133 hours

Vos, Wattana, and Crawley then reached Japan Ground Self-Defense Force Camp Yao. Because it was Crawley who drove the Townace, Vos gave his phone to the former with the document he received from Dirks earlier now open. Once Crawley received the phone, he used the document in the phone to show to the guard why they needed to enter, but despite that, the mercenaries had to wait until he was let inside as the guard needed to inform the commandant. Only after one were the mercenaries allowed inside.

As they parked their Townace, Vos, Crawley, and Wattana were then approached by Juzo Izubuchi and two guards. "I assume that you three came here because you were given that document for something urgent?"

"Armed men came to Hamada Church and kidnapped an asset of 'Smith's'," Vos explained. "We need one of the helicopters here."

"My men here will take you to the nearest available helicopter that is available."

"Before we go, there's something I need to take with us," Wattana said.

"What is it?" Vos exasperatedly asked. "We don't have time!"

"It'll be quick. I just need the rear trunk open."

"Fine."

Both Vos and Wattana rushed back to the Tonwace. Once the former got the rear trunk opened, the latter quickly got the AK-2000 they took along with the gunman's corpse.

"Got it," Wattana said.

"Close then I'll lock," Vos ordered to Wattana, who then exited the rear compartment and closed it. Vos then locked the Townace again, and the two returned to Crawley, Izubuchi, and the two JGSDF guards.

"Where did you get that AK?" Izubuchi asked.

"From one of the abductors that got killed earlier," Wattana answered. "And we're going to put it to good use."

"Then let's go," Crawley reminded.

"Get them to the helicopter," Izubuchi ordered his subordinates. "Now!"

"Ryoukai," one JGSDF soldier replied.

"Wait! I'm coming too."

Everyone now stood dumbfounded that Izubuchi made such a declaration. "W... Why you?" Crawley asked.

"The pilots don't know English," Izubuchi claimed. "But I do."

"Then we better hurry," Vos added to Crawley's earlier warning.

#

Studec'; Underneath Osaka Bay. 1140 hours

The Imperial Eurasian Navy submarine *Studec'* was now within Japanese waters. This submarine belonged to the *Vyšen'*-class of submarines that were used for not only reconnaissance, but also to deliver Spetsnaz units of the Imperial Eurasian Naval Infantry.

Like all submarines by 2030, the *Vyšen'*-class used a fusion reactor. Fusion power was a discovery yielded by the crash of *Revelator* and, as a result, ships such as submarines now use fusion reactors to avoid the need for refueling. Unlike every other submarine, the *Vyšen'*-class carried no weapons. Instead, the space that would have to accommodate torpedoes, and the tubes needed to launch them was instead used to launch and retrieve Naval Infantry *Spetsnaz*. In addition, the *Vyšen'*-class was built with a larger reactor in order to make it travel faster. As a result, it was longer than a *Rusalka*-class attack submarine without reaching the length of the *Dola*-class multi-purpose submarine.

"Kapitan, we're now at Kansai City," an officer said to his captain, Yelena Abramovna Samsonova.

"Spasibo," Samsonova replied to her subordinate. Forty-nine years old, Samsonova had blonde hair, dark brown eyes, and very light skin. Five years before, she was appointed as captain to the *Studec'* and that this wasn't the first time she had ever been to Japanese waters. Her first mission upon acquiring her commission was to deliver Tatiana Ioannovna Tsulukidze and her subordinates Pyotr Stepanovich Chadov and Karim Olegovich Zhakiyanov to Japan, as they were to operate an OVR cell in Kansai City.

Since then, whenever Tatiana needed to report to the OVR's director Vyacheslav Leonidovich Puzanov, Samsonova must provide transportation for Tatiana, in which the *Studec'* traveled to northern Sakhalin Island, held by the Eurasian Tsardom. There, Tatiana availed for a plane to take her to Nizhny Novgorod.

That mercenary Grand Duchess Tatiana told me about having to be quick, Samsonova anxiously thought. *We will be detected if we wait for him for too long.*

Samsonova then turned to the subordinate that talked to her earlier. "Egorov, are Stárshiy Serzhánt Danylo and his men ready?"

"They should have arrived at the water lock by now," the officer named Egorov answered.

"Open once they hear a knock. The knock will have to come from that mercenary we were told about by 'Elizaveta'. It'll be Stárshiy Serzhánt Danylo who'll tell us if there's a knock."

"Zametano, Kapitan."

The Chase

Higashiosaka Ward, Kansai City, Kansai Prefecture; State of Japan. April 20, 2030; 1221 hours (Japan Standard Time)

"What do we do now!?" the masked gunman with the AK-2000 asked to Serdar Muhadow, who drove their Odyssey after they successfully captured Maria Hoshikawa and escaped Hamada Church. "Gurdov's dead."

"We continue," Muhadow answered. "Just remember when to get out of the van."

"... Right."

Both Turkmens heard a police siren. "Kill them," Muhadow ordered.

Without saying anything, the masked gunman, Raşit Ghaemi, replied. He opened the rear right door and turned back to find the police car pursuing them. Ghaemi turned his AK-2000's safety off but moved the selective fire switch to the number 3. After that, he aimed the rifle at the pursuing police car and squeezed the trigger once. As a result, the three rounds hit the police car and only one of the three rounds hit the driver of the police car, making it spin until it stopped.

#

1230 hours

Elsewhere in the Higashiosaka Ward, Tarou Ganji and Frederick Dirks continued their pursuit of the masked gunmen that abducted Maria yet they took a different route to avoid attracting attention. While Tarou drove the PCX scooter they rode on, Dirks used his right hand for his smartphone in order to track down the gunmen as they didn't know about the tracking device Dirks installed on Maria.

"Where are those masked gunmen now?" Tarou asked Dirks.

"They might cross into the Higashi-Koya Highway like we are," Dirks answered. "Keep your eyes peeled for them."

"Roger."

Tarou then continued moving straight. Eventually, he and Dirks reached the Higashi-Koya Highway, which ran from Kashiwara to Shijonawate with Yao and the Higashiosaka Ward of Kansai City in the middle.

"Turn right," Dirks ordered to Tarou. "Hopefully we can catch up to those abductors before the police have."

"Acknowledged," Tarou replied before he turned right.

Both Tarou and Dirks were now at the Higashi-Koya Highway. As they got past the Shiritsu Shijo Library, they found the Odyssey they were looking for. They immediately gave chase.

In the Odyssey, Ghaemi saw the pursuing FIS agent and mercenary "Commander, it must those interlopers from the church!" Ghaemi warned Muhadow.

"Then kill them!" Muhadow screamed at his subordinate.

Ghaemi opened the door again. Like before, he turned off his AK-2000's safety but this time, he moved the selective fire switch to full automatic. He then aimed at Tarou and Dirks. Dirks in turned brought out his pistol, a Multi-Caliber Pistol (MCP) chambered at .45 Automatic Colt Pistol. Once Ghaemi fired his AK-2000, Tarou turned to evade the shots. Dirks fired back but the rounds he fired hit the van instead with no one hurt. This repeated until there was another turn that Muhadow used to evade his new pursuers. As Muhadow turned, Tarou and Dirks attempted to give chase but heard police sirens.

"Not good," Dirks said as he found police cars appearing. "If those policemen catch us, we're screwed."

"What do we do?" Tarou asked.

"Ganji, there's a police station near Nishi High School. I have an idea but it's highly risky."

"Understood. Taking us there now."

Hiraoka Police Station. 1302 hours

Both Tarou and Dirks approached the office of Kotarou Nanakawa, the Assistant Commissioner for Hiraoka Station. Fifty years old, Nanakawa only had his black hair between his scalp and his face.

"I hear you have information about the shooting near Hamada Church earlier this morning?" Nanakawa asked.

"We do," Dirks answered.

"And who's the one covering his head?" Nanakawa referred to Tarou, who kept his helmet on to avoid being identified.

"His face is need to know. Like how I have information I'm willing to offer to you in exchange for allowing us to assist in pursuing those gunmen?"

"What do you mean the information is need to know?"

Dirks then brought out his smartphone. He then opened the same document he gave to Wouter Vos earlier and showed the document to Nanakawa that read:

This man is a member of the Foreign Intelligence Service of the New United Nations. His presence in Japan is to monitor possible activity by foreign infiltrators. Assistance must be guaranteed to this man at all costs.

Miyako Nagare, Commissioner of the National Police Agency

Dirks then pushed the back to him and moved his right thumb, already pressing against the screen of his phone, downward. He then showed the document again to Nanakawa, now in Japanese writing. Now that it was in Japanese, Nanakawa read it extensively. He then pushed his upper body backward, allowing Dirks to move his phone backward.

"You know I can't act against an order from the Commissioner," Nanakawa continued. "But if we're after the same target, what do you wish to do?"

Outside Hiraoka Station. 1317 hours

Both Tarou and Dirks rushed out of the station and back to the PCX of the former. Once Tarou got on the scooter and started it up, Dirks joined him but brought out his smartphone and resumed using the application used for the tracking device on Maria.

"What do we do now?" Tarou asked before he moved the PCX.

"Something doesn't seem right," Dirks said as if he ignored Tarou's question. "The abductors seem to be headed toward Osaka Bay. Lest they have a submarine waiting to pick them up, it's as if they're going to kill themselves along with their hostage."

"Where are they now?"

"Near the Yaenosato Station."

"Then how do we cut them off?"

"I suggest we go to Tsutenkaku Park. If by some miracle that's the route of those abductors, we can stop them there."

"Roger that. Starting up the scooter but we need fuel."

"What do you mean we need fuel!?"

#

Gas Japan Higashiosaka Service Station. 1324 hours

Tarou, having paid for the fueling, rushed back to Dirks and his PCX. "Ganji, you're done?" Dirks asked.

"Yes," Tarou answered before he brought out a piece of paper and a ballpen. "Here's the receipt and the pen you lent me."

"Give those back to me later. We got bigger problems."

"What do you mean?"

Dirks showed his smartphone with Maps to Tarou. There, a blue dot was now at the Horikosicho neighborhood of the Tennoji Ward. "That's the route I use to travel to Taisho for picking up Dr. Hamilton when we're needed at the *Iron Dutchman*," Tarou said.

"We can at least join the police in pursuing those gunmen," Dirks replied. "Come on. We have no time to waste!"

However, Tarou and Dirks saw a UH-1H Iroquois utility helicopter. The former two knew who were inside the helicopter.

"Mr. 'Smith', I have an idea but it will take up some of our time," Tarou argued.

"What is it?" Dirks asked.

"I need to see if the shop here has tape."

"Tape? What for?"

#

1334 hours

"So you think this will work?" Dirks asked Tarou after the smartphone of the former was now taped between the throttle control grips.

"It has to," Tarou answered. "You can't track Maria with your phone nor keep up with Mr. Vos at the same time with my phone."

"Even so… Wait, did you call her 'Maria'?"

"I'm not allowed to?"

Dirks gave a smile that he kept away from Tarou before facing him. "Just be careful with my phone."

"I understand."

"We've wasted too much time here. We better move."

#

Higashinari Ward. 1345 hours

Tarou and Dirks now entered the Higashinari Ward. The latter was now using Tarou's smartphone to use IntMail. Upon using his conversation with Wouter Vos, whose name in IntMail was simply "Wvos", Dirks wrote "This is 'Smith'. Borrowing Ganji's phone because he needs mine to track the van were pursuing. What are our abductors doing now" and pressed "Send".

Although in a moving vehicle, Dirks had to keep an eye for a reply. He also had to hold on to Tarou's phone to avoid losing it, with Tarou having to make sure Dirks' phone didn't fall off while he drove his PCX. It was then that Dirks felt that Vos sent a reply, because he felt Tarou's phone vibrate. Upon opening IntMail, Dirks found Vos' reply that read:

Wattana, Crawley, and I have that van in our sights. They're giving the police a runaround, but for some reason, they're going to Taisho Ward. If we're all lucky, they'll hit a dead end and then we can get them. Also, Izubuchi opted to accompany us because the pilots don't know English.

After that, Dirks wrote "Do you have something to stop any of that Odyssey's wheels if neither Ganji nor I make it" before he pressed "Send".

Again Dirks waited for Vos' reply. Now, the former and Ganji crossed the Hirano River. Once they passed the river, Dirks felt Tarou's phone again, which meant that Vos replied. As he opened IntMail and his conversation with Vos, he found Vos' reply that read:

Wattana appropriated the AK used by the gunman Crawley shot at Hamada Church. If there's anyone who can shoot a van's wheels, it's her. Even if it's an AK without a scope.

Dirks' reply before pressing "Send" was "I wish you luck. Hopefully Ganji and I join up with those cops. We got the Assistant Commissioner of Hiraoka Station to get those cops to allow us to do what we need to do".

Dirks then put away Tarou's phone. "Ganji, increase the speed, but not too much," Dirks ordered. "We can't lose my phone."

"Roger that," Tarou replied.

#

Japan Ground Self-Defense Force UH-1H; Above Nishinari Ward. 1352 hours

"Wattana-san, do you see the target?" Juzo Izubuchi asked as he sat in the leftmost rear seat in the middle compartment of the UH-1H Iroquois while he faced Sunan Wattana, sitting on the front right seat wielding the AK-2000 she took from Gurdov.

Despite its age, the UH-1 Iroquois utility helicopter, commonly referred to as "Huey" due to its original designation HU-1, was still used by the

Japan Self-Defense Forces. This was part of making sure that the JSDF as a whole wouldn't be allowed to be powerful as helicopters more advanced that Iroquois was seen as force projection, which the respective militaries of the New United Nations' member-states weren't allowed to have as a price to remain independent.

"I do," Wattana answered. "It's nearing that building I told 'Smith' about."

"What building!?" Wouter Vos asked as he sat at the leftmost forward chair.

"The one where I first spotted Fahri."

"Get us lower!" Vos loudly ordered to the Iroquois pilots with Izubuchi repeating the order in Japanese.

"Wait! It's continuing to go straight!"

"Let me see!" Vos stood up, but moved slowly. He now joined Wattana as they saw the Odyssey and the police cars chasing it cross the Senbomatsu Bridge.

Izubuchi then commanded the pilots to move forward in Japanese with both pilots replying with a "Ryoukai".

#

OVR Safehouse. 1350 hours

Pyotr Stepanovich Chadov and Karim Olegovich Zhakiyanov then barged into Tatiana Ioannovna Tsulukidze's office. The latter showed anger through her face at the former two.

"This better be good!" Tatiana replied.

"A helicopter's on its way here!" Chadov replied.

"What!?"

All three OVR agents began to fear the worse. However, they found that not only did the Odyssey pass through them as if the former three didn't exist, so did the pursuing policemen. Both parties crossed the Senbomaru Bridge, with the former three looking with relief.

"Do you have your pistols with you?" Tatiana asked her two subordinates.

"Da," Chadov answered.

"Prepare them!"

All three OVR agents began to fear the worse. However, they found that not only did the Odyssey pass through them as if the former three didn't exist, so did the pursuing policemen. Both parties crossed the Senbomaru Bridge with the former three looking with relief.

"… That was close… " Tatiana remarked.

All three then turned to the Iroquois they first saw. In an instant, it began to leave, relaxing the OVR agents, prompting them to go back inside their safehouse.

#

Japan Ground Self-Defense Force UH-1H; Above Taisho Ward. 1355 hours

"And we're near home now," Jason Luke Crawley lamented as the Iroquois flew above Taisho Ward with Crawley looking below before he turned to Wattana. "Sunan, what are they up to?"

"Beats me," Wattana answered. "How are those policemen not running out of fuel?"

"Wouter, what are you doing?" Crawley asked as he saw Vos use his smartphone.

"Attempting to ask 'Smith' if we can fire already," Vos answered. "We need to end this now."

Vos finished writing his message to Dirks, which read:

We're near Hoshikawa land. It doesn't appear that the abductors have somewhere they intend on fleeing to and no one knows why and I doubt you do as well. Permission to have Wattana disable the wheels?

Vos then pressed "Send".

"What do we do now?" Izubuchi asked the mercenary leader.

"We keep pursuing," Vos answered as he turned to Izubuchi.

Nishinari Ward. 1357 hours

Both Tarou and Vos were now at the Nishinari Ward. While using the smartphone of the former, the latter received Vos' message in IntMail. After reading it, who composed his reply that read:

If those abductors are near Hoshikawa Shipyards, you have my permission to fire.

Dirks pressed "Send" as soon as he finished. "Was that from Mr. Dirks?" Tarou asked.

"That's right," Dirks answered. "We best join up with him. No doubt they're about to go near Hoshikawa Shipyards."

#

Taisho Ward. 1357 hours

"How long are we going to keep this up?" Raşit Ghaemi asked Serdar Muhadow while the latter drove across Taisho Ward. "We're already in the Taisho Ward. We need to find somewhere for you to take the real Maria with you and swim to that submarine 'Elizaveta' promised to pick you up."

"We're almost there," Muhadow answered.

Suddenly, both Turkmens heard the UH-1H Iroquois' rotor blades becoming louder.

#

Japan Ground Self-Defense Force UH-1H; Above Taisho Ward. 1359 hours

Now low enough, the Iroquois was at an altitude Wattana needed. She then moved the selective fire switch of the AK-2000 she took from Gurdov's corpse to semi-automatic. After that, she began to aim.

Seeing the left wheels of Muhadow and Ghaemi's Odyssey, Wattana counted on the AK's open sight to allow her to see the left rear wheel, her target. She then closed her left eye to focus her right eye against her target. However, Raşit Ghaemi opened the left rear door and began to aim his AK-2000, which Crawley noticed.

"Sunan, one of those terrorists has his AK aimed at you," Crawley warned to Wattana. "You better hurry!"

"Firing now!" Wattana shouted as she pulled the trigger. The 7.62x39mm bullet then flew out of the AK-2000's muzzle and toward the left rear wheel.

#

Taisho Ward. 1402 hours

The bullet then hit the rear left wheel of the Odyssey. It caused the van to spin, but despite that, Muhadow saw that he was near Osaka Bay.

"Opening trunk door!" Muhadow shouted as he moved his left arm to where the lock to the trunk door. As a result, the trunk door began to loosen and as the van made a full turn again, the door fell off, as did the crate with Ryoka Akagi inside.

"Ghaemi, get out!" the Turkmen mercenary simply kicked the left rear door and jumped out of the door. Muhadow then got out of the right front seat and reached for the still-unconscious Maria Hoshikawa. However, the police that had pursued him and Ghaemi now reached them, yet this was what Muhadow counted on as the Odyssey reached the edge of Japanese soil that led toward Osaka Bay.

The spinning stopped, but because the van was now at the edge, it began to fall off. Unbeknownst to the policemen and mercenaries pursuing Muhadow, Muhadow got the real Maria, yet he began to jump into the water. This ultimately caused the van to fall into Osaka Bay.

"No!" Vos shouted as he, Wattana, and Crawley rushed to the falling van as soon as the Iroquois landed. By the time they reached the edge, the van was now floating with Muhadow nowhere in sight.

It was then that Tarou Ganji and Frederick Dirks appeared. They saw some policemen surrounding Ghaemi while two looked at the crate that fell off the van. The former two joined the policemen, looking at the crate with Dirks using the same document he used when he talked to Nanakawa for the policemen.

"You must be Mr. 'Smith'," one policeman said.

"Hai," Dirks replied. "Where did this crate come from?"

"It fell off from the van that just fell into the water."

"Go to Mr. Vos and the others," Dirks ordered to Tarou. "I'll deal with this crate."

Tarou simply nodded and rushed to join Vos, Wattana, and Crawley. The former made it to join the latter three in looking at the empty van.

"Where's Maria?" Tarou asked.

"We don't know," Vos answered.

"There's a crate behind us. Mr. 'Smith' is looking at it."

"Maybe she's in there!" Crawley exclaimed, with desperate hope evident in his tone.

"Then what are we waiting for!?" Wattana asked.

The four mercenaries rushed to the crate. They found that the policemen and Dirks were unable to open it.

"Is anyone there!?" a girl's voice asked, shocking everyone that surrounded the crate.

"Hoshikawa-senpai, is that you?" Tarou asked.

"Who?" The question shocked the mercenaries and the FIS agent. *I... Impossible!* Dirks thought before he went to Maps in his phone, where he found that the blue dot that represented the tracking device he planted on Maria was now in the middle of Osaka Bay. By then, Wattana began to use the buttstock of her AK-2000 as a hammer by repeatedly hitting the crate. She kept on hitting the crate until she saw the girl, whom she, her fellow mercenaries, and Dirks mistook for Maria Hoshikawa.

"There is someone in there!" Wattana said.

"I'll get the rest of the crate open," Tarou declared by grabbing both ends of the hole Wattana made. Using his strength, Tarou tore open that end of the crate and as the pieces of wood flew out of the crate, they saw "Maria" inside, still pressing her knees against her body and gripping on them with her arms.

"Please calm down, Miss," one of the policemen said. "You're safe now."

"I... I am... ?" the girl asked.

"Hai," the other policeman said. "Just come out."

The girl then slowly began to stand up. However, Tarou rushed toward her and touched her blonde hair but he immediately pulled it out of her. It was as plain as day that the girl wasn't Maria Hoshikawa.

"What's going on here?" Crawley asked.

"Sir," said a policewoman as she approached Dirks. "We still have the man in the ski mask apprehended. I imagine you wish to take him with you?"

Dirks then turned to the policewoman. "Bring him to the helicopter." Dirks then pointed to the Iroquois and, by extension, Juzo Izubuchi.

"Ryoukai". The policewoman left with Vos, Wattana, Crawley, and Tarou now joining Dirks.

"What happens next?" Vos asked.

"We take our terrorist friend back to Camp Yao and keep him there for the time being," Dirks answered. "Naturally, we'll interrogate him, but it's clear he and his partners-in-crime have done a lot of planning. We wait until that van is extracted and then-"

"Tell me everything that happened." Dirks and the mercenaries turned to find Daisuke Hoshikawa and his wife, Miku. "What happened to my daughter?"

#

Underneath Osaka Bay. 1411 hours

Serdar Muhadow was now underneath Osaka Bay. He carried with him the unconscious Maria Hoshikawa as he swam.

I have to find that submarine the Grand Duchess sent to pick me up, along with Hoshikawa, Muhadow thought. *Hopefully, it's not too far because neither of us can last this long underwater.*

#

Studec'. 1501 hours

"Kapitan!" Egorov shouted as he rushed to his captain, Yelena Abramova Samsonova. "I've just heard from Stárshiy Serzhánt Danylo. He claimed to have seen the mercenary we were told about knocking on the glass bottom door."

"Was he carrying a girl with him?" Samsonova asked.

"Da."

"Then tell Stárshiy Serzhánt Danylo to open the door and let that mercenary in."

"Zametano."

#

1505 hours

"Zametano," Artem Viktorovich Danylo said while using the intercom located in the *Studec*'s launch bay. Thirty years old, Danylo joined the Imperial Naval Infantry Spetsnaz initially to provide for his family and after he finished his training, he fought in the Eurasian Tsardom's invasion of the Islamic Republic of Iran in 2023. Having found a wife himself, Danylo hoped that this was his last assignment as he intended on returning to civilian life to be with his wife and their son. He had light skin and blue eyes, with his brown hair underneath his diving suit.

"What did the Captain say?" Dahlia Vadzimirovna Kaminskaya asked. Only a year younger than Danylo, Kaminskaya served with Danylo since Iran, though unlike the latter, the former intended to stay. Like Danylo, she had fair skin but blue eyes with her blonde hair hidden by her diving suit.

"We let that mercenary in," Danylo ordered.

"I'll open the door." Kaminskaya rushed to a red lever found opposite to where the intercom was located. Once she pressed the lever downward, the glass bottom door opened. Muhadow then raised the unconscious Maria Hoshikawa through the door with two other subordinates of Danylo rushing to get her inside. After that, Muhadow then climbed up the door with Danylo himself raising Muhadow inside. Once the mercenary was inside, Kaminskaya pulled the lever upward, closing the door.

"Spasibo," Muhadow said to Danylo.

"You must have swum from Kansai City to here," Danylo remarked. "And you had your hostage with you. How were you able to do that without succumbing to the loss of air?"

"That's need to know. Might I please see your Captain?"

"Please be patient." Danylo then turned to Kaminskaya, who then joined him and Muhadow. "Dahlia, please get our guests a towel."

"Zametano, Artem," Kaminskaya replied.

"I have another question for you," Danylo said as he faced Muhadow again.

"And what is it?" Muhadow asked.

"How long will that girl you brought with you be unconscious?"

"She should come to. If you have a brig, take her there now."

"I'll see what I can do." Danylo then turned to his two other subordinates with Maria. "Surguladze, Popov, get that girl to the brig." "Zametano, Serzhánt," the two Naval Infantrymen named Surguladze and Popov replied in unison.

#

1520 hours

"So, you're Mansur Fahri?" Samsonova asked after Serdar Muhadow was brought to the command room of the *Studec'*. "Or should I say Serdar Muhadow? You're the most reckless person I've met other than 'Elizaveta'."

"I'll take that as a compliment," the Turkmen mercenary replied.

"I assume the girl you brought with you is need to know?"

"Da, I'm sorry to say."

"Then we best get out of here now. A NUN submarine might spot us."

"And now I must attend to my prized captive."

"I must warn you this and I hope you listen: I'll have you shot if you dare do *anything* to that girl."

"Noted." Muhadow then left the control room. Samsonova then turned to Eogorv. "Egorov, announce to the crew that we will leave in five minutes."

"Zametano, Kapitan," Egorov replied.

1526 hours

As Muhadow reached the *Studec*'s brig, he heard the announcement that the submarine will be leaving Osaka Bay. As a result, he pressed his back against the metallic wall beside. He knew that before it left Japan, the *Studec'* had to make an eighty-degree turn, making it face Osaka Bay as opposed to Kansai City. Luckily, the turn was only five minutes. After that, the submarine began to move. This wasn't to be the last turn the submarine would have to make, for there were to be more turns until the *Studec'* was to reach its destination. Once the submarine moved, Muhadow resumed entering the brig. In the brig, he found Danylo's two subordinates, Surguladze and Popov. Although Muhadow was a mercenary and that the former two weren't, salutes were exchanged.

"Has she woken up yet?" Muhadow asked.

"Not yet," Surguladze answered until Maria made sounds that she was waking up, surprising Surguladze and Popov, but now Muhadow.

"I need you two to leave," Muhadow requested. "I need to have a talk with our guest here. Also, she'll need food. She hasn't had lunch yet."

"Zametano," the Naval Infantrymen replied in unison before leaving. Muhadow then moved his left hand toward his crotch and, as fast as he could, found what he needed to get. Once he removed his left hand, Muhadow then placed the object he hid in his groin, a metallic ball. There was only one button on the device and Muhadow pressed it. He then laid the ball on the ground and it was then that Maria came to.

"W… Where am I?" Maria asked in English.

"Good morning, Princess," Muhadow replied in English.

Maria turned to see Muhadow. In one second, she widened her eyes and briefly moved her body backward and breathed heavily. "Y… You're that terrorist!"

"I find 'Terrorist' is too crude of a word to describe me, but I'm glad you recognize me."

"Where am I!?"

"In a submarine. There are some really important people that wish to meet you."

"Is that why you abducted me?"

"Yes. Cooperate with me and you will be released."

It was then that Surguladze and Popov returned with the meal for Maria with Muhadow, quickly grabbing his ball and pressing its button to turn it off. The latter two then turned to the former two. *This man can't be a mere terrorist,* Maria thought as she saw the two Naval Infantrymen as she correctly guessed that they're working with Muhadow. *I doubt that I will ever be released, but at this point, I can't afford to die just yet. I best cooperate to avoid getting killed.*

Surguladze then approached Muhadow and gave the meal to him. The former then opened the cell door, followed by the latter moving to give Maria her meal. "Don't try anything rash," Muhadow warned Maria; the latter complied by simply taking the tray before the former closed and locked her cell door. "How will we get her to come with us?" Surguladze asked in Russian to Muhadow; both assuming that Maria wouldn't understand them.

And now I feel like I'm in a Cold War story, Maria thought in her mind as she saw Muhadow and Surguladze speak in a language she couldn't understand. She started to pray.

Next Move

Taisho Ward, Kansai City, Kansai Prefecture; State of Japan. April 20, 2030; 1410 hours (Japan Standard Time)

"Tell me everything that happened." Daisuke Hoshikawa demanded, with his wife beside him, as he faced Frederick Dirks, Wouter Vos, Sunan Wattana, Jason Luke Crawley, and Tarou Ganji. "What happened to my daughter?"

"Since you just got back, allow me to elaborate," Dirks answered. "We pursued the men who abducted your daughter and just as when Crawley here shot the left rear wheel of the van the abductors used, it fell into Osaka Bay. The girl you just passed was a fake Maria Hoshikawa used by the abductors in order to trick us."

"Then where is she!?" Daisuke's fury was evident yet the mercenaries and their FIS handler weren't able to provide an answer.

"Calm down," Miku said to her husband before she faced Dirks. "What will you do now?"

"We captured one of the abductors so we're having him brought to JGSDF Camp Yao. We'll let the police take the girl we rescued and I'll go with them to learn what she knows."

"Ganji, go with the Hoshikawas," Vos ordered Tarou upon turning to him.

"Roger that," Tarou replied.

#

Hoshikawa Mansion, Higashiosaka Ward, Kansai City. 1449 hours

"I'm sorry it ended that way," Tarou said to the Hoshikawas after recounting the chase from Hamada Church up until Taisho Ward. He no longer wore his helmet.

"It's not your fault," Daisuke said. "It could have been mine."

"What do you mean?" Miku asked.

"I was told that a wagon was found near the hotel after the fire was extinguished. I assumed it to have been a prank or opposition to the- That could be it!"

"What do you mean?" Tarou asked as if he smelled suspicion coming out of Daisuke's mouth.

"The people who kidnapped Maria must have been behind the hotel fire and that they could be holding her for ransom."

"I doubt it. If it was opposition to your hotel in Nemuro, they would have announced it beforehand and contacted you as to what they want and how long you have to meet that demand."

"What do we do?" Miku asked.

"I'll contact Mr. 'Smith'." Tarou brought out his smartphone and after opening IntMail, he typed "Mr. Hoshikawa might have connected the hotel fire in Nemuro to the kidnapping". As he finished, Tarou pressed "Send".

"What will happen now?" Miku asked.

"That will depend on Mr. 'Smith'," Tarou answered.

"Damn it!" Daisuke screamed. "My daughter's life is on the line and you're talking about protocol!?" Neither his wife nor Tarou answered. Daisuke saw their faces and moved his head downward and closed his eyes. "I apologize for my outburst. It's an occupational hazard as a father."

"I understand," Tarou replied. It was then that Tarou felt his smartphone. "That must be Mr. 'Smith'."

The Hoshikawas looked as Tarou opened his smartphone again and began reading his IntMail. Dirks' message read:

Finished attending Ryoka Akagi's questioning. She was apparently told by her kidnappers to confess everything, or rather what she was allowed to tell us, as soon as we found her in that crate. I'm going to contact Vos for a meeting in your ship. Mr. Hoshikawa can attend if he so wishes.

"What is it?" Daisuke asked.

"We got a lead," Tarou answered. "Mr. 'Smith' even invited you to hear what he has to say."

"Go on first. I need to tell Ugaki."

#

Iron Dutchman, Taisho Ward, Kansai City. 1520 hours

"I have all we need to figure out who Maria Hoshikawa's abductors are and why they got her," Frederick Dirks announced to all members of Iron Dutchman Services in their briefing room with Daisuke Hoshikawa also attending. "We'll begin with Ryoka Akagi."

Managing to hear what Dirks said, Tatev Mirzoyan projected the page in the application on her laptop computer showing a profile of Ryoka Akagi with a picture of the girl in her school uniform. "To summarize who this girl is, Ryoka Akagi was simply a girl the terrorists opted to use because she was as old as Maria." Dirks continued. "From what she told the police, she first met Mansur Fahri while working at the Kitakagaya Café as a part-time job with Fahri as a customer."

"I heard from a client of a friend now running an air charter firm in the United Arab Emirates that Mansur Fahri was a falsified name because the one who provided the identity was arrested for falsifying documents," Daisuke said. "Most likely the abductor created the identity of Mansur Fahri to enter Japan and kidnap my daughter."

"Coincidentally, the police found Fahri's passport inside the same crate Akagi was trapped in," Dirks added.

"Any information from the FIS about this?" Wouter Vos, standing beside Dirks, asked.

"I imagine they have more than what we know but the one they sent to inform us won't be here until 2200 hours."

"What about the gunman who surrendered to the police earlier?" Tarou Ganji asked.

"We'll question him later," Dirks answered as he faced Tarou.

"What about the van?" Jake Crawley asked.

"According to the police, it was an Odyssey rented from Abenobashi Car Rental earlier this morning. According to Akagi, she was forced to go inside the crate after it was loaded into the rear trunk."

"Does she know where she was taken before being forced into that crate?" Sunan Wattana asked.

"No. Akagi claimed that when Fahri went to her café a second time, she fainted while attempting to get the bill to him once he finished the meal he ordered. When she came about, her head was covered and couldn't see anything. Even when her abductors took off the bag, she wasn't allowed to see her surroundings because she had an AK-2000 barrel on her head."

"What about the gunman I killed?" Crawley asked.

"He didn't have any form of identification with him. It's the same with his partner-in-crime currently in the custody of the JGSDF."

"When will you interrogate him?" Daisuke asked.

"Soon. I'd like to ask that man why Fahri allowed that passport of his to be found."

"Wait, there's something I need to share about what happened this morning," Tarou added.

"What is it, Ganji?" Vos asked.

"I think I know who Mansur Fahri is."

"What do you mean?" Dirks asked.

"During the shootout in front of Hamada Church, Fahri shouted at the gunman currently in the JGSDF's custody to get into the Odyssey after Mr. Crawley shot the other gunman. He spoke in Turkmen. While I'm hoping the gunman Mr. 'Smith' will interrogate later will provide more answers, I believe that Fahri's real name is Serdar Muhadow."

"Wait, did you say Serdar Muhadow!?"

"Who?" Sunan Wattana asked.

"A Turkmen mercenary. He's called the Butcher of Godana because during the Turkestan War of Independence, he and his fellow Turkmen mercenaries conducted an ambush that spared no lives. The governments of the Asian Pact protested about this as it was the Eurasian Tsardom who propped up the rebels with Muhadow and his men as part of that package. The Eurasians refused to humor the Asian Pact. Since then, the

Asian Pact along with the Eurasian Cooperative Sphere now have tense relations."

"But why would Muhadow abduct my daughter?" Daisuke asked.

"We'll have to ask his subordinate later."

"Take me with you," Tarou requested.

"Why you?" Dirks asked as he turned to Tarou.

"It may be a longshot, as you Americans would say, but hopefully I can get that gunman to talk by using Farsi."

"Why Farsi?"

"Because Muhadow's the one who turned me into a soldier at a young age." Open mouths from everyone else in the briefing room ensued.

"You're not lying, right?" Vos asked.

"I'm not. Muhadow was able to blend in because Iran hosted a Turkmen community. Muhadow was my unit's commander during the Eurasian invasion of Iran. I assumed him dead when I came to after that attack in Charmshahr."

"You're with me then," Dirks declared before he turned to Crawley. "Crawley, you'll be driving us to Camp Yao."

"Why me?" Crawley asked. "Can't you get Ganji to do it?"

"I intend to ask Izubuchi to let us leave with the Turkmen. We might have some use for him later."

Crawley sighed, resigning himself as if it came from Dirks, he automatically assumed it to be an order. "Fine."

"Then let's go."

#

Sumiyoshi Ward. 1652 hours

"By the way, how did you buy this van?" Dirks asked as he was seated in the left front seat of the Townace while Crawley drove and Tarou sat behind Dirks. Tarou still wore his PCX scooter's helmet.

"With the money you paid us with earlier this week," Crawley answered.

"But what about fuel and toll money?"

"Fed, Sem, and Vik pitched in. That's enough for one month."

"But what about after that one month?"

"We're hoping to ask Mr. Hoshikawa if we can find work with his company after this. Wouter knows of this."

"Nice planning."

#

Japan Ground Self-Defense Force Camp Yao, Yao. 1733 hours

Raşit Ghaemi was then brought to the interrogation room attached to the brig of JGSDF Camp Yao. Both Dirks and Tarou saw the Turkmen mercenary brought inside, and all three sat down.

"First, I'll offer you a deal," Dirks stated to the prisoner. "If you answer whatever questions we ask, we'll see to it you're set free. Isn't that a good deal for a mercenary like you?"

Tarou then interpreted Dirks' offer to Ghaemi into Farsi. This surprised the Turkmen as he didn't expected the teenage mercenary hiding his face with his scooter helmet to know Farsi.

Ganji's right, Dirks thought as he saw Ghaemi's reaction when Tarou spoke in Farsi. *Based on his face, it's seems that this terrorist knows Farsi.*

"I'll start with this question: your name, age, birthplace, and unit."

Ghaemi answered Dirks' question, yet it was in Farsi, surprising both Tarou and Dirks. *I knew it*, Tarou thought. *He really is a subordinate of Muhadow.*

Tarou then turned to Dirks. "He says that his name is Raşit Ghaemi. He's thirty-eight, he came from Ĉahârjuy in the Eurasian Tsardom's Turkmenia Governorate, which is alternatively called 'Türkmenabat', and that his unit's name is the Wolves of Turkmenia."

"Interesting. Next question: What's the name of the man one of my other colleagues shot earlier this morning?"

Tarou repeated the question in Farsi. *They're talking about Gurdov,* Ghaemi thought. *Strange for them to ask me such a question even though they killed him. I could deny them their answers, but they offered me my freedom.*

Ghaemi then answered the question. "His name was Dovran Gurdov," Tarou repeated to Dirks in English.

At this point, I could ask Ghaemi here the actual questions I have, but I get the feeling he won't tell for various reasons, despite my offer, Dirks thought. *Ganji already told me about Muhadow and if Ghaemi questions how I came across 'Fahri's' real name, I could have Ganji remove his helmet but no doubt I'm being watched by Izubuchi. Wait, that's it!*

"Please keep an eye on him," Dirks ordered Tarou as he began to rush out of the interrogation room's door.

"Where are you going?" Tarou asked.

"I need to talk to Izubuchi. Just prevent him from escaping."

"Roger that." Dirks then left the room. Tarou then stared at Ghaemi, managing to make sure he didn't make Ghaemi figure out who he was under the helmet.

I didn't think I would encounter someone from my past this fast, Tarou thought. *Not only that, Maria was kidnapped by Muhadow. Could I learn about my past from this? I'll never forget the day I joined Muhadow's unit.*

#

Semnan, Semnan Province, Region 1, Islamic Republic of Iran. June 1, 2023; 0830 hours (Iran Standard Time)

W… Where am I? a boy pondered as he woke up due to vibrations. *I don't remember the ground being this hard.*

The boy began to open his eyes. He was able to see the sun, but mostly, he began to see that he was on a metallic floor and that he was surrounded by children his age.

This must be a truck. But how did I end up here? Last I remember, I just left the refugee camp after it was bombed. Then…

The boy looked around. He then realized he wasn't the only one in the truck, but the other children didn't notice him. *If I remember what Farooq said, children were being grabbed by tall men and thrown into trucks. This could be it!*

The truck then stopped in front of a damaged and abandoned mosque guarded by armed men. As the boy laid on the metallic floor of the truck's rear, his entire body slipped to his left. He then got up but kept laying on the floor and crawled to avoid being heard. As he neared the edge, he saw that he was now in the damaged city of Semran.

Which city is this? The boy pondered before he looked around. After he looked to his left and its rear, he turned right. He saw two armed men talking to three more armed men. The former quickly hid his face.

The boy began to hear the conversation the two armed men were having. They used Turkmen, which the boy didn't know. *Now I'm going to know why children like me were abducted.*

Suddenly, one of the armed men appeared. "Hemmäňiz çykyň!" the man shouted.

The children, including the boy on the floor, subtly moved backward in fear. Mostly, it was because they didn't understand Turkmen. The man angrily aimed his Type 56 assault rifle. "Çyk!" the man shouted.

The boy on the floor got out. The man with the Type 56 put down his rifle and got out of the boy's way when he began to exit the truck. Once the former got out, another man with his Type 56 slung across his rear rushed to the former and led him to the mosque. The other children in the van, however, not moved. The man still carrying his Type 56 aimed the rifle into the air and fired but by now, the boy was inside.

#

Abandoned Mosque. 0905 hours

All the children were now gathered in a straight line inside the mosque. The two armed men that took them to the mosque guarded the door to make sure no one ran away. A man stood in front of the children, but unlike the other armed men, he kept his Makarov pistol holstered.

"Esme man Serdar Muhadow ast," the man said in Farsi, allowing the children to understand him. "I apologize for what we have done, but as you can see, we're in need of more people as the Imperialists have come to conquer your land. Your way of life will end if you don't do something and we are to inspire you to come onto that path. You will be fed, clothed, and sheltered if you listen to our orders. Now, I will go to each and every one of you and learn your names."

Muhadow moved to the children. The boy who left the truck outside of his own volition was the first one Muhadow approached. "Esmetun čiye?"

"Tarou Ganji," the boy replied.

Japan Ground Self-Defense Force Camp Yao, Yao, Kansai Prefecture; State of Japan. April 20, 2030; 1804 hours (Japan Standard Time)

Since then, I faced death many times, Tarou thought in the present as he continued to look at Raşit Ghaemi in the interrogation room of JGSDF Camp Yao's brig. *He's the one who brought me to Muhadow that day.*

Frederick Dirks then returned to the interrogation room, which Ghaemi and Tarou saw. "I've talked with Colonel Izubuchi," Dirks said to Ghaemi. "You're coming with us because we'll be continuing our interrogation elsewhere." This was followed by Tarou's interpretation of what Dirks said into Farsi to Ghaemi.

#

Iron Dutchman, Taisho Ward. 1915 hours

The interrogation now resumed in Tarou's room in the Iron Dutchman. It was for that reason that Ghaemi had two handcuffs that tied his legs to the left legs respectively found in the front and in the headboard.

"We're going to pick up where we left off at Yao," Dirks announced. Tarou held his tongue as there was no need because Ghaemi knew that they weren't done with him yet. "Where is Serdar Muhadow going?"

Tarou asked the question again in Farsi, with Ghaemi answering in the same language. "He says that he doesn't know who you're talking about."

Now I got you where I needed you to be at, Dirks thought before he brought out Muhadow's passport. "This passport was using a falsified identity and we know who 'Mansur Fahri really is so stop lying for him."

Tarou angrily repeated the question in Farsi to Ghaemi. The latter laughed, surprising the former and Dirks, followed by him saying something in Farsi.

"What did he say?" Dirks asked.

"He said you're bluffing," Tarou replied after managing to interpret what Ghaemi said.

"We're no longer in Yao. Take off your helmet."

"Yes, sir." Tarou did so at Dirks' order. This widened Ghaemi's eyes and opened his mouth as he saw Tarou. It was clear to Dirks that Tarou wasn't lying, that he and Ghaemi knew each other.

Ghaemi then screamed in Farsi. "He said that I was that boy who voluntarily climbed out of that truck seven years ago," Tarou said to Dirks in English.

Dirks then brought out his smartphone, still using the application for the tracking device he planted on Maria Hoshikawa. "And as you can see, I now know how Muhadow escaped with Maria Hoshikawa. You just have to explicitly tell me where Muhadow is going," Dirks added.

Tarou repeated what Dirks said in Farsi, frightening Ghaemi further. Ghaemi replied, but it took time for Tarou to interpret what he said.

"What did he say?" Dirks asked to Tarou.

"He said that Muhadow's going to an old Imperial Japanese Army bunker near Poronaysk," Tarou answered.

Dirks then turned around. "No… No… NO!" he screamed. "Not good!"

"What do we do now?" Tarou asked.

"We let Ghaemi here live for now. Though there is one last question I need to ask him for now."

"What is it?"

Dirks then turned to Ghaemi. "Why did Muhadow allow Ryoka Akagi to tell everything to the police?" Tarou's interpretation followed, as did Ghaemi's answer.

"He said that Commander Muhadow allowed Akagi to talk because he made sure that even if you got his passport, he wouldn't be in Japan for you to go after him."

"Figures. We need to gather everyone in the briefing room."

"We need to feed Ghaemi first."

"Fine. We can have Moura feed him. Tell Vos and the others."

2017 hours

"You mean to tell us that we might be dealing with the Soviets?" Wouter Vos asked Dirks at the *Iron Dutchman*'s briefing room after the latter and Tarou relayed to the rest of Iron Dutchman Services, save for Bartolomeu Moura, about what they learned from Ghaemi.

"We can't say that for certain," Dirks replied. "We need to wait for Vue to come here."

"You mean John Vue from the day Tarou and I settled at the condominium?" Anita Hamilton asked.

"That's right. He should have more information about Muhadow."

"So what do we do with Ghaemi?" Jake Crawley asked.

"This ship has a brig, right?" Dirks asked.

"Ja," Vos answered. "We never used it before."

"Clean up at least one cell and put Ghaemi there."

"I'll clean up the cell," Vikas Mistry said.

"Good." Dirks then turned to Ganji. "Ganji, go to the Hoshikawa Mansion and inform Maria's parents of what we just learned. After that, you and Dr. Hamilton go home and get your clothes because until we have our orders, we need you to stay here until we move out. We'll resume tomorrow."

"Roger that."

"We're dismissed," Vos ordered to everyone in the briefing room. Dirks, however, looked at Crawley.

"Except you, Crawley," the FIS agent said, surprising not only the mercenary but everyone else who had yet to leave the briefing room. "I need you to take me to Camp Yao."

#

Studec'; Underneath the Pacific Ocean. 2020 hours

The *Studec'* exited the gap between the western prefectures of the Kansai region and Shikoku Island. "Kapitan, permission to speak?" Egorov asked as he approached Yelena Abramova Samsonova in the submarine's control room.

"Speak," Samsonova replied.

"Because we waited a while for Gospodin Muhadow, we could be detected by the NUN fleet facing the East China Sea."

"What do you propose we do?"

"We stop the engines and launch the Zevat'."

"Very well." Samsonova then approached the intercom and, after grabbing it, she pressed the button for the engineering section of the *Studec'*. "Chief Engineer, we will be launching a Zevat' soon. I need you to stop the engines."

"Zametano, Kapitan," a female voice replied on the other end of the intercom.

The engines ceased to be heard. Samsonova put down the intercom but after two seconds, picked it up again but pressed the button pertaining to the *Studec'*'s torpedo room.

#

2039 hours

"Kapitan, we've loaded the Zevat'," a male voice said over the intercom with Samsonova listening.

"I'll tell Stárshiy Leytenánt Egorov to fire," Samsonova replied. "Standby."

"Zametano, Kapitan." Samsonova put down the intercom and faced Egorov. "Egorov, fire the Zevat'."

"Zamteno, Kapitan," Egorov replied.

"After the launch, we wait an hour, then contact Voloshyna to have the engines turned on again. I'll set the timer."

"Zametano."

Samsonova began to open her right sleeve as there was a watch worn on her right wrist. She began to press buttons on the watch.

NUNS *Vigan*; Off Yaku Island. 2110 hours

Samsonova's fear of being spotted by the New United Nations Maritime Force (NUNMF) was well-founded as one who repeatedly infiltrated Japanese waters. Between Japanese waters and the East China Sea were the Ryukyu Islands. Among the ships that patrolled these islands were two *Cheyenne*-class attack submarines.

One of these submarines was the NUNS (New United Nations Ship) *Vigan*. The design itself had its origins in the *Los Angeles*-class attack submarines of the United States Navy Navy. The name itself was also a relic of the US Navy, as during the Third World War, the US Navy still ordered more *Los Angeles* submarines. The *Cheyenne* itself was ordered on November 28, 1989 and despite the war, construction continued in the city of Newport News. Despite the dissolution of the US Navy, the nascent New United Nations Maritime Force opted to use the completed yet unlaunched *Cheyenne*. Subsequent ships became to be known as the *Cheyenne*-class as a result.

The *Vigan*'s captain, Abigail Ellison, picked up the intercom in the control room. Forty-nine years old, she hailed from Tuskegee and like her father before her, she opted for a career in the military but by the time she came of age, the United States Armed Forces as a whole began to downscale, seeing little need for more recruits by the time Ellison came of age. Undaunted, she applied for the nascent New United Nations Maritime Force. She managed to become the youngest submarine captain in the NUNMF.

"Conn sonar," a male voice said over the intercom.

"Conn aye," Ellison replied.

"Ma'am, we've received contact that left Osaka Bay more than an hour ago. If it's a sub, I've never heard anything like it before."

"That's strange. We'll investigate. Keep an ear out."

"Aye, ma'am." Ellison put down the intercom and walked to the chart table. The two officers from the fire control tracking party prepared themselves to hear what Ellison had to say.

"The only submarine that could enter Japanese waters like this is that 'Phantom sub' I've been hearing about from Kowalski," Ellison said as she began tracing from the Osaka Bay on the chart table's map a single line. She then drew a broken line facing the lower-left of the line she first drew and stopping as to where she believed was where the signal the Vigan's sonar room picked up was located.

"You said we'd investigate," one dark-skinned officer at the chart table said to Ellison. "With all due respect, how?"

"We'll simply approach him," Ellison answered. "However, we reduce our speed by five klicks."

Ellison turned to the officer of the deck. "Reduce speed to five klicks."

"Aye, ma'am," the officer replied.

#

Studec'; Underneath the Pacific Ocean. 2136 hours

At the *Studec'*'s control room, the watch on Samsonova's right wrist rang. After looking at the time, Samsonova made the ringing stop and turned to Egorov. "Egorov, tell Voloshyna to restart the engines."

"Zametano, Kapitan," Egorov replied before he walked to the intercom. At the same time, Samsonova traveled to the controls of the *Studec'*'s PA system.

#

2138 hours

Maria Hoshikawa pressed her hands toward each other while her head faced the deck and her eyes were closed. "O, God, whose only begotten son, by his life, death, and resurrection, has purchased for us the rewards of eternal life, grant, we beseech you, that by meditating upon these Mysteries of the Most Holy Virgin Mary, we may imitate what they contain and obtain what they promise," she said. "Through the same Christ our Lord. Amen.

"In the name of the Father, the Son, and the Holy Spirit." Maria crossed herself after that.

Suddenly, Maria began to hear Samsonova's voice across the submarine's PA system. *I can imagine that means there's an explanation as to why this ship hasn't moved for more than an hour,* Maria thought as she still didn't understand Russian. This was followed by the engines making sounds. *We're moving again. I hope someone finds this ship.*

#

Japan Ground Self-Defense Force Camp Yao, Yao, Kansai Prefecture; State of Japan. 2209 hours

A C-5 Galaxy transport plane landed at the runaway shared by both Yao Airport and Japan Ground Self-Defense Force Camp Yao. The Vue family, seated at the upper deck normally meant for infantrymen, got up.

However, John and Annerose's daughter Mary was asleep. Due to how long the flight was, it was natural the child would be asleep by the time the plane arrived at its destination. After removing her seatbelt, Annerose then picked up her daughter before she and John walked to the lower deck.

Once the Vue's reached the lower deck, the crew approached them with their bags. Because Annerose was carrying Mary, John volunteered to carry all of their belongings. Thankfully for John, he nor his wife and daughter brought much as they had no intention of staying in Japan for long.

After John got the bags, he and his family began to exit the Galaxy. As their feet touched Japanese soil, they found two men—Frederick Dirks and Jake Crawley—waiting for them.

"Who are they?" Annerose asked as she leaned her body to her husband's left ear.

"Their colleagues from work," Vue answered before facing Dirks and Crawley. "You're here to pick us up?"

"We are," Dirks answered. "Please follow us."

#

Iron Dutchman, Taisho Ward. 2250 hours

"I'm surprised this is still intact," Vue commented as he looked around the dining hall upon entering it with Dirks and Crawley.

"We do need a dining room, after all," Crawley replied.

"Everyone sit," Dirks ordered, with Crawley and Vue complying. As the three men sat down, Tatev Mirzoyan entered the dining room with Sunan Wattana.

Now I get to meet Tatev Mirzoyan, Vue thought upon seeing the adolescent girl.

"Sorry about this, Wattana," Dirks said as he approached the two women.

"It's alright," Wattana replied before she saw Vue. "That him?"

"I'd like you to meet John Vue." As Dirks, Tatev, and Wattana moved to the table where Crawley and Vue were seated at, Vue stood up and offered his left hand to Tatev.

"Nice to meet you," Vue said before Tatev grabbed his left hand with her right hand.

"I hear you have something for us?" Tatev inquired.

"I do. I see you brought your laptop."

"I figured that based on what Mr. 'Smith' said."

"How did you afford a laptop, anyway?"

"We worked *really* hard for it," Wattana answered. "When we first met Tatev, she was awfully smart that we needed her to scout for contracts."

"Anyway, please sit. I've been given installers for two more apps you'll be needing for future missions. Like with IntMail, you can only keep these apps until we put an end to this contract."

Relaying of Information

Studec'; Underneath the Pacific Ocean. April 21, 2030; 0600 hours (Japan Standard Time)

Egorov, the executive officer of the *Studec'*, found his captain Yelena Abramova Samsonova at her cabin. The former knocked on the metal that shaped the cabin, waking up the latter.

"Andrey, this better be good," Samsonova said as she woke up.

"Kapitan, we're about to approach the gap between Ichijo and Mikura Islands," Egorov reported. "I think it's time to use *that*."

"Very well. Wait for me at the control room."

"Zametano, Kapitan."

"When we're alone, you can just call me Lena."

"I'll do so next time."

#

0628 hours

Everyone in the *Studec'*'s control found their captain approaching and saluted. "How long until we reach the gap between Ichijo and Mikura?" Samsonova asked.

"Five minutes," Egorov answered.

"After those five minutes, we stop and turn. Then we use the *Chernyy Marlin*."

"Zametano, Kapitan."

0633 hours

At her cell in the *Studec'*'s brig, Maria Hoshikawa woke up to hear the submarine stop. *It happened again,* Maria thought. *How long is it until this ship reaches its destination?*

Across the *Studec'*'s PA system, Samsonova made an announcement. Like before, Maria wasn't able to understand it as it was in Russian. This was followed by the submarine's engines shutting down again.

I guess there's my answer as to what was announced, Maria thought. This was followed by the submarine turning. *And now we're turning again. What will happen now?*

#

0637 hours

"Engine's turned off," Voloshyna's voice said over the intercom in the *Studec'*'s bridge while she talked to Samsonova. "Spasibo," the captain replied. "Activate the *Chernyy Marlin.*"

Samsonova then put down the intercom. It was then that a loud spin was heard. That was the *Chernyy Marlin*, the name given for the largest propeller for all *Vyšen'*-class submarines. Based on the sole propeller used by the Project 945 series of attack submarines that were driven to extinction in the Third World War, the *Chernyy Marlin* was built to increase the speed of the submarine, making it travel faster than a torpedo. It was vital to make sure that a *Vyšen'*-class didn't stay in foreign waters for long and having done this before, Yelena Abramova Samsonova had nothing to feel about using the *Chernyy Marlin.*

Upon reaching the wheel, Samsonova pulled a key out of her jacket's right pocket. Plugging the key into the hole designated for the key at the console beside the wheel. After turning the key, a hatch opened. Inside the hatch was a lever and Samsonova moved her right hand to the lever. She began to push it slowly and as she did, the submarine moved again. She increased not only the speed of her hand on the lever but also the

Studec's. Once she had the lever at eighty degrees, Samsonova used all her strength to push the lever in earnest, making the submarine move faster than a torpedo.

As a result, everyone held onto what they could grasp in the moment. Samsonova opted to lay on the deck. "WE'LL STOP IN TWO MINUTES!" Samsonova shouted.

"ZAMETANO!" Egorov shouted back.

#

0839 hours (Shana Time)

"KAPITAN, I THINK IT'S TIME!" Egorov shouted to his captain.

"STOPPING THE PROPELLER NOW!" Samsonova replied while using what strength she had left in climbing despite the shaking.

Using the wheel, she climbed up. Barely managing to stand up, Samsonova reached for the lever with her left hand. Upon grabbing it, she pulled it as hard as she could but it was gradual, decreasing the *Studec*'s speed. Gritting her teeth, Samsonova continued to gather what little strength she could in pulling the lever. Miraculously, she was able to pull the lever back to its original position, making the submarine stop.

"Is… everyone… alright?" Samsonova asked as everyone began to stand up again.

"W… We're alright… Kapitan," Egorov replied as he and everyone else in the control room began to stand up.

"Good." Samsonova was now able to stand perfectly. "We need to turn again."

"Why?"

"By now, a NUN submarine has heard us. We must fire another Zevat'."

"Can't we get Muhadow and his captive to leave already?"

"We're still within NUN waters. Any of our aircraft will be shot on sight."

"Allow me to contact the torpedo room."

"You better hurry!"

NUNS *Busan*; Off Uruppu Island, Nemuro Subprefecture, Hokkaido Prefecture. 0910 hours

Casimir Kowalski, the Captain of the *Cheyenne*-class submarine NUNS *Busan*, rushed to his intercom. Fifty years old, he had short blond hair, light skin, and blue eyes. As he reached the intercom, he pressed the button for the sonar room.

"Conn sonar," Kowalski said.

"Conn aye!" a female voice said rapidly on her end. "Captain, we detected a projectile coming our way. Coming from where we believe the disturbance we heard thirty minutes ago to have come from!"

It'll most likely be a decoy torpedo again! Kowalski thought. *Every single time, we fall for that. No more!*

Kowalski then turned to his officers. "We follow, but up to three klicks and after ten minutes, we cease and return to our position."

"But ski-" one officer argued only for Kowalski to raise his right palm.

"I've had it every single time our sonar room picks up that same reading. This ends today!"

#

Studec'; Off Shikotan Island. 0915 hours

"Kapitan, shall we continue?" Egorov asked Samsonova at the *Studec'*'s bridge.

"We will, but this time, we'll travel between Iturup and Urup."

"But Kapitan, we'll be detected by that NUN submarine for sure."

"We've wasted too much time. All we need to do now is keep straight this time and as soon as we leave the Kurils, we surface. It isn't just us that risk being detected. We also have to consider the OVR agents sent to pick up Mukhadov and our captive. They'll be detected by Soviet patrols soon."

"Ya ponimayu, Kapitan."

Samsonova began to use the *Studec'*'s PA system again. "Attention all hands, this is your Kapitan speaking," she announced. "We're almost finished with our mission. However, unlike before, we will use the gap between Iturup and Urup. No doubt that we will be detected, but as soon as we make contact with a certain boat, we will end this mission. I've not asked for too much out of every man and woman in this ship, but I ask that no one waivers."

#

Vries Strait. 0955 hours

The *Studec'* was now traveling across the Vries Strait, which separated Etoroffu and Uruppu. These, along with Kunashiri, Shikotan, and the Habomai Islands, were among those in the Kuril Islands that were attacked by US and Japanese forces during the Third World War. Both nations were surprised that upon reaching the Pacific Ocean, the Eurasian Tsardom made no claim over those islands. Since then, they've remained a part of the State of Japan.

The *Studec'* surfaced upon exiting the gap between the two islands. As it surfaced, half of the submarine was now seen, especially the *Chernyy Marlin* propeller and the sonar array. Although half of the former was seen, it was taller and longer that the latter.

Unbeknownst to the *Studec'*, the NUNS *Busan* submerged behind it, yet it stayed in the entrance to the gap. After the *Busan* submerged, its bridge was opened. Coming out was Casimir Kowalski.

Kowalski wore a COOLPIX L320 camera with the camera hanging in front of his body because of its strap. He then removed the cover of the lens and turned on the camera. After that, he zoomed in on the *Studec'*'s *Chernyy Marlin* with the L320's lens and pressed the button needed to take its picture.

I finally got you, Kowalski thought. *I just need to relay this photo.*

#

Studec'; Sea of Okhotsk. 1002 hours (Sakhalin Time)

At the bridge of the *Studec'*, Yelena Abramova Samsonova saw a fishing boat. She then raced to the intercom on the bridge and pressed the button pertaining to the control room.

"I saw the boat 'Ivan' and 'Marko' are using," Samsonova said. "Egorov, prepare to announce to all hands that we'll be stopping. I'll contact the Chief Engineer."

"Zametano," Andrey Egorov replied on the other end of the intercom before Samsonova briefly put down the intercom. She then picked it up again and pressed the button for the engineering section. "Chief Engineer, we've found the agents ready to pick up Mukhadov and his captive. I need you to stop the engines."

"Zametano, Kapitan," Voloshyna replied before Samsonova put down the intercom for the second and, hopefully, the last time for the day.

#

Near Poronaysk, Poronaysky District, Sakhalin Oblast; Russian Soviet Federative Socialist Republic, 1233 hours

Muhadow, now controlling the "fishing boat", neared the town of Poronaysk in the southern half of Sakhalin Island. After the end of the Third World War, only the Russian Soviet Federative Socialist Republic (RSFSR) survived in the Sakhalin Oblast and in a portion of the Primorsky Krai. Northern Sakhalin was the last portion of the old Union of Soviet Socialist Republics that was conquered by the Eurasian Tsardom. Reluctantly, the RSFSR ceased what little complaints it had with the nascent resurrection of monarchical Russia in exchange for resources the Tsardom was willing to offer. Despite that, the RSFSR helped create the Asian Pact to avoid such a loss of territory from happening ever again. Mapmakers found that Sakhalin Island being divided between the Tsardom and the RSFSR was reminiscent of the island being split between Japan and Russia during the early 20th century.

As he drove the boat close to a beach, Muhadow stopped the boat. He then pushed the anchor off the water and after he left a bag beside the corpses of two men. Muhadow then took the still-unconscious Maria with him and jumped off the boat.

Muhadow pressed on and by the time his feet touched the sand that was RSFSR territory, two Turkmen with AK-2000s slung in their respective backs rushed to Muhadow and saluted him. Muhadow put Maria down and saluted them in return.

"We're glad you're safe, Commander Muhadow," one Turkmen mercenary said. "What happened to Ghaemi and Gurdov?"

"They're dead. We best move or their efforts to help me claim our prize will be in vain."

"Yes, sir."

"What about the boat?" the other mercenary asked.

"We're leaving it, along with the corpses inside. I even left their bag beside them as it contains proof they're OVR. That'll get the Asian Pact and the Tsardom at each other's throats while we simply guard the facility we'll be returning to."

#

Unknown Location. 1320 hours

W… Where am I now? Maria Hoshikawa thought upon waking up in a padded cell. She began to look around but only has a bed, a sink with a mirror, a toilet beside the sink, and the door.

Maria then began to grip on the door, but to no avail. *Figures it would be locked.*

She then walked up to the sink. She found a cup made of hard plastic filled with toothbrush, toothpaste, and a bottle of water on the other side of the sink. *Thank goodness they gave me toothpaste and gargling water.* Maria then turned to the toilet beside the sink. *Now why did they have to place the-*

A knock was then heard, forcing Maria's attention toward it. "Are you awake?"

It's that man, Maria thought. *The same one who abducted me.*

"Please speak up."

"I'm awake."

"Good." The sound of a key being inserted and being turned was now heard. After almost a minute, it stopped. The door was now open with Serdar Muhadow, as Maria correctly guessed, outside. He carried with him a tray filled with food and a plastic cup; itself filled with water.

"Where are we now?" Maria defiantly asked.

"Can't tell you," Muhadow answered. "I suggest you stop wasting our time and start eating."

"What's going to happen now?"

"I'll answer that question but after you've eaten. Also, you'll have to wait an hour. I'd rather not have any *complications* after you finished your meal."

#

1432 hours

Muhadow then returned to the outside of the padded cell where he kept Maria. He then knocked on the door.

"Are you done with your *business*?" Muhadow asked.

"I am," Maria answered. "Thank you for the bidet."

"Good. Just come forward once I unlock the door."

Muhadow began to use the key again. While inserting the key, he heard Maria's footsteps. Once the footsteps stopped, Muhadow finished unlocking the key, but he used his right hand as he prepared a syringe with his left hand and managed to remove its cover with the same hand.

The Turkmen then opened the door. As he finished, he saw Maria as if she was ready to die. Suddenly, Muhadow thrust the syringe against Maria's right side of her neck. He then pushed the same liquid he used to knock Maria unconscious in Kansai City the previous day onto her neck.

Not again… Maria thought before losing consciousness again.

#

1536 hours

Wh… What… happened? Maria pondered as she began to come to again. However, she wasn't able to see that she was now wearing a lab gown and tied to a metallic chair. As to why she wasn't able to see, her entire head was covered in a metallic helmet connected to the chair by way of wires.

Wait, I remember now. I was injected with that liquid again. But why can't I see?

"Initiating test," a female, monotonous voice said in the room where Maria was located.

What test? Sounds were now heard. In another room that was close to the room where Maria was but separated by a wall yet connected by a mirror and a door, men of varying skin colors looked at the monitors of the computers they sat in front of.

What was now shown on the monitors was everything about Maria: everything from her gender to recent accomplishments. "Test subject is now perfectly healthy," the same female voice said.

"Good," Serdar Muhadow said behind the men. "We can begin the test. Prepare to connect her chair to Solbein."

"But regardless of the results, we still need a pilot for Solbein," a scientist with light skin argued.

"I'll participate."

#

1614 hours

Muhadow then arrived at a hangar built to store Walgears. Walgears were bipedal vehicles with limbs reminiscent of a human's. Warfare was mostly dominated by these machines whose height was between three and four meters.

The Walgear was the result of what was found in *Revelator* that the Gatekeepers of Knowledge shared with the world. The first Walgear, the WG1 Warhorse, had four legs, but after the Eurasian Tsardom developed the first bipedal Walgear, the SH-5, supernational unions opted to create their own Walgears.

Muhadow stopped as he looked upon the only Walgear in the hangar. Currently, at two meters tall, it was painted gray with two machine guns located at its lower chest and a vent at its groin. The vent was needed to provide an exhaust for the miniature fusion reactor that powered the Walgear.

Suddenly, the yellow eyes on the Walgear glowed yellow. *Well, at least we know that Hoshikawa is needed for Solbein,* Muhadow thought.

1630 hours

"The test worked so far," Muhadow told the scientist.

"Even so, we need to test if it can be piloted. Only those *blessed* can do so."

"Then let's get to it. We need a target, though."

"We don't need one. We just need it to move around. After that, we'll send the results and the girl back to Enlightenment Point."

"Good. I just need to find my pilot suit and then we can get started."

#

1739 hours

Now wearing the pilot suit he spoke off for Walgears, Muhadow returned to the hangar where the Walgear he called "Solbein" was kept. The pilot suit was simply a flight suit worn by fighter plane pilots but most of it was covered by a ballistic vest. Between the groin and the belly button was a belt needed for certain items a Walgear pilot would need, one of which was a sidearm to protect himself. Muhadow had his Makarov pistol, the same one he used in Iran seven years before, holstered.

Muhadow then put on the helmet also needed for Walgear piloits. After that, he continued approaching Solbein. A ladder was now attached to the open cockpit, located at the rear of the Walgear as if it wear its backpack. Once inside, Muhadow found the button with the words "On/Off", colored white and separated by a slash. He pressed the button.

The Walgear was now functional. The maintenance personnel nearby rushed to remove the ladder and after they did so, Muhadow pressed another button, making Solbein stand and showing its actual height of four meters.

Muhadow then found the leg panels. They made the Walgear move with its legs, but this was only done if they were worn by the pilot. Muhadow then inserted each leg into their corresponding panel. After that, he pressed a button that closed the cockpit.

"Devotee-Colonel, this is Dr. Hovsepyan," the man whom Muhadow talked to said over the Walgear's communicator found in the control panel. "Now that you turned on Solbein, we can begin the test."

"Of course," Muhadow replied.

The Turkmen moved his left leg. However, the Walgear wasn't able to move.

"Devotee-Colonel, we're not seeing the Walgear move."

"I know," Muhadow replied. "I can't do this! I'm stopping."

#

1820 hours

"What happened?" Hovsepyan asked after Muhadow returned to the room with the monitors while he and Muhadow watched camera footage from the hangar an hour before.

"It's as you saw," Muhadow answered. "Solbein didn't move. And it was after I saw its eyes glow."

"What could that mean? Is she not *The One*?"

Both Hovsepyan and Muhadow turned to Maria, still tied to the chair in the adjacent room. *The One…* Muhadow thought before he widened his eyes. *That's it!*

"I have an idea," Muhadow said as he turned to Hovsepyan again.

"What is it?" the doctor asked.

"Get a sample of my DNA and we compare it to Hoshikawa's. Maybe, just *maybe*, we can salvage what happened today."

"If we rush the process, it'll take a day at most."

"That's fine."

"Then what do we do with Hoshikawa now?"

"We wait until your test is finished."

FIS Headquarters, McLean, Fairfax County, Commonwealth of Virginia; United States of America. April 20, 2030; 1802 hours (Eastern Standard Time)

Stanley McAllister opened the door to the Director of Foreign Intelligence's office as if he nearly slammed it. Although he didn't slam it, the way he opened the door acquired Alberto Pérez's attention.

"Yes, Stan?" Pérez asked.

"Caguiat just intercepted a message from COMSUBPAC. It's in here." McAllister came forward with a piece of paper and gave it to Pérez.

The Director of Foreign Intelligence then put on his reading glasses. The paper contained a message from the NUNS *Busan* sent to Commander, Submarine Force Pacific (COMSUBPAC). COMSUBPAC was the type commander in charge of all submarine operations for the New United Nations Maritime Force. One line in the message, however, widened Pérez's eyes as the line read:

Photographic evidence of the supposed "Phantom sub" was retrieved by the Captain of NUNS Busan. Busan will travel to Shikotan Island to await pickup of the photograph.

"Stan, when did 'Smith' last report in?" Pérez asked as he put down the paper and faced his Deputy Director of Covert Action.

"Eight hours ago, sir," McAllister answered.

"Tell Caguiat to have 'Smith' find the *Busan* and retrieve that photo. Those mercenaries and Vue will need it to figure out where to find Hoshikawa and how to rescue her."

"Yes, sir."

#

Café Aaaa, Taisho Ward, Kansai City, Kansai Prefecture; State of Japan. April 21, 2030; 0918 hours (Japan Standard Time)

Near Hoshikawa Group headquarters was Café Aaaa. The name was the sound made when someone opened his or her mouth when attempting to receive food from another's utensil, Frederick Dirks sat alone, drinking his coffee. After that, he resumed eating his loaf of bread filled with strawberry jam.

Once he finished the loaf, he heard a particular sound coming from his left pocket. He used his right hand to retrieve the source of the sound—his smartphone—and that he has a message for an application called "AudComm". Upon opening AudComm, Dirks found that the person calling him had the name "Maria Clara" and pressed the button for answering the call.

"This is 'Smith'," Dirks said.

"Where are you now?" a female voice, presumably "Maria Clara", asked.

"Having breakfast at a café near Hoshikawa Group headquarters."

"We've received information from the submarine *Busan* that might help identify where Maria Hoshikawa was taken to. However, you'll need to find a way to go to Shikotan Island because that's where the *Busan* is right now."

"Got it. Almost done.

#

Tennoji Zoo, Tennoji Ward. 0948 hours

At the Tennoji Zoo, the Vue family was at the section called the Friendship Garden. There, Mary Vue was petting the goats exhibited there. Her father felt his smartphone and found that Dirks sent him a message through IntMail. Upon opening IntMail, John Vue found the message that read:

"Maria Clara" contacted me. She tells me that the NUNS Busan has something we need to help us find Maria Hoshikawa. I intend to ask Daisuke Hoshikawa if he can lend me his private jet to go to Nemuro because I intend to hire a boat to take me to Shikotan.

Vue then wrote "Got it. Once you get back, we need to hold a meeting. I'll act out as a tourist for the time being", followed by pressing "Send". As he did so, his daughter called out to him with his wife Annerose encouraging him to do so.

Hoshikawa Group Headquarters, Taisho Ward, Kansai City, Kansai Prefecture; State of Japan. 1039 hours

"So, I assume you came here because you need my help?" Daisuke Hoshikawa asked in his office while entertaining Dirks. "If it means getting my daughter back, what is it you need now?"

"Your private jet," Dirks answered. "I can't say much. All you need to know is that I have a lead on how to get your daughter back."

"And where do you intend to go with my jet?"

"Sapporo. After that, I intend on taking a train to Nemuro, where I intend on bribing a fisherman into taking his boat with me on board to Shikotan Island."

Daisuke chuckled. "You never change, old friend," Daisuke remarked. "Very well. Just wait."

#

FIS Headquarters, McLean, Fairfax County, Commonwealth of Virginia; United States of America. 2039 hours (Eastern Standard Time)

Again was Stanley McAllister at Alberto Pérez's office. The latter looked at satellite footage being shown on McAllister's smartphone that showed a boat surrounded by men and women. On the lower-right end of the video were the words "Poronaysk, RSFSR" written in white. Below were the numbers 12:00 with "UTC+11:00" written beside it; both being separated by a semi-colon and a space.

"Anything from our station chief in Vladivostok?" Pérez asked.

"He heard that the corpses in that boat contained information that proved that they were OVR infiltrators," McAllister answered. "The KGB has yet to do to forensics on who shot them."

"Have Nizhny and Vladivostok started talking about it yet?" Pérez sternly asked, as he knew what two dead OVR agents in RSFSR territory meant with McAllister knowing as well.

"The Tsardom's ambassador to Vladisvostok has yet to finish talking to the Premier about it."

"Either way. This will complicate the situation, as we might have to infiltrate Soviet Sakhalin to rescue Maria Hoshikawa. No doubt this is related to what 'Smith' got from that Turkmen he and Iron Dutchman Services captured. I need to tell the Chairman of Intelligence and she has to report to the Secretary-General about this. After that, have Caguiat inform 'Smith', Vue, and those mercenaries, but tell her to tell them not to do anything until we hear from the Secretary-General on what to do with the Tsardom and the Soviet Remnant."

"Yes, sir." McAllister then left the room.

#

Iron Dutchman, Taisho Ward, Kansai City, Kansai Prefecture; State of Japan. 1140 hours (Japan Standard Time)

In her room in the *Iron Dutchman*, Tatev Mirzoyan found that she was receiving a call from her laptop computer's AudComm application. As she opened AudComm, she found that it was "Maria Clara" calling.

"You needed something, Miss Clara?" Tatev asked.

"Thank goodness I reached you, Miss Mirzoyan," Alicia Cagiuat, using the alias "Maria Clara", replied. "Listen, we have an update on the situation. Where's Mr. 'Smith'?"

"He left for Sapporo. He said something about retrieving a photo from a submarine captain."

"Good. We have an update on where Maria Hoshikawa is, but I'd rather share what I've just been told after Mr. 'Smith' has come back. Don't forget."

"I won't."

#

Fishing Boat; Off Shikotan Island, Nemuro Subprefecture, Hokkaido Prefecture; State of Japan. 2249 hours (Shana Time)

"Sore da," Dirks said to the fisherman whose boat he was riding on as they arrived off Shikotan Island and that they spotted the surfaced NUNS *Busan*. "Chikazuite kudasai."

"Hai," the fisherman replied as he altered his boat's direction toward the *Busan*.

As the boat neared the *Busan*, Dirks raised his smartphone into the air with both of his hands. He began to repeatedly press the screen with his right thumb. On the submarine's bridge, Casimir Kowalski saw this with his binoculars.

#

Iron Dutchman, Taisho Ward, Kansai City, Kansai City. April 22, 2030; 1500 hours (Japan Standard Time)

Dirks ultimately returned to the *Iron Dutchman*. He found Wouter Vos waiting for him.

"I can assume that since you're here to greet me, 'Maria Clara' contacted Mirzoyan, and that she warned you?" Dirks guessed.

"You're correct," Vos answered. "However, we need Hamilton, Ganji, and Vue here."

#

1813 hours

"You're late," Vos said as he and Dirks saw Tarou and Anita Hamilton rush inside the *Iron Dutchman*.

"Sorry about that," Hamilton replied. "Tarou had to deliver homework for Miss Hoshikawa because Misa Todoh asked him to do it."

"It's alright," Dirks replied. "I should have anticipated that. In any case, we can start the meeting after dinner. We still have to wait for Vue."

"Then let's eat," Vos ordered. "Mirzoyan found us something from her native Armenia and Barto felt like trying it out for dinner."

Preparing for the Rescue

Iron Dutchman, Taisho Ward, Kansai City, Kansai Prefecture; State of Japan. April 22, 2030; 2036 hours (Japan Standard Time)

All members of Iron Dutchman Services were now at their briefing room with Tatev at the projector room. Using an Internet browser, Tatev opened a website that showed all the world's time zones represented by clocks. One clock was under UTC-05:00 which corresponded to the United States of America's Eastern Standard Time whereas another clock was under UTC+09:00, corresponding to Japan Standard Time. The former was because FIS Headquarters, where Alicia Caguiat worked at, was located in the US's Eastern Seaboard, which used UTC-05:00. Tatev needed that website to know when Caguiat would report for work in FIS Headquarters as she was to talk to all members of Iron Dutchman Services.

It was then that John Vue arrived. "Glad you made it," Frederick Dirks said upon seeing Vue.

"Sorry," Vue replied. "The Kansai Metro started to get full by the time I left the hotel." He then sat beside Jason Luke Crawley.

"Now that we're all here, we can begin," Dirks declared before he turned to the projector room. "Mirzoyan, I think it's time. Contact 'Clara' now."

"Roger," Tatev Mirzoyan replied before turning on her laptop computer's AudComm, as it was now connected to the projector. After that, she pressed the name "Maria Clara" found on the list named Contacts. Upon pressing the name, a ringing sound was heard across the briefing room. This was because the speakers for the theater that the briefing room used to be still functioned, a necessity that was to be used soon.

"Miss Mirzoyan, I assume you're calling because that meeting of yours is about to start?" Alicia Caguiat asked, ending the wait.

"Yes, everyone's gathered," Tatev answered. "Mr. Vue's here too."

"Good. Yesterday, we've heard that two Eurasian OVR agents have been found dead in a fishing boat off the town of Poronaysk in Soviet Sakhalin. We have to hear anything from our station chief in Vladivostok, but I've been told that the Director intends to take this issue to the Chairman of Intelligence, who will then report about this to the Secretary-General."

"And what does that mean?" Wouter Vos, standing beside Dirks as usual, asked.

"We can't do anything until the Director has been given instructions on how to handle this. In case you're wondering, this does concern how we are to rescue Maria Hoshikawa. Mr. 'Smith', please elaborate."

"Yesterday, I traveled to Shikotan Island because we were warned of activity underneath Japanese waters by the NUNS *Busan*," Dirks explained. "I went to Shikotan to meet the *Busan*'s captain Casimir Kowalski about what he found." Dirks turned to the projector room again. "Mirzoyan, show them the photo."

There wasn't any need for a reply this time as Tatev rushed to the program in her computer used for presentations. Once she opened the program, the photograph Kowalski took of the *Studec*'s *Chernyy Marlin* propeller was now shown on the screen.

"This is the only proof Kowalski found of what he and other Maritime Force sub captains call the 'Phantom sub'," Dirks continued. "Chances are, this is what Serdar Muhadow must have used to escape while taking Hoshikawa with him."

"I get the nickname, but how does that explain the dead OVR agents in the Soviet Remnant?" Vos asked.

"That could be it," Vue announced as he came up with an idea.

"Then tell us," Dirks demanded.

"Muhadow might have worked with the OVR to get Maria. He must have that phantom sub ready to pick them up after that car chase throughout Kansai City. That big propeller in that photo must have allowed that submarine to travel fast in order to make sure it wasn't detected before the *Busan* spotted it."

"But if Muhadow was working with the OVR, would he have killed those agents?" Tarou Ganji asked. "Not only that, why?"

"Tatev, please open the Device Tracker," Vue loudly requested to Tatev while turning to the projector room.

Tatev immediately opened Device Tracker, the same application Dirks used in his smartphone connected to the tracking device he sneaked into Maria. Now projected on the screen was a map of Japan with lines from Osaka City until Poronaysk. "This, ladies and gentlemen, might be your answer." Vue then pointed to a smaller line that went past Poronaysk.

"That could be the bunker Ghaemi spoke of," Dirks surmised.

"So let's recap what we now know," Vos interrupted. "Muhadow must have worked with the OVR to infiltrate Japan and bring in Ghaemi and Gurdov. He and his henchmen grab Maria after Black Saturday Mass and clearly engineered that van of his to sink into Osaka Bay in order for him to reach this phantom sub while taking Maria with him. The sub then uses that big propeller to travel awfully fast once it hit the Pacific, and despite the *Busan* detecting it, the sub reached Soviet waters and met up with the OVR agents only. And now, we can presume Muhadow murdered those OVR agents to go to Poronaysk."

"Then is he a Soviet agent?" Sunan Wattana asked.

"Probably not," Dirks answered. "Otherwise, he wouldn't have left the town that fast."

"Either way, we cannot make a move until we hear from the Director," Caguiat reminded.

"Don't worry, we won't," Dirks replied. "We still have things to do. Just let us know what happens next."

"Got it. I'll be ending this call." Dirks then resumed facing most of Iron Dutchman Services. "So, what do we do now?" Crawley asked.

"You heard the lady," Dirks answered. "We wait." Dirks then turned to Tarou. "Ganji, I need you with me because we'll need to start interrogating Ghaemi again."

"What for?" Vue asked.

"Depending on what we'll hear next, we need to be prepared. If we'll allowed to find that bunker and save Hoshikawa, we need to know how to enter and exit that bunker."

"Good idea."

2100 hours

Both Dirks and Tarou arrived at the cell they kept Raşit Ghaemi at in the *Iron Dutchman*'s brig. Tarou then yelled at the Turkmen in Farsi, which Dirks easily understood would be the Persian equivalent of "Get up". In turn, Ghaemi asked a question in Persian.

"He asked 'What do you want now'," Tarou said to Dirks.

"We need you to draw what the bunker you spoke of looks like," Dirks demanded. "Don't bother denying that you can draw. Ganji here knows you can draw."

Tarou repeated what Dirks said in Farsi. Ghaemi's eyes widened again upon listening to what the child had said. *He… he remembers!* Ghaemi thought.

"It seems like you know," Dirks added before he turned to Tarou. "Keep an eye on him. I need to get the keys from Vos, along with a pencil and some paper."

Tarou nodded. Dirks then left the brig with the former continuing to look at Ghaemi.

#

Unknown Location; Enlightenment Point. 1635 hours (EP Time Zone)

"No… No, No!" Sergei Akulov screamed at his throne with Reinhard Frühling having to listen.

"Grand Gatekeeper, we've compared the test many times," Frühling replied. "Maria Hoshikawa is one of the *blessed.* As is Devotee-Colonel Muhadow."

"But if Muhadow can't use Solbein, then everything we've done so far has been for nothing!" Akulov then slammed his right palm against his face. *And I doubt there's anything that could be done at this point.*

"Might I make a suggestion?"

Akulov then removed his palm from his face and faced his Gatekeeper of Intelligence. "What is it?" the Grand Gatekeeper asked.

"We give Maria Hoshikawa to the Tsar."

"Are you insane!? We do that, the Tsar will ask many questions as to how we came across Hoshikawa."

"But surely he knows."

"That's the problem. It'll cause trouble that he might suspect Tsesarevich Iosif. And unlike the Tsar, we might still have a use for the infertile Tsesarevich. Hoshikawa's presence will stir up trouble that we don't need just yet."

"Then what do we do?"

"We allow Hoshikawa to be rescued. You did say the Director of Foreign Intelligence is on his way to meet with the Secretary-General of the New United Nations, right?"

"Yes?"

"Then we allow the FIS and Iron Dutchman Services to stage a rescue mission. In order to do so, they need to infiltrate Soviet Sakhalin easily. To do that, we need to have the Soviet Remnant and the Eurasian Tsardom fighting each other so that they won't pay attention to whosoever infiltrated Soviet Sakhalin. But we need to make sure that the FIS and those mercenaries leave before it mutates into a war between the Asian Pact and the Eurasian Cooperative Sphere."

"How should we start the border war, then?"

"We use 'SB'."

"But don't we need to tell Devotee-Colonel Muhadow of this?"

"We can't. Muhadow might sabotage the whole thing if we do inform him. He might even give Hoshikawa to the Tsardom to spite us."

"We trained him too much to think like a mercenary."

"Then contact 'SB'."

#

Unknown Location, Poronaysky District, Sakhalin Oblast, Russian Soviet Federative Socialist Republic. April 23, 2030; 0021 hours (Sakhalin Time)

In front of the door leading to the padded cell where Maria Hoshikawa was kept, a figure whose entire body was covered save for the face looked at the door. The head and body were covered by a black raincoat, while the individual wore black pants tied by a black leather belt and boots of the same color. This individual was "SB", the woman responsible for setting the hotel in Nemuro owned by Daisuke Hoshikawa, and she was joined by Serdar Muhadow.

"What are you doing here, SB?" Muhadow asked the individual.

"I apologize, Commander," "SB" replied upon turning to Muhadow. "I just wanted to know where we're keeping the guinea pig."

"Ask me next time before going to this cell. By the way, our communication room intercepted a message from Enlightenment Point. For your eyes only."

"By the Grand Gatekeeper's will." "SB" then left the door. *No doubt Tarou will try to save her. He did the same for me ten years ago.*

#

0037 hours

"SB" then reached the communication room. Accessing an unused computer console, she found that the message at GOKMail. The individual accessed the message as it read:

Tengru Redro Morf Eht Dnarg Repeeketag,

Reenigne a Raw Neewteb Eht Naisarue Modrast Nad Eht Naissur Teivos Evitaredef Tsilaicos Cilbuper. I Nac Emussa Ev'voy Draeh Taht Eht Tset Htiw Niebleb Deliaf Os T'si Rof Taht Nosaer Ew Deen That Raw. Ev'ew Depto Ot Wallow Eht Wen Detniu 'Snoitan Ngierof Ecnegillentni Ecivres Nad Nori Nambctud Secivres Ot Eucser Airam Kawakihsoh.

No wonder it's for my eyes only, "SB" thought. *No use keeping Hoshikawa. I best take a photo of this message and reply to Gatekeeper Int later. The Commander cannot know of this message.*

"SB" then brought out a smartphone and began to use its camera. Unbeknownst to the individual, Muhadow approached the room but stopped as he saw the Devotee in charge of the communications room waiting outside. Muhadow knew that the Devotee waited outside because of the fact the message was for "SB" only.

For the latter, the wait was over as "SB" left the room. "That was fast," Muhadow remarked.

"You know a message like cannot be kept in GOKMail for long," "SB" said. "I need one of our Loshads."

"What for?"

"All you need to know is that I've been given a task separate from yours."

"Very well. Just be on your way." "SB" then left. *I guess I do owe her for asking her to burn that hotel in Nemuro,* Muhadow thought.

#

New United Nations Headquarters/St. Anthony Crater, Newfoundland and Labrador Province, Canada. 1119 hours (Newfoundland Standard Time)

Alberto Pérez was now at the headquarters of the New United Nations, carrying a suitcase. This building was almost a replication of the old United Nations headquarters that was located in New York City. The destruction of UN Headquarters by an Afghan refugee using a home-made nuclear weapon caused the Third World War.

Near the present-day NUN Headquarters was the crater where the town of St. Anthony in Canada's Newfoundland Island once stood. St. Anthony was the only casualty Canada's Atlantic coast suffered throughout the war when a Soviet Project 667M Andromeda ballistic missile submarine attempting to attack the United States of America, was intercepted. Before being sunk, the captain launched one P-750 Meteorit-M nuclear-tipped cruise missile from the Andromeda but instead of hitting a US city, it hit the Canadian town of St. Anthony.

Upon the creation of the New United Nations after the war, the nascent supernational union opted to have their headquarters situated near the crater where St. Anthony once stood to symbolize that the mistakes of the past must never be repeated. With assistance from the Gatekeepers of Knowledge, who helped clear the area of radioactive material, construction of NUN Headquarters took four years.

Pérez then saw a woman as old as he is with very light skin and brown hair, also carrying a suitcase, approaching. He then turned to the woman as a way to make sure she would divert her attention to him and it worked as the woman stopped before him. She wore a pantsuit and heeled shoes that were both navy blue. This woman, Cecilia Parnell, served as the

Director of Intelligence, whom Pérez answered to as all intelligence agencies of the New United Nations formed the Intelligence Collective. The Director of Intelligence was to report to the Secretary-General of the New United Nations in matters such as Maria Hoshikawa's kidnapping and why the Eurasian Tsardom would be involved.

"I apologize for being late, Al." Parnell said.

"Luckily for the both of us, the Secretary-General has yet to show up," Pérez reminded. "We best hurry then."

"Agreed."

#

Soviet Ground Forces Outpost, Zabaykaletsky District, Sakhalin Oblast, Russian Soviet Federative Socialist Republic. 0210 hours (Sakhalin Time)

A loud beep resonated across a border outpost of the Soviet Ground Forces in Poronaysky District facing the northern half of Sakhalin Island, dominated by the Eurasian Tsardom. Two men left the outpost using a UAZ-469 light utility vehicle. Their uniform consisted of SSh-68 helmets and the M73, which consisted of a tunic with four buttons and trousers, both of which were colored beige. A brown-colored belts system was strapped on their upper bodies and it contained ammunition for their AK-05 assault rifles that were kept beside them. Their footwear consisted of black boots.

"Yuri, can't you hurry it up?" one Soviet infantryman seated at the right front seat of the 469 asked to the other infantryman driving.

"It's not that far," the other infantryman named Yuri replied. "Just wait until we put an end to this madness."

"Fine."

#

Near the Outpost. 0214 hours

The two Soviet infantrymen arrived near another 469. Upon seeing it, they stopped their vehicle. Once they removed their seatbelts and opened their respective doors, they got their AK-05s and got out of the vehicle and walked to the other one. One of them carried a flashlight with his left hand while he kept his AK on his right hand.

"Who owns this one?" Yuri asked. "The Tsarists?"

"We best answer that our-" the other infantryman, carrying a flashlight, said until he stopped moving his entire body.

"Gennady, what's wr-" Yuri joined the infantryman named Gennady in looking at what made him froze.

Both saw a dead Turkmen at the second 469. His neck was slit with blood flooding out of it. His eyelids kept the eyes open.

"Who could have d-" Gennady attempted to say before he and Yuri heard the respective safety of two pistols being switched off.

Behind Yuri and Gennady was "SB" as she aimed two Makarov pistols at the respective heads of the former. The two Soviet soldiers froze where they stood with fear emanating from their respective faces.

"Ignore the corpse and do as I say," "SB" demanded.

"And what is it that you want?" Yuri asked.

And now, I got what I need to start the war, "SB" thought.

#

Near an Imperial Eurasian Army Border Outpost, Smirnykhovsky Uyezd, Sakhalin Governorate, Eurasian Tsardom. 0520 hours

Yuri, Gennady, and "SB" arrived near an outpost of the Imperial Eurasian Army (IEA) in the northern half of Sakhalin Island held by the Eurasian Tsarsdom. "SB" rapidly pointed her pistol at Gennady, forcing him to remove his seatbelt, open his door, and get out after getting his AK-05.

"Now charge against that outpost and shoot until they shoot you," "SB" commanded.

Gennady opted not to reply. He then charged against the outpost.

"What happens next?" Yuri reluctantly asked.

"As soon as we hear shooting, we leave," "SB" answered.

The sound of automatic fire followed. Yuri immediately began to start up the 469.

Near the Border with the Russian Soviet Federative Socialist Republic. 0601 hours

An IEA *Loshad'* began to come across the 469 that was used by Yuri, Gennady, and "SB". The driver stopped. He and another infantryman began to get off their *Loshad'* to investigate. Unlike their Soviet Ground Forces counterparts, the Imperial Eurasian Army uniforms for their infantrymen were different.

The two men wore a beige-colored uniform that comprised a helmet, a tunic with four pockets and five silver buttons, a ballistic vest above the pockets in the upper half of the tunic, a brown leather belt separating the tunic and hiding the fifth button, trousers, and black-colored boots. Unlike the Soviets, who use the SSh-68 and M73 combination, the uniform combination of the IEA was that of the M88 uniform worn by Soviet infantrymen during the invasion of the Democratic Republic of Afghanistan that was infamously interrupted by the crash landing of *Revelator* in 1985 and a new helmet designated the SSh-10. The usage of the M88, nicknamed "Afghanka", was due to the Tsardom's creator Ivan Vladimirovich Tsulukidze having in mind his time in Afghanistan as to what his soldiers ought to wear.

Once the *Loshad'* was stopped, the two infantrymen riding on it removed their seatbelts, grabbed their AK-2000 assault rifles, and got off the *Loshad'*. As they got close to the 469, they stopped as they found the driver dead with his AK-05 awfully close and his chin torn open by a 5.45x39mm round.

#

Iron Dutchman, Taisho Ward, Kansai City, Kansai Prefecture; State of Japan. April 24, 2030; 0806 hours (Japan Standard Time)

Save for Tarou Ganji and Anita Hamilton, all members of Iron Dutchman Services ate their breakfast at their dining hall. Wouter Vos then heard his smartphone and upon picking it up, he found that it was a call from "Maria Clara" on AudComm.

"This is Vos," the South African said.

"Thank goodness I reached you, Mr. Vos," Alicia Caguiat said on the other end. "Listen, something terrible happened and that we need to launch the operation as soon as possible."

#

Nishi High School, Higashiosaka Ward. 1533 hours

Vos now appeared at Nishi High School. Everything about him made him acquire the attention of teacher and student alike throughout the school. He stopped in front of Class 2-2's room just as classes had ended.

Tarou Ganji then came out of the door to the right of the locker, but he caught a glance of Vos and turned to his left. He was unable to move as a result, causing those behind him to congest to the door.

"Mr. Vos, what are you doing here?" Tarou asked.

"I came to tell you we have an emergency," Vos answered before he leaned to his right ear. "Doc needs you."

Tarou managed to realize in time what that meant. However, Yumi Hasegawa pushed herself out of the room to confront Vos as she knew he was responsible for why her students weren't able to exit the room.

"Excuse me, but if you don't have anything urgent to do here, please leave the premises," Hasegawa said in English to Vos.

"My apologies," Vos said as he turned to Hasegawa. "I needed to inform Mr. Ganji here Dr. Hamilton needs his assistance. I'll be leaving now."

"I see."

#

1555 hours

Tarou now approached his PCX scooter. He then heard loud footsteps approaching his way and turned to find Misa Todoh rushing to him.

"Ganji-kun, where are you going?" Misa asked as she stopped. "We're starting Judo club."

"I humbly apologize for this, but I need to leave right away," Tarou replied. "Hamilton-sensei needs my help."

"Very well."

#

1600 hours

Both Vos and Crawley saw Tarou using his scooter to leave. Crawley carried a plastic bag from the nearby pharmacy.

"Our work here's done," Crawley declared.

"Then let's go," Vos ordered.

#

Iron Dutchman, Taisho Ward. 1705 hours

Save for Bartolomeu Moura, all members of Iron Dutchman Services, along with Frederick Dirks and John Vue, were now gathered in the briefing room. At the adjacent projector room, Tatev Mirzoyan prepared her laptop computer's AudComm and with the computer connected to the projector, everyone else now saw the AudComm open. However, the name used to indicate whom Tatev will be talking to isn't "Maria Clara" but "Langley 3".

"Langley 3, all members are now gathered," Tatev said. "Mr. 'Smith' and Mr. Vue are here as well."

"Good," Stanley McAllister replied from the other end of AudComm. "For those listening, allow me to introduce myself. I'm the Deputy Director of Covert Action, but you are to refer to me as Langley 3."

"Why are you contacting us?" Dirks asked.

"Because this is highly urgent that 'Maria Clara' needs her rest to concentrate."

"How urgent are we talking?" Vos asked.

"We've heard from our station chief in Vladivostok that a Soviet soldier barged into Eurasian territory and attacked an Imperial Eurasian Army outpost. He's dead, as is his accomplice, who was found dead in his UAZ and that he killed himself with his AK."

"That can't be, sir!" Vue argued. "What happened to the meeting between the Eurasian ambassador and Vladivostok?"

"It happened as soon as that meeting ended. It doesn't matter how it'll end. We need to get Hoshikawa out now before what happened in Sakhalin turns into a war between the Asians and the Eurasians and we got the green light from the Secretary-General to do whatever it takes as long as we don't get dragged into it. I've reviewed those pics of those drawings Ghaemi made and we've already thought of how you're to get in, get Hoshikawa, and get out."

"How?" Vos asked.

"The Director of Foreign Intelligence met with the Secretary-General and the Joint Chiefs of Staff. They're pooling what you'll need to get the job done. We have a Commando on its way to Itami and you're to enter Soviet Sakhalin by way of parachutes the Commando will be carrying. I assume some of you know how to use them."

"Wouter, Jake, and I do," Sunan Wattana replied.

"Also, once you get Hoshikawa out, you'll have to race your way to Lake Nevsky to the northeast of Poronaysk. The Chief of Staff of the Maritime Force already contacted the NUNS *Ronald Reagan* to take in a SWF team that will ride on a Surion that will extract you."

"But why Itami?" Crawley asked.

"We know that you lack sufficient equipment," McAllister answered. "Colonel Armstrong has what you need. Just tell him that this is an order from the Secretary-General."

"Will do," Dirks replied.

"I have one request and it'll require that I go to Itami personally to see Colonel Armstrong," Tarou said.

"And what might that be?" McAllister asked.

"We might need an Osprey Walgear carrier. Based on those drawings Ghaemi made, there's a Walgear hangar and should there be one, I intend on using it to escape."

"A good suggestion. It'll go with the extraction team."

"How long will it take for the Commando to arrive at Itami?" Anita Hamilton asked.

"11 hours. It left Comox at 0730 hours Pacific Standard Time."

"Then it'll arrive tomorrow," Vue deduced.

"Then make your preparations before it arrives. Going to Itami should also get Armstrong to allow that Commando to land there and pick you up. 'Smith', I need you to lead the infiltration team."

"Yes, sir," Dirks replied.

"Langley 3 out."

#

1st Light Mechanized Assault Regiment Headquarters/Itami Field, Itami, Hyogo Prefecture. 1840 hours

Dirks, Vos, and Tarou were now at the office of Henry "Hank" Armstrong, the commanding officer of the 1st Light Mechanized Assault Regiment. Tarou wore his scooter's helmet like he did during the car chase the previous week to avoid being exposed as a teenager.

Armstrong then appeared. Because they were guests, Dirks, Vos, and Tarou remained in their respective seats. Forty-four years old, Armstrong had very light skin, blue eyes, and blond hair in a crew cut. His post was only recent as he was previously assigned to the Democratic Republic of Congo, where his original unit fell into an ambush that was only thwarted by Wouter Vos, who assumed responsibility to avoid diplomatic problems between the New United Nations and the African Federation as Vos commanded the unit that saved Armstrong's subordinates.

Both men remembered as Armstrong turned to Vos first as soon as he sat down. "Figured you'd go to the Company," Armstrong remarked to Vos.

"I'm actually a mercenary," Vos retorted. "The Company just recruited me."

"And how are Wattana and Crawley?"

"Crawley's outside. He drove for us. Wattana's still at our ship."

"You have a ship?"

"It's our base. Anyway, I'm not here to talk about the past." Vos then used his right thumb to point at Dirks, who was seated between him and Tarou. "He's here to avail for your equipment."

"For what?"

"Everything I'm about to say must not leave this office," Dirks demanded. "Got that?"

"… Fine."

#

Pervomaisk Training School, Pervomaisk Volost, Nogliksky Uyezd, Sakhalin Governorate; Eurasian Tsardom. 2040 hours (Sakhalin Time)

Vladimir Nikolayevich Mirov, a man in his late twenties with black hair in a crew cut, average height, very light skin, and dark brown eyes, was inside the office of the Pervomaisk Training School's commandant Iroda Olimovna Sobirova. Although from separate branches of the Imperial Eurasian Armed Forces (IEAF); the former wore the officer's uniform of the Imperial Eurasian Navy that hid his body with an athletic build, while the latter wore the officer's uniform of the Imperial Eurasian Army. That was because the Pervomaisk Training School was built to train new Walgear pilots for both the IEA and the Imperial Eurasian Naval Infantry; the latter being the service branch Mirov was a part of. Mirov's post at the Pervomaisk Training School was because he managed to destroy five main battle tanks during the Eurasian Tsardom's invasion of the Islamic Republic of Iran. Destroying five tanks was a Herculean task even for a Walgear pilot as Walgears were built with metals that were built to sustain the weight of their human pilots, yet heavy rounds, particularly from tanks, can easily penetrate their armor..

"You called for me, Generál?" Mirov asked as she stopped saluting.

"You've heard of the attack against the outpost near Koshevoy?" Sobirova asked."

"Da."

"Then read this." Sobirova offered a letter that Mirov wasted no time in grabbing from her. As he opened it, he read it thorougly, but he was slow in finishing it due to its contents with Sobirova realizing what was in the letter without reading it.

1921 hours

"You're nuts!" Armstrong exclaimed after listening to why Dirks came to him. "And a Commando is on its way here to pick you up and drop you off into Soviet Sakhalin?"

"He's serious," Vos warned.

"So, what do you need?"

"Assault rifles, a sniper rifle for Wattana, grenades, earpieces, and vests."

"And also a Walgear carrier," Tarou added. "If those Turkmens have one, I'll use it to escape and it'll need to be picked up if assuming it'll survive by the time we reach Lake Nevsky."

"I'll have what you need ready by tomorrow and get that Osprey to the *Reagan.* You better give me back the rifles, the earpieces, vests, and Osprey once you're done with them."

"We will."

#

Unknown Location, Poronaysky District, Sakhalin Oblast; Russian Soviet Federative Socialist Republic. 2100 hours (Sakhalin Time)

"Damn you, Ananaev," Serdar Muhadow cursed while he and a subordinate of his were at a men's restroom in the underground complex beneath the bunker. "Thanks to you, we'll be discovered."

"So what do we do now?" the subordinate asked.

Muhadow, however, didn't reply to his subordinate's question. He found a camera above them and opted to lean toward his subordinate's right eye. He then whispered his answer, which surprised the latter once Muhadow finished and stopped leaning on him.

"When do we get started?" the subordinate asked.

"We observe the upcoming war first," Muhadow answered. "Send out a team to observe what will happen at sunset and when we hear from them, put the plan into motion."

The Rescue

Iron Dutchman, Taisho Ward, Kansai City, Kansai Prefecture; State of Japan. April 24, 2030; 2039 hours (Japan Standard Time)

All members of Iron Dutchman Services, Frederick Dirks, and John Vue gathered at the Iron Dutchman's briefing room again. This time, Moura joined them. Projected onto the screen was a drawing that consisted of a square shaped structure with longer rectangles below it. Separating the square from the rectangles was a line. There were five rectangles below the line, with the second one connected to the line by another rectangle that was smaller and that it faced upward diagonally to its right.

"This is one of the drawings Ghaemi made about that bunker he spoke of," Dirks explained to Vue and the mercenaries. "As you can see, Muhadow and his men aren't using a mere bunker because it's a front for the underground complex you're seeing. I know what most, if not all, of you are thinking. However, we're against the clock, so rescuing Hoshikawa takes priority. We don't have time to find out about the facility."

He then pointed to the smaller rectangle. "This is the exit that Ganji must use to escape the underground complex as soon as he locates Hoshikawa. If he's right and that there is a Walgear there, those mercenaries might close it. Therefore, we'll split into two teams."

Managing to hear 'split into two teams', Tatev Mirzoyan used the program showing the drawing to switch to another slide. Now projected was a map of central Sakhalin with a long white line dividing it to represent the northern half that was the Eurasian Tsardom's Sakhalin Governorate and the southern half to represent the Russian Soviet Federative Socialist Republic's Sakhalin Oblast. Also on the map were dots in purple and red. There was one dot that, in contrast to the purple and red dots, was colored green.

"The dots in red are Soviet outposts," Dirks continued. "While the dots in purple are Eurasian outposts. No doubt that they'll be busy gearing up for war, so that should allow the Commando to infiltrate Soviet airspace, in which we drop. As for the two teams, Ganji and I will drop directly into the bunker, which is here."

Dirks then pointed to the green dot, which represented the bunker. "I gleaned this from the tracking device I planted on Hoshikawa."

"So why the splitting into two teams?" Jason Luke Crawley asked.

"One team needs to go to that bunker, while the other team is to infiltrate a Soviet outpost and steal a UAZ from them. Once Ganji and I reach the bunker, he'll go inside by himself to find Hoshikawa. As for me, I'll find the exit of that tunnel connected to the second underground floor and I'll start setting up explosives once I find it. I'll blow it open once the other team joins me with the UAZ."

"Then Crawley, Wattana, and I will get the UAZ," Wouter Vos declared.

"What about weapons?" Sunan Wattana asked.

"Ganji will only have his P226 and the AK-2000 we took from Gurdov," Dirks answered. "He'll need them if in case he has to fight his way out. As for me, Vos, and Crawley, we'll use the ADRs Armstrong will be providing. As for you, Wattana, you'll use the ADR Sniper Armstrong's also providing while you'll take the Lusa II as your secondary weapon."

"When do we launch?" Tarou Ganji, no longer wearing his helmet, asked.

"Tomorrow. As soon as the Commando arrives, we get on, the plane launches, and we drop as soon as we near Poronaysk. It'll have to leave us because if it stays for too long, then the Soviets will think NUN as a whole will be backing the Tsardom."

Dirks then turned to Anita Hamilton. "Hamilton, I'll need you to explain to the principal of Nishi High School the cover story you and Ganji have as to why he won't be attending school tomorrow."

"Roger that," Hamilton replied.

Dirks turned to Vue. "Vue, I need you to go to Camp Yao and avail for a helicopter so that you can go to the *Reagan*. They'll need to be notified that the Walgear carrier from Itami will be joining with them. If you'll have a problem with the guards, just show them your FIS card. It'll attract Colonel Izubuchi's attention."

"Got it," Vue replied.

"Now we discuss the next slide." Upon hearing Dirks' words, Tatev switched to a new slide, showing another drawing. This time, it was a floor plan that showed one of the underground floors. "This is the third floor of the underground complex. According to Ghaemi, Hoshikawa was meant to be kept in the padded cells located on that floor. Ganji is to primarily infiltrate that floor and, by any means, find which cell is she kept in."

"But how will Ganji get inside that bunker leading to the underground complex?"

"After Ghaemi made those drawings, Ganji and I discussed something that he'll explain now."

Tarou then stood up and reached the stage. He now stood in front of the other mercenaries and Vue. "As Mr. 'Smith' and I discussed, we plan on using Ghaemi," Tarou explained. "We'll be taking him with us."

"But what about his parachute?" Vue asked as he raised his hand. "No one knows about this idea."

"I'll think of something."

"Then you may return to your seat," Dirks ordered as he turned to Tarou. The latter complied by getting off the stage. "Anything else?" Dirks asked to the mercenaries and Vue.

"What about communication?" Wattana asked. "How will we keep each other updated?"

"Armstrong's men will provide us with earpieces," Dirks answered. "However, they will be useless for Ganji once he's in the underground complex."

"So how will we know if he got Hoshikawa?" Vos asked.

"Once I detonate the explosives on the tunnel connected to the second floor, that should allow Ganji to use the earpiece," Dirks answered before he turned to Vos. "Though I expect that once I do blow up the door, you join me with the UAZ."

"Count on it."

"Anything else?" Dirks asked as he resumed looking at the other mercenaries and Vue.

"What about Ghaemi?" Vue asked. "If he does manage to land without any injuries, what will happen to him?"

"Mind if I be allowed to answer that?" Tarou asked as he raised his hand.

"Please enlighten us," Dirks ordered.

Tarou stood up and turned to face the rest of Iron Dutchman Services and Vue. This time, he chose not to climb up onto the stage. "Having fought under Muhadow, he might execute Ghaemi should he appear in front of the bunker. Seven years ago, he executed a subordinate for failing in his task."

"And you think it's a good idea to bring him with you and give him to Muhadow? Why not grant him asylum in any NUN member-state of his choice?"

"He's a mere subordinate of Muhadow. Other than the layout of the bunker and what it's hiding, that's all he has to offer. Besides, with what's about to happen, he can distract the guards long enough for them to give me an opportunity to enter the bunker, allowing me access to the underground complex."

It's even more saddening that a child like Tarou knows how to take advantage of an enemy than to take advantage of his youth, Vue thought grimly.

"Other than communication, what about mapping?" Hamilton asked. "How will you know your way?"

"We take our phones with us and count on D-Maps," Dirks answered. "As for me, as long as Hoshikawa is at that underground complex, I can use the coordinates to relay it using Device Tracker to Vos and his team. It'll be up to them to find me and Ganji."

"Anything else?" Vos asked. "Once I say we're dismissed, there's no going back from this."

"None," every other member of Iron Dutchman Services and Vue replied with resolve evident from their respective tones.

"Then we're dismissed, everyone. We rest up now. We have a big day tomorrow."

NUNS *Ronald Reagan*; Pacific Ocean. April 25, 2030; 1010 hours

A Japan Ground Self-Defense Force UH-1H Iroquois helicopter neared the NUNS *Ronald Reagan*, one of the three aircraft carriers of the New United Nations Maritime Force. This carrier was the namesake of the class she shared with the two other carriers. The design was also a relic of the United States Navy as it's a continuation of the *Nimitz*-class aircraft carriers, which were all sunk during the Third World War.

After contacting the control tower with John Vue, the sole passenger of the Iroquois, explaining why he and the Iroquois were coming, the helicopter was granted permission to land. As soon as Vue stepped out of the Iroquois, the latter immediately left the *Reagan*.

Vue then found himself face-to-face with a female Marine. Her uniform consisted of a utility cover cap, a camouflage blouse and trousers in blue, and tan suede boots. She had an MCP holstered on her left hip.

"Admiral O'Flaherty is expecting you," the Marine said. "Please follow me."

#

1039 hours

Vue was now at the flag officer's quarters of the *Reagan*. He now faced Nora O'Flaherty, the commander of the 1st Carrier Battle Group of NUNMF's North Pacific Fleet. Despite her looks, O'Flaherty was fifty-two years old; her red hair showing no visible signs of graying maintained the illusion. She had very light skin and green eyes.

"So, what brings you to the *Reagan*?" O'Flaherty asked.

"I've been instructed to tell you that we're to be expecting an Osprey Walgear carrier from Itami," Vue explained. "The Walgear pilot of Iron Dutchman Services thinks the ones who kidnapped Maria Hoshikawa might have a Walgear, and he intends to steal it to help in the escape once he's saved Hoshikawa."

"And it'll accompany the Swiffs in the extraction?"

"That's right."

"Very well. Now please make yourself comfortable. We have a long day ahead of us."

#

1st Light Mechanized Assault Regiment Headquarters/Itami Field, Itami, Hyogo Prefecture. 1056 hours

The party from the *Iron Dutchman* arrived at Itami Field, the headquarters of the 1st Light Mechanized Assault Regiment. Originally a military airfield, it became the civilian Osaka International Airport in 1959 but when Osaka was struck by a nuclear warhead during the Third World War and that Kansai International Airport near Izumisano was built, the airport in Itami became a facility for storing old aircraft.

When the New United Nations Defense Forces was created and that NUN's member-states had to downscale its respective militaries, the Japan Ground Self-Defense downsized its Central Army. When the New United Nations Ground Force (NUNGF) created the 1st Light Mechanized Assault Regiment as the first unit primarily dedicated to the usage of their new Walgear, the MWG3 Minuteman, they needed their own headquarters that would allow them first-response capabilities.

As a result, the former headquarters of the JGSDF's Central Army in Itami, along with the old Osaka International Airport, were given to this regiment. This allowed the regiment to launch as soon as transport planes from the New United Nations Air and Space Force arrived at Itami.

After Jake Crawley parked the party's Townace, he got off. Frederick Dirks, Wouter Vos, Tarou Ganji, and Sunan Wattana followed. The latter two forcibly made Raşit Ghaemi follow. Armstrong and two armed guards then appeared.

"This your crew?" Armstrong asked.

"That's right?" Dirks answered.

Armstrong primarily focused his attention on Crawley and Wattana, the latter two being his former subordinates back in Africa. Both parties showed that neither have forgotten nor forgiven each other for what happened. "Should have known you two would have become mercs," Armstrong remarked.

"What's that supposed to mean?" Wattana asked.

"I just hope you don't mess this one up." Armstrong then turned to the hooded Ghaemi, then to Dirks. "You said nothing about him."

"He's part of our plan to infiltrate that bunker," Dirks explained.

"Really now? Luckily, the plane isn't here yet. We still have time to listen to your plan. Now follow me."

#

1116 hours

"So that's your plan?" Armstrong asked after having listened to what was discussed between Dirks and Iron Dutchman Services the previous night at the briefing room of Itami Field. "I guess that explains the need for a Walgear carrier."

"What about our equipment?" Wattana asked.

"Major Ngor here will take you to the hangar where we're keeping the equipment." Armstrong gestured to a male subordinate with black hair underneath his patrol cap and dark intermediate skin. "Just follow him."

#

1130 hours

"This is the earpiece you asked for," Ngor explained as he grabbed one of five earpieces from the top of a crate now that he, Dirks, and the mercenaries were at a hangar. "Sadly, though, we'll be able to hear everything because these are ours. As to how it works, it has one button for turning it on. Press it multiple times to access a certain frequency. Instructions on how to access a frequency will be added."

"It's fine," Dirks replied. "Thanks."

"Now it's time to stock up. Your plane will be here in a matter of minutes."

1142 hours

An MC-130J Commando II special operations military transport aircraft now landed at Itami Field. Dirks, Vos, Wattana, Crawley, and Tarou now had their vests, weapons, and earpieces. Two of Armstrong's men now restrained Ghaemi.

Once the rear ramp of the Commando II was erected, everyone proceeded to the plane. Upon seeing the plane's commanding officer, Joanne O'Leary, stepping out, the group stopped.

"Didn't think I'd be working with you again, 'Smith'," O'Leary remarked.

"Sorry about that," Dirks replied.

O'Leary looked at the mercenaries, but her attention was mostly on Tarou before returning her gaze to Dirks. "Should have known having a kid with you was suspicious."

"He's done well so far."

"But what about him?" O'Leary asked as she pointed at Ghaemi.

"He's part of the plan," Dirks answered. "I'll explain on the plane."

"Very well. Everyone, get in. As for our guest, turn him over to Singleton and Norton."

Dirks used his head to instruct Armstrong's men to move ahead with Ghaemi. Both Andrew Singleton and Grace Norton grabbed Ghaemi, allowing the two NUNGF soldiers to leave. Once they entered the Commando II, everyone else followed.

#

New United Nations Air and Space Force Special Operations Command MC-130J; Above Ishikawa Prefecture. 1216 hours

"You're joking, right?" O'Leary asked as her command panel, after listening to Dirks about how he and the mercenaries will be arriving at Soviet Sakhalin. "We'll have to decrease altitude to avoid detection!"

"You'll have to," Dirks replied. "I've already been told that you're not going to wait around for us."

"We can't because we didn't have a chance to refuel. I'm just hoping we fly low enough that we're not detected."

"Then we'll jump as quickly as possible but we jump in teams. Ganji, Ghaemi, and I first. Vos, Crawley, and Wattana will have to drop after us because they have to secure us a UAZ from a Soviet outpost and we need that UAZ to rush to Lake Nevsky."

"Very well, but I need to remind you that once we leave, you're on your own. You'll have to be fast in escaping to Lake Nevsky and make sure no one is following you by the time the Swiffs come."

"We'll make it quick."

"Now return to your seat. I'll have the pilots decrease altitude once we leave Japanese airspace."

#

Smirnykhovsky Uyezd, Sakhalin Governorate; Eurasian Tsardom. 1436 hours (Sakhalin Time)

Four SH-6 Walgears now faced the border between the Eurasian Tsardom and the Russian Soviet Federative Socialist Republic at Sakhalin Island. The SH-6 was now the workhorse of the Imperial Eurasian Armed Forces for ground warfare. This was shown with the differing colors of the four Walgears. One was purple while the other three were beige. The purple one, piloted by Vladimir Nikolayevich Mirov, was the color for the Imperial Eurasian Naval Infantry, whereas beige was used by Imperial Eurasian Army SH-6s.

"Leytenánt, how long are to attack our targets?" a male voice asked over the communicator of Mirov's SH-6.

"Until we attract a large force," Mirov answered. "Remember, we're limited to hit-and-run."

"Zametano."

Suddenly, the sound of missiles filled the air. Mirov and his three IEA subordinates knew that their time to attack was near.

Gatekeepers of Knowledge Laboratory, Poronaysky District, Sakhalin Oblast; Russian Soviet Federative Socialist Republic. 1533 hours

"So it's come down to this," Muhadow said after having listened to his subordinate about the Eurasian attacks. "Start whispering to all our men that we'll be launching the plan. I'll be having a chat with Dr. Hovsepyan."

"What about Maria Hoshikawa?" the subordinate asked.

"We'll take her with us. We'll surrender to the Soviets and tell her who she really is. That will add more fuel to the fire 'SB' started."

#

1535 hours

At his office, Hovsepyan hurriedly grabbed a hard disk drive from his desktop computer after uninstalling it from the computer. He then put it in his small sports bag, along with belongings. He then grabbed a PM-01 semi-automatic pistol and started shooting at his computer.

It was then that Muhadow arrived at the office, interrupting Hovsepyan. "I… It's you, Devotee-Colonel," Hovsepyan said.

"Started cleaning up?" Muhadow asked.

"We have to. This laboratory will be discovered."

"Why don't I get you to the second hangar already? We best make haste."

"Agreed."

Both Hovsepyan and Muhadow began to exit the room. Muhadow glanced at the camera. *By now, all the cameras must be disabled. Soon, they'll detonate the explosive already attached to the* TPR *to make sure Enlightenment Point isn't contacted*, Muhadow thought.

New United Nations Air and Space Force Special Operations Command MC-130J; Above Makarovsky District, Sakhalin Oblast. 1535 hours

Dirks barged into O'Leary's command panel in the Commando II; now flying below its earlier ceiling height in order to evade Soviet radar. "What is it?" O'Leary asked as she turned to Dirks.

"We're near the target zone," Dirks answered. "Please turn on the red light. Like you said, you want us out as soon as we reach the target? Then allow us to get into our chutes already."

"Got it. Once we're one klick near the target, I'll turn on the green light for Ganji to prepare Ghaemi."

#

1601 hours

Dirks and the mercenaries were now in their respective parachutes. Tarou Ganji, however, put the parachute meant for him on Raşit Ghaemi.

"Really?" Andrew Singleton asked. "He gets the chute?"

"That's part of the plan," Tarou answered.

"Then how will you land?"

"I'll improvise."

#

Gatekeepers of Knowledge Laboratory. 1605 hours

Muhadow and his men now surrounded a circle of corpses they made in another hangar that contained another Walgear. Corpses that were once the staff of the laboratory. Only Hovsepyan was spared, but as far as the Turkmens knew, he would follow his colleagues soon as Muhadow aimed his Makarov pistol at Hovsepyan's head.

"W… What on Earth are you doing?" Hovsepyan asked.

"I'm going to betray the Gatekeepers because of this war," Muhadow answered. "My men are about to secure the self-destruction module and once we escape with Hoshikawa, I intend on giving her to the Soviets while telling them who she is."

"But what about the test results?"

"I'll find some use for them. All that matters is making the Gatekeepers pay for using 'SB' to start this war. Thanks to your paranoia, they'll never know of my treachery, and by the time they do, it'll be too late."

Muhadow then shot Hovsepyan. Because the former shot the latter at his forehead, the bullet flew immediately out of the head, creating a tunnel throughout Hovsepyan's brain. Muhadow then went through Hovsepyan's corpse after it fell onto the floor and found a key around his neck. After getting the necklace with the key off, Muhadow stood up.

"Berdiýew, Rejepow, secure Hoshikawa's cell," Muhadow ordered.

"Yes, sir," the two men named Berdiýew and Rejepow replied.

Muhadow then turned to his current second-in-command. "Geldiýew, you're to accompany me to the self-destruction panel. Once I've activated it, we pass by for Hoshikawa, then we escape."

"Yes, sir," Geldiýew replied.

"Sir!" another subordinate shouted as he rushed into the hangar, making Muhadow look at him as he stopped and paced himself.

"What is it, Esenov?" Muhadow asked.

"Someone claiming to be Raşit Ghaemi appeared on a parachute," the subordinate named Esenov answered. "Chayev and Saparow are taking care of him now."

How could he be- Never mind, Muhadow thought. *It seems things are about to be more interesting around here.*

Muhadow then turned to Geldiýew again and offered the key he took from Hovspeyan. "Geldiýew, you handle the self-destruction module. Esenov and I will see to Ghaemi."

Above the Old Imperial Japanese Army Bunker. 1614 hours

As they continued falling to their destination, Ghaemi continuously creamed in Persian. Tarou, knowing what it meant, ignored him. While falling, Tarou and Ghaemi now saw the bunker.

Ghaemi pleaded again, but Tarou had something else in mind beyond ignoring the mercenary. Luckily for Ghaemi, Tarou didn't think for too long as he managed to rotate himself in the opposite direction and once that was done, Tarou activated the parachute and separated from Ghaemi.

However, the gap between the bunker and Tarou was still high, especially when the latter moved around to see what he was falling to. The latter remained undaunted, but the lower he got, he saw that he was now close to the bunker. Miraculously, Tarou had yet to suffer the consequences of such a fall, but those weren't in his mind, as the bunker was now close.

He then prepared both of his arms with his palms open. As he got close to the bunker, he managed to use the hands to touch the bunker as his way of landing. Ghaemi in the parachute soon followed.

Time to hide, Tarou thought. *Once the door in front of me opens, I'll rush inside.*

Tarou then swung his entire body backward, putting him into the air again, but this allowed him to get closer to the bunker's roof and, unlike earlier, he prepared his feet for the landing, which miraculously succeeded. It was then that Serdar Muhadow and his subordinate, Esenov, appeared outside.

Tarou immediately turned and rushed to the entrance. He found that it was going to close, forcing him to jump off the roof, but while managing to avoid the attention of Muhadow and his men, Tarou used his arms to prevent the door from closing. With what strength he could muster, Tarou used the arms to keep the door from opening while pushing his entire body forward to slide himself, his arms included, inside just before the door closed.

Finding the panel where machine guns were once placed, Tarou now saw Ghaemi talking to Muhadow. However, he had no time to watch and hid again before bringing out his smartphone. Using the Pictures application, Tarou accessed a drawing Ghaemi made: a floor plan of the bunker used to hide the laboratory. He found that there were stairs leading to the underground complex and once he put down his phone, he saw the same stairs and rushed to them.

Near the Old Imperial Japanese Army Bunker. 1641 hours

Elsewhere, Dirks landed without issue. He then took his sunglasses from his shirt and resumed wearing them. After that, he used his earpiece and pressed its only button thrice.

"Ganji, do you read me?" Dirks asked.

"This is Ganji," Tarou replied on the other end of the earpiece. "I'm inside the underground complex. Muhadow's men must be removing all traces of this lab because I smell gasoline."

"Just go to the third floor and get Hoshikawa. I'll make my way to where the tunnel ends."

"Roger."

#

Gatekeepers of Knowledge Laboratory. 1715 hours

Tarou hid at the wall of the stairs leading to the third floor of the laboratory. He looked at his phone again to find at Photos another drawing by Ghaemi. This time, the drawing was a rectangle with eight squares total; four on each side. Two squares facing each other near another staircase had "Bathroom" in them; one was for men and the other for women. Tarou then put down the phone and briefly got out of his cover to look at both sides.

This must be it, Tarou thought, until he saw two guards in front of one cell, causing him to hide again. *If there are two guards, then they must be guarding the cell Maria is kept at. I better hurry because Muhadow's bound to know I'm here thanks to Ghaemi.*

Tarou then readied his P226 and turned off its safety. *These two shots must count. Not only that, I have to hurry.*

#

1716 hours

In her padded cell, Maria Hoshikawa heard two gunshots coming from outside her cell and a female voice that spoke in Russian throughout the bunker's PA system. *Wh… What could that be?* Maria anxiously pondered. *Is this it?*

"Hoshikawa-senpai, are you there?"

That voice, Maria thought. "Ganji-kun, is that you?"

"It's me," Tarou Ganji said from the other side of the door. "Now that I know you're alive, I'm going to need you to trust me. Please cover your ears."

"What fo-"

"Just cover them!"

Maria did as Tarou requested. Outside, Tarou had removed the trousers of one of Muhadow's men after killing him and the other one. He then took the belt off and grabbed one of his grenades. Tying the grenade to the doorknob with the belt, Tarou then removed the pin and ran as far as he could away from the door, specifically to the men's bathroom. As he made it to the bathroom, the grenade exploded. He then rushed back to the now-open cell and turned on the lights. He found Maria sitting on the floor of the cell.

"It's time to go," Tarou said.

Maria raised her head to find Tarou now carrying his P226. "G… Ganji-kun, w- why are you carrying that gun?" Maria asked with Tarou realizing she's referring to his P226.

"There's too little time to explain," Tarou replied. "For now, all you need to know is that I'm part of a mercenary group hired by the Foreign Intelligence Service to keep an eye on you. My cover was to act as a transfer student in order to get close to you."

"Does my father know about this?"

"He and your mother. Now we best hurry. They've started a self-destruction sequence and if we don't go, we're both dead." A man shouting "The cell's open" was soon heard.

"Not good!" Tarou cursed as he briefly looked outside the cell before he turned to Maria again. "Maria, while I open fire at those guards, please grab one of the corpses outside and bring him in here. He has ammo for the rifle in my back and I really need that ammo."

"I'll do what I can," Maria replied.

Tarou then immediately rushed outside and used his P226 against the Turkmen. This allowed Maria to crawl toward the nearest corpse she could find and upon reaching the corpse, she grabbed him and dragged him inside the cell. Tarou was able to glance at what Maria did, allowing him to withdraw back to the cell.

Tarou then rushed to the corpse and grabbed the first AK-2000 magazine he could grab on such short notice from the dead Turkmen. After that, he turned to Maria and saw her praying.

"If you're done, get the other magazines out of the corpse," Tarou instructed. "It's as simple as that. And you better hurry."

"… Right," Maria hesitantly replied.

Tarou then loaded the rifle with the magazine. He hugged the left cell wall and seeing more of Muhadow's men, he fired the rifle. Maria then finished her prayer, grabbing the rest of the magazines.

Escape

Poronaysky District, Sakhalin Oblast; Russian Soviet Federative Socialist Republic. April 25, 2030; 1744 hours (Sakhalin Time)

At a metal door mostly hidden by leaves until he discovered it, Frederick Dirks planted C4 explosive in the middle of the door followed by connecting it to the detonating bars. As he finished, he pressed his earpiece thrice.

"Vos, what's your status?" Dirks asked.

"Green, I guess," Wouter Vos replied on the other end. "If you count being chased by Eurasian troops that is."

"What do you mean by 'being chased'?"

"We found an outpost but Eurasian troops had occupied it. Wattana came up with a plan for us to take their truck but now we're being chased by them."

"Damn it! Just get over here now! Ganji most likely has Hoshikawa now, and he's in trouble!"

"Jake's at full speed with this. Please be patient."

#

Gatekeepers of Knowledge Laboratory. 1750 hours

"It sounds there's more, no matter how much you keep on shooting," Maria Hoshikawa warned while Tarou Ganji reloaded his AK-2000 assault rifle and that the padded cell they were trapped in had empty magazines scattered beside the corpse of the Turkmen mercenary Tarou killed earlier.

"I know," Tarou replied. "And this is my last magazine from that man whose corpse you dragged in here."

"What do we do?"

"Cover your ears." Tarou then put down his AK and got a grenade and placed his left index finger in its pin. Maria saw the grenade and immediately covered her ears.

Tarou then pulled the pin and threw it, causing Serdar Muhadow's subordinates to stop firing and run upward. After he threw the grenade, Tarou grabbed his P226 semi-automatic pistol and just as he turned off its safety, the grenade exploded.

Once he finished removing the safety of his pistol, he immediately used his left hand to grab Maria. "We run," Tarou commanded. "Now!"

Maria made no response once Tarou simply dragged her with him out of the padded cell. While Tarou ran, Maria had to run as well as her left arm was held by Tarou's. Both now saw one of Muhadow's men in the stairs in front of them, whom Tarou shot with his pistol. In a stroke of luck, the Turkmen mercenary fell onto the stairs with one shot.

As soon as Tarou and Maria were now at the second floor of the laboratory, they now found themselves surrounded by Muhadow and his remaining subordinates. Had the former two continued, the latter would have killed them. Despite that, Tarou still aimed his P226.

"I'm glad you're still alive, Tarou," Muhadow said, appealing to their time together in Iran. "Give us the girl and you'll live."

Suddenly, the sound of a truck was heard followed by an explosion. Everyone initially forgot what they were doing until Muhadow was rapidly approached by Tarou, with his pistol on his right hand and Maria and her left arm on his left. As soon as Muhadow turned his head, it was too late as Tarou kicked him. Every other Turkmen mercenary was too stunned to act but as soon as Tarou and Maria turned to their right and found a room to run to, they immediately ran for it.

By the time Muhadow's men aimed at Tarou and Maria, it was too late as Maria opened the door and Tarou fired his pistol at them, killing a few of them and forcing the others to hide. By the time Tarou needed to reload, he was inside and Maria immediately closed the door and locked it.

"What was that explosion just now?" Maria asked.

"My handler, Mr. 'Smith'," Tarou answered. "Before the explosion, I heard an engine. Mr. Vos and the others must have gotten a UAZ to use."

"Now how do we get out of here?"

"Hold on." Tarou turned his entire body away from the door. He now saw the tunnel leading to the surface. He then turned to his left and found the Walgear Solbein.

"And now we have our way out," Tarou answered with Maria joining him in looking at the Walgear.

"A Walgear?" Maria asked. "Do you even know how to pilot that thing?"

"I do," Tarou answered while turning on the safety of his pistol and hiding it. "Come on."

Both Tarou and Maria rushed to Solbein. The Walgear was now crouching and that its cockpit was open, allowing Tarou to climb first. "What about me?" Maria asked.

"Bipedal Walgears can only fit one pilot in the cockpit," Tarou answered as he was halfway to the cockpit. "Please wait. I just need to tu-"

A kick then resonated across the hangar. Tarou rushed getting into Solbein's cockpit but as he was now seated, Muhadow and two of his men entered.

Good luck getting that thing to- Muhadow thought until he saw Solbein standing up and turning to him and his men. All were frightened that the machine whose height was four meters stared at them as if it were a vengeful god yet Muhadow simply looked at it while desperately avoiding to flinch his eyes as a contrast to his henchmen, who knew that fighting a Walgear with their SR-2 submachine guns was suicide.

Impossible! Muhadow exclaimed in his mind with fear. *He got that Walgear moving and yet I couldn't!*

However, Tarou moved Solbein's left arm and opened its hand. Maria then jumped onto the Walgear's palm. One of Muhadow's subordinates screamed and started firing at Solbein. Although the shots missed, Maria covered her eyes.

"You fool!" Muhadow screamed at his subordinate yet Solbein stood up with the sound making Muhadow and his men continue looking at it.

That was foolish of them! Tarou thought after he got Maria into Solbein's left palm and covered her with the Walgear's right hand. He then used the computer that was a vital component of Solbein's control panel and finding that the only weapons it has were two machine guns chambered at 12.7x108mm, he used one of them by pressing the topmost button on the right handle of the steering wheel found below the computer.

Once that button was pressed, the Walgear fired its right machine gun located directly above its groin. Muhadow and one of his men miraculously dodged the shots but the other subordinate, the same one who fired at Solbein, wasn't as fortunate.

Tarou saw what he did through the Walgear's front cameras, located on the eyes. However, he saw everything on all directions as Solbein's cockpit was shaped like a ball. *Despite the 360-degree view, this Walgear still functions like the Minuteman I used in Suriname,* Tarou thought.

Maria, still hidden by Solbein's hands, felt her heart beat. *Wh... What is this feeling?* Maria pondered until the firing stopped.

Tarou then moved Solbein toward the direction of the tunnel. He then pressed a small switch on the control panel that was above two words, both of which were colored white. Above the switch was "Legs" and below was "Wheels". Tarou chose wheels and upon doing so, he began to use the Walgear as if it were a car, ultimately pressing the right pedal with his right foot. As a result, Solbein moved using all four of its wheels; two of which were attached to each leg. Muhadow and his surviving subordinate simply watched as Tarou and Maria escaped.

Suddenly, this night has become even more interesting, Muhadow thought as if his confidence was a man who came out of a bathroom break before he turned to his subordinate. "We're going to pursue them."

"But si-" the subordinate argued until Geldiýew appeared only to stop as he saw the subordinate who was filled with holes after Tarou killed him. Muhadow then turned to him.

"Thank God you're here, Geldiýew," Muhadow said. "Get everyone onto the trucks. The mercenaries we were told of are here and they took Hoshikawa."

"Y... Yes, sir!" Geldiýew replied. "Also, the men went over Hovsepyan's corpse and they found this." Geldiýew brought out Hovsepyan's external hard disk drive.

"Give it to me now then instruct the men to get to the trucks!"

Outside the Laboratory. 0623 hours

Tarou and Maria then came out of the tunnel, which was now open, yet some of the fire remained. The former, through Solbein's camera eyes, saw a *Begemot* truck, but he saw someone waving at him. Tarou then briefly stopped the Walgear and zoomed in on the individual waving at him. He saw that it was Dirks.

"Mr. 'Smith', is that you?" Tarou asked with his voice transmitted through small but powerful speakers, which allowed Dirks and those in the *Begemot*, consisting of Wouter Vos, Jason Luke Crawley, and Sunan Wattana inside, to hear Tarou's question.

"Yes!" Dirks shouted. "And your hunch was right!"

"Nice Walgear!" Wattana commented as she popped out of the closed cab of the *Begemot*. "You have Hoshikawa? Where is she?"

"Bringing her down now." Tarou then lowered both of Solbein's arms. He then opened the right one, showing Maria. Having heard everything, she jumped out of the left palm with Dirks running up to her.

"Call me 'Fred Smith'," Dirks said. "I can imagine that Ganji told you everything, so I'll make this quick. Worked with your father a long time ago in the military and joined the FIS after that. Now, I'm the handler for the mercenary group Ganji is a part of and that your father and I helped arranged for Ganji to be transferred to Nishi High School."

Didn't think Ganji-kun is the type to join a mercenary group, Maria thought.

"Come on, we gotta move!" Vos shouted.

Wattana directed Dirks and Maria to rush to the cab of the *Begemot*. Wattana helped Maria inside while Dirks followed on his own. As soon as the latter sat down, Crawley started the engine again, allowing Dirks to summon his smartphone and use its AudComm. He then tapped into a certain frequency with the name "History Buff" attached to it while the *Begemot* moved.

"This is 'Smith', we have Hoshikawa and we're en route to Lave Nevsky," Dirks said.

"Thank God you're calling," John Vue said on the other end of the smartphone. "You better hurry and make sure you're not followed. As soon as we saw Hokkaido, the Swiffs have launched in their Surion along with the Walgear carrier Tarou asked for. Is there a Walgear Tarou found?"

"He's following us with it." Dirks turned to see Solbein following the *Begemot.* "It's something we've never seen before in terms of Walgear design. You'll have to wait until it's fetched by that Osprey to see it yourself. Also, we hit a snag."

"Don't tell me-"

"We'll be expecting pursuers any minute no-"

"We have company!" Crawley shouted.

It was then that Tarou moved to the truck's right before making a half-circle turn. Now Dirks, Maria, and Wattana saw that two vehicles pursued them, yet they couldn't be easily identified as it was past sunset.

"I got this," Wattana boasted as she aimed her Adaptive Rifle (ADR) sniper at the left light of the first vehicle she, Dirks, and Maria could see. However, Tarou used Solbein's left machine gun to destroy it but Wattana cared little as she started to aim at the second vehicle's right headlight. Using the light itself to find it, Wattana pulled the trigger. The 7.62x51mm bullet flew out of the *Begemot*'s rear cab and toward the headlight. However, as soon as it hit the target, the vehicle would also be destroyed, but someone, or rather, something else.

"Damn it!" Wattana screamed. "Those were my kills!"

"We got more pressing matters!" Dirks shouted as he, Wattana, and Maria now saw beige-colored Walgears appear.

"Great!" Vos shouted as he moved half of his body out of the front right seat and turned it to his rear to see the pursuing Walgears while Tarou fired his Walgear's machine guns in vain, causing the beige Walgears to dodge them. "Imperial Eurasian Army Donians!"

"Flooring it!" Crawley announced, making him use the full force of his right foot to press the gas pedal of the *Begemot*, increasing its speed.

While the *Begemot* continued on, Tarou continued to fire the machine guns while he was able to see the enemy Walgears despite the night sky normally making it impossible, but to no avail. Two of the four SH-6s of the Imperial Eurasian Army that he could see, carrying the same assault rifle for Walgears Tarou was familiar with, fired at him, but he evaded.

Damn it, Tarou cursed in his mind. *If I don't do something, they'll keep on shooting me. If I do something, they'll evade. Maria and the others won't last without my protection. I got to do something.*

Now, it was Tarou's turn to hear the loud heartbeat. At that instant, another SH-6 fired its rifle. Tarou managed to evade its shot and then rushed against it fast enough that the opposing pilot was too late to do anything as it came up close. Tarou then used the Strike Knuckle of his Walgear's right arm, the weapon to be used for close quarters combat, and punched straight through the head of the SH-6, disorienting it. Tarou then grabbed the headless SH-6's rifle and fired it at its former owner, killing the pilot and destroying the SH-6. The other SH-6, which fired at Solbein earlier, attempted to fire again, but after one squeeze of the trigger, Tarou dodged it again.

"On bystryy!" the female pilot of the SH-6 shouted before Tarou fired a split second after he dodged. The pilot, however, was also too late to see and was shot by a 30x155mmB bullet, while the others from that burst simply destroyed the cockpit, causing the SH-6 to stop.

W… What was that? Tarou thought. *It was just like when I first turned on this Walgear.*

"Incoming at 12 o'clock," a female voice said across Solbein's cockpit.

Tarou now saw two more SH-6s charging at him. One was beige, but the other was purple. *A purple one?* Tarou instantly pondered. *He or she must be Imperial Eurasian Navy.*

Tarou fired the Walgear's rifle again, but the two SH-6s evaded it. Not only did he miss, but he saw that he was now out of ammunition, forcing him to throw the rifle away.

"Another target approaching from 12 o'clock," the female voice said.

Both Eurasian Walgears now saw the new target and turned to see it. To everyone's surprise, including Tarou's, it was an SH-5, the first bipedal Walgear. While they both looked alike, there was one fundamental difference between the SH-5 and the SH-6; the former wasn't built with the cockpit protruding out of the rear, as that was a feature introduced with the latter.

"Leytenánt, leave that interloper to me," a male voice said over the communicator of Vladimir Nikolayevich Mirov's cockpit. "You continue pursuing the ones who stole that truck."

Mirov closed his eyes and gripped his teeth. "Spasibo, Kursant Klychev."

The beige SH-6 charged at the SH-5. Meanwhile, Mirov and his SH-6 charged against Tarou and Solbein and fired its rifle.

I have no time for this, Tarou thought before Solbein's yellow eyes increased the glow.

As Mirov's Walgear pulled the trigger, Solbein evaded the shots again. The latter then came across the rifle it discarded with Tarou grabbing it while using Solbein's arms. As it lifted the rifle, Mirov got close, but this allowed Tarou to use the rifle as a club. He made Solbein swing it against Mirov's SH-6, damaging its head.

With Mirov now disoriented, Tarou used the Strike Knuckle of Solbein's left fist. As the fist and brass knuckle got close, lightning manifested on the knuckle and when it hit the SH-6, the lightning was now transferred to the former. This caused damage to Mirov's control panel, but before Mirov did anything, Tarou moved his right leg and, as it was attached to the right leg panel in his cockpit, Solbein used its right leg. By the time Tarou made his kick, Mirov managed to find a certain button and press it. Upon pressing it, the top hatch of the SH-6 were the damaged head was opened with the cockpit ejected into the sky.

Tarou then turned his attention to the fight between the beige SH-6 and the SH-5. *I best get out of here while they're distracted,* Tarou thought until he felt tension at the rear of his head, making him close his eyes and grit his teeth. *What was that?* Luckily for Tarou, it was brief, allowing him to the original direction he was moving in and pressed the left pedal again. While moving, he pressed his earpiece twice.

"Mr. 'Smith', are you there?" Tarou asked.

"Ganji, you okay?" Dirks asked on the other end of the earpiece.

"I'm fine. How near are you to Lake Nevsky?"

"Vos can see Lake Nevsky. Just get back to us ASAP. The extraction team will be low on fuel by the time they get to the lake."

"Roger."

Near Lake Nevsky. 0700 hours

"Why were you assigned to keep an eye on me?" Maria asked in the *Begemot's* cab while Dirks put away his smartphone.

"We don't know," Dirks answered. "That's what we're supposed to find out because the Soviets seem to know about you and, as we found out now, the Eurasians."

"Could explain why I was repeatedly knocked unconscious. While those armed men cornered me and Ganji, he and their leader seemed to know each other."

"I believe that man is Serdar Muhadow. He was what made Ganji what he is now."

How despicable, Maria thought. *To be forced to use a gun and to fight at a young age…*

"When we first met, Tarou saved my life, along with Wouter, Jake, and Doc," Wattana added.

"Doc?"

"Dr. Anita Hamilton. She's our medic. She posed as Tarou's guardian for the mission."

"I've only known him for weeks and couldn't see him much outside school. What's he like?"

"Quiet, but he's the type to make his actions speak louder than his words. I can say for certain because I thought him Muay Thai."

"That explains how he kicks."

"I'm seeing a chopper!" Vos shouted.

Dirks and Maria moved their bodies to the outside to see a spotlight on the truck. "It's not firing at us, nor the pilot shouting in Russian," Dirks said. "It's definitely ours."

"Stopping now," Crawley said before he turned the truck to its right and stopping it.

Everyone then got off the *Begemot.* Dirks then brought out his smartphone and aimed it at the truck knowing that the helicopter was watching. He then turned his phone's flashlight on and off repeatedly while it was aimed at the truck.

"He's using Morse," one pilot said in the helicopter's cockpit.

"It says 'We're to be picked up'," the co-pilot said. "Landing this bird now."

The helicopter began to descend near the lake. Dirks then turned on his phone's flashlight again and aimed it at the helicopter. He, the mercenaries, and Maria now saw that it's a KUH-1 Surion transport helicopter.

"It's a Surion," Dirks said. "That's our extraction team."

"Does that mean we're saved?" Maria asked.

"More or less," Vos answered.

Once the Surion landed, four men in black jumped out. Carrying ADR carbines, they quickly moved to Dirks, the mercenaries, and Maria. These men belonged to the Special Warfare Flotilla (SWF) of the New United Nations Maritime Force. While the name originated from the special operations force (SOF) of the former Republic of Korea Navy (ROKN) whose role they took up, they're also seen as the spiritual successors of old naval SOFs from NUN member-states such the United States Navy's SEAL (Sea, Air, and Land) teams and the British Royal Navy's Special Boat Service (SBS).

"You 'Smith'?" one man in black, who had dark skin and dark brown eyes, asked.

"That's right," Dirks answered.

"Call me Mpax. Pronounce it with the spelling 'E-M-P-A-X' in mind." The SWF team leader then turned to Maria, with Dirks doing so as well. "Is she Maria Hoshikawa?"

"That's me," Maria answered. It was then that Tarou and Solbein appeared. All SWFs then pointed their carbines at Solbein, but Dirks got in their way. "The pilot's with us," Dirks explained.

"Good," Mpax replied. "Osprey's just behind. The Walgear and its pilot will have to be the last to leave."

"Incoming!" a female SWF member shouted as Tarou turned to see the SH-5 coming.

"We gotta go, now!" Crawley shouted.

Everyone ran to the Surion. "What about Tarou?" Maria asked before Dirks grabbed her by her left arm like Tarou did.

"He can deal with him," Vos replied. "Now come on!"

While the SH-5 fired its rifle at Solbein, the latter evaded. This allowed everyone to board the Surion. Once everyone was inside, it began to lift off. By the time it turned away, the SH-5 threw away its rifle and distanced itself from Ganji.

"You've improved," a male voice Tarou was familiar with said over the communicator of Solbein's cockpit.

"Muhadow!" Tarou shouted.

"Surprisingly, that Eurasian pilot gave me a warm-up. I could end this exercise now by killing you or you surrender so that Hoshikawa can trade her life so that you can go free."

"No."

"Then die!" Muhadow then charged against Tarou with his SH-5's right fist using its Strike Knuckle. The latter evaded it and attempted to use its right machine gun, but Muhadow evaded it.

"You call that an attack?" Muhadow asked mockingly.

Tarou screamed as he attempted to use Solbein's Strike Knuckles, but Muhadow evaded every blow. When Tarou attempted to use the left fist, Muhadow used his Walgear's right fist. As a result, sparks flew literally as Solbein and the SH-5's respective Strike Knuckles met.

#

New United Nations Maritime Force KUH-1; Off Sakhalin Island. 0756 hours

Heavenly Father, please help Tarou Ganji survive the tribulation he is enduring at this moment, Maria Hoshikawa said in her mind as she pressed her hands against each other. *Please, Lord. He's endured so much, so please end it. You're the only one I can turn to. Amen.*

It's like watching my wife pray for me, Frederick Dirks thought as he watched.

Near Lake Nevsky, Poronaysky District, Sakhalin Oblast; Russian Soviet Federative Socialist Republic. 0759 hours

"Give it up, Ganji!" Serdar Muhadow demanded over Solbein's communicator, while Tarou Ganji continued to defy him.

"Never!" Tarou screamed. *Though I can't keep this up forever! There must be something I can do!*

Tarou then remembered the *Begemot,* which was still intact. He then heard the loud heart beat again. He screamed as he increased the strength of his thumb pressing on the topmost button of the handle used to control Solbein's left arm. This allowed Solbein to push its left arm and, by extension, the right arm of Muhadow's SH-5.

"I… Impossible!" Muhadow shouted as he saw the incredible display of strength.

Tarou then moved close to the SH-5's left arm while the latter and its pilot were still off balance. Reaching the arm, Tarou grabbed it with both of his Walgear's hands after pressing the topmost button on the right handle for the Walgear's right arm and moved further behind the SH-5. He then slid the SH-5's left arm above Solbein's right shoulder.

"W… WHAT ARE YOU DOING?!" Muhadow screamed. "LET ME GO!"

Tarou then said nothing as he managed to make Solbein lift the SH-5 into the air and flip it in front of him by using the left arm to hold on to. The SH-5 now flew toward the *Begemot* and once it made its crash landing, the truck was damaged. From his cockpit, Tarou now saw gasoline spill now that the *Begemot* was damaged and because Muhadow was too slow to get up, Tarou repeatedly fired at the already damaged truck with the machine guns until he saw more gasoline spill out of the truck.

As a result of the flip Tarou and Solbein did to it, the right hand of Muhadow's SH-5 was damaged that there was a spark of electricity coming out of the hand. The spark touched the gasoline pouring out of the truck. An explosion soon followed, with the SH-5 caught in it.

I doubt he could survive that, Tarou thought.

"Ganji, do you read me?" Dirks asked over Tarou's earpiece. "The Osprey's close. Please respond."

"This is Ganji," Tarou replied. "Enemy Walgear eliminated. Notifying Osprey that I'm a friendly."

Tarou then made Solbein kneel and opened its cockpit. Once he jumped off the Walgear, he hurriedly faced it and aimed his smartphone at it. He then turned his flashlight on, then turned it off. He repeated this until he heard the tiltrotors of a V-22 Osprey vertical take-off and landing military transport aircraft built to carry only one Walgear. The pilots then saw the flashing lights on Solbein.

"That means 'Pick me up'," one male pilot said.

"Aim the light at that Walgear," the other male pilot ordered. "If he knows how to use Morse, he can understand if we use it."

The light was now big enough to engulf both Tarou and Solbein. Then it disappeared, only to appear again. The former knew it came from the Osprey and walked away to read the spotlight, turning on and off again as he knew what it meant.

Tarou then rushed back to Solbein's cockpit and, after turning it on, made the Walgear stand up again. The Osprey now flew above Solbein and turned around after flying above the Walgear. It then used its two magnets, built to make a Walgear stick to it, to lift Solbein. Once it was attached to the Walgear, the pilots lifted off the Solbein and proceeded to leave while carrying the mysterious Walgear.

Unbeknownst to everyone, Muhadow managed to survive the explosion Tarou caused to kill him. However, he survived with severe wounds, causing him to crawl out of the burning wreckage that was his SH-5. He kept on crawling despite his broken bones and a few burns on his skin, yet he began to lose consciousness.

Before his eyes closed, Muhadow saw feet. It was "SB", his "subordinate" that abandoned him a day before. She wasn't alone as four men in black appeared with their faces covered in masks of the same color. Two carried assault rifles, while two carried a stretcher.

"Once we get him, we leave," "SB" ordered to the men in black. "While we have until sunrise before the nuclear bomb underneath the laboratory will detonate, we have to rejoin the team recovering the corpses and then leave to avoid detection from either the Soviets or the Eurasians."

"Yes, Devotee-Lieutenant," one man in black replied.

NUNS *Ronald Reagan*. April 26, 2030; 0149 hours (Japan Standard Time)

The Osprey with Solbein in two now reached the *Ronald Reagan*. As it was dark, lights were on throughout the *Reagan*'s flight deck. This was never attempted before on an aircraft carrier, especially if it was to receive a Walgear.

As soon as the Osprey was above the *Reagan*, it descended but to land Solbein on the carrier first. Due to its height, Solbein was able to stand on the carrier as soon as it touched the flight deck without causing the carrier as a whole to sink. Once the Walgear's feet touched the carrier, the Osprey disabled the magnets, letting go of Solbein. It then regained altitude and flew forward for almost forty seconds before landing itself on the carrier. Tarou then made Solbein kneel. After opening the cockpit, he got off the Walgear. Vos, Crawley, Wattana, Dirks, and Maria all ran up to Tarou.

"I knew you'd win!" Crawley excitedly said to Tarou.

"You did it!" Vos added. "I knew you'd kick its ass!"

Maria, however, rushed to Tarou and hugged him, that both fell into the flight deck, surprising the mercenaries and Dirks. "Thank goodness you're alive!" Maria exclaimed.

"T… Thank you, Maria," Tarou replied. His tone mostly showed surprised because of how everyone greeted him upon arrival, but there was a faint of happiness that only he could sense. "C… Could you please get off me?"

"R… Right." Maria was the first to get off Tarou and resume standing. Tarou then followed.

"Now then, we have to get debriefed," Dirks announced.

"Right," Tarou replied.

"That goes for you too," Dirks said as he turned to Maria. "Mr. Vue will need to hear everything that happened to you."

"Of course," Maria replied.

Nizhny Novgorod Kremlin, Nizhegorodsky District, Imperial Capital of Nizhny Novgorod; Eurasian Tsardom. February 1, 2030; 1100 hours (Novogord Time)

At her father's office, Tatiana Ioannovna Tsulukidze kneeled before her father, Tsar Ivan Vladimirovich Tsulukidze.

"You may rise, my daughter," the Tsar commanded with Tatiana obeying. "Now, what brings you here?"

"Your Majesty, I've retrieved this piece of hair from a subordinate of mine that got it on him while he assisted a high school with its trash," Tatiana explained before she gave a small plastic bag that contained a strand of blond hair to Ivan. "That shade of blond made me think it I should give it to you."

"Why?"

"Because it belonged to a girl named Maria Hoshikawa. She looked like us. I ask that we have that strand of hair be used in a DNA test and compared to yours?"

"What do you wish to know if I willingly participate in such a test?"

"Father, please. Maybe this girl might be-"

"I'll keep the strand with me, but I will not disrupt my schedule just to spoil you. Now, return to your post."

"Da, Vashe Velichestvo."

#

OVR Safehouse, Nishinari Ward, Kansai City, Kansai Prefecture; State of Japan. April 26, 2030; 1000 hours (Japan Standard Time)

And now I regret giving Father that hair strand, Tatiana had in her mind at the present. *Maria ended up kidnapped because of what I did. Now I fear what will happen once Father does have the strand's DNA compared with his.*

Tatiana then heard SatCom and rushed to respond.

NUNS *Ronald Reagan*; Pacific Ocean. 1100 hours

Alone in the enlisted mess hall, Tarou Ganji ate his breakfast. He wasn't alone for long as Maria Hoshikawa appeared with her breakfast and arrived at his table.

"Mind if I join you?" Maria asked, making Tarou stop to see her.

"Sure," Tarou answered.

Maria then sat down, but Tarou realized that Maria didn't come to him simply for a vacant chair. "I suppose you've come to ask me what will happen once we return to Kansai City?"

"You're a mercenary. Will there be other jobs after this?"

"There might be, but those are additional jobs Mr. Vos can accept or reject. We'll remain with you until we figure out why people want you."

"Enough about that. Mr. Vue told us not to talk about that after we were debriefed."

"My apologies."

"There's something I wish to share with you after what happened."

"What might that be?"

"I've always known that I must have come from somewhere else. I've always felt it despite my parents' love. When I asked them one day because I received my first insult over my blonde hair and blue eyes, they told me once I'm older, they'll tell me. Now, I fear what they'll tell me."

"I don't want to make comparisons, but unlike me, you have parents that love you and friends."

"But what about the rest of Iron Dutchman Services?"

"I still need my past. It's why I'll continue to protect you. I apologize if I'm taking advantage of why people want you."

"The world is a scary place. Father warned me once that the wealthier people are, the attention they attract can be dangerous. For saving my life, I'll help in any way I can. I am your client, after all."

"Thank you, Maria."

"But I must remind you that once we return to Kansai City, we're back to being senpai and kouhai."

"But what about the Todoh siblings?"

"… Right. I honestly don't know what will happen but will you help me see it through?"

Epilogue: What Comes Next

Unknown Location; Enlightenment Point. April 27, 2030; 1930 hours (EP Time Zone)

"The one who defeated Muhadow, find out about him," Sergei Akulov ordered to Reinhard Frühling. "Now."

"By your will, Grand Gatekeeper," Frühling replied.

Whoever defeated Muhadow cannot be trifled with if he can use Solbein yet Muhadow couldn't, Akulov thought. *Yet that cannot make us falter.*

It was then that "SB" entered with Akulov turning to her. "How is Muhadow?" Akulov asked to his subordinate as she saluted him.

"The doctors have begun treating his wounds," "SB" answered. "His bones will recover while the doctors treat his burns."

"Good. He may have betrayed us by attempting to make money out of Maria Hoshikawa but he still has some use to us. This will be the last time I will tolerate failure. Is that understood?"

"By your will, Grand Gatekeeper," both Frühling and "SB" said in unison.

#

FIS Headquarters, McLean, Fairfax County, Commonwealth of Virginia; United States of America. 1000 hours (Eastern Standard Time)

"Order 'Smith' to get our station chief in Vladivostok out of there now," Alberto Pérez ordered to Stanley McAllister.

"I'll have Caguiat contact him, but what of Iron Dutchman Services?" McAllister asked.

"Let them rest. As for their payment, get them a bonus for that Walgear they brought with them. Vue's report got me thinking that there was more to this than Maria Hoshikawa being kidnapped. Especially after that laboratory became an irradiated crater."

"But the last thing the station chief told us was that the Osprey Tarou Ganji asked for was spotted. What do we tell the Soviets?"

"We have Yeom. Have 'Smith' make a pass for Guantanamo to pick him up. We can use Yeom as a bargaining chip to tell the Soviets to keep quiet about the Osprey."

"What about the Walgear?"

"The mercenaries can keep it. If they need spare parts, they can always contact Armstrong."

#

Nishi High School, Higashiosaka Ward, Kansai City, Kansai Prefecture; State of Japan. April 29, 2030; 0749 hours (Japan Standard Time)

Tarou Ganji arrived at Nishi High School in his PCX scooter. Once he arrived, he got off the scooter and dragged it toward the school complex. Reaching the bicycle rack, Tarou parked the scooter at the section dedicated to motor scooters.

Once he parked the scooter, he removed his helmet and hid it underneath his seat alongside his P226 semi-automatic pistol. After that, he began to walk to the school when he now found himself walking beside Maria Hoshikawa.

"Ohayou gozaimasu, Ganji-kun," Maria greeted.

"Ohayou," Tarou replied.

Everyone surrounding them took notice of how Tarou and Maria approached the school together. The Todoh siblings, Misa and Riku, stopped and saw the former two.

Those two must have done something throughout their absence last week, Misa thought.

"Doshita no, Nee-san?" Riku asked to his older sister.

This interrupted Misa, who then turned to Riku. "Nandemo nai, Riku," Misa replied. "Enough of that, we best hurry!"

"Hai."

Outside Nishi High School. 0752 hours

Outside the school, Maria's limousine left the school. Unbeknownst to everyone, Pyotr Stepanovich Chadov watched from the nearby pharmacy. He then brought out a smartphone and used it to contact "Elizaveta". However, he left as he was still inside the store and that he found it improper to use his phone while inside.

"What is it, Chadov?" Tatiana Ioannovna Tsulukidze asked on the other end.

"Maria Hoshikawa is now at school," Chadov answered.

"Good. Return there later in the afternoon. Right now, Zhakiyanov's prepared breakfast."

#

OVR Safehouse, Nishinari Ward. 0754 hours

At her office, Tatiana put down her smartphone. *The time to get Hoshikawa will come,* Tatinana thought. *But we can't rush it. We must be patient.*

Plugging the smartphone again to the dish needed to use SatComm, Tatiana left her office.

#

Sevastopol Base, Sevastopol Volost, Crimea Uyezd, Ukraine Governorate; Eurasian Tsardom. 1500 hours (Novgorod Time)

Vladimir Nikolayevich Mirov approached the office of Levon Samvelovich Khachikian, the commander of the Imperial Eurasian Navy's South Seas Squadron, and saluted him. Although an Armenian, Khachikian was able to have a career in the IEN that allowed him to reach *Contre-Admiral.* He was fifty-five years old with black hair in a crew cut, light skin, and gray eyes.

The jurisdiction of the South Seas Squadron was the Black Sea and the Caspian Sea with plans to build a shipyard and a naval base in the Iran Governorate. Khachikian's career in the Imperial Eurasian Navy began during the Unification Wars where, upon coming of age, enrolled at the Nakhimov Naval School in Murmansk after the city's government, which went independent due to the collapse of the Union of Soviet Socialist Republics, swore its allegiance to Ivan Vladimirovich Tsulukidze after the surrender of the Byelorussian Soviet Socialist Republic. Once he finished his studies, he started his career with the newly established Northern Fleet until reaching *Contre-Admiral* and was assigned to the South Seas Squadron.

"How goes your recovery?" Khachikian asked.

"I'm fine now, Admiral," Mirov replied. "Spasibo."

"I'm going to tell you that you have another assignment in two days."

"Two days?"

"It should be tomorrow, but the government still thinks you need one more day of rest because this assignment doesn't involve the war in Sakhalin?"

"Why?"

"Your new assignment involves that mysterious Walgear that killed your students in Sakhalin. I can imagine you wish to exact your revenge."

"I would sell my soul to the Devil in order to defeat that Walgear."

"But first, you need to go through a list of potential team members."

"Team members?"

"You're to have your own team. I have the files with me and out of ten candidates, you can only select three of them."

Mirov came closer to Khachikian's desk to receive the files. The latter gave one file at a time to the former, until Mirov now held all ten files with both of his hands.

"I expect to hear whom you wish to recruit tomorrow."

"I won't let you down, Admiral."

Because his hands were full, Mirov raised his arms with the files upward. Khachikian smiled as he saluted, since what Mirov did was the best he could think of as a substitute salute until Mirov's hands were free. Regardless, Mirov began to leave the room with Khachikian pressing a button underneath his desk as Mirov didn't have any free hands to open the door to leave.

I will avenge my students, Mirov thought just as the door opened in front of him. *Whoever you are, pilot of the silver Walgear, you will regret not killing me that night.*

AUTHOR'S NOTES

- Prologue (A Faltering Voyage)

➢ *Muay Thai* – commonly translated as "Thai boxing". Alternatively known as the "Art of eight limbs" as it involves using the body's pairs of fists, elbows, knees, and shins. Original Thai: **มวยไทย**

➢ Senhor Crawley – Portuguese for "Mr. Crawley"

- Chapter I (The Iron Dutchmen)

➢ *Movimento Popular de Libertação de Angola* – Portuguese for "People's Movement for the Liberation of Angola"

➢ *Instituto Técnico Militar* – Spanish for "Military Technical Institute"

➢ ITM José Martí – located in Marianao. It was established in 1967 to train cadets into being officers. After five years, a cadet will graduate to be a lieutenant. The institute was named after Cuba's national hero José Martí, who died in the War of Independence he started at the first battle fought between Cuban rebels and Spanish forces, the Battle of Dos Ríos, on May 19, 1895.

- Chapter II (Movement)

➢ *Revelator* – a title given to John the Apostle as he wrote the Book of Revelation from the Bible's New Testament.

➢ *Otdeleniye Vneshney Razvedki* – Russian for "Foreign Intelligence Department". Cyrillic: Отделение внешней разведки

➢ *Gospazitza* – Russian equivalent for "Miss". Tatiana being addressed as "Gospazitza" is to treat her as a stranger yet Puzanov used it rather than "Grand Duchess Tatiana" or using a dimunitive. Cyrillic: Госпожица

➢ *Spasibo* – Russian for "Thank you". Pronounced "spa-si-bah". Cyrillic: Спасибо

➢ Tachyon – derived from the Greek word "*tachy*" (ταχύ), which means "swift". Apt for particles that allow instant communication.

➢ *Hoteru Soreiyu made onegaishimasu* – Japanese for "Please take me to Hotel Soleil". Original Japanese: ホテルソレイユまでお願いします

➢ *Koko de ii desu* – Japanese for "Here is fine". Original Japanese: ここでいいです

➢ *Roku hyaku roku-jyu en ni narimasu* – Japanese for "That will be 660 yen". Original Japanese: 660 円になります

- *Hai douzo* – Japanese for "Here you go". Original Japanese: はい、どうぞ
- *Arigatou* – Japanese for "Thank you". Original Japanese: ありがとう
- *Irrasaimase* – Japanese for "Welcome to our store". Original Japanese: いらっしゃいませ
- Chapter III (Meeting)
- *Mamonaku, densha ga mairimasu* – Japanese for "The train will be arriving at any moment." Original Japanese: まもなく, でんしゃがまいります
- *Katakana* – *kana* used for transcribing foreign words into Japanese.
- *Kanji* – Japanese for "Han Character" (original *Hanzi)*. The name was the result of material written during China's Han Dynasty arriving in Japan.
- *Pandoh* – Japanese for "Bread Way." Original Japanese: パン道
- *Hontou ni gomen nasai* – more sincere variation for "Please forgive me" in Japanese. Original Japanese: 本当にごめんなさい
- *Hai desu* – more sincere way of saying "Yes" in Japanese. Alternatively, it can be translated as "That's right". Original Japanese: はいです
- *Kami ni kansha shimasu* – Japanese for "Thanks be to God". Original Japanese: 神に感謝します
- *Otou-sama* – Japanese for "Father". Unlike the casually respectful *Otou-san* and the stereotypically casual *Oyaji*, *Otou-sama* is used in formal households. Maria addressing Daisuke with *Otou-sama* is a reminder that she is the daughter of the President of Hoshikawa Group. Original Japanese: お父様
- *Wakarimashita* – Japanese for "Understood" in the past tense. Original Japanese: わかりました
- *Keiretsu* – a Japanese term for companies with interlocking relationships and shareholdings. The successor to the *zaibatsu* after the Second World War. Original Japanese: 系列
- *Gochi sou sama deshita* – Japanese for "Thank you for the meal". Original Japanese: ご馳走さまでした

- Chapter IV (Preparations)

➢ "Fuijoka Hana desu" – In Japanese, full name order is one's surname followed by his or her forename. In English, "Fujioka Hana desu" will be "I'm Hana Fujioka".

➢ *Kochira e douzo* – Japanese for "This way, please". Original Japanese: こちらへどうぞ

➢ *Chashi* – a hilltop fortification made by the Ainu. Originally romanized as *casi* in the Ainu language. Original Japanese: チャシ/砦

➢ *Wakatta* – like "wakarimashita", this can be translated as "Understood". "Wakatta" is more casual as a contrast to "wakarimashita". Original Japanese: わかった

➢ *Yoshi* – Japanese for "Okay then". Original Japanese: よし

➢ *Sate, hajimemashou* – Japanese for "Now then, let's begin". Original Japanese: **さて、始めましょう**

➢ *Namae* – Japanese for "Name". Original Japanese: **名前**

➢ *Oikutsu desu ka* – Japanese for "How old are you". Original Japanese: おいくつですか

➢ *Jyu-nana sai desu* – Japanese for "I'm seventeen years old". Original Japanese: **十七歳です**

- Chapter V (Update Part 1)

➢ *Shachou* – Japanese for "Company President". Original Japanese: しゃちょう

➢ "Nishikoyama-san" – Japanese equivalent for "Mr. Nishikoyama". "-san" can be used as the English equivalent for "Mister/Mr." for men and "Miss/Ms." for single women.

➢ *Hiragana* – the writing system nowadays learned first for those learning Japanese. Originally learned by women only in Japan because their education was restricted as a contrast to men.

➢ *Sugoi* – Japanese for "cool" "awesome". Original Japanese: すごい

- Chapter VI (Update Part 2)

➢ Sanzu as a callsign – the name of the Japanese Buddhist equivalent of the Styx River where the souls of the deceased must cross a bridge, a ford, or go through snake-filled waters depending on how he or she had sinned prior to death. Prior to crossing, six *mon* (Japan's currency from 1336 until 1870) was to be paid. This was used as the callsign for the unit O'Leary's MC-130J Commando II belonged to as

Sanzu refers to spirits and that Commando II is used for airborne special operations. O'Leary referring to her Commando II as "Sanzu 2-3" is to shorten the chain of command of her unit: Commando II #3 of 2nd Flight, Sanzu Squadron.

➢ *Dewa, shitagatte kudasai* – Japanese for "Please follow me". Original Japanese: では、従ってください

➢ *Suwatte kudasai* – Japanese for "Please sit". Original Japanese: 座ってください

➢ *Mochiron desu* – Japanese for "of course". Original Japanese: もちろんです

➢ *Khrushchyovka* – a type of apartment building built across the former Union of Soviet Socialist Republics during the premiership of Nikita Krushchev, hence its unofficial name. Cyrillic: Хрущёвка

➢ *Baikal* – a non-alcholic beverage that originated in the USSR. Created as the Soviet equivalent of Coca-Cola. In the 1970s, Pepsi Cola found more fame in the USSR as a contrast to the United States of America because Coca-Cola still dominated the drinking habits of US citizens at the time and in exchange for importing and marketing their cola into the USSR, PepsiCo was allowed to export and market Stolichnaya vodka to the US. The recipe for *baikal* was altered as a result. Cyrillic: Байкал

- Chapter VII (Relaying Messages)

➢ *Net* – Russian for "no"; pronounced "ni-yet". Cyrillic: Нет

➢ *Shako* – a tall military cap that had its origins with the ceremonial hatd worn by Hungarian shepherds. This hat came to be known as *csákó* ("peak") when the Hungarian Grenz infantry adapted the hat but added a visor, hence the name *csákó*. Militaries across the world would come to wear this cap, nowadays for ceremonial purposes. Marching bands would come to wear such caps in this day and age.

➢ *Da* – Russian for "Yes". Cyrillic: да

➢ *Vashe Velichestvo* – Russian for "Your Majesty." Cyrillic: Ваше Величество

➢ *Serzhánt* – Russian for "Sergeant". Cyrillic: сержáнт

➢ *Zametano* – Russian for "Roger that". Pronounced "ze-me-ta-nah". Cyrillic: заметано

➢ *Odnako* – Russian for "However". Pronounced "ad-na-kah". Cyrillic: Однако

➢ *Chto eto takoye* – Russian for "What is it". Pronounced "Sh-to e-toh tako-e". Cyrillic: Что это такое

➢ *Vy Serdar Mukhadov* – Russian for "Are you Serdar Muhadow". "Muhadow", a Turkmen surname, is turned into "Mukhadov" in Russian. Cyrillic: Вы Сердар Мухадов

➢ *Gospodin* – Russian for "Mister". Cyrillic: господин

➢ Ohkrana – short for "Otdeleniye po **Okhran**eniyu Obshchestvennoy Bezopasnosti i Poryadk**a**" (Отделение по охранению общественной безопасности и порядка; "Department for Protecting the Public Security and Order"), the state security and secret police of the Russian Empire from 1881 (created as the union between a part of the Imperial Russian Army's Special Corps of Gendarmes and the Third Section of His Imperial Majesty's Own Chancellery) until 1917. Because the Eurasian Tsardom was Ivan Vladimirovich Tsulukidze's attempt to recreate a monarchical state in the former Soviet Union, he opted to recreate the Ohkrana.

➢ *Hawa* – Turkmen for "Yes"

➢ Iraqi Turkmens – Turks who settled across the Middle East. The first wave of Turks settling in the Middle East were the result of the Seljuk conquests of the Middle East, followed by refugees fleeing the annexation of the Khwarazmian Empire by Genghis Khan's Mongol Empire in the 13th Century and the Ottoman conquests of Sultan Suleiman I three centuries later. Muhadow had in mind the Turkmen communities in Iraqi cities such as Kirkuk, Tal Afar, and Mosul. Despite the name, these Turkmen (including those in Syria) ought not to be confused with the Central Asian Turkmens; the latter where Muhadow comes from.

• Chapter IX (First Day)

➢ *Nani ka tasuke ga hitsuyou desu ka* – Japanese for "Do you need any help". Original Japanese: 何かて助けが必要ですか

➢ *Doushita no, Ugaki-san* – Japanese for "What's the matter, Mr. Ugaki". Original Japanese: どうしたの、宇垣さん

➢ *Tadaima* – Japanese for "I'm home". Original Japanese: ただいま

➢ *Okaerinasai* – Japanese for "Welcome home". The standard reply to "Tadaima" above. Can be shortened to "Okaeri". Original Japanese: おかえりなさい

➢ *-chan* - a Japanese honorific used for two individuals who are close to each other. For both Misa and Maria, the former calling the latter

"Maria-chan" and the latter calling the former "Misa-chan" indicates how close they are. Original Japanese: ちゃん

- Hasegawa calling Tarou "Ganji-san" – this was to show that it was still Tarou's first day in Nishi High School. Hasegawa will use "-kun" after this.
- *-kun* – a Japanese honorific used normally for men, especially teenage boys. Riku is addressed as "Todoh-kun" by Hasegawa as they're teacher and student. Original Japanese: くん
- *Todoh Riku desu. Douzou yorushiku* – Japanese for "I'm Riku Todoh. Pleased to meet you". "Douzou yoroshiku" is actually "Please take care of me". Original Japanese: **藤堂竜孔です。どうぞよろしく**
- *-senpai* – this Japanese honorific is used when a student is addressing another student one grade above them. In Maria's case, she's above Tarou by grade, hence why Miku addressed her as "Hoshikawa-senpai". Original Japanese: 先輩
- Donian – an alternate term for the Cossacks that populated the middle and lower basins of the Don River that ran from Novomoskovsk until the Sea of Azov. The Don Cossacks played significant roles in Russia's military history, mostly as cavalry. The Eurasian Tsardom's Walgears being named "Donian" was fitting as these machines allowed men to act out as the cavalry of old.

- Chapter X (First Challenge Part 1)

- *Teriyaki* – a combination of the words *teri* ("to shine") and *yaki* ("to broil" or "to grill"). That is because when something is finished cooking, the food shows grill marks that make it stand out. Original Japanese: 照り焼き
- Bloke and Sheila – Australian slang terms for men and women respectively.
- *Dare da* – Japanese for "Who's there". Original Japanese: 誰だ
- Spook – a slang term for spy.
- Maria Clara – a character from Jose Rizal's Noli me Tangere. She was based on Rizal's cousin and lover Leonor Rivera, who was wedded to one Henry Kipping in 1890. The individual whom Dirks talked about knows that "Maria Clara" is an alias for Alicia Caguiat.

- Chapter XI (First Challenge Part 2)

- *Öte jaqsı* – Kazakh for "Nice"

➢ *Kashikorimashita* – a more formal way of saying "Understood" in Japanese, moreso than "Wakarimashita". Original Japanese: かしこまりました

➢ *Tasuke ga hitsuyou desu* – Japanese for "I need your help". Original Japanese: 助けが必要です

➢ *Coup de grâce* – French for "blow of mercy". Originally used to refer to giving dying animals a quick and painless death, now it means striking one last attack against someone.

➢ *Mládshiy Leytenánt* – Russian for "Junior Lieutenant". It's seen as the Russian equivalent of "2nd Lieutenant", a rank used in English-speaking ground warfare forces.

• Chapter XII (Invitation)

➢ *Domo arigatou gozaimasu* – most formal way of saying "Thank you" in Japanese. Original Japanese": どうもありがとうございます

➢ *Kiritsu* – a Japanese order used by a class representative to make the rest of the class to stand up when a teacher appears. Original Japanese: きりつ

➢ *Mondai nai* – Japanese for "No problem" or "Don't mention it"; the latter translation making more sense in context when Nonaka thanked Muhadow for helping her with the food she bought. Original Japanese: 問題ない

➢ *Eigo ga hanasemasu ka* – Japanese for "Do you speak English". Original Japanese: 英語が話せますか

➢ *Itadakimasu* – Japanese for "Let's eat". Original Japanese: いただきます

➢ *Mamekan* – Japanese for "Bean Hall". Original Japanese: 豆館

➢ *Yakitori* – Japanese chicken that is grilled after it is skewered. Literally means "grilled bird". Original Japanese: 焼き鳥

➢ *Gomaae* – a Japanese side dish that consists of spinach and sesame sauce. "Goma" is "sesame" whereas "ae" means sauce. Original Japanese: 胡麻和え

➢ *Sake* – Japanese rice wine. Original Japanese: 酒. The actual term for rice wine, however, is "nihonshu" (*Japanese alcoholic drink*; 日本酒)

• Chapter XIII (Adjustment Part 1)

➢ Demeter – the Greek goddess of harvest and agriculture. Her name made sense for a fancy restaurant in a hotel.

- *Hajimemashite* – Japanese for "Nice to meet you". Original Japanese: はじめまして
- *Filet mignon* – French for "tender, delicate, or fine fillet". Original referred to cuts of pork tenderloin, English-speaking countries use the term for steak made from the psoas major of a cow.
- Maria going from "Ganji-kun" to "Tarou" – she opted to do so because she and her parents were using English while talking to Tarou and Hamilton. Maria opted to do away with surname and honorific from Japanese and used the forename.
- *Konbanwa* – Japanese for "Good evening". Original Japanese: こんばんは

• Chapter XIV

- *Pochemu* – Russian for "Why". Cyrillic: Почему
- *Ohayou gozaimasu* – Japanese for "Good morning". Original Japanese: おはようございます

• Chapter XV (Final Preparations): Nemuro Subprefecture – while the northern Japanese island of Hokkaido is a prefecture itself, the city of Nemuro and the nearby towns of Betsukai, Nakashibetsu, Rausu, and Shibetsu, as well as the nearby islands of Shikotan, the Habomais, Kunashir, and Iturrup, were made into the Nemuro Subprefecture. However, the nearby islands, claimed by Japan to be their territory, are still internationally recognized as Russian territory. Not in this story, however. That will be discussed in later chapters.

• Chapter XVI (Abduction)

- *Gideli* – Turkmen for "Let's go"
- Providing overwatch – a modern-day tactic where one unit is positioned somewhere that offers high vantage for another unit. When spotting an enemy, the unit positioned at the high vantage point can contact the other unit, allowing the latter to respond.
- *Mizu mou ippai onegaishimasu* – Japanese for "Please give me another round of water". Original Japanese: 水もう一杯お願いします
- Ugaki using "Miss Maria" – in-universe equivalent of ""'Maria ojou-sama" Ugaki came up with in English.
- *Studec'* and *Vyšen'* - pseudo-deities mentioned in the Book of Veles, text pertaining to passages in Slavic mythology found on wooden planks in 1919 by White Russian Army lieutenant Fyodr Arturovich Izenbek, who attempted to make money off the planks after he fled Russia. However, they were discovered to be forgeries because the text in the

planks was written in modern Slavic as opposed to how it would have been written in 7th Century BC - 9th Century AD, where the writing was believed to have dated at. Another reason was that Izenbek was able to give the planks to one Yuri Miruyulbov in Belgium, who didn't let anyone access them. Since the New United Nations isn't aware of the *Vyšen'*-class submarine and that the Eurasian Tsardom wish to keep it that way, these submarines bearing the names of these deities is apt as their existence is to be unknown to NUN.

➢ *Spetsnaz* – short for "*Voyská* ***spets****iálnogo* ***naz****nachéniya*"; Russian for "Special Operations Forces" or "Special Purpose Military Units". Most assume "Spetsnaz" referred to one unit but in reality, it refers to units tasked with the name. For this story, the Imperial Eurasian Naval Infantry's *Spetsnaz* are different from the *Spetsnaz* of other branches of the Imperial Eurasian Armed Forces. Cyrillic for "Voyská spetsiálnogo naznachéniya": Войска́ специа́льного назначе́ния

➢ *Kapitan* – Russian for "Captain". Cyrillic: Капитан

➢ *Stárshiy Serzhánt* – Russian for "Senior Sergeant". Danylo holds such a rank because he's Naval Infantry. Cyrillic: Ста́рший сержа́нт

• Chapter XVII (The Chase): *Ryoukai* – Japanese for "Roger that". Original Japanese: 了解

• Chapter XVIII (Next Move)

➢ *Ĉahârjuy* – Persian for "Four Brooks". Original Persian: چاهارجوی

➢ Persian Languages – the Persian languages are given names depending on where they're spoken. In Iran, it's called "Farsi" while in Central Asian countries such as Afghanistan and Tajikistan, they're respectively called "Dari" and "Tajiki". Tarou and Ghaemi use Farsi because the former came from Iran while the latter infiltrated it.

➢ Iranian Administrative Divisions – in real life, the Islamic Republic of Iran is divided into multiple provinces, where they're grouped into regions. That was the case in the 2023 flashbacks Tarou has about his time in Iran but wouldn't be the case in the present as Iran was conquered by the Eurasian Tsardom, turned into the Iran Governorate.

➢ *Hemmäňiz çykyň* – Turkmen for "All of you get out"

➢ *Çyk* – Turkmen for "Out"

➢ Turkmen being used in Iran – the gunman using Turkmen at the children his partners-in-crime abducted to turn into soldiers used Turkmen because they're Turkmens living in Iran working with Muhadow, a Turkmen from Afghanistan. Ghaemi was an Iranian Turkmen, hence why he uses Farsi.

➢ *Esme man Serdar Muhadow ast* – Persian for "My name is Serdar Muhadow". Original Persian: است سردار محدو من اسم (In Persian writing, it's an inverse of a sentence in English. Translating one word at a time, that sentence would turn into "is Muhadow Serdar name My").

➢ *Esmetun čiye* – Persian for "What's your name". Original Persian: اسمتون چیه (your name What). There are many variations but this is the most informal way of asking one's name. I opted to use it because it fitted Muhadow's character.

➢ *Ja* – Afrikaans for "Yes". Same for languages such as German, Dutch (where Afrikaans originated from), Danish, Norwegian, and Swedish.

➢ *Zevat'* - Russian for "Yawn". Cyrillic: Зевать

➢ *Stárshiy Leytenánt* – Russian for "Senior Lieutenant". Cyrillic: Старший лейтенант

➢ Klick – short for "kilometer" for military usage.

• Chapter XIX (Relaying of Information)

➢ *Chernyy Marlin* – Russian for "Black Marlin". A fitting name for a large propeller meant to make the *Vyšen'*-class submarine travel really fast as black marlins are supposed to be the fastest aquatic animal in the world. Cyrillic: Черный марлин

➢ *Ya ponimayu* – Russian for "I understand". Cyrillic: я понимаю

➢ Vries Strait – named after one Maarten Gerritsz Vries, a Dutch explorer who discovered the southern Kuril Islands. Not much about him was recorded other than dying during the Dutch Republic's failed campaign to conquer the Philippine Islands, then a Spanish colony, in 1646 (Battles of La Naval de Manila).

➢ *Chikazuite kudasai* – Japanese for "Please take me there". Original Japanese: 近づいて ください

• Chapter XX (Preparing for the Rescue)

➢ Difference Between Eurasian and Soviet Administrative Divisions – for this story, the Russian Soviet Federative Socialist Republic uses the real-life administrative divisions of the old Soviet Union and the present-day Russian Federation, which is multiple districts making up one *oblast* (область; "Region"). For the Eurasian Tsardom, they use the administrative divisions of the pre-1917 Russian Empire where multiple *volost*s (во́лость; rough equivalent in English is "district") make an *uyezd* (уе́зд; closest equivalent would be "County") with many *uyezd* making up a Governorate (губе́рния; *Guberniya*). It should be noted that the usage of *volost* ceased with the creation of *raion*s (whose equivalent is "District" as I've used when I took the story to Sakhalin Island) in Soviet times, which I didn't apply for the RSFSR in this story ("Poronaysky District" ought to be "Poronaysky Raion") because the former rang better in the throat comapted to the latter.

➢ *Loshad'* – Russian for "Horse". Cyrillic: Лошадь

➢ Armstrong calling the FIS "The Company" – a reference to how the CIA is called "The Company" in real life. In-universe, this is because the FIS inherited the resources and most of the personnel of the foreign intelligence agencies that the member-states of the New United Nations dissolved when creating NUN. Most of those resources and personnel came from the United States of America's Central Intelligence Agency and the joke that they're called "Comapny" was inherited for the FIS.

➢ *Generál* – Russian for "General". Save for the a-acute (á) in the former, there isn't any difference between it and the latter from English because the Cyrillic is Генера́л

- Chapter XXI (The Rescue): Swiff – an in-universe nickname for those serving in the Special Warfare Flotilla as it's shortened into "SWF". It's similar to how anyone serving in United States Navy SEAL teams are called "SEALs" even though "SEAL" means "SEa, Air, and Land".

- Chapter XXII (Escape)

➢ *Begemot* – Russian for "Hippopotamus". Cyrillic: Бегемот

➢ *On Bistryy* – Russian for "He's fast". Cyrillic: он быстрый

➢ ASAP – short for "**A**s **S**oon **A**s **P**ossible"

➢ *Kursant* – Russian for "cadet". Cyrillic: Курсант

➢ Mpax – short for *Istiompax indica*, commonly called "black marlin".

➢ *Kouhai* – Japanese for "Junior". The term refers to how between two people, one must refer to the other because he or she is older. Because Tarou is a second-year student at Nishi High School and Maria is one year above him, Tarou is Maria's "kouhai" as a result despite being the same age. Original Japanese: 後輩

- Epilogue (What Comes Next)

➢ *Nandemo nai* – Japanese for "It's nothing". Original Japanese: なんでもない

➢ *Contre-Admiral* – Russian for “Counter Admiral”. No longer used in English-speaking navies. Cyrillic: Контр-адмирал

About the Author

A.I.V. Esguerra, from the Republic of the Philippines, was born in 1996. Throughout elementary and high school, Esguerra opted to be a writer after being exposed to various works of fiction. In college, Esguerra started writing while waiting to graduate, beginning with the short story Before Death, published by Mistwood Entertainment in 2019. Two years later, Esguerra's first novel was The Young Knight of the Desert and wrote it to be uploaded it to Honeyfeed.fm as part of the MyAnimeList X Honeyfeed Writing Contest but lost the contest. Despite that, Esguerra continued writing, starting with The Young Knight and His Metal Steed.

Esguerra intends on not only writing more books but also to venture outside books. The desire to write comes from exposure to various works of fiction and Esguerra hopes to share the same interests in fiction unto others with the stories already written and what will be written.